Interrogating Ellie

JULIAN GRAY

cloiff books

Published by cloiff books, 2015

Cover design: John Featherstone

Author's note

I should like to thank the many people who helped me write this book, giving me practical assistance, information, constructive advice on drafts and, above all, encouragement to continue. I cannot name them all here, for reasons which should be obvious to them, but they know who they are. The Documentation Centre for Austrian Resistance in Vienna was an invaluable resource in that city. The staff of the Kaprun museum, and the Zell am See town hall, were helpful in answering my questions about events and places as they were in the 1940s.

The web site associated with this book is

www.interrogating-ellie.com

It contains pictures of people and places mentioned in the book and you can learn more about the true story on which *Interrogating Ellie* is based.

'the great ideological storms [of the twentieth century] have altered the lives of virtually all mankind…it is well to realise that these great movements began with ideas in people's heads: ideas about what relations between men have been, are, might be, and should be; and to realise how they came to be transformed in the name of a vision of some supreme goal in the minds of the leaders, above all of the prophets with armies at their backs.'

Isaiah Berlin

'Fateful moments are times when events come together in such a way that an individual stands, as it were, at a crossroads.'

Anthony Giddens

1

DASHWOOD HAD FED well on the soft green farmland of
Carinthia. His cheeks had broadened and flesh hung beneath
his chin. He ground his teeth as he completed the cover sheet.
What was her bloody name? He should have got her to write it
down.

Subject: Vetting: BAUER Elise
    To: District Security Office, Carinthia
    From: 428 Field Security Section
    Ref: your 101/DSO/RR dated 31st July '46.,
    herewith vetting in quadruplicate, of BAUER Elise.
Personal Details
    Name: BAUER Elise. Name at birth: PICOT Elise.
    Date of birth: 22.1.1915.
    Place of Birth:
    St. HELIER, JERSEY, CHANNEL ISLANDS.
    Nationality at Birth: British.
    Present Nationality: Austrian.
    Religion: Catholic.
    Present address:
    JERGITSCH Strasse 4, KLAGENFURT
    Present occupation: Translator and Interpreter at
    M.C. KLAGENFURT.
    Languages spoken: English, German, French.
    Language used for Interrogation: English.

This was the routine he had done a hundred times in his Field Security Service career, since Naples back in '43. All the way up Italy his unit had set up shop in abandoned or requisitioned palazzos, hotels, barracks, town halls. He had grilled the accused and those who had denounced them, given the third degree to black marketeers filching from army stores, screened local women planning marriage to British soldiers, tricked the guilty into confessions, interrogated undernourished prostitutes, the poor, the desperate, the defeated citizens of ruined nations left in the wake of fighting armies.

He ploughed on, writing up the account of his most recent cross-examination. The problem of her first name was irritating. 'Elloweez' it had sounded like when she said it, or was it 'Elleez?' One of those French spellings. Bloody French tart basically, faking it. How could she claim she was British with a name like that? Well, she counts as Austrian now. So he gave it an Austrian look: 'Elise'.

He wrote on as the light faded, summarising her answers. He knew how to make it look objective; record the facts separately from interpretations – like the report of a science experiment in school, the way they'd taught them at the Corps Depot. But then there was the concluding section where he could express himself. He always looked forward to that. In this case it would be a particular pleasure. He continued writing:

That'll put a stop to her, he thought

There were visitors to the house who could have told me more about Ellie. If only I had known to ask. Once she came in with a man whose face was strained and pale, clothes hanging loosely off his thin frame. She made him sit down, which he did slowly with a grunt of pain, as if he had some injury deep inside his body. As Ellie lit a cigarette for him he looked over at me and managed a laboured smile. Then she said something to him and I knew enough to realise that I was hearing German.

They spoke in low voices in that language, which I had never heard my mother speak before, with the man mumbling a lot and putting his head in his hands. Ellie sat sideways to him and he seemed so miserable it looked like she might put her arms round his shoulders, but she didn't. I went next door. They didn't say anything to me as I left.

Then Richard came into the kitchen. After that I heard shouting so I went upstairs and shut the bedroom door, like I always did when my mother and father yelled at each other.

They never told me who this was, but I found out much later: it was her first husband, Michael Bauer. He had come back to see her for one last time. He had lung cancer and he knew he was dying. Richard must have found this visit too much to take and he wanted the man out of the house.

There were a lot of things that Richard and Ellie didn't want their children to know. And it turns out that Ellie knew a lot more than Richard ever did. That was what she did, you see: she covered things up. She thought she had to.

She was ablaze with colour. Her skin was brown, her hair was black, she wore scarlet lipstick and painted her nails and toenails. On long car journeys, with kids jammed in the back, her frustration with our bickering would boil over. A jangly purple-stoned bracelet around her wrist, she would flail her hand and blood red nails about, seeking angry contact, like a dragon's claw, shouting 'Christ all bloody mighty will you brats stop belly aching and shut up!'

And she poured her passion into an extravagant and hardly believable love for us. She enfolded each of us in her arms, crushed us against her when the mood took her. Each one of us was told we were her favourite. And although we all thrilled at this attention when we could get it, we also knew enough to fear her and, in the end, never to trust her.

Who could trust her really? Apparently Richard's father tried to buy her off when he found out she was going to marry his son. And Richard himself eventually came to feel she had hoodwinked him, although he stayed with her all the same.

Louis Nicholson and his wife Ruth visited too. They were a friendly, laughing couple who made a fuss of us so we liked it when they came. But I could see from the little glances they gave each other and Ellie that they had some kind of secret going on, which my dad wasn't allowed to share.

Much later the two Austrian girls came over for a visit. I learned a lot more once I got to know them.

And just recently I found the records of her interrogation. Now I know that that she had always had to look after herself because no-one else could be trusted to do that. By the time she met Richard it was a chronic problem for her. The war had seen to that.

2

WHEN ELLIE FIRST met Michael Bauer she knew straight away she liked the look of him. Tall, fair-haired, elegant in his formal waiter's suit, he'd gone outside the hotel kitchen to have a smoke. She made sure she was there too, ready to oblige him with a light.

'It's going all right in there,' she said, holding a match up.

He cupped her hand in his to get the flame in the right place. His hand felt warm on hers.

'Yes, it goes really well,' he said, 'I am tired – it is a long day. But Mr Maurer will be happy.'

He had a funny accent, she thought, sort of a lisp even, something a bit exact in the way he said his words, like he was trying out each one, a word at a time.

'Oh yes, he's happy all right,' said Ellie. Just at that moment he turned sideways and she got a good look at his face in the beam of light coming out of the kitchen door, the smoke from his cigarette curling across the illuminated space. He was pretty nice, she could see. Well, very nice in fact.

'Mr Maurer told me it's a much better turn-out than last year,' she said.

'Oh really? How many last year?' he said, looking straight back at Ellie, right into her eyes in fact, even though she knew he couldn't have seen them too well in the dark. So she laughed.

'Well, his brother owns the café where I work and he told me it was a disaster last year. They only sold half the tables.

You're in his good books.'

He looked puzzled.

'I mean, he's pleased with you. Good books – it's an English saying.'

He nodded. Michael had suggested to Mr Maurer that the hotel could celebrate Christmas Eve 1934 with an Austrian-themed *Weihnachten* celebration. With a couple of young Austrian women who, like him, had come to Jersey to work in the hotel trade, he had set it up and it had been a complete success. Every table was sold and the guests inside were cheerfully singing along to a French accordionist, brought in to play German sounding tunes to put them in the mood.

He seemed so easy about chatting with her, she thought. He didn't stumble over his words or anything. She knew he must be clever to learn another language so well. And she could see he was interested in her, which pleased her.

She took his cigarette from his fingers, put the tip against her own, her fingers brushing over his as she gave it back.

'You're one of the Germans aren't you?' she said.

'Austrian, you mean. It's not the same as Germany.'

Ellie had never paid much attention to maps at school.

'But you sound German.'

'Yes, of course I do to you,' said Michael, who seemed offended then. 'We speak German in Austria you know. It is most complicated you know.'

'Oh, I see. Well what are you doing here then?'

'Working,' he replied. She sensed he was going to have a bit of fun with her now.

'I know that. But I mean what are you *doing* here? You know what I mean!'

'Working I said, I am of course working here. Is that not enough for you?' and then he had a little laugh at her expense.

She grinned at him and shoved his shoulder, mucking about, and he smiled a little too.

'I know, I know. Well, if you won't tell me, I don't care.'

She finished her cigarette. 'I've got to be back in the reception. I'm filling in for Margot.'

'Oh do not say this,' he said, now sounding disappointed. 'I will tell you about myself if you like.'

So then it was her chance. 'No, I really must get back,' she said, trying to sound serious. 'They'll miss me soon and what if someone rings? I'm the only one at the desk.'

Then she flounced off, leaving him hanging there, she supposed.

After that, Michael made sure he often passed by the café on the front where she worked, calling in for a coffee. He asked her out to a dance, introduced her to his sister. He was a good-looking, popular lad, enjoyed a drink when he could afford it and she liked how he made such a fuss over her. Every now and again she saw him strolling along the front with his sister, enjoying the sea air or whatever. Eva was like him, fair haired and slender, a pale face. Once, seeing the winter sun shining on them and the sea whipped up by the wind behind, she had the idea they were like a pair of angels.

At that time they told each other a lot of things that weren't true. Much later she figured out he'd wanted to impress her. He said he'd been caught up in the fighting after some Nazis had tried to overthrow the Austrian government. They'd managed to kill the prime minister, Dollfuss, but then it hadn't gone so well for them and they'd had to get out, so he'd come to Jersey.

Ellie eventually found out who told him that story— a friend of his to whom it had really happened. It must have sounded exciting to Michael, a bit of derring-do, and she was duly impressed, thinking he was some kind of fugitive hero. She wasn't sure which side he'd been on in the fighting. She hadn't got any idea about politics in those days, and not much more about men.

Yet she knew she needed a man in her life by then, really needed one. She was only eighteen, but by that stage she felt she'd been mucked about so much, more than most people get in a lifetime. He felt like a breath of fresh air. More than that – she thought he'd magic her into a different life. And he did of course, but not one that she could ever have expected, or would have wanted.

She told Michael her own mother had died when she had her. Her father had had been killed a year later in the war in France and she didn't know anything about him. She said her Grandmère was too busy running her dressmaking shop to look after her and her brother Billy, so she'd put them with the Lebrocqs, who had looked after them.

As children every now and again she and Billy had been brought over to Grandmère Picot's house, dressed in their best clothes. They sipped lemonade in the garden, keeping as quiet as mice, listening to the old lady, dressed in black crêpe, belching after a meal of rabbit braised in red wine, a phonograph playing Beethoven in the background. Then they were sent back to the LeBrocqs. That much was true anyway.

She wasn't going to tell him that her mother was actually alive and well and living in Birmingham, kicked off the island because she'd had two children out of wedlock, or about the other children at school who she and Billy had to fight because of what they said about their mother. She told him nothing that might put him off her. No fear, she thought, none of it.

She had no idea who her father had been. She didn't tell him that. Michael teased her a couple of times about her father being a wandering tinker, which felt a bit close to home. But she told him flatly she didn't see the joke and there had never been any tinkers on the island, so he shut up about it. She knew what he thought about gypsies. He used to go on about how there were a lot of them roving around where he came from in Austria, pinching things, cheating, the kids begging, the men who knocked their wives about. When she heard this she thought of what that bastard Scragg had done to her own mother, and what a fool her mother had been to stick with him. Scragg had even tried to touch her up, so she'd run away.

But most of the time she managed not to think about the bad things. Michael was such a handsome man and she could see he was falling for her. She liked it that he was foreign too, and when he wasn't with her she heard again and again in her mind his lovely soft accent when he spoke English. He really was like an angel. Not that he'd come down from heaven of course, but he might as well have done as far as she was concerned. He came from another world and it had *nothing* to do with the people on the island who had given her such a hard time growing up. She knew that was a really big part of his appeal for her.

His sister Eva had an English boyfriend called James and the four of them used to go round together a lot. They took the bus up to Grève de Lecq on their days off. James was dark-haired like Ellie and she thought they made a good match for the two pale blonde angels.

Ellie knew it was very important to look right. She was too dark to copy Eva's look but she plucked her eyebrows and used red lipstick which she thought was just nice against her hair, jet black in those days. It felt good to her when the four of them strolled down the sea front, arm in arm, laughing as the sea wind blew in. They had something special, young, full of beans, having fun. She could see the looks people gave them, dead curious and maybe a bit jealous.

But after a bit, Michael wanted to be alone with her and she felt the same way. Eva could see what was happening and had the good grace to back away. She had her own pals anyway, young ones mostly, chamber maids, kitchen staff, waiters, reception staff, all working in the big hotels in St Helier.

All that time Ellie was sure he'd leave her if he found out too much.

But then things took a turn which gave him other things to think about. She gave him what he really wanted and it was what she wanted too, thinking bugger the consequences. At one point during their lovemaking she wondered if her own mother had been the same way with her father, before she had her and Billy. Sometimes, she thought, you've just got to have your heart's desire.

He had such a smooth, slender body that felt so lovely against her, and then he was all over her. And he had this cool white skin, which felt gorgeous. She couldn't think of anything else and just wanted it again and again. He was the first man she'd done it with. She didn't know about him; she didn't like to ask and figured that he would only have told her some story anyway. But after they got going on sex he didn't seem too bothered about finding out more about her past, nor she about his, it was all now now now, lovely glorious now, so they shut up about those other things.

Then it was all just fine for a long while really. Anna came along, as babies do, she told him ruefully, if you get up to that kind of activity. But that was fine too, they would manage. They both had jobs didn't they? They got married. Anna was a sweet little soul. They were a proper family, the first one she'd really had.

After that it was just a matter of getting on with things, in blissful ignorance of what was round the corner.

There's a battered, creased photograph I found after Ellie died, taken in 1934, Christmas Eve at the St Helier House hotel. It seems to have been organised by the hotel management, to commemorate the occasion. There are perhaps thirty people in the picture, most of them women, many of them young, in a ballroom festooned with Christmas decorations. The top of a Christmas tree, covered in lights, is behind them. Mr Maurer, dressed up as Charlie Chaplin is seated in the centre at the front, with young women arranged on the floor on either side of him, others in chairs. More staff stand behind the chairs. To the left, kneeling and holding a menu, with an arm on the shoulder of one of the women, is Michael Bauer. On the right stands a rather chunky looking woman in *lederhosen*, with her hand on her hip. Behind this figure, her face half-hidden, stands a slim young woman with dark hair in a long dress. Everyone is smiling.

Three years later, on an afternoon in October 1938, Ellie sat opposite Michael and her brother Billy at a café table on the front at Havre des Pas, with Eva at her side. The sun umbrellas had been taken down at the summer's end but the weather was warm for the time of year so they were outside.

'What do you mean, Ellie?' asked Eva. She wore a light green dress and her hair was fashionably bleached and shaped into waves. She leaned forward on her elbows as she held a cup of hot coffee that threatened to spill onto the table as her shoulders shook with suppressed giggles. 'He said what?'

It was good to see Eva looking so cheerful, thought Ellie. She knew Eva was upset to be losing her brother. Michael was laughing too, through the smoke of his cigarette which curled up through his fair hair.

'The man in the passport office told me 'You have not made a very good swap' when he gave me this. Those were his very words. I can't believe it! What a cheek! He's a pompous idiot dishing out his opinions like that. Not a good swap, he said. I'll give him a good swap, I'll swat him on the face if I ever see him again, I can tell you.'

Ellie held up a brown passport document and waved it about. Then she opened it and they all looked at the photo-graph inside, passing it around, making comments.

'You're not looking your best there you know Ellie.'

'Oh I don't know, she's got her serious look on.'

'It's a passport after all Michael, you don't expect her to…'

'Reminds me of the time she stood on a clam shell on the beach. You should have seen her face then, all screwed up,' and Billy, the joker, scrunched up his face and squealed, the rest of them laughing.

'Oops, don't spill,' said Eva as the document was put down on the shaky outdoor table next to the cups of hot drink, 'you're going to need that tomorrow Mrs Bauer.'

The brown booklet lay with cover upwards, showing an eagle with wings widespread, a swastika below in a wreathed circle.

'It's not as nice as the good old British one,' said Ellie, suddenly contemplative. 'I once saw one: a proper little book with a hard cover and all that gold, royal stuff on the front. I never had one of those, never needed to, so that little man was wrong – it's not really a swap. What have I got to swap?'

Michael picked up the new passport. *Deutsches Reich, Reisepass,* it said on the front. A number was punched with holes, running all through the pages, even the front and back covers. Eva turned to her brother.

'*Deutsches Reich,* what is that supposed to mean Michael?' said Eva, suddenly irritable. 'What was the matter with the old Austrian eagle? The Germans have taken over in our country. What have we got to do with them? We can't even call ourselves Austrians any more.' Michael gave her a concerned look but before he could answer Ellie butted in.

'It looks as if it's made of paper,' she said, snatching it from Michael's hand. 'It's not built to last is it? It'll fall apart if you're not careful.'

'Well you'd better take good care of it then Ellie, else you'll be in trouble. Keep it somewhere safe,' said Michael seriously.

Ellie's eyes glittered. 'Oh I know where I'll keep it! I'll keep it somewhere safe all right. Somewhere no-one will be able to get it!' and she tucked it down the front of her blouse. There was more laughter when Billy jumped up, pretending to be about to reach in to retrieve the passport.

'I'll have that out of there in a German jiffy,' he shouted.

'Hey Billy, that's enough of that,' said Michael, standing up quickly in turn and putting his arm out to bar the way. 'That's my wife you're molesting there,' he added with a laugh as he saw the wounded look on Billy's face.

'Come on,' said Eva, 'It's time I got back,' and turning to Ellie she said 'and remember Ellie, you're picking up Anna at four o' clock today. Don't be late. I want to get James to the shops before they shut.'

The party split up. Ellie shouted to Alfred, the café owner, 'Hey Alfred, can we owe this one to you? I'll pay up before we leave,' to which Alfred, glasses in hand, gave a pleasant nod.

Michael and his young wife nodded goodbye to Billy who headed off towards the boys fishing on the rocks and the couple walked the other way together, along the short promenade. Ellie turned her head to the familiar shore, a stretch of seaweed-strewn sand below, with the autumn waves whipped up by the breeze. She tried to fix the image in her mind.

James had agreed to look after their little daughter Anna that afternoon, while Ellie went to get her new passport from the consulate office in Ingouville House, after which they had met up on the front for what would probably be a last get-together with Eva and Billy.

They headed for town where the two of them, along with Eva and James, still shared a place, though she knew that was coming to an end tomorrow. They were cramped in that flat of theirs, she thought. At night they didn't dare move for fear of waking the baby next to them. The partition wall that made one bedroom into two was as thin as paper and Eva and James were on the other side. Each couple could hear every movement the other two made in the night, and although in the morning there was a mutual, tactful agreement to stay silent about the night time sounds, it was pretty embarrassing. It was also frustrating. They were still young after all, they were married now, and it was only natural…

Tomorrow they would be packing their bags and taking the afternoon ferry to St Malo where they would stay the night.

The next day, a train to Paris, retracing the steps Michael had taken four and a half years before.

Michael had come to Jersey not because he was fleeing from political persecution, but because he had been sacked from his job as a hotel bell boy after Hitler introduced his tax on German tourists, designed to bring the Austrian economy to its knees. He had met a wealthy English guest, holidaying in the mountains, who had advised him to come over to Jersey where there were jobs.

He told Ellie he had never seen the sea before or been in any vessel larger than a rowing boat. All he had known was the lake at Zell am See, with the little craft that took tourists and the occasional fisherman out, surrounded by high mountains.

Ellie hadn't wanted to go when Michael had got the letter from his parents urging him to return with his new bride and child. He had been away for four years, they wrote, and they had not seen him all that time. Letters were not enough, his mother said.

Michael pointed out to Ellie that he was his mother's only son, born bang in the middle of four sisters. That made him special in her eyes. But up to now, he had resisted her pleas for him to come home, whose intensity had increased after the baby was born. Anna was nearly a year and half old now, running around and getting into everything. His mother wanted to see this new granddaughter, she said. And they knew, too, that there was another baby on the way, though they hadn't yet told his mother about it.

But that wasn't what had made him take them seriously this time. The more pressing issue was to work out where the money was going to come from to support this new family he had acquired. That should always come first, he explained to Ellie, whatever they might feel.

'We've got to provide for Anna and this new little one,' he said, patting her stomach as he spoke. 'My mother says things are looking up at home. The Germans are pouring money into the country now that they've taken over. There's a good job for me at the hydro-electric works up at Kaprun that pays well if I want it. I could earn a lot more there than in the hotel and we could find a place to live that would fit us all in. We could really live well for a change!'

His words had an ominous truth for her. Their life together in St Helier had been good at first, but now…

It was getting harder for her to find regular work that gave enough to make it worth paying for someone to look after the child. Everyone else either had their own work to do, or they looked after other children. She couldn't call on anyone for free favours any more. And now there was this other one on the way.

So she had agreed. They would try it. Look on the bright side, he said to her, it would be great fun to see a new place. He could show her where he grew up, introduce her to his parents. They would love her like a daughter, he said. Yes, like a daughter. And if they decided they didn't like it, or for whatever reason, then why, they could just come back! That's the beauty of a mixed marriage across the waters, he told her, you've always got the option of moving to the other place. They were lucky really. And they were so young.

Now that they were about to go to Austria, Ellie remembered Michael's story of political conflict and flight, although she still wasn't too clear about whose side Michael had been on, or what the Nazis had stood for. Were they the socialists she thought? After all, they were called National Socialists by some people weren't they? Michael's story seemed to come from a world completely removed from the one she knew in Jersey. And that was part of his attraction for her after all.

'Do you think we should be worried?' she asked him. 'It doesn't seem like a very safe country. Are there any of these Nazis where your parents live? Eva told me to steer clear of them. Are you sure we're doing the right thing?'

But Michael told her not to worry, that his parents would

look after them and they'd be delighted with their new granddaughter and the prospect of a second on the way. She realised he'd say anything to persuade her, whether he believed it to be true or not. With the money he could earn, they could live well, he said. They had to take this opportunity.

On 10th October 1938 they visited a photographer's studio where they had a picture of themselves taken, with Anna on Ellie's lap. A separate one of Anna, then just 18 months old, was taken, standing next to a teddy bear with a large bow around its neck. On the back Ellie wrote the date and her daughter's name: 'Anni 1 ½ years.' She gave a copy of the photographs to Eva.

And two days later they took the ferry over to St Malo on the French coast, the first leg of their long journey. As they waved goodbye to Billy, Eva and James standing on the dockside, Ellie saw a figure dressed in black standing some way behind them. It was Grandmère Picot whose white unsmiling face stared out at the boat drawing away from the shore.

3

THE HOUSE WAS a small, single storey, whitewashed building squashed between two larger, better houses on two floors. It looked old, as if from some previous era, before a town had surrounded it. Michael explained that it was an old council property, leased to his father as a part of his job.

The old man – she always thought of him like that, although he was only in his 50s, but looked so old and tired – had a job as a handyman with the town council services department. He stuck with his job through thick and thin, turning out in all weathers, so that now the town hall officials would no more think of sacking him than of demolishing their own comfortable, heated offices.

But it was his wife, Ilse, who ruled the roost at home. She had been all smiles when Ellie and Michael had first arrived on a cold October evening after an exhausting journey by boat, train and bus. Then, she appeared overwhelmed with joy at the return of her son, kissing and crying and hugging and kissing and crying again, little exclamations of distress mixed with pleasure, patting and smoothing his head, waving her husband away when he tried at first to embrace his son, so she could have her precious boy all to herself.

Then, in the kitchen, a blue apron tied around her substantial waist, she bustled around, hair coming out of its bindings as she fussed about him, settling them all down on stools around the little table, asking Michael solicitously about the journey while the old man stood by the door, unable to get into the tiny room. Plates of hot stew were put in front of them in chipped earthenware plates, mostly peas and vegetables tasting of onions, some coarse bread to have with it. Gherkins lay on a plate between them. The food was welcome.

As Ilse Bauer watched them eat, she chattered in German with Michael. Ellie kept her head down, not understanding the talk, wondering when she would become the focus of attention. It meant she had time to take in her mother-in-law's appearance: a powerful-looking woman with a somewhat masculine face and full lips, hands worn from a lifetime of manual labour. She had an air of intelligence that was somehow disturbing. It made Ellie feel instantly questioned whenever the woman's eyes rested on her. She never managed to get rid of this feeling.

The old man, her husband, continued in the doorway, shifting his gaze from one adult to the other, unsmiling but not unkindly, then noticing the little girl Anna on the bench next to Ellie, eating the soupy stew with the help of a spoon she gripped, enclosed by her mother's helping hand, her other hand dipping pieces of bread into the greenish liquid. Anna stared at him, said nothing and turned again to the food.

Michael's mother said something in German and Michael gave Ellie a nudge so that she looked up and smiled. Frau Bauer smiled back and spoke.

'She says she hopes you like the food,' translated Michael.

'Oh yes, do tell her thanks, thanks for the food. It is very good after this long journey. Say thank you Anni' and she turned to her child, getting her to look towards Frau Bauer. Anna was too shy in this new place to say anything. Ellie decided to take a risk with the German Michael had been teaching her: 'Danke schön Frau Bauer, danke für das schöne Essen,' she tried, hoping it was right.

Michael beamed with pleasure and his mother laughed, prompting a lengthy exchange between the two of them and much further laughter.

'What are you saying?' asked Ellie.

'Oh nothing darling, she likes your German that's all.'

His mother said something else more sharply this time, and pointed to Ellie. Michael looked concerned as he replied but Ellie decided not to ask about it. She was exhausted and so was Anna, who could hardly keep her eyes open through the meal.

'Let's get our things sorted out shall we?' said Michael cheerfully in English, and his mother said more in her language, pointing to the room where they could stay. It had been where Michael had slept as a child – the only other room in the house apart from the parents' bedroom and the kitchen. Michael explained that it had been cleared out for them to stay 'until we get something of our own.' Ellie was too tired to ask him more.

With Anna already asleep in her arms, mother and daughter collapsed onto the mattress and fell, more or less straight away, into a deep sleep that was to last until morning.

She did her best to fit in at first. Learning German was her most pressing problem. Michael had taught her some phrases back on the island and even on the train journey from Paris he had been writing down a list of words for her to learn as Anna slept beside them.

But soon after their arrival Michael had to get involved in work up at the dam and wasn't around so much to teach her. It would be too expensive for her to join him up there. The free accommodation for the dam workers wasn't for wives and children so he would have needed to rent a place. He said they couldn't afford it. It made more sense for her to stay in Zell am See in his parents' house.

She could soon hold simple conversations with people in shops. Nobody spoke a word of English, so she had no alternative. Then she found that if she went out into the streets or settled down on the grass near the lake with Anna playing nearby, other women would try to talk to her. As a foreigner who was not a tourist she was an oddity, which sparked people's interest.

The lake was beautiful, a picture postcard, little boats, a steamer doing excursions, mountains rising high at either end, green fields and forest on the opposite shore. A tourist place, just like St Helier really, only with a lake rather than sea. Lots of big hotels too, just like home.

After a while, she managed to get hold of newspapers, one or two magazines, even books from the lending library van that visited the town square once a week. Reading helped a lot, she found. She was particularly fascinated by the *Völkischer Beobachter* which her father-in-law brought home regularly. The sentences were short and easy to understand and she didn't really care what the articles were about. Once she understood more of the language though, she couldn't help being fascinated by the pieces about Jews. There were cartoons that made them look like goblins. The stories about them taking everyone's money and kidnapping children reminded her of fairy stories she had heard as a child and gave her a similar thrill of horror. Could there really be people like that?

Michael told her that when the Germans had come in 1938 his father had applied to join the NSDAP like every other council employee but he'd been unsuccessful. Apparently there had been a flood of people wanting to join after the Nazis took over so they decided to make it a bit more exclusive and a lot of people were disappointed. Luckily old Galther, the head of the transport and maintenance department, had also put in a failed application, so he couldn't put on any airs and Johannes Bauer had been kept on.

It wasn't long before the two married Bauer daughters visited to take a look at their brother's new wife. They were courteous but distant, without quite being unfriendly and made Ellie feel they were judging her with a critical eye. Their husbands were great thick-set men with solid, slab-like faces and large hands, who worked on the land, to whom their wives were unbelievably subservient. These men planted themselves in the seats in the kitchen taking up the whole of the tiny table and expected their food to be brought to them on a plate by their women, their beer to be poured for them, and to smoke a pipe or two while the women cleaned up. Only then did the women eat, and it was rare at that point for any meat to be left in the stew.

Michael told her that his sisters hadn't lived with them as children but instead were looked after by peasant families in the countryside. His parents had sent small sums to pay for the upkeep of their girls. Michael was the only one allowed to stay with Johannes and Ilse in the tiny house in town and as soon as he was old enough he had got himself a job in the hotel, trying to ease their burden.

With Michael away in Kaprun, returning only at weekends or on his occasional weekdays off, Ellie and Anna faced the winter more or less alone. Anna found the snow delightful at first, making little balls and throwing them at the wall, scuffing it with her tiny feet and laughing, but soon she understood the meaning of cold as the weather worsened. They learned to wrap up warm, both outside and within the house, to keep the snow from penetrating their clothes so that there was dry material against their skins, to put on lots of layers and plug any holes near the neck or wrists so the frozen air couldn't get in.

The kitchen was the best place to be from that point of view, as it was kept warm by the stove which Frau Bauer lit early in the morning. The two of them kept it going throughout the day and into the evening with the plentiful wood from the council yard. Ilse Bauer informed her she would teach the younger woman cooking 'to make you into a proper *hausfrau*' and at weekends they produced special stuff for Sundays when both Michael and his father would be at home. Michael's favourite was beef stew with dumplings, although Ellie liked it best when they had fish from the lake, fried in butter with plenty of potatoes. In the week, it was usually back to pea soup and bread in the evenings.

As her understanding of the language improved, Ellie was able to join in with conversations. She began to realise that Michael's mother was worrying about where they were going to live. Although they had pestered Michael to come home, the older couple had in fact got used to having the tiny house to themselves, seeing the stay of their son and his new family as a temporary measure.

Things came to a head in the new year when it became obvious that Ellie was expecting a second child.

'You will have to find somewhere by the spring Michael,' said his mother, her husband nodding his head in agreement. 'There isn't enough room here for four of you.'

'What about those new places they're building out beyond Waibel's place, in the fields where he used to have those chicken sheds,' suggested the old man. 'That's housing for young couples isn't it? They're going up fast.'

'No that's for all the people coming from Germany,' said Michael. 'They're going to be flats for the families of the bosses and the foremen at the dam.'

'But you're working up at the dam, Michael!' exclaimed his mother. 'What's to stop you from applying for one of those for your family? You always put yourself down you know. It's about time you learned you've as much right to things as any other man in this town.'

Michael looked a bit shamefaced at this and his head hung down as he twiddled his fingers, not responding to his mother. Ellie didn't really understand what was going on, but put her hand on his arm to sympathise.

'I've heard Waibel made a lot of money on that land deal,' interjected Michael's father, helping out with his son's embarrassment. 'That land was worth nothing with chickens on it, but when they decided to put the housing there he flogged it for a tidy sum.'

'Oh, you hear a lot of gossip these days Johannes,' replied Frau Bauer. She transferred her irritation to him. 'You don't want to believe everything you hear. Waibel just happens to be one of the lucky ones.'

'He got the deputy mayor job pretty fast though, didn't he?' said Michael, looking up again.

'That's because they needed someone with a bit of ability,' said his mother. 'Waibel gets things done, not like the rest of that crew. They don't know their arse from their elbow when it comes to running a council department. You remember Julius Grabner? He got the housing job. I knew him when he was a kid. You don't want to know what he got up to in those days – his mother used to talk to me, but I don't think she told me the worst of it. He never did anything at school and mooched about the town looking for work, half the time never did what he was paid for, went from job to job doing nothing right, eating his way through his parents' larder.'

'He got that job because of service to the Party,' offered Johannes Bauer. 'I heard he joined back in '33 because he thought he was in love with that girl Marianne from the Streubel house – he thought it would impress her,' said the old man.

Ellie felt Michael's arm pull away from hers as his mother smiled, saying 'Ah, yes, the Streubel's. I wonder what happened to that girl? But you're wrong you know. He didn't join to impress her. If he did, he wasn't going anywhere with it – that Marianne Streubel was never likely to be attracted to a fat, good-for-nothing like Julius Grabner. You remember her Michael?'

'Yes of course I do,' said Michael, now reddening a bit. Ellie saw this – this woman wasn't someone he'd ever mentioned to her.

'Look,' said his mother, focusing on her son, 'I think you

should see Grabner about getting a place. Why don't you make a time to visit his office? You can't stay here for ever you know.'

They went to the housing department in the town hall the next morning, taking Anna with them, and met a junior official there. He was a neatly dressed, fair haired young man. Piles of printed forms were arranged in rows on a shelf near his desk. He wore a little lapel badge ringed with red, a black swastika in the centre.

With Anna wriggling on her lap, Ellie listened as he patiently explained the rules to them. Most of the new places would be ready by the summer, he said, but they weren't really for local people. The town was being transformed. The project at Kaprun needed a lot of extra workers. The labourers, people from all over the place, could be housed up at the dam, but the managers, mostly German engineers brought in for the job, needed something better. Until now these managers had lived on the site in barracks, without their families. Now they'd be able to bring their families and commute up to the dam site, like Michael.

Michael said he was a manager too, and his family badly needed somewhere to live. He didn't want to live on his own any more either.

Ellie watched his performance beside her, seeing his graceful hands with their long fingers gripping the side of the table ever more tightly as he spoke. She wished he wouldn't sound so desperate.

The young man sighed and took a form from one of the piles on the shelf. This would have to be filled in, he said, and then the application would be considered at the next meeting of the housing allocation committee. There wasn't much chance though. If you were local you had to be a Party member to get one of these flats. Had they tried asking around town if anyone had something to rent? Perhaps there was something up in Kaprun itself?

The couple could hear the discouragement in his message and went away despondently, Michael clutching the paper form in his hand. They headed back down towards the lake in silence, past the tourist hotels until they stood outside the grandest one of all, where only the wealthiest German tourists stayed. From the cold street they looked up at the glittering window lights, radiating warmth.

'Don't worry,' Michael said to his wife, 'my folks will look after us for a bit longer yet. I'll fill in the form and we'll see where it gets us – you never know. And if they don't give us a flat, we'll think of something else.'

Ellie smiled at him and squeezed his hand. She had wondered where all the money was going that Michael earned in his canteen job but he had explained to her that he gave most of it to his parents while they were staying at their place.

'So would that be enough for us to get a place of our own do you think?' she asked him.

'If you want to live in a rabbit hutch it would be,' he laughed ruefully. 'They don't pay me much. Anyway, I still have to help Mutti and Vati.' He often used the childlike German words for his parents, which now suddenly irritated Ellie.

'But what about us?' she exclaimed. 'Can't your sisters help? Why do they need our money?'

'You don't understand dearest,' said Michael pleadingly, 'these are my parents. I didn't come back here just to feather my own nest. I have to help them – I'm their only son. My sisters can't do anything for them – two of them are married themselves and have their own families to think of. The other ones just about keep body and soul together working on that farm over in Rauris. They can't spare anything.'

Ellie felt frustrated and upset. Michael had disappointed her about several things now and his promises about the good life they could expect in Austria were looking increasingly hollow. She was sick of living in the one little room with Anna, her husband away most of the time, having to be on her best behaviour with his mother. She was starting to think there was no way out.

'But what about your father? He's got a job hasn't he? We need somewhere to live, Michael. We can't stay with them for ever and she keeps on dropping big hints whenever I am alone with her about what she wants to do with that room. It's not fair!' She began to cry.

Michael, though, was unsympathetic. 'You just don't understand do you?' he said angrily. 'His work brings in almost nothing – the neighbours are always pointing at them or laughing behind their backs. All that food you cook at the weekends has to be paid for somehow. Who do you think has been paying for that?'

This didn't make any sense to Ellie. His parents had managed before she and Michael had arrived. How could they expect them to continue giving them money out of Michael's meagre income and still put pressure on them to leave and get a place of their own?

But Michael then produced a final outburst in his attempt to win the argument, something that really dug the knife in: 'What do you know about having parents anyway?'

There was a silence as this sank in.

'You shouldn't have said that Michael,' she said as her tears really started to flow. A man looked over at them as he came out of the hotel entrance.

'I don't know what you expect me to do,' he continued, as if he had not heard her. 'I'm sorry but I really don't. You would understand if you knew this place. I have to help my parents.'

'Look, I know Michael, I know. It's just that…' and she began to sob again, feeling defeated. After all, she reflected, he was right. What did she really know about having parents?

Finally he seemed to soften and put his arm round her.

'Don't cry darling, don't cry,' he said more gently. 'I'm sorry I shouted. Let's not argue. Things will work out.'

It was their first major fight since they had arrived in Austria and it had frightened her. He seemed chastened too, perhaps realising that he had gone too far.

But there were more disappointments to come, and more arguments. The form was filled in but got them nowhere. It was because Michael wasn't a member of the Party, repeated the young man in the housing office the following week, and nor was Ellie. Anyway, she was foreign and that hadn't counted in their favour either.

'But I thought these houses *were* for foreigners!' protested Michael, 'All the Germans are getting them!'

'We are all Germans now in the Ostmark,' said the young man smugly, fingering his little lapel badge, 'although your wife is British of course.'

So they walked away with Anna holding her father's hand down to the side of the lake that bordered the town. Anna was two years old now, and Michael carried her in his arms when she didn't want to walk. It was April and the weather was getting warmer.

Ellie moved slowly, rubbing her belly from time to time, feeling heavy with the weight of her developing baby. Her thoughts were churning over with resentment at the unfairness of it all. Couldn't the man see they needed somewhere decent to live? What was so special about these other people who got the houses and flats she and Michael so desperately needed?

But Michael now affected cheerfulness about the outcome of their housing application, saying he had always known it would be like this, they mustn't worry, something would turn up. She found his complacency irritating, sensing that it came from a timid side of him that she was increasingly coming to dislike. Where had the cheerful young adventurer she had known in Jersey gone? Back home, with his parents, he seemed like a child.

They settled down in the grassy area by the lake. Michael and Anna went down to the waterside and poked stones in the shallows with a stick. Ellie stayed on a bench; the walk had made her tired and she was glad Michael had taken Anna off her hands. The town was behind her and she looked out over the water, where small rowing boats and a single sailing vessel plied up and down in a freshening wind.

Across the lake, the green hills stretched up away from the water side to forested heights that, compared with the low undulations of the Jersey countryside, she would once have thought were mountains. She knew better now. These were just foothills. Over to the right she could see the snow peaked mountains of the Kitzsteinhorn. To the left, towards Saalfelden, a valley stretched out, eventually rising into another ridge of mountains separating the Ostmark from Germany. Just over there, Michael had told her, was where the Führer had a mountain retreat, somewhere he went to rest and plan: an 'eagle's nest.'

Well, I suppose I am resting and planning now, she thought, although my eagle's nest isn't up to much. She reflected on the smallness of her plans next to the grand plans she imagined must be made over in Berchtesgaden. People like me, she thought, what does it matter what plans I have? What weapons have I got? Where are the armies of men to help me? The rest of the world isn't exactly awestruck when I turn up.

On second thoughts, she reflected, perhaps I am just resting. Her eyelids began to droop and she lay down sideways, putting her head on her bag. It had been an anxious night knowing that in the morning they would learn the fate of their housing application and she hadn't slept well.

Out of the corner of her eye she saw a young woman talking with Michael. He pointed down towards Anna. The young woman smiled and laughed and so did Michael – they seemed to be having a very animated conversation. The woman bent down and picked up Anna as they continued to talk. Anna laid her head over the women's shoulder in the same trusting way she did on her own mother's, putting her little arms around the woman's neck. The woman laughed and hugged Anna and continued to talk to Michael – a conversation which Ellie could see but not hear.

The woman had thick blonde hair, braided and piled into a large bun. Her face was lively, sharply pointed. She wore traditional Austrian clothing, a long rose-coloured dress with a white apron and puffed white sleeves coming out from under the shoulder straps. There was some embroidery work on the bodice, so it was a particularly elaborate *dirndl*. This was an unusual sight in the town during the week – most women wore work clothes and kept that kind of thing for special occasions. Ellie saw Michael pointing and the woman looked in her direction, the smile still on her face. After a little more conversation, the child was put down and they parted, laughing and waving goodbye.

Michael and Anna came back and she sat up.

'I thought you were asleep,' he said.

'No, just dozing,' she paused. 'Who was that you were talking to just there?' and then said to Anna as she chucked her under the chin, 'You liked the lady didn't you?'

Anna hung on to her mother's fingers and her face beamed with pleasure as she pulled them about, her little pink tongue poking out of the side of her mouth.

'Oh, that was Marianne Streubel, she's back in town. I thought you were asleep otherwise I would have brought her over.'

'That woman you were talking about the other day?'

'Yes, that's the one. I knew her at school. She's from the town but she's been away in Vienna for a couple of years. She got back this spring.'

'What was she wearing all that stuff for Michael? It looked a bit elaborate to me. Not very practical.' Ellie looked down at her own very workaday wear – a brown skirt with a dark blouse, colours that would hide the dirt of the kitchen and the wood shed and save on washing. Her middle pushed at the waistline of the skirt.

'She told me she's got a job with the tourist office. That's what she was learning about in Vienna – the tourist trade. Things have picked up a lot since I was a hotel boy here.'

'*Kraft durch Freude*, yes I know, I read about it in the paper.'

'That's it Ellie. It's great. It's bringing money to our town. This is a beautiful place you know and lots of people want to visit it. You'll see this summer, the German tourists will fill the place!'

'So she's working for the tourist office is she?' said Ellie, sensing that Michael was straying away from the topic.

'Yes that's right. She was just at a reception for the big wigs over in the hotel. She's some kind of hostess at things like that, has to act as one anyway, and they like to see some of the traditional stuff. I don't think she wears those things all the time.'

'No, but she looks very nice in it I must say.'

'Yes, I suppose she does, I wouldn't know…' said Michael, tailing off.

'You were at school with her you say?'

'Yes that's right. We were at school together. Old friends you might say.'

'She's very pretty. Wasn't she a pretty lady Anni,' said Ellie, as her daughter continued to play with her fingers. 'You liked her didn't you?' she said, addressing her child. Michael said nothing.

Then they went to break the news to his parents that they would be staying a few more weeks yet.

4

As spring came to the mountains, the snow melted away from all but the highest peaks and the green grass on the slopes outside the town invited walkers and tourists to explore the meadows and hike further into the mountainside forests. Ellie paid special attention to her daughter. This, she reflected, was the last time Anna would have her to herself alone – after the baby was born she would have to share her mother. Ellie felt she wanted to make the most of this time, whatever troubles there were with money and housing.

Enjoying Anna's company was not difficult for her. She was an easy child, affectionate, playful and pretty. She loved to splash about in the water on the edge of the lake, a straw hat on her head, from which the curls of her hair tumbled down. The two of them walked out of town into the fields, or around the lake, picking spring flowers to bring home, going as far as Ellie could manage as she grew heavier and the little legs of her daughter would tolerate.

Anna was her special first child. Her birth had been easy and she had always slept and fed well. As she had held her baby daughter in her arms, watching her at her breast, feeling the little mouth as it gave both her and the baby warmly delicious sensations of pleasure, Ellie wondered what it could have been like for her own mother, who had left her behind when she was only a few days old. Holding Anna close to her, she could not bear to think of what such a parting must have been like. Why had her mother not insisted on taking her with

31

her? How could she have allowed such a separation?

Anna's little hands and face, her sweet and complete dependency on her mother and on her mother's body for sustenance and care, filled Ellie with happiness. She watched the child smile, begin to sit up, to crawl, to speak, to walk, to run, to become everything that a mother might want her little baby girl to be. She realised that her daughter's birth was perhaps the best and most profound thing that had happened to her in her life. She loved her as completely as the love Anna so completely gave to her, and she knew that this love was greater than anything she might ever feel for any other person. Certainly no man could come close to this in her affections.

So the second child continued to grow within her through the months of April and May. It was the middle of the week when her waters broke. Preparations for this moment had been made. A local woman, Frau Hirsch, who attended births came round within the hour and Anna was taken away to be looked after by Frau Hirsch's daughter while she and Ilse Bauer busied themselves around the bed where Ellie was experiencing increasingly frequent contractions.

It was a long and difficult birth and all night the two women were encouraging and supporting Ellie in her labour. This was a big baby and somehow it wouldn't come out in the same easy way that Anna had made her entry into the world. Frau Hirsch said this was unusual – the first birth was usually the difficult one – and she hinted that her fee would need to be increased if it went on much beyond morning. Hearing this didn't help Ellie much, the anxiety making her tense.

But eventually, with what seemed like enormous effort, the two helpers encouraging Ellie's deep breathing and pushing, through waves of pain, the crown of the baby's head appeared. A little more of the baby came out and then with a spectacular crescendo of pain, along with a rush of fluid and bloody material, the baby slid out onto the bed. The midwife picked it up, slapped it on the back to make it cry and, once she had cut and tied the cord and mopped up a bit of the bloody mess on its body, wrapped it in some towelling and laid it next to its mother. It was another girl.

Ellie was torn by the passage of the baby, although the pain of this could not be separated in her mind from the other sensations of the birth, and the stinging, throbbing soreness of that part of her body seemed natural after such an experience. Frau Hirsch told her about the tear and stitched her up, saying ominously that a doctor might have to be called if things weren't looking right in a day or two. After the sheets had been changed and some cleaning up had been done, she then left, saying she'd call in to take a look at how things were getting on in a couple of days. Her daughter would bring Anna back later that day. The two women were left on their own with the baby.

Ilse yawned, seeing the baby apparently quiet next to Ellie, who looked with dull eyes at the little creature lying next to her.

'She'll need to feed soon I shouldn't wonder,' said the older woman. 'I'm surprised she didn't latch on straight away. I'm going to lie down for a bit. They'll bring Anna back soon and I need a bit of rest. Are you going to be all right?'

Ellie turned to her and nodded weakly and Ilse Bauer left the room.

This baby is different, thought Ellie. All of this is different. I'm not at home. I'm in a strange place. This baby is a stranger to me. What's its name?

The baby stirred next to her and one of its pink hands gripped the side of the towelling. Its face was wrinkled and its black hair, plastered onto its scalp, glistened wet. It made a kind of squealing noise and its mouth opened in what looked like a yawn, stretching the skin on its thin cheeks.

I suppose I must try to give it some milk, she thought, and she moved her breast to the baby's mouth. At this point, Anna had latched on eagerly and sucked hard. But this baby did nothing. Its lips seemed to have no purchase. She pushed the nipple into the baby's mouth a little further, holding its head, and the baby gave a couple of weak sucking movements and stopped.

Then its head moved away from the nipple and the real bawling started.

It went on for an hour and Ellie could do nothing for the baby. Then Ilse Bauer, unable to sleep because of the noise, came in and tried to help, putting the baby up against her daughter-in-law's breast, asking if Anna had been the same, worrying about the baby's distress, saying nothing like this had ever happened with her babies. After a couple of hours of this, the baby eventually settled and began to suck, but it was a bad start and it set the tone of the next few days, as far as breast feeding was concerned.

The weekend came and Michael was able to return from Kaprun to see his new child who they had named Maria. By that time Anna was also back at home, excited to see her sister. But the baby cried when it was put on Anna's lap and the little girl soon lost confidence and gave it back to her mother. It was floppy and fractious, taking the breast intermittently, not seeming to get much out of it, and crying in between times. Ellie complained of soreness everywhere and was uncommunicative, seeming increasingly hopeless about getting the baby to suck. Ilse Bauer was fussing around, tut tutting in between attempts to latch the baby on and soothe it to sleep. Ellie had done no more than sit up in bed and had only got up to go to the toilet. She seemed exhausted.

Frau Hirsch came round after a week of this, during which neither woman had got much sleep, assessed the situation and had a private conference with Frau Bauer. After this, it became clear what needed to happen and Ilse explained things to Ellie.

'My dear, this is not working out and Frau Hirsch and I have had a word about it. You mustn't worry you know, but this sort of thing happens from time to time and we know how to manage it. I am sure that what I am going to suggest will be helpful to you.'

Ellie was hardly listening, distracted by tiredness and the thoughts and feelings that seemed to be welling up from deep within her. Her mother-in-law seemed to be talking from behind a screen, her voice distant.

'We are very worried about your baby my dear. Maria needs to get some food into her or else there will be a bad result. You must know this yourself. We need to try her on someone who can provide her with milk. It'll give you a chance to rest and recover and when things are more even, you can have her back.'

Later, Ellie realised that her main emotion at this proposal was one of relief. At the time though, she neither felt nor said anything, but simply nodded to indicate her assent and the baby was taken away. Maria was given to a woman in her early thirties who lived in town and had just given birth herself to her fifth child. She was grateful for the money she earned by wet nursing Maria, which she did easily and without fuss. The baby responded well to the new mother and after a couple of weeks began to put on weight. Later Maria was sent to Rauris, to a country family who had looked after two of Michael's sisters when they were small, as it was clear to everyone that Ellie was still in a bad way and that it was a matter of indifference to her where her baby was.

Ellie's feelings were in fact very dark for several weeks after the birth, although she had no energy to tell anyone about them. She knew that she felt no love for her second child, but she had no idea why. After the baby had been away for a week, she still felt constantly tired but, at the same time, could not get to sleep herself and lost her own appetite for food. She ceased wanting to be with her husband or with Anna, who was looked after more by her grandmother as a result.

She found herself wondering what she was doing in this strange country, with these alien people who spoke a different language, yet she was unable to think where her real home was. She felt she had no home and belonged nowhere.

When Michael was around he would find her crying for no apparent reason and, when he asked her what was the matter, she snapped at him. She accused him of not loving her, complained again about his giving money to his parents. She found herself becoming suspicious about Michael being unfaithful and sometimes thought about Marianne Streubel who she had seen at the lakeshore that day with him.

She also thought about Anna and imagined she had been a bad mother to her, that she was allowing Ilse Bauer to take over too much, so she would call her daughter into the room but then be unable to think of what to do or say to her and the little girl would wander back to her grandmother. The one person she never thought about was her baby, whose very existence she began to find hard to imagine.

There was no doubt about it: it had been a mistake to have a second child. But how was she to prevent it from happening again? As she started, after a few weeks of these moods, to feel a bit better, she concentrated more and more on this thought: how to stop having another child. She knew there was an easy solution to this in the short term, but it would not work for ever. Sex was too important, both to Michael and her.

One day in mid-July Ellie found that she had slept well for a change and felt stronger. She was no longer plagued by the bad feelings that had been swirling about in her mind since the birth and she could see that the sun was out, the air was fresh and that it was summer in the mountains. She got out of bed and went into the kitchen. She looked around at its white-washed walls, pegs screwed into the bricks with pots and cloths hanging from them, the rough wooden table. Her mother-in-law was there, at the sink.

'Oh it's you is it?' said Ilse grumpily when she saw her. She pushed a strand of hair out of her eyes, her deeply veined hands making a contrast with her face, which to Ellie had always seemed unnaturally smooth in a woman of Ilse's age. 'Arising from your bed finally? We don't see you in here very often.' She had been making it clear to Ellie that she was getting tired of doing all the cooking and child care herself.

'Oh don't be like that Ilse' said Ellie. As she spoke she realised she had never used the other woman's first name before.

If Ilse was surprised by this, she said nothing about it. But it seemed she didn't like Ellie's attitude.

'I think it's fair enough for me to let off steam a bit, don't you think? It's not easy at my age you know, holding the fort here while you have been lying in bed.'

Ellie ignored the provocation. 'I feel so much better today though. I think I've been ill. Thank you Ilse. I don't know what I would have done without you.' And unusually again in their relationship, she put her hand on the other woman's sleeve in a gesture of affection.

Ilse softened immediately. 'Thank you my dear, those words mean a lot to me.'

At this the two women both began to cry a little and Ilse gave her a little hug in an uncharacteristic burst of warmth. Ellie felt it was the closest they had ever got to a real mother-daughter feeling.

'I wanted to ask you about something Ilse,' Ellie started hesitatingly, 'you being older and more experienced than me. I wanted to ask you about babies…'

'What do you mean, babies? I've had five of them myself and you have had two now. What can I tell you about them my dear?'

'No, it's not that. It's about, well, how to stop them.'

Ilse's eyes widened.

'I want to know if there's a way. Can you tell me? This one has been so bad, I don't think I can go through it again. Can you help me?' Ellie pleaded.

At this point Ilse Bauer clearly decided to make her feelings and her beliefs known, which she did at some length, while Ellie listened patiently, her own eyes now widening at what was revealed.

Ilse told Ellie in no uncertain terms that she was a Catholic, true not a very good one, she did not go to church very often, or take confession, but a Catholic she had been born and bred and a Catholic she would always stay. Yes, she knew the Party had had difficulties with the church, and Cardinal Innitzer had not always said the right thing, but that was the church as it was in Austria at this time, and that did not affect her fundamental beliefs, which were that you did not interfere with the will of God when it came to birth or death. God decides on these things and it was up to us to take the consequences.

She knew that not everyone agreed with her on this, she told Ellie, not even all Catholics, but she had consulted a priest about it after her third child and had satisfied herself on this matter. In the 1920s, when she was a younger woman than she was now, some people had come from Vienna to set up a clinic in the town offering advice to women who wanted to place limits on their families, but the priest and other local citizens had put a stop to their activities. And there had been books that had been circulated too, showing how everything worked, with pictures. Some local schoolboys had got hold of a copy, she had heard, and had to be punished by their teacher.

At any rate, she knew times were changing and that new thinking was coming in, but she for one wasn't going along with it, for the reasons she had already explained. She had heard that some of these *Kraft durch Freude* people were peddling some filthy ideas about sex that had nothing to do with the way in which decent people behaved, and that could be why you heard so many stories these days about divorce. In her younger days divorce was unheard of – you made your bed when you got married, and you had to lie in it, come what may. No, you could say what you wanted in favour of the Party, and there was a lot you could say in its favour, chiefly that it had made us all a lot stronger and more positive about the future, and that it was a relief that someone was finally prepared to do something about the Jews and the Gypsies and other unspeakable types, but if there was one thing where she parted company with them it was over the way they had tried to undermine Christian teachings, persuading people to leave the Church and cease to pay their dues, which she had heard was becoming more and more common, even in this town...

Ellie could see that she had unleashed a torrent, indeed a veritable waterfall of sentiment, and that there was no hope of getting any useful advice about avoiding pregnancy from that quarter. On the other hand, she had finally found out, because of that brief moment of intimacy, what made this bloody woman tick.

After this time Maria's birth and the events around it became matters about which nobody spoke. Anna stayed at home and regained much of her natural sweetness, Michael visited from Kaprun at weekends, baby Maria continued to live with her new family in the country to whom Michael paid a small weekly sum which he could ill afford. Ellie decided she must get a job and, in August that year, found temporary work in the council's housing department.

The housing office was located in the town hall on the main road through town, above the tangle of streets that led down to the lake, an ancient white building with black turrets pointing up to the sky like a witch's castle out of a fairy tale. Julius Grabner, the head of the housing department, had been appointed to that position after the previous incumbent, a man with a history of involvement in socialist politics, had been dismissed from his post. Grabner was a small, rotund man with thin spectacles who believed absolutely in the ideology of the Nazi party. In fact, he believed in it so much that all of the staff in his department were obliged to be blond and, preferably, blue-eyed. He himself, being dark and not at all Aryan looking, presented quite a contrast. However, he made up for this by dressing in semi-military jodhpurs and leather boots so that he struck an appropriately martial air, modelled, it seemed, on pictures he had seen of Heinrich Himmler, who was said to be one of his inspirations. It was rumoured that he engaged in regular shooting practice at the weekends with a pistol.

Knowing this about the man – for the whole town spread rumours about the personalities and quirks of the people who had been put in charge of their affairs since the regime change – Ellie held out little hope that she would find employment in Grabner's department, for she was dark skinned, with black hair and not in the least Aryan in appearance. What she did not realise at the time, though, was that Grabner's prejudices about the physical appearance of his employees did not always extend to his sexual fantasies, into which Ellie, who had recovered her shape well after the birth, must have fitted extremely well: she got the job.

Pretty soon it was evident that she was very good at her work. She had never done clerical work before, and the language was relatively new to her, but she was intelligent and hard-working, popular with her colleagues (who all hated Grabner) and she could see ways of streamlining the records system that no-one else had thought of. Coincidentally, she worked most closely with the young man who had interviewed her for the housing application, whose name was Peter. He turned out to be surprisingly amenable and friendly as a colleague. By September the two of them had put the filing system for housing applications into much better order.

The money she earned was very useful and took the pressure off their finances, even giving her hope that she might save enough over the next few months to be able to afford to rent a place.

Then came a day in early September when she was called into Grabner's office on the second floor. She went to him unsure what to expect, but apprehensive. The room was too warm and Grabner's desk was so big that it took up most of the room.

She felt his hot, wet hand on her back through the fabric of her dress as he guided her to a chair.

'How are those delightful babies of yours?' he asked, making himself comfortable in his own capacious seat on the other side of the desk, an empty expanse of shining wood.

She smiled in spite of herself at the thought of Anna, but felt it best not to tell him too much about Maria. 'Oh they are in very good condition Herr Grabner, thriving. My Anna has just turned two and the baby is doing just fine, thank you very much. My mother-in-law looks after them while I am here. My husband has to be away in the week you see.'

'Yes,' said Grabner, 'he is away, I know. You must be very lonely sometimes,' he said, leaning forward towards her with an oily smile, a bead of sweat appearing on his forehead.

Ellie said nothing to this.

'So he's working up at the dam?' Grabner continued, unabashed.

Ellie nodded and smiled cautiously.

'Such an impressive project! He must be proud to be a part of it I would think.'

'Yes he is proud I think,' she said doubtfully. 'He is certainly very pleased to have the work. He manages the workers' canteen.'

She was exaggerating – Michael was not the only 'manager' up there. In truth, he would count only as a deputy manager – there were three of these under-managers, on a shift system as work on the dam continued around the clock, and the *Höhere Aufseher*, a Bavarian German brought in to oversee the whole catering operation at the work camp, kept them all in line.

'He must be well paid then,' said Grabner speculatively.

'No, no, not so well paid,' said Ellie, confused and wondering what this interview was really all about. 'You'd be surprised. And we have growing children you know, and it is expensive staying here in the town. And we have the costs of his travel when he comes home. That is why I must have this job Herr Grabner, I am so pleased to have found a place here; I do hope I can continue.' And she smiled again at him, which seemed to charm him utterly. His face looked hot.

Then he got to the point.

'Well, I've called you in because of that. We would like to employ you here permanently,' he announced. 'It really is quite remarkable how you have managed to bring a sense of order to the housing files.'

Ellie was pleasurably surprised. She hadn't realised she was so good at the job.

'But I'm afraid you will have to get one of these new certificates if you are to work here permanently. We have no alternative; it is the law.'

He explained that Zell am See was a bit behind the times in complying with the new ancestry laws. She would need an *Ahnenpass,* stamped and signed correctly, if he was to issue her with a permanent contract of employment. Until then, it would be hourly paid work only, on a purely temporary basis.

'It's straightforward,' he said, spreading his fat little palms upwards on the table in a gesture conveying how routine this all was. 'You just need to tell the authorities who your parents were, where they were born, that kind of thing. Everybody is doing it now. It doesn't have to be a problem Frau Bauer. Just show your birth certificate and answer a few questions and you'll be done in an afternoon.'

But Ellie was worried. What might happen if these people discovered her parentage?

'Please don't think I'm trying to make a fuss Herr Grabner,' she said, trying to control her anxiety. 'Please believe me I am not. But it won't be so easy for me to get hold of documents like that. I am not from around here as you know. I only became Austrian when I married. How could I get a birth certificate from Jersey?' She gave him a pleading look. 'I really need this job Herr Grabner. What can I do? What would you advise?'

'I can't help it my dear,' said Grabner, 'I have to do what the law requires. I simply can't issue that contract as things stand. I am sure you can write to the records office – there must be a records office in that place – what is that place you come from? Jersey you say?'

'Yes,' said Ellie hurriedly, 'that's it – a little island off the coast of France.'

'Well, you can write to them can't you? Ask the French authorities for your birth documents. Everyone has to do it these days you see. We must all be able to show our ancestry you know, especially if we are in the public services,' and he smiled, as if this were a self-evident fact of life.

'Yes of course' she said, giving up the struggle. She had learned in her time in Zell am See that the town hall bureaucrats could be sticklers for the rules. A combination of pigheaded rural stupidity, she thought, and fear of their superiors. It didn't pay to make mistakes in this country.

'I'll try Herr Grabner, I'll try. And meanwhile, perhaps I can continue...'

'Of course my dear, you can continue working in the Department for now. We all think you are doing so well. Just let me know if you run into any difficulties over this little matter of the *Ahnenpass* and I will do all I can to help. We Austrians like to be helpful you know.'

He stood up and came round the desk to let her out of his overheated, cramped office, making sure that he slid a sticky palm down from the small of her back and over her bottom, giving it a little squeeze as he ushered her out. She turned her head and forced a smile as she walked out of his reach. It wasn't worth antagonising him.

The Jews were at the heart of this *Ahnenpass* thing, she knew from reading the *Völkischer Beobachter*. And it wasn't just the Jews, it was a whole lot of other people too: Gypsies, Slavs from the East, all sorts attracted suspicion and hostility whenever anyone mentioned them. Michael had said some were working up in the mountain camp at Kaprun, had worked there all through the winter. He seemed strained when he talked about this and hadn't wanted to look her in the face, so she had avoided asking him more.

But there weren't any Jews living in Zell am See. She had never seen one in her life. So why was everyone here so bothered about them?

No point in mulling over that one, though. She had a job to do and money to earn. In her lunch break, she walked through the streets of the town towards the lake. It was mid-week, so it was odd that all the shoe and clothing stores were shut; a notice on one said 'Temporary closure notice' but no more. But she was more concerned about what to do about the *Ahnenpass*. Finally she had an idea: she would go and see her friend Kurt Steinhauser. He'd know what to do.

She had got to know Kurt Steinhauser when she had gone with Michael and Anna to his studio to have their photographs taken, shortly after their arrival. Michael wanted to record the auspicious moment, at the point in his life when he returned to his home town with his wife and child. He made Ellie dress up in a *dirndl* and pose against a painted backdrop of snowy mountains, smiling for the picture.

After that first visit Ellie made a habit of dropping in on the photography shop, which was not very busy in the winter months, and chatted with either Kurt or his wife Irma, depending on who she found tending the counter. They were always pleased to see her and Kurt was particularly helpful in her efforts to learn German in the first few months. The friendship was important to her as she recovered from the birth of her second baby too, as the older couple were good at listening to her troubles and did not seem to judge her harshly for what had happened. In fact, she had trusted the couple with some of the secrets about her own parentage that she shared with no-one else.

Today, Irma was at the counter. She found Kurt seated upstairs in the studio, reading. He was a man in his mid-fifties whose greying hair stood upright at the centre. Irma used to tamp it down, complaining that he never brushed it, a charge he laughingly denied, getting out a little comb to bring it under control, a state of affairs that never lasted more than a minute or two, as the hair then stood up again. Irma called him her *igel* – her hedgehog.

Ellie told him about the *Ahnenpass*, about how hard it would be for her to obtain the required certificates of birth. His face grew strained as he heard the story and he put his book down, leaning forward.

'I'm afraid this is a serious matter. You must take some steps to make sure that you are all right. It is a problem about your father. Are you sure you know nothing of him?'

'Yes, my grandmother knew who he was, but she wouldn't say anything about it to anyone. I'm sure there is no record of him anywhere.'

'But this is not something that can be hidden. The Germans who control these things are very thorough and they will find out if you tell any lies, believe me.'

'But what will happen if I tell them Kurt?' she exclaimed anxiously. 'I could lose my job! I am good at it and I need the money – why do they need this thing?'

'You know why, my dear.' His face was sad.

'But I'm not Jewish,' she exclaimed. 'My mother was from a French family. They lived in France for ages before I came along!'

Kurt fell silent for a while. Then he explained patiently that it wasn't just about proving that you were not from a Jewish family. You had to provide positive proof of racial ancestry and to eliminate the possibility that any parent, grandparent or great grandparent had had impure blood in them too.

'But how can I do that if I don't know who my father was,' she said despondently. 'The bloody Jews – why are they causing all this trouble for us?'

There was another silence and she realised that she had said something very wrong. Kurt was more than pained as she looked into his face. There were tears in his eyes. She felt mortified.

'What have I said? Why are you upset? I am so sorry, if there's anything…' and she stood up and came over to him, putting her arms around his shoulders to comfort him. He put his arm around her waist from where he sat and eventually looked up, somewhat recovered.

'It's all right my dear. There is so much you don't know. Why should you after all? You have your child and your husband, who is not much wiser than you,' and he laughed a bit at this, blowing his nose on a handkerchief. 'Look, I must tell you a few things, because we are friends and we trust each other, I think. It is time you knew a little more about me.'

Kurt Steinhauser then explained to her that he was a Jew, although his wife was not. He had met her in Vienna in the 1920s. He had grown up in the great city, in an area called Leopoldstadt where many Jews lived. Irma was also Viennese. Their marriage, which had divided the families, meant that it was best to leave Vienna and set up somewhere far away from either family. With money that he had inherited, they moved to Zell am See where he had set up his photography business.

He told Ellie about what had happened to his relatives in Vienna after the *Anschluss*. Within hours of the German entry into the country Leopoldstadt had been invaded by hordes of young men shouting *Sieg heil!* and *Jude verrecke!* and other crazed, angry slogans. Many were in the brown shirts and uniforms of the SA, roaming around the streets smashing shop windows, breaking into houses, stealing property, beating up Jews and terrorising them, a real witches' Sabbath. His father had been caught on the street by a bunch of these thugs and had been forced to perform physical exercises, crouching down, standing up, crouching down, standing up, until he could raise himself no more, all the time surrounded by the brownshirts, with an outer ring of onlookers who watched half horrified, half with pleasure, at the sight. Kurt's sister had written to tell him of this.

Ellie thought of what she had said about the Jews causing trouble and tried to apologise again, but Kurt waved her off, saying he forgave her. But he needed to tell her more.

The mobs in Vienna subsided after a week or so, leading some to think the worst was over. But the violence of the first week was then replaced by a more systematic persecution. Kurt described how members of his family – his parents, his sister and her husband – had been desperate to emigrate and had spent days queuing at various offices for the paperwork that would allow this to happen. Kurt was with them by this stage, trying to help them make sense of the forms they had to fill in, providing moral support and comfort. His family had all gone to America and he had heard that they were in New York, though he knew little of their circumstances there.

'They left with nothing, Ellie, nothing but the clothes they stood up in and a suitcase each,' and Kurt seemed on the verge of tears again, with Ellie beside him, appalled at the story.

Kurt himself was protected, he explained to Ellie, because his marriage to Irma meant that he was not subject to the same laws. He wondered how long that would last though. He kept his Jewish origins quiet in his dealings with the townspeople, although he knew many people were aware of it, and he and Irma had been in Zell am See so long, and were so well liked that he thought he was safe there. But he worried all the time that this situation might not continue for ever. In Vienna Jews married to non-Jews were being forced to live in 'Jew houses', especially if they had no children, and had had their livelihoods stripped from them. Some non-Jews had even divorced their Jewish other halves – the new laws allowed that. People who had *mischlinge* children were desperate to get them reclassified. There were Aryan mothers who had got Jewish fathers to swear on oath that they were not really the father of their children.

'How could they do such a thing?' Ellie exclaimed, astonished. 'And how could they persuade the authorities that it was true?'

'It's not so unusual,' said Kurt, laughing now. 'You really are a bit more innocent than I thought. Some men have got good reasons to get their wives pregnant by other men!'

Ellie couldn't understand this at all and her face must have shown it. Kurt explained: some men were impotent, some had had syphilis. He seemed quite easy about discussing these facts of life with her, but she suddenly felt self-conscious and embarrassed to be hearing of such things, especially from a man. Kurt seemed to sense this and deflected the subject

As a photographer he had been involved in this *Ahnenpass* nonsense first hand, he told Ellie. He didn't know of any other Jews in Zell am See, but there were people who had trouble proving their ancestry with the right kind of birth records. In the scramble for jobs in the town hall, that mattered. Some of them got referred to the Office of Kinship Research in Vienna for a physical assessment, but the people there were overwhelmed so they got him to take technical photographs which he then sent to Vienna for assessment. The pictures allowed measurements of all kinds of physical features – the thickness of the lips and earlobes, the breadth of the forehead, whether the eyebrows met, the angle of the nose. They sent him a little measuring device in a frame that the people had to press up against when the pictures were taken.

'I feel terrible doing this work Ellie, terrible. The people are anxious about the outcome and ask all kinds of questions that I cannot answer. I just follow the instructions that those devils in Vienna send me, and put the photographs in the envelopes they provide. I feel I have to do it. To refuse would bring attention to myself. When I think of my own family so far away…'

Ellie had listened to this story with a growing sense of horror about what had been going on. She realised how naïve she had been. How could she have blurted out that thing about the Jews to Kurt Steinhauser? What was the matter with her? Then she thought about Ilse and some of the things she had heard her say – about Hitler, about the Sudeten Germans coming back into the Reich and about the Jews of course.

'You must think I am a complete idiot Kurt,' she said. 'I can't believe how stupid I have been. I had no idea…..'

'Yes, Ellie, I suppose you are,' said Kurt through his tears again, 'but I am very fond of you, so I forgive you.' And he smiled at her so that she felt overwhelmed, yet at the same time a little awed by him. With all that he had been through, how could he have taken her under his wing? She felt very small beside him.

Kurt then said that she would need to fill in the forms to say there were difficulties getting the relevant birth certificates. The people in Vienna would no doubt then require a physical assessment and perhaps an interview with a local official. He did not think they would ask her to go to Vienna, although he didn't know for sure. But he thought she would be all right. He was no expert in racial science but with her type of dark skin and hair he suspected she would be regarded as being Mediterranean in appearance rather than Jewish. She certainly wouldn't be categorised as Slavic – her eyes weren't the right shape.

They laughed at that and, after a little more talk she took her leave of him, pressing his hand and apologising once again, thanking him for his advice, promising to see the couple again soon.

This, as it turned out, was a promise she could not keep.

*

When she got home, she found Ilse in the kitchen clutching a newspaper. Her hair had come loose and hung around her shoulders so that grey streaks in it were more visible than usual and she looked suddenly older.

'Have you seen this?' she said, thrusting the front page almost into Ellie's face. 'England has declared war!'

Ilse was tense and angry, a wild look on her face. It was as if the war was Ellie's fault.

'This is like my childhood again. I never thought I would live to see this happen a second time. There will be rationing again soon. Have you seen the High Street? Half the stores are closed while they work things out. How could they do this? Can your people not see that the Poles only meant trouble for Germany? Something had to be done to…'

'I don't know anything about this Ilse,' Ellie objected angrily. 'Don't say my people. I am Austrian remember! I have Austrian nationality, same as you or anyone here!'

This was ridiculous and she knew it, but in the heat of the moment, feeling instantly attacked, it was all she could think of. Anna came into the room and stood in the doorway, attracted by the noise of the two women's voices, but they were too worked up to pay attention to her.

'Austrian, my eye!' said Ilse. 'You are British. You know it too, I can tell. The British are warmongers. They love war so much that they oppose the Führer's just demands for our land and people. Why do they do this? Why?'

She was working herself up into a frenzy.

'I know nothing about this Ilse, I told you. It is nothing to do with me. I grew up in Jersey remember, which is French as far as I'm concerned. Remember my name? Eloise Picot. A *French* name! My family were all from there. I'm not part of them. I don't know anything about these political things,' and she threw down her shopping bag angrily.

Ilse paused at this. The French, of course, were one of the countries ranged against Germany now, but it seemed she didn't make the connection. For her, the British were leading the charge.

'What do you mean, you are not part of them?' she said suspiciously.

'I mean I'm not part of Britain, that's what I mean. I never was and I am certainly not now.'

'I thought you meant something else,' said Ilse with a sly look on her face. The atmosphere was calmer now, but Ellie was still feeling very worked up.

'I suppose you are talking about my father!' It was a topic that had never been raised between them before. 'Well I'll tell you about him if you must know. My father is called LeBrocq. He's the person who brought me up and he is Jersiaise through and through – not British and not French, but Jersey. You don't know much about that kind of thing do you, stuck in this little place all your life?'

Ilse was undaunted. 'But I heard he is not your father Eloise. Michael told me…'

And Ellie knew the game was up. That idiot Michael with his fawning approach to his mother. She should have known he would give away all her secrets. But by now she felt so outraged she could have said anything. She was sick of all the tip-toeing around the truth that was necessary to get along in this rotten little town.

'Ah, so he told you did he? Well to me he's my father. He brought me up. I don't know who my real father is and I don't care. I don't see why I should be ashamed of that either. He could be German for all I know, Dutch, French, Italian. I don't care! He could be Jewish for all I give a damn about it! He never took an interest in me or my mother after he had ruined her life and I don't care who he is or where he is now.'

At this, the older woman smiled.

'Look, let's calm down about all of this shall we?' she said. 'Take your coat off and we'll have a cup of coffee together. I was upset at this news of war, you see. I'm sorry to have laid into you for it. I know you're not to blame. We shall see what we shall see, and our lives will go on, come what may.'

Ellie saw that Anna was nearby, listening, and she drew the little girl towards her and sat her on her knee. Anna's face was tense with anxiety and bewilderment so Ellie put her arms around her to squeeze her against her own body, feeling her own sensations become calmer as she did so. The two women studied the paper together, reading some of the details of what was going on in Poland and the rest of the world and speaking more quietly to each other.

Much later Ellie realised that this was the moment when Ilse starting making new plans for her son.

5

The *AHNENPASS* ISSUE did not work out as Mr Steinhauser had imagined. Because of the war, getting birth certificates from Jersey, now enemy territory, was impossible. Ellie got a letter from the Vienna officials with a document recording her as *Vorübergehend nicht klassifiziert* – 'temporarily unclassified'. She was informed that as a citizen of the Reich by virtue of her marriage to an Austrian she was protected from internment as an enemy alien, but she would have to report to the police once a month. This she did for a couple of months, but when she missed the third month nothing happened so she didn't go back. But she lost her job at the town hall.

Through the autumn of 1939 she worked in hotel kitchens until the dregs of the summer tourist trade dried up. Then she put cards in local shops, advertising herself as a domestic help. Michael objected to her doing such demeaning work, but she brushed him off, telling him they needed the money – an unspoken accusation at him for the way in which he was allowing his parents to take a cut out of their finances. She cleaned the houses of local worthies and sometimes looked after their children while Anna stayed at Ilse's place. For a while she even got a job looking after the children of Frau Waibel, the deputy mayor's wife.

She and Michael did not speak of baby Maria. If the money which Michael gave his parents had been his guilty secret, hers was her inability to look after Maria and her eventual rejection of the baby. The couple generally avoided both topics. And the time Michael spent with them in town became less and less as the winter progressed. He said the snows made it difficult for him to get down from Kaprun. Things were hard up in the mountain camp he said, and again she found him looking down at the floor as he spoke of conditions in the camp, unwilling to say more.

The newspapers grew less filled with news of the war, since nothing much seemed to be happening. Instead, there were notices about the growing numbers of restrictions in their everyday lives. The clothes shops in the town had re-opened after a couple of weeks but there were now new rules about clothing allowances to follow. The *Völkischer Beobachter* ran a cheerfully worded article on how to re-cut old clothes to make them more fashionable.

Ilse laughed at that: 'That's for the Viennese so they can keep up their airs and graces,' she said.

Soap was also rationed so Ilse nagged at Johannes about the amount he used shaving – why did he have to wash out the brush? Surely there was enough there for another day?

That autumn young men in brown shirts appeared in the main square rattling collecting cups for winter war aid, while a military band played marches. From mid-November the weather turned unusually cold so when the newspapers announced that the price of fuel was going down a lot of people in the town were relieved, especially the people in the new housing over near Waibel's fields, since their heating depended on supplies of charcoal briquettes. It made no difference to the Bauer family though and Ilse crowed about this. There were plentiful supplies of firewood in the council yards, to which Johannes had access. Then the flour ration was increased a bit, which did make a difference to them, so they could all be pleased.

Marianne Streubel visited occasionally in the evenings or at weekends. She had known the Bauers as a young child it seemed, because of being a school friend of Michael's, and although her parents were too important in the town to pay much attention to the family, Marianne seemed less snooty. Ilse was keen on her visits and whenever she departed called out to her 'Come again soon.' But Ellie felt wary of her. If Michael's visits coincided with Marianne's, and it seemed they often did, he paid a lot of attention to her.

On the other hand, the tales Marianne told of Vienna made it seem an exciting and glamorous place to Ellie. She had been there as an apprentice in the tourist office when the Germans had arrived and she told them about that crazy week in March the year before when the crowds had gone wild. Ilse was very interested in all this and asked her a lot of questions about the speeches in the Heldenplatz, about which German leaders had been there apart from the Führer, what they had said, the reactions of the crowd, who was running the city now.

But Ellie wanted Marianne to talk about the shops and the restaurants and the grand buildings she had seen there. She particularly enjoyed Marianne's description of women in the coffee houses, 'eating cakes piled so high with cream you wouldn't think it was possible to get it down you.' Cream was banned from the coffee houses now, Marianne said, although it was clear from her figure that she herself hadn't indulged in that particular vice very much: she was a well-proportioned young woman with smooth white skin and lovely long blonde hair which she wore in plaits which most of the time were pinned up. Ellie wondered how her hair would look if she brushed it out.

Christmas passed and the New Year brought even more freezing weather. Although Ellie struggled out of the house into the icy conditions to her various jobs, the cold, dark evenings meant that she and Anna spent long hours cooped up in the small space with the older couple. It was much harder to spend time down at the lake, as they had in the summer, as it was so cold Anna's fingers froze after an hour or so and she wanted to go home to the warmth. Ilse said Ellie was a bit soft about cold and egged her on to take the child out more, which caused tensions, although there was no repeat of the row they'd had when war had broken out.

It was a relief, therefore, when in March the weather began to warm and the days grew longer. Anna made a new friend down at the lake, a boy of her own age from a neighbouring family, and because this boy knew other children, Anna would often beg her mother to take her to the lakeside where she might meet up with her other little friends.

Then Michael brought welcome news. There was a job and somewhere to live in Kaprun for Ellie. Marcher, one of his colleagues in the catering operation up at the dam, came from Kaprun itself and his son was away for now, in the armed services.

'Probably in France I shouldn't wonder,' said Ilse.

'Yes,' interjected Marianne who was there on one of her visits, 'I heard Josef Marcher joined up back in November with the army. He's a soldier now. His mother's very proud of him!'

'And so she should be,' remarked Ilse, 'they are achieving great things in France. The French and the British went down like skittles.'

The whole town was following the news of the German invasion avidly, but Michael gave his mother and Marianne a stern look.

'Oh I'm so sorry Ellie,' said Marianne, 'I forgot.' Ilse put her hand over her mouth and fell silent.

Ellie shrugged. 'It makes no difference to me what these men get up to with their guns and tanks; what do I care?' and she laughed defiantly, saying no more about it.

She thought about it all the same. It wasn't as if she didn't realise she was living in a country that was at war with hers. But, she reflected, she had meant what she had said to Ilse about not feeling British. What had the British ever done for her?

'What's this job Michael?' she said, 'Tell me about it.'

Michael explained that Frau Marcher ran a gasthof just out of town which prepared food for some of the workers building the power plant at the bottom of the valley. She needed someone to help out and had a spare room they could have.

'It's only a small room darling, but it'll be big enough for us and the best news is about the job. You'll be able to earn some money and the work is nowhere near as hard as it is in the mountain camp.'

By now she knew that the workers at the mountain camp where Michael worked were mostly either prisoners, or what he called guest workers from Poland. Michael said conditions were tough for the men up there, really tough. It was hard getting supplies up the narrow track into the mountains and he had to fight the transport people all the time, who were under pressure to get the dam built as fast as possible, so that food supplies for the workers' canteen were low down on their priority list. People were so hungry, he started to say, looking up at her with a pleading look in his eyes. She could tell that he wanted to say more, but then he stopped himself, switching back to what she'd be doing in the work site lower down.

The job in the Marcher gasthof sounded good to Ellie and she could see Michael was pretty pleased with himself for getting it all set up. It would be so great to get out of this place. But then she thought of her daughter and her new friends at the lake. 'What about Anna?' she asked, 'It'll be quite a change for her, just when she's got the summer to look forward to.'

'Oh, we'll look after her my dear,' said Ilse, and smiled at the little girl, giving her a squeeze. Anna was listening silently and looked like she didn't know what was going on. 'You can stay with your granny can't you?' Marianne smiled too at this, leaning over and stroking Anna, who went over to her and got on to her lap. Anna stood and reached up to play with Marianne's hair, which was pinned up as usual, but Marianne pulled her head back and gently but firmly got the little girl to sit down.

'There's no room for children I'm afraid,' said Michael. 'Frau Marcher specified that. And anyway, who would look after her while we're at work? It's a full-time job you know. You'll be on a shift system and we'll have to get your shifts to fall in the week so we can get down here together. It'll be all right, you'll see.'

It did indeed sound like a good plan, which would solve a lot of problems. They'd have more money and they'd finally be together. And she'd get away from this house, which had become like a prison to her.

A week later Anna was in tears about her mother leaving for Kaprun. She stood on a bench at the bus station and had her arms gripped tightly around her mother's neck as Ellie tried to soothe her, patting her back and saying she would be back to see her very soon. The little girl, though, was inconsolable, wailing and struggling against Ilse who held her back as Ellie got her bags onto the bus.

Seeing Anna's reactions was another thing that gave Ellie pause for thought. She knew that she didn't feel unhappy about leaving Anna behind and part of her wondered why. Overwhelmingly, she was filled with thoughts about what was to come and almost deliriously happy to be escaping from Michael's parents' house, where she had now spent two long winters.

Anna would be all right for a bit she said to herself. They'd be back to see her and they'd soon find a bigger place for them all. This Marcher place was just a temporary solution.

Frau Marcher proved to be a large, middle-aged woman who welcomed her warmly. It turned out she wasn't going to be staying at the gasthof, but in the Marcher's house in Kaprun itself. She'd have to walk half an hour up the valley to her work. The Marcher house was twice the size of the Bauer's, which wasn't saying much, but there was a spare room with the

son away at the war, and although it was tiny, she liked it –
finally a place she could call her own. Frau Marcher said she
could have her own cupboard in the kitchen and could come
and go as she pleased.

'Can we eat in the kitchen too?' asked Ellie.

'How do you mean?'

'I mean Michael and myself – in the kitchen? We won't be
in your way.'

'Well, this is a room for one person you know,' said Frau
Marcher, her broad forehead frowning with concern. 'I did
stress that to your husband when we made this arrangement.'

This was news to Ellie. She realised she hadn't really
thought through how all of this would actually work, although
she thought she remembered Michael saying they could both
stay there. On the other hand, it wasn't the first time his promises hadn't quite worked out. She thought quickly.

'Oh, of course,' she said, 'I understand. You mustn't worry,
I won't be in your way.'

She could sense that this woman was someone who could
get tough when she wanted to. This situation had to be made
to work, at least for now, else it was back to Zell am See for
her and no job at Kaprun.

After that she had to feel her way carefully with her new
landlady. Frau Marcher proved true to initial impressions –
friendly enough, but defensive of her territory. Her husband
turned out to be a younger copy of Johannes Bauer, silent most
of the time and always tired from his work, which was up at
the mountain camp with Michael. When he came down from
the camp to home he wanted to put his feet up and be served
by his wife in what Ellie now recognised as the customary
Austrian fashion.

Her own relations with Michael seemed to improve. Frau
Marcher was happy for him to stay the night with Ellie when
he came down from the mountain, which he did from time to
time in the narrow bed. But neither of them wanted to do this

all the time as he had a room in the worker's barracks on the power station site which he had got used to. She couldn't stay with him there overnight, but she could visit the room in her breaks or after work for an hour or two in the evening if she wanted. They promised each other they would find a bigger place soon, although neither took any steps towards making that happen. If Ellie thought about it, she realised their money probably wouldn't have stretched any further anyway.

The work at the gasthof proved more demanding than Michael had led her to believe but for the most part she loved it. She appreciated having something she could do for herself and enjoyed walking up the road to work each morning, unencumbered by husband, child or parents-in-law, getting stuck into the busy atmosphere of the kitchen and getting to know the others who worked there, who were a good lot.

The food Ellie made was for the senior managers of the hydro-electric project, who were billeted at the gasthof. The men always had to have a choice between two or more dishes – fish or chicken, stew or sausage, beer or wine. Not that Ellie got involved in the cooking itself. Her job was to prepare vegetables for the cooks, wash and clear up and do anything else that was needed to keep the kitchen tidy and clean. What mattered with a job like this was getting on with the people you were working with and staying on the right side of your boss. That, and avoiding peeling potatoes if you could. From that point of view, it was all just fine.

Once in a while, though, she got sent to the canteen serving the workers who were building the power station at the bottom of the valley. Most of these men were Austrians, but some were prisoners or Poles. She had to clean the hotchpotch machine in the kitchen. This was a huge steel drum into which two grinders fed material that boiled everything up together, usually starting with a basic mix of dried pea powder and water. All kinds of stuff got fed into the stew through the grinders.

The first boiling was for the Austrian labourers, people who had been signed up in the labour exchanges in Vienna, Graz or Linz, men who had been down on their luck and had jumped at the chance of a job. Fresh vegetables – mostly potatoes and carrots – were put in, the rotten stuff having been thrown into a pile. Any meat was cut up and put into the mix in lumps, avoiding the grinders. The result was a passable stew, which the workers had with bread every other day. They didn't always like it but there was a lot of sea fish available nowadays, shipped in from Germany, and that was a good substitute, baked in trays.

The second boiling was for the Poles and the prisoners. They were the people who did the dirtiest, most dangerous jobs, the ones shifting heavy cement bags and steel rods off the trucks and into the warehouses, or digging foundations. The meat for them was generally rancid and fatty stuff or bits that had been discarded earlier, so it had to be mashed up in the grinders before it went into the hotchpotch. The pea powder often came from old or broken bags and if there were insects they went in too. Then the vegetables were added, sometimes cut into lumps if the kitchen staff had time, otherwise they were just added to a general mix that usually included rotten stuff kept from earlier, sent through the grinders to produce a paste that was mixed into the boil. The prisoners never got anything else. Ellie wondered what they ate up at the mountain camp.

At the end of a shift, the whole thing had to be dismantled and cleaned, something that took Ellie and another kitchen worker an hour of hard work. The smells and sights as the grinders were opened were foul and everyone tried to avoid getting assigned to that job.

As the summer approached, they got used to their new living and working arrangements. Michael came down from the mountain every ten days for a few days off and that was the time they had hoped to get down to Zell am See to see Anna together. But Ellie couldn't always be sure of getting those days off as her shifts – organised by Frau Marcher – had to take account of the other kitchen workers. So when they couldn't coincide one of them would go down alone, usually just for the day.

Ellie found, though, that these visits often upset her because of the fuss Anna made. Once, Anna was out with Marianne when Ellie arrived and the two of them took ages to get back to the house, Marianne explaining that Anna wouldn't be prised away from her friends at the lakeside when she was told to come home to see her mother. More usually, when Ellie got to the house, Anna would be playing outside at the back of the house and wouldn't come in when she was told her mother was home.

Ellie couldn't understand this. Surely Anna must be missing her and was looking forward to her coming home? What was the matter with her? She tried hard to get Anna's attention, taking her to the lake herself if she hadn't been that day, going to the main street with her and buying her a biscuit at the bakers, until she had got Anna back into a good mood. All too soon though, it would be time to leave again and Anna would start up with her bawling and crying. Increasingly, Ellie found these visits draining and discussed it with Michael, the two of them agreeing that it probably wasn't a good idea for Anna to be upset so often by her visits. This was a perfect reason to cut down on them. That summer Ellie focused instead on finding new friends in Kaprun.

6

THE FIVE COMPANIONS set off up the mountain path one hot August day, the men carrying water, bread and sausage in their back packs, the women with alpine walking sticks they had borrowed from the Marcher house.

Josef Marcher had come home on leave from France and his companion, Paul Schneider, an older man, was a fellow soldier. Paul had been wounded in the fighting in France and his left arm dangled loose in its sleeve. Marianne had joined them for the day.

'I know a path up through the forest,' called out Paul. 'There's a lake up there where we can have a swim.'

'I haven't got a costume,' said Marianne to Ellie. 'Have you?'

Ellie shrugged, indicating that she hadn't either, but Josef overheard them. 'You don't want to worry about that!' he said, his eyes bright with laughter. He was a wiry young man with thick black hair, cropped short, and white teeth. His upper body was muscular and he sprang along the stony path without any apparent effort while the civilians panted to keep up.

'Slow down a bit will you?' said Michael, 'we're not all in training you know.'

They made their way across the alpine meadow where cows grazed and birds flew from one grassy tussock to the next, through a gate and into the belt of conifers, which surrounded them with a cool, slightly damp, darkness. The path went on, with glimpses of sunlight through the trees. After half an hour, the trees began to thin out and they found themselves out in the open again, on barer ground. They stopped to look back at the view over the tops of the trees.

Far down below was the valley where the power station was being built.

'There's a farmhouse that'll have to move once we've built the dam up there,' said Michael, indicating upwards.

'That won't be for a while yet, at the rate things are going,' replied Josef Marcher. His older companion nodded and spoke in a deep, quiet voice.

'I've known that valley since I was a boy. I used go up there sometimes. You can just about get up and back in a day. It'll be sad to see it gone. It can take as long as it likes as far as I'm concerned.'

Ellie looked at Paul as he gazed down the slope, his right hand cradling the useless left arm as he stood. Unlike Josef, whose muscular energy seemed to burst forth in everything he said or did, Paul was calmer. He had allowed his hair to grow since his wound and it flopped forward over his eyes, giving him a dreamy look as he stared into the distance. Ellie thought his face seemed worn with experience. She knew that he had spent two months in a hospital after he was wounded. These two soldiers must have seen some terrible things.

She spoke for the sake of something to say.

'I'd like a swim when we get to the lake. It'll be good to get into some water. In Jersey I was always in the water.'

Paul looked at her for a while with a thoughtful expression and she found him beside her as the party resumed their walk, although he said nothing.

An hour later, they worked their way around the shoulder of a treeless pasture with a jagged rise of rock rising up to the left. There was a little mountain rest hut up there, but it was empty. Below them was the dark Brandlsee lake.

'Let's have a swim boys!' cried Josef, and ran down the slope. The other two men made their way more carefully across the rocky ground and joined Josef at the waterside. The girls watched as the men took off their clothes and ran into the water, laughing and splashing.

'Let's stay up here and watch them show off,' said Marianne.

'No, I want to go in,' said Ellie and pulled Marianne by the arm.

'You can't do that Ellie,' she said, resisting, 'we'd be naked!'

'Who cares? I've seen it all before and I expect they have too. Come on. We can go over there behind that little rise. If we take our clothes off there the men won't be able to see us, and then we'll be in the water.'

The water was icy and became deep very quickly. Marianne kept her head above water, doing a sedate breast stroke along the shore towards the men. Ellie struck out for the centre with a powerful crawl and got there rapidly, stopping and paddling her legs to keep her head above water.

'This is amazing!' she shouted and looked back at the men sitting in the shallows. Marianne was near them at the shoreline, crouching with her upper body above the water, her arms crossed over her breasts. Ellie swam towards the group and Michael came out to her so that they were standing in water that came up to their necks. Her back was towards him and she felt his erect penis against her.

'I didn't know you could do that in water this cold,' she whispered, laughing. She glanced up behind her at the same time and saw that he was gazing at Marianne.

He became aware of her and joked, 'Well I suppose there's still some life in our marriage yet!'

Then they swam apart.

On the shore again, drying off in the mountain sunshine where the men could not see them, Ellie looked at Marianne's smooth pink body with breasts heaving with the effort of the swim.

'I must teach you to do crawl Marianne. It's much faster.'

'No thanks, I don't like to get my hair wet. You swim like a fish Ellie – like you've been doing it all your life.'

'Well I have, I suppose. I grew up on an island remember, surrounded by sea. And it's warm, too, for quite a bit of the year. We were always in and out of the water as children. This lake water is a bit different though.'

As they got their clothes on Ellie found herself remembering a trip she'd made once to La Grève de Lecq in Jersey with Michael, Eva, James and Billy, when they had found a conger eel on the beach and brought it home to eat. Five of them then and five of them now. She had felt strands of weed curling around her legs while she was in the lake and wondered if there were any lake monsters in there that could rival the conger eel.

'So you're from the Channel Islands,' said Paul as he got food out of the rucksacks. Michael and Josef Marcher were smoking.

'Yes that's right,' replied Ellie. 'Born and bred.'

'I think that's where I'm headed.'

'Don't be silly Paul, they're English,' said Michael.

'Not any more they're not. We took them a few weeks ago,' said Josef, proudly.

'What! You took them?' exclaimed Ellie. 'What do you mean, took them?'

'That's just what I mean. We took them – the glorious German army that is, with a bit of help from Paul and me here. We occupied the islands back in July. Didn't you hear?'

'It's not exactly big news over here,' said Marianne. 'Everyone thinks they're a part of France but it's the only bit of England we've got so far. My father was saying the British are foolish, trying to be heroes. They can't hold out for ever. When they ask for peace, Germany will accept.'

'Do you really mean there are Germans there now?' asked Ellie.

'Yes I expect it takes a bit of getting used to,' reflected Josef, taking a bite of sausage and spitting out some skin.

'Rumour is that I'll be posted there soon,' said Paul. 'That's where they put people like me, the walking wounded. I'll be on occupation duties.' And then to Ellie, 'You must tell me what it's like.'

'Did they report this in the papers?' she asked. She was beginning to wonder whether this news had been kept from her deliberately. Michael wasn't saying anything and when she looked at him he looked away.

'Yes of course,' said Josef, 'although as Marianne says, it's not such big news I suppose, compared with our entry into Paris,' and he was off on one of his favourite subjects. While Paul had been languishing with his wound in a field hospital, he had got to Paris. He hadn't taken part in the famous victory parade down the Champs-Elysées. Austrian troops were excluded from that, he said bitterly, even though we had fought as well as the next man. But he had seen Paris. And what a time to be there!

At that, Marianne was full of questions and curiosity about what the city had been like. Josef enjoyed this attention and described gorgeous houses, grand boulevards, majestic palaces and churches, the shops, the women.

'I can tell you, they were all over us!' he said. 'We were the conquering heroes as far as the French girls were concerned. You wouldn't have thought their men had been trying to fight us just weeks before. Not that they put up much of a fight.'

'Not like the Tommy who got his bayonet into me,' said Paul ruefully at that point. The men still had their shirts off after the swim, Josef's thick mass of dark chest hair and muscular torso contrasting with Michael's slim, almost hairless frame. Ellie's eyes were drawn to the scar below Paul's shoulder.

'Is that where it went in?' she asked.

Josef answered for him. 'Yes, that's where it went in. The Tommies fought bravely at Dunkirk, at least some of them did. Old Paul here got the Iron Cross for what he did that day, and he's got the close combat award too. He's too shy to tell you. He's a fine soldier.'

'Was,' said Paul, looking down miserably, 'was.'

'Oh don't be so downhearted. You've done your bit. People in the town respect you for that. No-one could have done more.'

'I don't know. There are those that didn't come back.'

'No, I don't mean that Paul. You did your best, performed your duty, showed courage when courage was needed. You didn't get those medals for nothing. And now look at you. You've got a restful berth to look forward to on Ellie's holiday island, you lucky devil. Cheer up.'

Paul looked up and smiled, 'Oh, I suppose you're right.'

'Let's have a drink,' announced Michael, bringing a bottle out of his ruck sack.

'You clever lad,' said Josef, 'a nice surprise to help us wash things down.'

'Warm us up, more like,' said Marianne, who was shivering.

They handed round cigarettes too and all took swigs from the bottle. It was schnapps and it burned Ellie's throat so that she coughed. Paul patted her on the back with his good hand.

As they went back down the mountainside Ellie thought about Billy back in Jersey. Images of men in uniforms with guns flashed through her mind and she felt a cold rush of fear. Billy was pretty patriotic and he knew how to stand up for himself: would he fight back? He could get hurt or killed. She looked at Josef Marcher's back, just ahead of her and thought of him, up against Billy.

And she sensed she must keep these thoughts about Billy and the occupation to herself. It wouldn't do to let people round here know she had any sympathy for people who were their enemies.

Down in the streets of Kaprun, walking back to the Marcher's house after parting their ways with Michael and the others, Josef slipped his hand around Ellie's waist. She quickly moved away and walked separately from him. Later that evening, squeezing past her in the corridor near her room – he said he needed some of his things from the cupboard – he made sure he touched her breast as he passed. She gave him a slap and his hands sprang away from her.

'I'm married. You know that. Leave me alone!'

'Take it easy darling, it's not like that, I'm just being friendly.'

'I don't need that kind of friendly, thank you very much.'

'Okay okay, calm down. Hands off. I understand,' he said, laughing. 'You could take pity on a poor soldier going back to the wars next week.'

'From what I understand there's no shortage of willing women where you're going.'

Josef sniggered. 'You don't know what you're missing.'

'Go on, get away with you, go to bed' said Ellie, laughing at him in spite of herself. He seemed impossible to shame. It had been a long time since any young man had shown interest in her, although when she had been working as a cleaner down in the main town there had been one or two Julius Grabner types she had had to fend off. But something like that was the last thing she needed in her life right now, she thought.

Josef Marcher's leave ended and he went back to his

army posting the following week, causing Frau Marcher some tears. After that, life went back to normal, with weekly work, occasional visits to Zell am See, and even more occasional nights with Michael.

She used to see Paul Schneider in Kaprun quite often. He had nothing much to do, waiting for his posting to come through, and he seemed to enjoy spending time with her. He asked her a lot about Jersey. The two of them became friends and she looked forward to bumping into him on her walk back from work, when they would spend time together chatting in the street before she returned home for her evening meal.

One time, he asked her to his sister's house. She wasn't too sure about this – after all, Michael might have something to say about it if he got to hear of it – but his sister Susan turned out to be in, and nothing happened. Her husband, Franz Zainzinger, was a farm worker and the house was a typical farm cottage on the outskirts of the little town, clad in dark wood, a little balcony running around the upper storey. They all had a nice meal together and Paul walked her home. Unlike Josef, he didn't try anything on.

After that she often went up the hill to his sister's place. Susan Zainzinger was a woman of her own age who had lived in Kaprun all her life, although – unlike many of the women Ellie had met there – her outlook on life was a broad-minded one and she had an intensely curious turn of mind. She was a dark-eyed, motherly woman too, large both physically and in the feeling of warmth that she projected, who gave Ellie a welcome sense of being somehow enfolded in her presence, comforted – even cherished.

One day Susan confided in her. As a young woman, before her marriage, she had visited Vienna on several occasions and had met a man there with whom she had fallen in love. One thing led to another and she had found herself pregnant with his child. Then she discovered her lover was married. She stayed in Vienna, afraid to return to Kaprun and had the child who was given up for adoption. Susan cried bitterly when she told Ellie about this and, in comforting her, Ellie found herself telling her about her own mother and her absent, unknown father.

Susan's husband had known about her affair but had married her anyway and she was profoundly grateful to him for this. But he knew not to talk about it to anyone in Kaprun, and Ellie must not say anything either. They both swore to keep each other's secrets.

Susan had been unable to have any more children with her husband, a source of great sadness to her. So she had become an avid reader. She borrowed a new book each week from the travelling library, sometimes asking the man to get her books she had read about in the newspapers, so that she was well informed about the most surprising topics. She asked Ellie a great deal about England and told her stories about Vienna, making Ellie feel even more that she wanted to experience life in the big city. She was the first true woman friend Ellie had made in Austria and they became very close.

One day in the autumn – it was a Thursday – Ellie took the bus down to Zell am See to see her daughter. She thought she'd stay until the weekend and put up with sleeping at Ilse's place. Her shift started on Saturday that week. It would be harder to get there once the winter snows set in. When she got there Ilse told her that Anna was at the lake with Michael.

'But Michael is in Kaprun,' she exclaimed in surprise.

'No, didn't he tell you? He's here. I thought you were working,' replied her mother-in-law.

She headed down to the lake. As she approached she could see Marianne in the distance, standing at a wall that ran along a path, with Michael next to her. She looked around for Anna and saw that her daughter was playing with another child, under the watchful eye of its mother. Her eyes turned back to Michael and Marianne and she saw him put his arm around her waist, their heads touching as she leaned against him and curled her own arm around him. He moved to kiss her but as their lips touched she pulled away seeing people nearby, put her finger on his lips and drew away with a laugh, caressing his cheek with her hand.

Ellie felt a red flush go across her face and a feeling of intolerable tension rose up in her chest as she realised what was going on. How long had they been lying to her? She took a step towards them. But even as she did so, the couple began to turn to go back to where Anna was playing. Something in Ellie made her shrink back, and she hurried away from the scene.

She couldn't go back to the house, she thought. What was she to do? She wandered through the streets of the town and found herself outside Mr Steinhauser's photography shop. Except that it wasn't Steinhauser above the door now, but Gruber. She decided she had to talk to someone and went into the shop. Behind the counter stood a large man. When she asked for Steinhauser he laughed and said hadn't she heard? The Steinhausers had moved on. He grinned and said he ran the business now, how could he help her?

She ran out of the shop. Just ahead, she saw Marianne coming towards her, this time without Michael. Anna was with her.

'Ellie' she cried, half friendly, half apprehensive, 'I didn't expect to see you here.'

'No I don't suppose you did,' was the grim reply Ellie made.

'What do you mean?' said Marianne. 'Here's Anna, say hello to mummy,' and she pushed the little girl forward, who took a couple of reluctant steps and then stood sucking her thumb while Ellie glared at the other woman.

'What were you doing with Michael down there at the lake? I saw you,' said Ellie angrily.

'What do you mean? We were taking Anna for a walk. You know she likes to go to the lake.'

'That's not all you were doing, you bitch, I saw you,' and she pushed at Marianne.

'Don't you touch me! I don't know what you're talking about.'

People had stopped to watch the two women. Marianne continued aggressively. 'Maybe if you were here a bit more often to see your daughter you could have taken her for a walk. And who is calling who names!'

'Don't you talk to me about my daughter – it's none of your business.'

'It is my business you know. It's very much my business what happens to a little girl who has been abandoned by her mother.'

'What? Abandoned? How dare you!' and Ellie found angry tears falling down her cheeks.

'Yes, and that other little girl of yours. Don't tell me you haven't abandoned that one!'

At this, Ellie launched herself at the other woman, tearing at her clothes and beating her face and body with her fists. Marianne fell back, defending herself. Anna stretched her arms out pleadingly towards both of them and started to cry. One of the women looking on ran over and picked her up.

'Hey, stop that you two,' said a man, but without doing anything to follow up. There were others nearby with grins on their faces.

Ellie had Marianne on the ground by now and was trying to pummel her face, with Marianne fending off the blows with her arms. 'Get off me' she shouted and pushed at Ellie who was thrust back and found herself holding a rope of yellow hair. It was one of Marianne's plaits. She realised this woman's famous hair was artificial and began to laugh.

Marianne was mortified at her unveiling and, struggling to her feet, feeling her head where the plait had been attached, screamed at Ellie, 'Give that back!' At which Ellie threw the thing at her and launched forward for another assault, only to find herself lifted off her feet, arms pinned to her side from behind by a huge man.

A woman helped Marianne pick up the false hair plait and put her arm around the sobbing woman. 'You should be ashamed at yourself Frau Bauer, attacking a woman in the street like that in broad daylight! And in her condition too!'

At this Ellie, arms still pinned down by the big man who had set her down again on her feet, looked again at Marianne Streubel and saw that her belly was stretched tight against her dress.

'Oh my God!' Her body slackened as the man let her go, sensing that the will to fight had left her. 'Oh my God, not that.' She took a last pitying, hostile look at her enemy, her rival, and turned to Anna, still sheltering in the arms of the passer-by.

'Give me my daughter. I'm taking her home.'

After that, she marched off with Anna in her arms, filled with distress and outrage, unsure what she would do next, only knowing that she would go to the Bauer house. Michael opened the door and looked shocked at her appearance. Angrily, she thrust Anna into his arms saying, 'Here, take your daughter' and she turned on her heel. As she walked away she threw at him, 'and you can find your girlfriend in the high street sticking her hair back on.'

*

Then Ellie went back to her room in Kaprun. She told Frau Marcher what had happened, and the lady sympathised with her. Over the next few days she simply locked down all her emotions and carried on with her life, going to work, coming home, going to work again, coming home. Nothing mattered any more and she had no ideas, no feelings, no plans of any sort. She was sealed into an impenetrable ball of anger and misery that belonged to her alone.

Michael came over to the gasthof once and tried to talk to her in the kitchen, but she angrily pushed him away, refusing to respond to his protestations of innocence. He came to the house too, but both times Frau Marcher showed him the door while Ellie sat frostily inside. She took satisfaction in the hurt she hoped this might cause him.

Paul waylaid her on the road back from work and tried to talk to her but she refused to discuss it with him. She said he had been sent by Michael, and she wouldn't give him the satisfaction. He protested that he was acting out of friendship alone, but she wouldn't give him a hearing.

And so it went on, through the months of October and November as the snows came and winter closed in on the town again. She did not visit Zell am See again that year.

Then, one day in December, Paul stopped her on the road and said he had news for her – he was deemed to be recovered from his wounds and had received his orders. He was being posted to the Channel Islands, as expected. He invited her to his sister's house for a last meal before he left – the snow would be too heavy if he left it much beyond Christmas and he had to report for duty in Munich at the start of January. Softening, she agreed, but, she said, only on the condition that he did not to get her talking about Michael. Paul agreed.

That Sunday she visited Paul and renewed her old

acquaintance with Susan and her husband. Susan had prepared pork and warm pickled cabbage for them and she fried red berries she had found in the mountains with sugar. Although Susan was not a mother, she had all the physical attributes of an intensely motherly person, a large softness to her body, wrapped comfortably in a plain grey skirt and blouse, and an air of calmness which she shared with her brother and managed somehow to broadcast to the people around her.

In spite of herself, Ellie found some of the tensions she had held in her body over the past few weeks to be relaxing. But that also made her want to cry, so she kept fairly quiet as the others chatted in front of the fire and spooned up the red sugary mix.

She found herself listening to a story, told by Susan's husband, Franz. 'It's going round the town,' he said. 'There was this girl, you see, this girl and she'd had an affair with a Polish labourer. It's dreadful what happened.'

'Oh you don't know how to tell stories do you?' said Susan. 'Tell us who they are and how they met. You get to the punch line too soon.'

This gave her husband pause for heavy, slow thought, and he resumed. He explained that there were too few people to work the farms these days.

'So many young chaps are in the armed forces, and them that are left have gone to the towns to find jobs in the factories. Even the young girls have joined them. In some places there's no-one left except the old people. But farmers still need to milk their cows and sow their crops, even though the prices they get for milk and grain aren't enough to live on these days.'

'Stick to the point Franz,' laughed his wife.

At this, there was more ox-like rumination before he took up the story again. 'Well,' he said, 'it is a great thing that the Polish labourers have arrived to take up the slack.

A lot of them are good chaps who ran their own farms back where they come from but, for one reason or another, they've had to leave those places and come over here.'

Paul gave a derisive snort at this, but said nothing.

'So anyway, over in Uttendorf, on the Feichtinger's farm, a Pole called Tomek arrives last spring. He came bound up with a whole lot of rules and regulations, but the Feichtingers didn't take much notice of them. They weren't to give him money, they were told by the people down at the town hall, just his food, and he wasn't supposed to sleep in the house or eat at table with them. Blah blah blah. Just do his work and keep himself to himself, which he did and he made himself very popular with them. He was a hard worker and he knew his stuff. When the harvest came, he did the work of two men. It didn't seem fair to keep him out of the main house. 'People who work to-gether should eat together' said old Feichtinger, and any-way, who was there to see what was happening? The town hall people don't go up there much. So that's what they did and he became part of the family like. Apparently he had a wife and children back in Poland where he come from, but no more was said about that.'

'You can't do much about those things,' interjected Susan philosophically.

'No you can't,' said her husband, 'this is true. Anyway, there was a young woman who lived with the Feichtingers, their niece I believe. She hadn't gone off to the city with the others as she had a club foot. That made it hard for her to do farm work but she made herself useful about the place and she earned her keep. Didn't have anywhere else to go anyway, I suppose. Still, it seems she took a fancy to this fellow Tomek and he took a fancy to her and before you knew it they were at it, if you know what I mean, like a pair of farm dogs.'

'Oh really, you don't have to put it like that Franz,' said his wife, laughing a bit.

'Look,' said her husband, 'this isn't a pretty story I'm warning you. They were at it, as I say, and it got talked about and then someone reported them back to the town hall. Next thing you know, the police were up there and the pair of them were arrested.'

'Why, what happened to them?'

'Well that's what's so terrible. I'm sorry to say that it seems there are laws against that sort of thing nowadays. He should have known better I suppose. There was a trial and – well you'd hardly believe it – he was sentenced to death!'

'I don't believe it!'

'You should believe it my dear, and that's what happened. A bunch of soldiers turned up with a German officer and everyone was lined up in the square to watch, the Feichtingers included. That's how I know about it. Some say there were people there who crapped their pants at the sight of the poor man swinging there. It seems like a terrible thing to do to a man, to my mind, and for what? They read out some sort of proclamation so I'm told, something along the lines that he would be an example for everyone.'

'What happened to the girl?'

'She was taken away somewhere and hasn't been seen since. The Feichtingers are going crazy about it, but they hardly dare make a fuss because the police told them they were responsible in the first place for letting it all happen. I don't know what the world is coming to. It is truly shocking. The poor man.'

Ellie suddenly she felt she was going to be sick. She got up and ran to the kitchen where she vomited up red juice into the sink. She felt like the berries had been fermenting inside her. Susan came and fussed about her, apologising for feeding her the fried-up mix. 'It can sometimes do that

I'm afraid, if you're not used to it. I should have known.'

The story had unlocked something in Ellie's feelings and as the conversation turned away from the horrors of the tale itself she found her body loosening still further. She began asking Paul about his forthcoming time in the Channel Islands and he reciprocated without moving the conversation on to the topic of her own difficulties, which she knew he was interested in. She felt thankful for his sensitivity.

'You know you should write a letter home. I could take it for you. They must be wondering what's happened to you,' he said.

Ellie had had no communication with anyone in Jersey since the war had started and postal services had been suspended. Even with the occupation now placing Jersey in German hands, it was impossible to get a letter through.

'That's a good idea, I will, thanks Paul. Only I don't want to get you into any trouble,' she added, suddenly apprehensive, especially after the story they had heard. 'Do you think you're allowed to carry a letter?'

'Oh don't worry about that Ellie. I can look after myself. I won't take any risks.'

After that she didn't see Paul again but she gave Susan a letter to Billy, her brother, for Paul to take to St Helier.

Dearest Bill,

You haven't heard from me in a while but now I have a chance to write and let you know what has been going on with me. Where to start? I suppose it's best to tell you the bad news first: Michael and I have had a bad row and I don't know what's going to happen about it. The cause of it is that he is up to no good with another woman. She is someone he knew before he came to the island and he took up with her again when we got here.

I thought she was a friend, but I can see now that all the time they have been carrying on. I don't know what will come of it. I know I want nothing to do with him now, at least unless he finishes with this other woman once and for all.

So that's the worst of it. It is getting me down a lot as you can imagine but the great thing is that I have very good friends here to see me through my troubles, so it is not all bad. I am up here at a place called Kaprun where I have a job and a place to live, so you'll be pleased to hear that. I have plenty to eat too, although we have ration cards for lots of things. I suppose you do too now. I heard what has happened at home with the Germans coming and hope you and everyone else at home are bearing up. I think of you all a lot and would like to see the old place again, but I don't think there's much chance of travelling so far and anyway I am not sure it would be allowed. Anyway, there is Anna to think about. I can't just leave her. She is going to be three soon, in January, and she is a sweetheart, a real character and she chats away if you get her in the right mood. You should see her!

Speaking of Anna, she is being looked after by Michael's mother who she is very fond of, so she is all right, although I would prefer to have her with me here. There is no room for her though, so we have to make do and I see her as much as I can when I can get a day off work, although it's going to be difficult now with this trouble going on with Michael. The snow in the winter is heavy too, which makes the road down to the main town difficult, although you can walk it if you wrap up warm. Still, we must hope that things improve, I always say. They usually do! Life is funny isn't it?

This place is very different from the island. There are high mountains and lakes and it's very cold in the winter with lots of snow. I've had two winters here now and a third one coming up, so I've had a chance to get used to it, though I'm not sure I ever will be though. The people are so different from Jersey people. Most of them have never seen the sea! They are mostly pretty friendly although they say things have changed a lot since the Germans came here, some for the better, some for the worse, but I'll say no more about that.

I'm thinking I might try my luck in Vienna when the spring comes. I've heard it's quite a place and a lot of people from round here have got jobs there. I could get set up and then Anna could join me there. I'll let you know if it happens if I can.

I'm not sure I should be writing to you like this Billy, but a good friend has said he will carry this letter for me and it has been so long and there is no harm in it. If anyone else sees this letter on its way to you, it's just family news isn't it?

So that's the news of me Billy, some good some bad. I miss the old place a lot and think of you all often 'with a fond heart' as they say in the flicks. Tell everyone what I said. I don't want to say more, but write back if you can. What's up at home? I'll try and write again.

Your loving sister, missing you with all my love and fond kisses,

Ellie.

7

Billy Picot to his sister Ellie
From Jersey, undated

Dearest Ellie

We got your letter for which thanks. It is very good to here from you. We are all well. Your frend Mr Maurer had to leave with the others for the main land, France that is. Mrs M went with him even thogh she is Jersey born and bred. I have joined the police now you may like to know. I had to see Mr and Mrs M to the boat. It was not plesent I can tell you, but that is what you have to do sometimes. I am sorry for your troubles and hope they sort out soon. Your M. has been a bit of a devil hasn't he, but it may not last and you must hope and pray for better times. I know what I'd say to him thogh. Give my love to your little one, a big kiss from Uncle Bill.

Life here is allright but diferent as you may imagine. The Germans are not so bad and we rub along with them for the most part as long as our blokes don't give any trouble. Papa turned 45 and we had a cake. Not sure I should be writing again for a bit Ive got a job to keep but its innusent stuff isn't it. Keep your chin up.

Your loving brother, Bill.

PS: Your pal is a nice chap, considering.

Dear Susan,

I have arrived! I am free! It is wonderful to get away from all the 'misery in the mountains.' Vienna is just as you said. It is a big place with all sorts of people and things going on in the streets, 'some good and some bad' as they say. But I have kept my head, like you said, and got down to business and I am now set up with a room and a job. It is not hard to find work here you will be pleased to know. I looked in the papers and I am trying my hand at a bit of dress-making with a woman who has a little shop making patterns, just outside the centre, which will do for now. She has let me live above the shop in a room she has, which is all right. There's not much money in it but it will do for now while I look around.

This is just a short note to let you know I am well. It is good to think of you back in Kaprun. It is boiling hot here though I suppose it's a bit better in the mountains. They say the rich people get out of Vienna in the summer, so I suppose they're all with you now! I wouldn't mind a bit of 'riches' myself right now, but I suppose there is not much chance of that, not unless I meet the right person (ha ha!). You should see how some of them are in the Karntner-strasse. I have to rush now, but I'll write you a longer letter soon, I promise. I am just starting out here and thought it best if you get some news.

Have you heard from your brother? It would be good to know that he is all right. I suppose he is in Jersey now. Do write back and tell me your news, and any news of Paul.

My best regards and fondness, Ellie.

PS: Mrs G, the dress lady, says I should cut the patterns for a very important client – one of the theatre actors here who has been in the films too. I'd love to go to see her in a play. PPS: If you have news of Anna please tell me. I have written to her but she is so young and there is no word back about her.

Ellie to Anna
From Vienna, January 1942

My dearest darling Anna,
Happy Fifth Birthday to you with all my love! Five today! I hope you have a lovely day.

I miss you so much darling and I long to see you. Perhaps Daddy can explain to you why I have not been able to come to see you for so long. But I think about you all the time my dearest, you should always remember that and I hope it won't be too long before we see each other again.

I am living in Vienna, working with a lady who makes pretty dresses. It is very hard work and I am very tired a lot of the time, but I think of you all the time.

I love you so much. All my love darling, your loving mummy

xxxxxxxxxxxxxxxxxxxxxxxxxxxxxxxxxxxxxxxxxxx

Michael to Ellie
From Zell am See, January 1942

Dear Eloise,
As you have not contacted me since your departure I have had to find out where you are from Susan Zainzinger. She tells me that you are well and staying in Vienna and that she is in touch with you. I am glad to hear that you are safe and well.

Your letters for Anna have arrived and we have told her of their contents. They have a bad effect on her and it would be better if you do not write to her from now on.

You would not talk to me when I tried to tell you this, but I hope you will read it now. Your suspicions about myself and Marianne are all wrong. It is true that before I left to go to Jersey in 1934 there was something between us, but it wasn't serious. We were just teenagers then. But like you always do, you have leapt to the incorrect conclusion, which is quite typical of you and you have ruined our marriage as a result. Marianne told me how you behaved with her in the high street, which was shocking in such a public place. Everyone is talking about it in the town. I know you saw us by the lake but I was only comforting her after she had told me her troubles, which you know about.

Marianne has had her baby now, a daughter, and I am most certainly not its father and I will deny that to my dying day. I do not know who he is and I refuse to ask her as it would only upset her, but out of my old friendship for her I am doing my best to help, as is my mother. It is not so easy in this town if you have a child in such circumstances. Her own family has not been very good to her either so she needs some friends.

I will be frank with you and say that I suspect Josef Marcher in this affair. He is away with the army now, but I suppose you know what he is like. I will say no more about that.

You would not hear me out in Kaprun when I tried to talk to you about this, but I hope that you will read this letter and think about your actions and remember the times we have shared together. It may not be too late for us to make up. Please write to me.

Your husband, Michael

From Vienna, Stumpergasse 13, February 1942

Dear Michael,
If you think I am going to believe your nonsense about Marianne and Josef Marcher you should have another think coming. I saw the two of you down at the lake together and I know what I saw. Josef wasn't even around when Marianne got herself pregnant as you surely must know. He was away in France. It is revolting that you are trying to blacken Josef Marcher's name like this just so you can cover up for yourself. I wish I had never met you and I have no wish to 'make up' with you as you put it. I am perfectly fine where I am, thank you very much, and I don't want any more of these lying letters from you.

About Anna, she is my daughter and I will continue to write to her if I want. You may not like it but you have obligations towards me and my daughter and I will be in touch again about that. Anna needs her mother and I am going to see what the law has to say about her living with her father when you have been carrying on with another woman and driven me out of the home.

You will hear more from me about this all right, don't you be mistaken.

Eloise Picot.

Ellie to Susan Zainzinger
From Vienna, Stumpergasse 13, March 1942

Dearest Susan,
Thank you for kind letter which has been a great comfort to me. It is very good to know that Paul is well and I think of him in my home town with fondness. It is so wonderful that he has been able to meet Billy there, which gives me

the feeling that at least there is a real link that I have with my old life. I am forever grateful to you and your brother.

Things have not worked out so well with the dress-making business. I couldn't get by on what Mrs G paid me so I had to take another job which gives me a bit more. There is an air force hospital nearby where they needed help, so I am cooking and cleaning for them and just doing a bit of the dress cutting in spare moments, which Mrs G. is fine about. She is a kind old bird and she is happy for me to stay on above the shop as long as I can pay the rent.

Some of the airmen are not a pretty sight and the burned ones are the worst. But they like a joke, those boys, and when they are feeling better we can have a laugh, even though most of them know where I'm from. Some of them aren't too badly off, so will be going back to the flying business soon enough – they are the happy ones. I sometimes wonder what makes them do it but it's not something I can ask is it? For the Führer I suppose they'd say. Fair enough.

I am starting to get around a bit more and see the place. I saw a good film the other day about Robert Koch, who was a scientist who made all sorts of medical discoveries, which was wonderful. Most of the stuff in the cinema is thrillers usually, which I don't go for so much, or else they are like that terrible 'Soldiers of Tomorrow' one which must have reached Zell am See by now. Did you see it? The British really aren't like that you know. But this one about Koch was great. Makes me realise how little I know about science and things like that.

So I've decided to take a leaf out of your book and start borrowing books from the library. There is a good one here. I have heard the university runs courses in this and that which anyone can go to, but that's a bit beyond me for now I think, but I might look into it. There are some lovely pictures in the art galleries here and they are free to go to. I'd like to find out more about art and painting. I met a painter who calls himself Rudofsky the other day – don't know his first name. Perhaps he'll show me.

Another chap I met is someone involved in the theatre here. Not the big Burgtheater across from the Rathaus but little places he says. I went with him to one of his shows. It was in a cellar they'd cleared out for the audience. It was hilarious, with music and songs too. All about the people in a small town where they want to build a public toilet off the main square and the fights that go on between the people about it. Some of them want it and some of them don't. It reminded me of some of the things I used to hear about in Zell am See. I can tell you, the audience were just roaring with laughter at some points. My friend said he had a musician friend who had done the songs and it was all based on a French book he had read. We had a great time.

Look, I don't want you to think I am just having a lot of fun and games here. I had a letter from Michael the other day telling a pack of lies about him and Marianne. He says he spoke to you to find out where to send it. I don't mind that you spoke to him Susan, but please don't tell him anything about me. I wouldn't want to give him the satisfaction.

If I want to come and see Anna for a few days, could I stay with you in Kaprun? I don't think I could stand it in the main town with all of the people there.

I hope all is well with you and your husband. I remember his funny ways and what fun you have with him. You are a lucky woman!

With love and kind affection, from your good friend, Ellie.

From Ukraine, May 1942

My darling girl,

Greetings from the East! I can't say exactly where I am but I am sure you have heard the news of our progress. You have no idea what fun we had! The air boys smash things up ahead and then we just come in and roll over anything that's left. The enemy collapse when faced with our lads. I took a whole bunch of them back with me after one attack, like a little flock of sheep following their leader. They were only too happy to give up the fight when they saw our tanks. My division officer said I could be due for a gong, how about that? It's a shame Paul couldn't have been there. Have you heard from the old fellow? It would be nice to know how he is getting on.

Well that's enough of me and my news. I mostly want you to know that I am due some leave in early June and that I plan to come to Vienna and look you up again. It's all very well running around in foreign lands but home is where the heart is and you must know that means you my dear girl, where I am concerned. You were right to leave that pathetic fellow you were with in Kaprun, a real mummy's boy if you don't mind me saying. You must see there's no future with him now. I felt so sorry for you that time in Kaprun.

Oh, remember, that time in Kaprun? I can't get it out of my head. You were so beautiful that night. I am desperate to see you again my darling Ellie and to hold you in my arms again. I know the big city is a dangerous place for someone as lovely as you, but I want you to know that I long to see you again.

Well sweetheart I must say goodnight for now and a million kisses. Write often sweet. I love so much to get your letters and I haven't had any for a week now. Please reply quickly.

Your loving Josef.

Ilse Bauer to Ellie
From Zell am See, June 1942

Dear daughter-in-law,
Michael has given me your address and I must write to you now about the important matters that affect us all. It is time to face facts.

It is clear to me that your marriage to my son is at an end and I have spoken with the priest about this who said I should write to you. Michael has told me that you believe he is the father of Marianne's child. I cannot help but feel that you are only saying this because of your own selfish wish to go and live a life of your own in Vienna, which I know has always been something you wanted. I told Michael when he married you that he was making a mistake and I have been proved right. The fact that you are from a country that has made war on ours did not stop Johannes and I from doing our best to make you feel welcome, as was our duty to God and common decency. Believe me when I say this did not make us popular with our neighbours. But you have decided that this is not enough for you. So you have abandoned your husband and child to run off and live a life of your own.

I will not try to persuade you to return here and make it up with Michael. The poor boy is devastated by your behaviour and it is my duty to make sure things come right for him and for Anna.

It would be better if the two of you get a divorce. This is not something I ever thought I would say, but the law allows for it and I think it would be a better thing for Michael if he was free to marry again. I have known Marianne and her family all my life and I am sorry to have to tell you quite bluntly that she would make a much better mother for your children than you have done. Many people agree with me in this.

Michael is seeing a lawyer who will tell him the best way to proceed. You will then be free to do what you will. May the Lord forgive you for what you have done.

Yours sincerely, Ilse Bauer.

Michael to Ellie
From Metz, June 1942

Dear Eloise,
I am writing from Metz because I was called up for service in the Luftwaffe in March this year and have been posted here in the air defences.

You will know from my mother's letter that I have seen a lawyer and he said to write this letter to you, a copy of which he will keep. He has explained to me how divorces are given.

My mother has told me about the conversation you had with her about your father, who you always told me you knew nothing about. Now she says you told her that he was probably a Jew and I am very shocked about this.

The lawyer has told me that under the new laws this means our marriage can be considered to have been invalid, since I was mistaken in person about you. This is not, therefore a divorce but an annulment of our marriage which my mother thinks would be a better thing in the eyes of God, in which I agree with her.

So in case of any doubt this is to let you know that I married you in 1934 without knowing that your father was a Jew, and that this is something that I only recently discovered. You will hear more about this from the lawyer.

Yours sincerely, Michael.

Ellie to Michael
Vienna, Stumpergasse 13, June 1942.

Dear Michael,
You must be mad. I never told Ilse my father was a Jew. It is exactly as I have said to you. I do not know who he was and if your lawyer friend gets hold of the records in Jersey he will see that this is true. I went through the whole Ahnenpass thing ages ago and it has never been resolved properly. Even if he was a Jew, I'd only be a half one, and MY lawyer tells me you haven't got a hope of getting that through the courts even if they are packed with Nazis. Yes, I can go and see lawyers too you know! I have got friends in Vienna believe it or not and I know my rights and how to use them.

Nice try Michael, but it won't work.

I am coming to see you in Metz because I have my own ideas about this, and they involve Anna.

Ellie.

Ellie to Susan Zainzinger
Vienna, Stumpergasse 13, June 1942

Dear Susan,
Michael and his mother have been writing me some ridiculous letters that I must tell you about. Please keep it a secret though – this is just for us. First, Ilse wrote to me saying she thought it would be better if I divorced Michael and he married Marianne instead. How could she suggest such a thing? I thought she was supposed to be against divorce. She says she spoke to her priest about it, believe it or not. Imagine getting a letter like that, just when I was building up a life here and starting to feel a bit happier.

Then Michael wrote to say he had seen a lawyer who

told him there is a new law that says that because I am a Jew (I am NOT!!!!) and didn't tell him, he can divorce me, or that our marriage wasn't even supposed to happen or something like that. I have suffered from this kind of persecution all my life Susan, as you know, because of my father. When will they leave me alone about it? It's not my fault that I don't know who he is. Back home no-one would tell me who he was they are all so ashamed about it, and I am supposed to carry the can.

Men are terrible beasts aren't they? I don't mean your dear husband, please don't get me wrong. It's just that men generally can get away with so much with us poor women. Who the hell made Marianne pregnant if it wasn't Michael? Whoever it was, and I am not letting Michael off the hook believe you me, he was one of the 'bad guys' wasn't he. There are a lot of them about it seems. Men can go spreading themselves around and making babies all over the place and it's we women who have to pick up the pieces, clapping our hands all the time at their exploits. Not that I am forgiving that bitch Marianne for what she did with Michael. He is so weak!

Oh I am sorry Susan. I am quite upset this evening. I really hope you don't mind me writing to you like this.

The men in Vienna are just as bad, I must say. A woman on her own here is easy prey to those vultures and I have had to fend a few off I can tell you. You don't know how lucky you are with your nice man! Stay in the country Susan, don't rock the boat, I'm warning you from bitter experience. The city isn't safe for the likes of us!

There you are, I have cheered up a bit. Not all men are bad, I must say and they can be useful for us girls too, at times. One or two kind gentlemen have taken me to some nice places recently, all expenses paid! And believe me there are some nice places here if you have the money.

Josef Marcher was in Vienna recently, did I tell you?

Fresh from the wars and full of himself as usual. What a baby he is, but fun to see again, although he hasn't got much money to pay for his fun. I believe he's coming back to Kaprun for a bit to show off his medals before he goes off on his next adventure.

I will tell you more when I see you. I am going to visit that husband of mine in Metz next week and give him a good talking to. I plan to come back via Kaprun so I can see Anna again, poor little thing who I miss dearly – thank you so much for putting me up at your place. I look forward so much to seeing you again, my dearest friend.

With much love, Ellie.

Susan Zainzinger to Ellie
Kaprun July 1942

Dear Ellie,

After last week you must be wondering what is happening in the town. First, though, I want to say how sorry I am that the meeting with Anna did not come off as you wanted. As I said to you, when I went down to the town to fetch her Frau Bauer seemed willing enough to let her go after I had explained the situation to her, but Anna herself simply refused to come with me. She was so distressed, I have never seen such wailing and tears. As you know, I don't have children myself, so I am perhaps not the best person to manage a child when they are in that kind of state. I even suggested to Marianne that she could come with the child up to Kaprun but, perhaps understandably, she refused. In the circumstances I thought it best to leave without her and perhaps try another day, as I tried to explain to you.

I am sorry that this was so upsetting for you, especially after your long journey back from Metz. I think you are probably right that they have turned Anna against you.

But I expect you want to know more about the reaction in the town to that other matter.

I am afraid the news got out pretty quickly once Josef Marcher started boasting about what had happened between you and him. There is not a lot to be done about that Ellie and I hardly know what to say to you myself. You know that I am a person who has an open mind about most things and you and I have always got on very well, but it was not sensible to try to solve your problems like that. In fact, I think you will find you have made them worse. They now have what they want I am afraid, if Frau Marcher is willing to act as a witness. You will just have to hope that she will not do that because it will also reflect on her son. She is very proud of him you know, as he is quite a soldier.

I won't say any more in this letter. You should know that I am your friend and always willing to hear from you and to help you if I can. It is a little dull in Kaprun as you know, and it is good for me to have some excitement from time to time! (I hope you won't mind my little joke).

Do keep in touch and let me know how you are once you have settled back in Vienna.

From your dear friend, Susan.

PS: Paul sends his best regards. He arrived back on a ten day leave after you left and will take your letter when he goes back. He and Josef met and had some kind of argument but I don't know what it was about – he wouldn't say.

Dear Bill,

Thanks so much for your news. It's so good to hear how things are with you and that you are all right. It's been ages, I know, but I have heard our carrier pigeon is back over here, so here is my news.

I am living in Vienna now, as Michael and I have separated. I am just in Kaprun for a few days, visiting. I am afraid the problems I mentioned in my last letter have not gone away. I have seen Michael just recently to talk about what to do, but things are not decided yet. Meanwhile I am keeping in touch with Anna, who is still at her grandmother's.

I don't want to go into the ins and outs of all that now Billy, but I hope things will work out. I will let you know, if I can.

Here, the people I meet talk a lot about the war. I have a friend who has been in Russia and he has told me what it was like. I don't know if he will go back there now.

You have to be careful what you say and who you say it to these days. Our carrier pigeon said a few things he shouldn't have done and one of his old army pals got upset about it I heard. He will need to be careful. Could you tell him I said this, or he might get himself into trouble.

There is a lot to do in Vienna. You would be impressed with the place. You will never believe it but I have been going to talks in the university about all sorts of subjects that anyone can go to and I am finally getting some education into me. Last time there was a chap talking about Shakespeare and the place was full. It seems the Germans like the old boy a lot and the fact that they are at war with England makes no difference. They even had a Shakespeare play on at the main theatre here, although I didn't get to see it. The *Merchant of Venice* it was. Anyway, I am going to spend some of my hard earned cash on a copy of some Shakespeare plays and I will see if I can read them. I don't mind what language they are in, German or English. Perhaps I'll get both and I might learn both languages a bit better by comparing them. Well that's what my plan is anyway. We'll see if it happens.

I was down in the market the other day, early in the morning before work and there was a round-up. They were looking for Jews and went through all our papers. There was some big fat woman who shouted at one of their blokes and he pulled a gun out of his pocket and pointed it at her until his boss came over and told him to leave off. They drove off with the ones they found, I don't know where. That kind of thing can happen here and no-one likes it much. But what can you do?

Well that's enough for now Billy. I will write again. Keep sending me your news if you can.

Your loving sister, Ellie.

Ellie to Susan Zainzinger
Kufstein, September 1942

Dear Susan,
Things have got a bit awkward for me in Vienna and I have decamped to Kufstein in the mountains for a bit. That friend I mentioned, do you remember, the one who made up the funny play about the French town, got arrested the other day. It seems he was Jewish and hiding from the authorities. Apparently he saw a man selling someone a packet of cigarettes in the street and he went out to get some himself, at which point one of them said where is your papers and he didn't have any. So that was that for him and I don't know where he is now.

After that, there were policemen knocking on doors of people he knew and I was one of them, so I have done a flit back to the countryside.

I think I might go over to Rosenheim soon. Enough said. I will be in touch again

Ellie.

PS. I am sorry to hear about Paul. You must be very worried. Things should come out right for him I think. After all, he was quite a hero in France wasn't he and that must count for something?

9th December 1942
In the name of the German Nation!

The High Court of Justice at Salzburg represented by (LGR) Dr Tusch as Judge in the petition of the plaintiff Michael Bauer, Camp-Captain, at present sergeant, Army Post No. L.44.323, LGPA Berlin, represented by Inspector Dukat of the Court of Salzburg as lawyer to the poor against the defendant:-

Eloise Bauer nee Picot, resident at Kufstein, Tyrol, Hotel Stern

The defendant EB is guilty on account of adultery [with Josef Marcher]

The cost of the proceedings have to be borne by the defendant

Reasons: by reason of the deposits of the witnesses of Anni Marcher and of Joachim Blecher it is evident that the defendant committed adultery about four times during the period summer 1942 to October 1942.

The petition of the plaintiff is therefore justified according to paragraph 47 Matrimonial Law (E.G.).

The plaintiff did not file a claim to refund of expenses.

High Court of Justice Salzburg

Dear Ellie,

Regarding your letter I think it is time I set the record straight. You say that Susan Zainzinger has been telling tales about her brother and myself. I am sorry about what has happened to Paul, but I think you need to know the facts and not just hear things from her point of view.

When I was last in Kaprun, after you had gone back to Vienna, I went out with Paul to the coffee house down in the main town and we got talking about the progress of the war. You should know that your old enemy Marianne was there by the way. We'd had a bit to drink and Paul started talking about things he'd heard were going on in Russia that he didn't like the sound of. He's always been a soft hearted fellow, so I didn't mind much. But then he cranked it up a bit and started going on about all sorts of wrongdoing and injustice in the *Wehrmacht* that he knew about and how it was all going to end in defeat now the Americans had come into the war and that kind of thing. It really was sickening stuff.

I was pretty shocked I can tell you and so was Marianne, I could see. But I promise you I wasn't going to say anything about it to anyone until I got back to my posting here and happened to tell my corporal that I'd had this conversation with a chap back home. I suppose that was my mistake because he wouldn't let it drop, this corporal. He's seen a thing or two in his time in the East and he doesn't like defeatists and he ordered me to report it officially to the Captain. What could I do? I had to obey him or else he might have told his own version to the Captain and then I could have been in trouble. I didn't see why I should suffer. Paul is a good man I'd say, but he's had a cushy number over on that island and I think it had got him soft in the head. If it's one thing I've learned as a soldier, you can't afford to give in to that kind of soft stuff when you're facing the Russians, who are devils.

After that it was out of my hands and you know the rest. I am sorry for Susan over this and I know you are fond of her, but she ought to know the facts and stop running me down over this. I didn't do anything wrong and I am not responsible for whatever happens to Paul. That's a military matter now.

I hope you understand. It is a hard fight we have here, you wouldn't believe it if I told you how hard, but every day I hope for victory and then I will get some leave and come home. Keep me in touch with your address. It would be wonderful to see you again. You know how I feel about you.

Josef.

Ellie to Susan Zainzinger
Graz, September 1943

Dear Susan,

I am so sorry not to have written for so long, and not to have heard from you. So much has happened and I've ended up in Graz. It's pretty bad for me right now. I'm wondering if you can help your old friend one more time.

They've put me to work in a factory which makes chains, all kinds of chains. They tell us it's for the war and we need to work harder all the time, and longer. We only get paid 60 pfennigs an hour. It's not enough to keep body and soul together. Sometimes I have to sleep on the factory floor. It's too far to get back home for the night and be here again by the morning. I didn't want to do the job but the labour people said I had to.

I have to check every link, once the chains come out, file off any spikes and uneven bits, lug them over to the boxes for packing. Some of them are so heavy. My hands are sore and I'm hungry all the time. I've been sick too, but I can't afford a doctor. They say I've just got to keep working. I think they know I'm English and they hate me because of that.

I told them I wanted to do something else, find another job, but they said I'd be in trouble if I left and I believe them. There are people here who've been in that kind of trouble. Worse I think. Remember the prisoners who were working on the dam? They've got some here too, doing the outdoor work. They bring them in on trucks from a camp in Peggau. It's all right in the summer but I dread to think how they'll manage when the snows come. Some of them are so thin.

I've got to get out of here Susan. Can you get your husband to write a letter? He could say I'm needed on his farm, important for the war effort, something like that. I'm desperate Susan. For old time's sake. The address to write to is this:

Aufseher A. Frankel
Verpackungsabteilung
Pengg-Walenta
Graz
Please Susan. Please help me.
Ellie

Interrogation report: Klagenfurt, 1946

While she was in Vienna, her husband had been conscripted into the Luftwaffe. During that time her husband had written and told her that he had met an old girlfriend and that his parents thought she would make an

excellent mother for the subject's child
Anna. She went to Metz, where her husband
was stationed, to try and find a solution
to their unhappy circumstances. This visit
however was not a success and, after a
brief visit to Zell am See to see her
daughter after her return from Metz, she
moved to Kufstein in the Tirol at the end
of the summer of 1942.

She was soon sent by the local Arbeitsamt
to work in a factory there, where she was
employed making electrical parts for flying
instruments. Subject did not like the work
here and claims that the people in the
Arbeitsamt at Kufstein had a grudge against
her, and so she rented an attic just over
the border into Germany and by doing so
came under the direction of the Arbeitsamt
at Rosenheim, in Germany.

It was while she was living in Kufstein
that she paid a visit to Josef Marcher who
was then at Saalfelden. At the same time
her husband came to Saalfelden where he met
Marcher and shortly afterwards divorced
subject.

In January 1943 subject was called up by
the Arbeitsamt in Rosenheim, into the
German Air Force, and was sent for her
initial training as a telephone operator at
Freimann in Munich, the course lasting
three months. Some 300 girls took the
course which consisted of learning the use
and the mechanism of field telephones. Many
secret numbers were also given to the girls
and she learned the various telephone
numbers of high-ranking Nazi personalities.
Subject could give no reason why she was
conscripted into the Luftwaffe or why she
was among those who learned the secret
numbers. She was never asked by the
Luftwaffe authorities to become an interpreter. (Subject also states that in an

enrolment form for the service she stated
that she was of British birth, but that
this was perhaps not noticed).

On completion of the course in April
1943, the majority of the girls were sent
to France, attached to Luftwaffe units.
Subject states that at this time she was
dismissed from the service as papers had
been sent to her O.C. from the Nazi
authorities in Zell am See, pointing out
that she was an Englishwoman and as such
unsuitable for service in the German
forces. Subject states that the letter
writer was one Julius Grabner who had
briefly employed her in his department at
the Zell am See town council. Before being
dismissed she was warned of the consequences if she devolved any information
learned during the course

Her next move in April 1943, was to Graz,
travelling on a warrant issued to her on
her release from the Luftwaffe. She can
give no specific reason why she wanted to
go to Graz, except that it was 'for a
change'. She stated that it just 'occurred'
to her to go to Graz.

She became employed by a Frau Bettig
living at the Adolf Hitler Platz 2, as a
governess to her two children and helping
with the housework. She left in August 1943
as she says it was too much to do for one
woman.

She was then sent by the Arbeitsamt to
work in the Pengg Walenta chain factory, in
Graz. Here she worked alongside slave labour
from Russia, Greece, France, Poland etc, and
was often forced to sleep in the factory
through lack of money as she was very poorly
paid. Subject was employed here for about
three months and then she was able to see
the manager who gave her a 'sympathetic
hearing', and allowed her to leave.

It was while in Graz that she met
(through Frau Bettig) Franz Schollmann, a
Croat, who was the director of the Opel
works in Cilli in what was then occupied
Yugoslavia. It was on the advice of this
Schollmann, described by subject as a 'man
of the world', that she went to Vienna for
the second time in October or November
1943.

8

RUDOFSKY, WHO SHE had had met in her first stay in Vienna, continually pestered Ellie to pose nude for him and made no secret of the fact that he also wanted to sleep with her, although he had the tact to make these requests out of his wife's hearing. He was a peculiar man, or perhaps it was just that he had an unusual marriage. He told her his wife, Alma was a plain woman. Alma, who was with them at the time, just laughed, appearing genuinely unhurt by the comment, perhaps mollified by his adding 'and I love her dearly of course.' Ellie suspected they had an arrangement. Plain though she might be, Alma was often out of the house all night. She never objected to Ellie's visits. At any rate, Ellie knew she herself wasn't going to sleep with Rudofsky, who was a tiny gnome of a man.

Today he didn't need her to model for him. He was absorbed in painting a fish, which he said wouldn't last much longer. It was in front of the easel, decomposing on a plate. Green streaks were appearing near the fins and the clouded eyeballs rested in red rimmed pockets. The smell was strong.

'I took it from Alma as soon as I saw it!' he exclaimed. 'Someone caught it for us in the Danube. She thought we would eat it but I could see a better use straight away, don't you think?'

He turned the painting to her. The fish had been transformed into a kaleidoscope of colours, laid on a green table cloth under a window. Outside, the sky was painted red.

'It is a picture of the Devil himself!' he exclaimed wildly.

'But where can you show that Josef?' she pointed out. 'You'll have to find a private buyer who'll hide it away.'

'Nonsense! Böckl had blue trees in a gallery on the Karntnerstrasse the other day and nothing was said. If Böckl can get away with it, so can I. '

'So you're copying his style are you?' she said playfully.

'Don't be ridiculous Ellie. That fellow…' And then he realised she was teasing and shut up. There was silence for a minute while he fiddled with the paints on his palette.

'When are you going to take up that offer I made?' he asked, his pinched, intense face looking up at her.

'Which one? You make so many.'

'Oh no, I don't mean that, can't you be serious for a minute? I mean the job at the Academy. They need someone like you to model for them. You've got a fine head even if you won't let them see anything else. What else have you got to do? And they'll pay you for it you know.'

'How much – you never said.'

'Oh, I don't know. I think it could be a couple of marks an hour, more if you, you know, go all the way.'

Ellie laughed, 'I suppose you'd turn up then, Josef? I'm not taking my clothes off for a bunch of men I've never met.'

'Come on darling, they've seen it all before. They're not all men in life drawing anyway. Models aren't usually so precious you know. Of course, if you're shy you could try it out here in my studio, where you're amongst friends,' and he smirked hopefully.

Ellie was getting tired of this. These days the conversation always somehow came round to Rudofsky's sexual needs. She resolved to spend less time in the artist's studio.

'I've got to go now. I've got a class this afternoon. Some new pupils according to Julia – military types I think. They want conversation in English.'

'Ah, Ellie, you know what they say,' remarked the painter, wagging his finger. She expressed puzzlement. He said it was a riddle. 'How do you tell an optimist from a pessimist?' he asked.

'I don't know, tell me,' she played the game.

'Pessimists learn Russian and optimists learn English!' said Rudofsky, laughing at his own joke. 'These will be the optimists. I wonder whose army will get to Vienna first when the time comes?'

'Don't say that too loudly Joseph – the neighbours'll hear and you'll be in trouble,' she said grinning widely. Rudofsky was all right, a lot of fun to be with even if he did pester her. But she had to get back. 'I'm off now,' she said, putting on her coat and shouldering her bag.

Outside she caught a tram which took her all the way down Mariahilferstrasse. Rudofsky's place was out near the West-bahnhof where studio space was cheap and it was a long way back to the centre, too long to walk if she was to make it in time. She wondered about these new customers Julia van der Lye had been so excited about.

As the tram rattled along she looked down Nelkengasse to see where the new construction work had got to. The huge concrete tower planted in the middle of the Esterhazypark seemed to be sprouting wings at the top and round platforms jutted out at the corners. There were other flak towers going up around the city – two of them near Mrs van der Lye's place. It was making everyone nervous.

Since the Russians had sent a few planes over this time last year, there had been no bombing. Many people said the Allies would avoid destruction from the air out of respect for the ancient and beautiful city. But the temperature had been raised when caretakers went round pestering people in their blocks about air raid precautions, which meant clearing out inflamma-ble rubbish and stocking up on preserved foods. There were limits put on coal storage too, which had hit people hard over the previous winter, although of course there were those who fiddled the rules, as always. They had been told the flak towers would function as air raid shelters too, if things came to it.

'Bloody monstrosity,' muttered a woman next to her who glanced in the same direction. Ellie knew instinctively not to respond. Trams were notorious places for provocateurs who might scuttle off to the Gestapo if you indulged your opinions too freely. And Ellie wasn't officially registered for work, so knew she needed to stay low. She kept her mouth shut, just smiling at the thin, middle-aged woman clutching a huge cloth shopping bag that seemed to be part of the uniform of Vienna's servant class.

'Going home?' she asked Ellie.

'No, off to work now,' was the reply.

The woman shrugged and said nothing for another couple of blocks.

'Where's that then?'

Ellie muttered in reply, sensing somehow that this was a conversation to be avoided. She turned back to look across the tram through the other window. A police truck with horns wailing a double note flashed past in the opposite direction.

'The streets never used to be this filthy you know,' said the bag woman, plucking at the shoulder of Ellie's coat to get her attention, 'before the war.'

Paper bags and cigarette ends blew about amongst the autumn leaves on the pavement as they clattered past.

'I suppose so,' replied Ellie and then, as the tram slowed to its stop on the Ring, 'I need to change now.'

'Don't I know you from somewhere?' said the little woman persistently, but Ellie shook her head and got off. She watched the red iron vehicle grinding away from her past the museum. The woman's white face was looking out at her through the window. It reminded her of Grandmère Picot's face staring at her from the quayside at St Helier on the day she had left the island.

*

At the Rennweg house, the language school was on the fourth floor. In reality, it was Mrs van der Lye's apartment, but it was spacious and since her husband's death she only needed a small part of it to live in. Two large rooms at the front were 'cleared for action' as she put it, using the English phrase with a jolly shake of her head. Soft chairs and a couple of sofas were arranged in two circles in the one room, for the conversation classes. In the next room rows of fold-up seats were arranged in front of a blackboard – the classroom where the proprietor gave formal lessons in English, French or (though no-one wanted it) Dutch if need be.

Ellie found her friend – for that, she felt, was what Mrs van der Lye had become to her in the months since she had arrived back in Vienna – pacing up and down anxiously in the classroom. She was a heavy, middle aged woman who suffered from arthritic pains and moved slowly, but today she seemed disturbed.

'Oh there you are Eloise,' she exclaimed, 'I was wondering.'

'Sorry Julia, I got held up. That old goat Rudofsky insisted on showing me his fish.'

'Fish, what are you talking about? What is he doing with fish? Oh never mind, you are here now. Look, they are coming any minute and they are bound to be on time. Come next door.'

She had arranged some chairs in the conversation room around a low table. There was a bottle of water and some dry biscuits laid out, with glasses. 'Do you think that's going to be all right for them? I didn't want to overdo it. It is a business arrangement after all, and these military men can be very formal. I could offer them coffee.'

Ellie tried to calm her down. Julia van der Lye depended entirely on the language school for her income and the business had not been doing so well recently. Interest in French tuition had almost entirely dried up and her French conversation assistant, Walther Günth, only had a few loyal clients left.

Walther shared Julia's worries about this. He was an old friend of her husband's from their theatre days together, a man who had clearly once been very handsome but now had a tense, hunted look about him which had faded his youthful charms. His acting career, never very successful, had dried up now and he lived on the proceeds of his language teaching. Ellie used to enjoy trying out her French on him – he had lived in Paris for a while before the war. The differences between the Jersey patois she had known and his formal Parisian vocabulary kept them entertained.

There had been an approach to Julia from some soldiers in the local city command who said they wanted to learn some English. Julia was excited – it could be an important first step in tapping a new client base. Until now, the school had largely catered for the needs of well-off families from places like Hietzing who brought their sons and daughters to the school in the evenings and weekends to learn one of the languages. It was a good arrangement from Ellie's point of view. She could earn decent money outside normal working hours just for chatting to children and wealthy housewives in her native language – Julia covered the formal lessons – and go cleaning or working in art studios during the day. The cleaning work had dropped away more and more as the other two had picked up. It was no fun scrubbing and polishing in some rich apartment under the beady eye of the woman of the house. At Julia's place she felt like she was the boss when faced with such people.

'If this works out we could get more business from the Army,' said Julia. 'Let's really impress them!' she said, grabbing Ellie's shoulders and planting a big kiss on her cheek.

'We will Julia, I know we will,' said Ellie, returning a broad smile as the apartment's doorbell chimed.

Three men entered the room in some style, in Wehrmacht uniform, their shining leather boots clacking on the wood floor. Their leader, a round-faced young man in his mid-twenties, introduced himself to Mrs van der Lye as Carl Mayer.

'I know your husband's work, Mrs van der Lye,' he said graciously as he shook her hand, his heels clicking together. 'It is a pleasure to meet you.'

'It is a pleasure for me too, Captain Mayer,' said the Dutch woman, her cheeks growing noticeably redder. 'Do you mean you saw him on stage? Forgive me, but you seem hardly old enough…'

'No, no, his film work.'

'You mean his film!' Mrs van der Lye was pleasurably flustered. 'I had no idea! Where did you see that?'

'As a boy here, Mrs van der Lye. I was an avid cinema-goer as a child and *Die Goldratten* was a wonderful adventure for me. I shall never forget the get-away scene – so exciting, and Nora Herbert was wonderful in it – she was a particular favourite of mine when I was a boy. Your husband must have enjoyed to work with such people. How lucky to be in the film business. '

'Ah, I see,' said Julia, seemingly less impressed with this news of his boyhood interest in the actress. 'Henk died in the 30s. It was his only film.'

'Ah, I thought he was involved with that film about the Jews, too – what was it? *Die Stadt ohne Juden*. A wonderful film I think, a masterpiece – prophetic even, if you think about it.'

'No, that wasn't him,' said Julia, 'I'm afraid those times are gone now, but I am so glad you liked his film.'

The other two men were introduced as Sergeant Rudolf Berger and Lieutenant Alfred von Weyr. 'But we won't mention military ranks in this house – we are Carl, Rudolf and Alfred when we are here, just like children at school,' said Mayer cheerfully.

As Ellie was introduced to each of the smiling young men she recognised that all were Austrians. Berger looked no more than a child, his sergeant's uniform hanging from his thin frame. Von Weyr was older and wore a wedding ring. They seemed full of energy and good will and readily acceded to

Julia's offer of coffee. Ellie joined her in the kitchen while the men made themselves comfortable in the conversation room. She was troubled by what Mayer had said.

'Why do we have to deal with people like this?' she said to Julia angrily. '*Die Stadt ohne Juden* – City without Jews, eh? What's all that about? More nonsense about the Jews?'

Ellie had moved on since her conversation with Kurt Steinhauser in Zell am See. The morning in the vegetable market when she had witnessed Jews being rounded up and the attitudes of her fellow Luftwaffe trainees in Munich towards the Jewish 'question' had hardened her own feelings on the subject, though she knew not to express them openly in the wrong company. It stuck in her throat to think she would have to be nice to a bunch of Nazi zealots.

Julia smiled, 'No it's not what you think dear.'

'Come off it Julia, you heard what he said. He liked the film.'

'No, no. It's the exact opposite of what you think. He was sending us a message. It will be all right, don't you worry. Look, I haven't got time to talk about this, but please don't worry. You are so quick with your feelings my dear. We must get this coffee to them and you and I can talk later.'

The men were particularly appreciative of the coffee, which was made with real beans from a secret store Julia kept. They were keen to learn some English, Mayer explained, and they had found Mrs van der Lye's advertisement in the newspaper. They hadn't expected, though, to be taught by a real English speaker!

Ellie blushed and replied in German. 'Oh, I am not the real teacher you know. That is Mrs van der Lye's job. I am here to help with conversation, accent and so on you know. I am not so much a teacher.'

The men beamed at her over their coffee cups, 'That is understood, Mrs Bauer, quite well understood. We shall put ourselves in the hands of the experts then!' said Mayer, and he laughed with the other men, who sat forward on the edge of their seats balancing their saucers. Such fine, clean young men thought Ellie. It's true what Rudofsky had said – these are the optimists!

They rapidly agreed terms with the proprietor. They would make a regular weekly time to begin with, starting this Saturday, although this might need to be varied if events in army command required their presence. But for now, next Saturday afternoon? After a few more pleasantries and thanks for the coffee, the men departed.

'Well that went well,' said Julia as the two of them cleared the coffee cups. 'They agreed to my first price – didn't try to bargain like some of those hoity toity types from Hietzing. This could be a new beginning for us.'

'Why do you suppose they want to learn English?' Ellie said. 'They never told us that.'

'Ours not to reason why my dear. Oh, and by the way, you really don't need to worry about that talk about the film. He was probably sounding us out you know – typical Viennese caution. That film wasn't the usual stuff we see these days about the Jews. It was a story about them being expelled from Vienna, but then being called back because the city couldn't manage without them. The Nazis hate that film. Captain Mayer was telling us where he stood by saying he liked it.'

Ellie shrugged her shoulders at this as Julia went on.

'All that was a long time ago and I don't like to think about it. After *Die Goldratten* Henk went crazy for making films – it was all he wanted to do after he met Nora Herbert, his big star, but it wasn't possible. It was a very difficult time for me too you know, very hard. The film was a flop, whatever Captain Mayer thought of it. Henk spent all his time trying to raise money for film projects after that but they never came off. His stage career suffered for it and we only survived because I had this idea of a language school. Anyway, these visitors of ours want to learn and we must be happy to teach them and that is all we need to know for now.'

Ellie could see the sense of this but still wondered about the visitors. She couldn't see why they wanted to learn English.

The next Saturday morning was spent with Julia giving lessons to children while Ellie saw different groups for an hour each. It was tiring work and the mothers could be irritating. Some of the pupils were brought by servants, of course – governesses she supposed they were, and these people generally dropped their charges off at the door and used the morning to get some time to themselves. Some of the mothers did the same, going off to the shops, cafes, hairdressers and manicurists in the inner city. But two or three always stayed, spreading their expensive coats over the sofas and chatting loudly on one side of the room while Ellie took the children through their paces in another group. The women were obsessed with the most trivial matters. Once a whole gaggle of them spent the morning complaining about the rationing that meant there was no longer extra cream to pile onto the cakes at Sacher's. She sometimes had to ask the women to keep their voices down as the children could be timid as they attempted to pronounce the difficult words. She wondered what the women's husbands did for a living, to have wives with such leisure on their hands. It was clear that none of the women worked.

The children and their mothers had all gone by the time Mayer and his friends arrived, this time in civilian dress. Now she could see that Mayer walked with a limp. She noticed too that his face, while round, was strangely angular, almost sculptured. Julia said that since they all claimed to have a bit of English already, they should start with conversation so that she could assess what formal help they needed. She would take part.

As the conversation developed it became clear that Mayer's English was already very good, although the other two were at a quite basic level. Mayer explained that he had spent time in London once and that he was coming now just to brush up on the finer points. Julia announced that the other two would need to take her intermediate classroom course, but Mayer was beyond all that, to which he replied that he wasn't averse to reading and discussing some literature, if that would be acceptable.

'We could look at some Shakespeare if you like!' said Ellie. 'I have an edition that has German and English side by side.'

'That would indeed be of great interest to me,' he responded, 'and my two friends here can join us when they have finished their lesson and try out what they have learned.'

In fact, Mayer was already very familiar with the majority of Shakespeare's plays, having seen several during his stay in London, more so than Ellie who had never been to the theatre in England. She had treasured her edition, which she had bought when she was last in Vienna in 1941 and taken with her everywhere she went, but although she had gained a deep familiarity with the works in evenings spent in numerous lonely attic rooms, barracks and dormitories over the past couple of years, she knew she was no literary expert. She felt quite intimidated. He must have sensed this, suggesting to her they could proceed by him simply reading the English text out loud. 'That way, you may help me with my accent. It is too strong I know.'

So that was their pattern for the first few visits made by the new pupils. Mayer read aloud with Ellie helping his pronunciation for a bit, and then they would fall into a more natural conversation particularly after he pronounced words in a way that made her laugh. She found herself telling him things about herself, about Michael, her time in Zell am See and her subsequent wanderings, and he told her more about his life. He had been in the Austrian army before the Anschluss and had seen it change as the men learned the ways of the German military. He had been with the Wehrmacht in France, in an Austrian division, where he had got the leg wound that had brought him back to Vienna, his home city. He'd had a desk job ever since.

Then, in a surprisingly personal disclosure, he told her he

had been engaged to be married before the Anschluss, but the woman was Jewish so it had to be put off, maybe for good. This had stopped him from rising far in the ranks he told her, but that was all right with him. Time would tell.

'Where is she?' Ellie asked, anxiously thinking of the round-up of Jews in the market she had seen. Mayer hesitated a bit, then answered.

'Oh, she left with her parents before the war. They are in England now. One day…' And he shrugged. 'Let us read that speech from the Lady Macbeth again – the one about the spot of blood! I love it!'

Ellie wondered at the ease with which he spoke of the engagement being put off. He was either a cold fish or good at covering up his real feelings.

Later, the other men would come in from their class next door and the conversation would turn to how many loaves of bread mother had bought, how to ask for directions to the flower market, whether it would rain today, and other such scintillating topics to test their command of tense and vocabulary. It was hard work, occasionally relieved by soldierly joking that slipped back into German as the banal English sentences were issued forth, and for the most part Mayer sat back and looked on while Ellie worked her way through the stilted conversation with his two colleagues.

'That's enough now I think,' he would say after about twenty minutes of this and Ellie learned in time that this was a signal for her to get up and leave the room to join Julia in the kitchen or the next door classroom. She usually then heard the three men conversing in German in low voices next door, talking shop it seemed from the snippets she was able to pick up. Then one of them would come and find the women to pay for the lessons and to say their goodbyes until next time.

After a while, they brought other men with them and Berger and von Weyr became only intermittent attenders. The others were fellow soldiers they said, who had heard of the classes and wanted to join in, and some civilians who they introduced as friends, including an intense young woman called Laura Gadoll. Saturday afternoons spread into Saturday evenings and they were even talking about expanding into Sunday. There seemed to be quite an urge to learn English amongst the Viennese, joked Rudofsky when Ellie told him about the turn things had taken. 'A lot of optimists!' he chuckled.

9

On a cold day in March Ellie, wrapped in coat, gloves and hat, was walking hurriedly across the Stadtpark to get home after a stint at the language school. The newspapers were full of news from the Eastern front, all of it wildly optimistic about the prospects for holding back, no, *turning* back the Russian tide that everyone guessed was sweeping away the German defences. Julia had some maps on the walls of her classroom, one of Europe, the other a world map. Walther had a good knowledge of geography too and together they had listened to the place names mentioned in the radio broadcasts and could see that since Stalingrad the movement had all been westwards. Names like Rostov, Voroshilovgrad, Izyum, Smolensk, Dnepropetrovsk: who or what could live in such places, with such incredible names? She wondered what had happened to Josef Marcher, whose last letter had been from Stalingrad, but thought she could guess. The newspapers published pages of little black crosses recording the deaths of soldiers and there were more and more women in mourning clothes in the streets.

As she paced along she thought too of Zell am See, Michael and Anna, places and people whose memory always caused her pain. She had not seen or heard from Anna since April. She'd be seven this January. She had been to see her after the Luftwaffe threw her off the telephonist training course, but it had been another difficult episode, with relentless hostility from Ilse. She knew she must stop thinking about it because it got her down, and she pulled her coat tighter around her, striding through the park. After that, Graz and the factory had been murder – what a shit heap – but things were looking up now. Franz Schollmann had been right about the move to Vienna – it had done her prospects no end of good. Her mind was wandering. They'd been good together, she thought, it was a shame Franz had a wife. Funny how it's always foreigners she seemed to make friends with. Julia was lovely, she thought, how good to have a friend like that. You need friends when you're on your own. But there was no doubt about it, Vienna was the place to be, even if there was a war on. These random thoughts and memories spinning round in her mind, she strode on.

She went over a little bridge that crossed the canal running through the park and turned to go through the trees, looking over to the little bandstand near the Kursalon. The roses had gone now and the trees had lost their leaves. The park benches were empty, except for one where a small woman wrapped in a dark coat sat leaning forward, her head in her hands. As she hurried past she heard moaning and against her better judgement looked sideways at the woman. There were a lot of down-and-outs on the streets these days and it didn't pay to give them too much attention. But the woman's face, stained with tears, looked up at her and she held out her hands to Ellie. She realised with a shock that this was the woman she had met in the tram.

'Help me!' she cried.

Ellie could do nothing else but move towards the distressed woman. What was the matter, she asked, what was she so upset about?

It seemed the small woman was suffering both in her feelings and in her strength. Ellie tried to help her up on to her feet, but she could not – or would not – stand.

'It's my heart I think,' she managed to say. 'I feel so weak. I need to stay here a bit longer.'

'You can't stay out here in this cold. You'll freeze.'

At this, the woman beat her fist against the back of the bench with a show of extraordinary force. 'I had to sit down on this thing, although I said I never would,' and she raised herself to look at Ellie with a desperate and angry expression on her tear-streaked face.

The benches, like all of those in the Stadtpark, were stencilled with *NUR FÜR ARIER* – only for Aryans.

The woman seemed confused, maybe a bit mad, but also in need of help. Her coat was thin and she would freeze on this bench if she stayed here much longer. There was no-one else about. Ellie decided she would have to do something.

'Come on, let's get you to somewhere warm,' she said, picking up the woman's bag and putting her arm around her shoulder to lift her up. 'Where do you live?'

She learned that the woman's name was Poldi and that she lived on the other side of the old city, 'on the Ring,' she added.

This wasn't very plausible, but she could see this Poldi wasn't going to be making much sense until she was warmed up and given a chance to recover. 'You'll have to come home with me,' she told her, 'and we'll try and get you sorted out. Perhaps there is a doctor you can see. Come on, I'll help you. It's not far.'

They struggled along the edge of the park and turned off into Biberstrasse, Ellie helping Poldi as she stumbled along with small steps, periodically stopping to catch her breath and regain strength. At the entrance to the apartment block the curtains on the caretaker's window twitched as they entered. Frau Steiner emerged from her station straight away to see what was going on, arms folded as Ellie helped Poldi through the doorway.

'What's all this?' she barked.

'She needs help, she's had a funny turn,' replied Ellie, struggling with the door with one arm around Poldi, whose small frame was light even when she stumbled and Ellie had to support her full weight. Ellie didn't bother to ask the caretaker for help. 'I found her in the park and I'm taking her in for a bit to warm her up. It's all right. I know her.'

'I didn't know you were such a good Samaritan,' said Frau Steiner with her customary cynicism. 'Just make sure there isn't any trouble,' she threw in as she returned to her cubby hole.

Luckily there was a lift up to the fifth floor and she helped Poldi up the final staircase into the top corridor which had doors to single rooms along it, running along under the roof. She got the woman into her room and sat her down, then went out to the kitchen down the corridor to put a kettle on.

'You look so like Mrs Kremenezky,' said Poldi, opening her eyes when Ellie came back with the tea. 'Are you sure you don't know her?'

'Mrs who? I'm afraid I don't know what you're talking about. Look, take this and have a few sips. It will make you feel better.'

Poldi was quiet for a while, holding the cup in both her hands against her lips. The steam rose in front of her white face in the cold air of the apartment, as she stared into the empty fireplace. Ellie watched her. She was about forty or fifty years old, she guessed, small but with a sturdy build, her coarse black dress under a patched woollen coat, brown hair streaked with grey. Hair grew on her top lip.

'Where do you live again?' asked Ellie, hoping Poldi might have got her wits together by now.

'On the Ring my dear – it's a bit of a walk, but I'll be all right. It's not so far.'

She wasn't making much sense, thought Ellie. A place on the Ring for someone dressed like that? It couldn't be true. On the other hand, perhaps this was some rich eccentric. Ellie felt worried for Poldi and she didn't trust this story about a weak heart, but also felt curious.

'Let me help you home,' she said, 'I'm not doing anything this afternoon and perhaps you could do with some help still. I don't think you should be out on your own if you've got a heart problem like you say.'

She expected her to reject the offer of help, but in fact it was accepted readily, making Ellie more convinced that Poldi must somehow have engineered the meeting.

After tea and a bit of bread and butter the two of them got their coats on again and went down in the lift, past Frau Steiner's spy hole and out into the street again. Poldi's energy seemed restored and she was able to lead the way, albeit somewhat slowly, through the city centre to Schottengasse.

'Here we are,' she said, looking up at a massive palace, five storeys high, with Italian-style corner towers, golden balcony railings, rows of pillars topped with classical statues above cream coloured stone.

'You can't be serious,' gasped Ellie. 'This isn't a house a person can live in. You *can't* live here!'

'Oh but I do,' said Poldi with a proud little smile on her face, 'I do.'

She led her to a side entrance and they stepped through a door cut into huge wooden gates studded with brass rivets. Poldi led her across a courtyard and in through another door, smaller this time, through winding corridors and down a short flight of stone stairs.

'I'm afraid I have deceived you a little – forgive me. This is where I live.'

Poldi lived in just two small rooms in the basement of the magnificent building. Lit by a single weak lamp, the room they entered was dark, the window to the courtyard being a narrow slit above their heads. Through a door Ellie could see a bed spread with a white cover, a crucifix above a small table on which there were some faded flowers. Two surprisingly ornate chairs were pulled up at a table and Poldi drew one back for Ellie to sit down.

'You are noticing the chairs? They belonged to the Kremenezkys. The Germans let me have them.'

She dug out a half-full bottle of barack and popped the cork out, pouring them a drink into little glasses. The fiery spirit made Ellie cough as the warmth spread through her chest.

'Who are the Kremenezkys? How is it that you live here Poldi? Who else is in the rest of the building?'

'You have a lot of questions all at once don't you,' Poldi laughed, in a more cheerful mood now she was back in her home with a restoring drink. 'You can't be from round here I think. People in Vienna know better than to ask so much.'

'Oh, I'm sorry, if you – it's just that…'

'No, don't worry. I don't mind telling you,' said the little woman.

Poldi said she had been a servant to the Kremenezkys, the Jewish family who had built the palace and lived in it for most of her life. She had come to them many years ago at the age of fifteen, sent there by her peasant family in Burgenland.

'Here, I'll show you some photographs,' she said, pouring them another drink and taking an envelope out of a drawer.

They were family snaps, one or two where a younger looking Poldi had been invited to pose with groups of Kremenezkys at home or at play. One of the photographs showed a woman with a huge white wig topped by a massive feathered hat balancing on her head, a silk dress sweeping down to the floor, a velvet jacket and an ornate walking stick held theatrically in her left hand. Oil paintings formed a background and sculptures and rich furniture sat on a patterned carpet beneath the woman's feet.

'That's amazing. Who on earth is she?' asked Ellie.

'That's Mrs Kremenezky. She decided she wanted a picture of herself looking like Marie Antoinette! I helped her with her dressing up that day. It took three hours to get her into that, and then she never wore the clothes again. I've no idea what happened to them, but she was like that – money to burn. It was just for the photograph. You could have fed a family for a year on what she spent that day. But she wanted to see what she would look like.'

'She's quite fat for that dress isn't she?' Ellie said.

Poldi sniggered. 'She had plenty of lovers though. I used to let them in through a side entrance in the evening and out the same way the next morning.'

Ellie felt a surge of anger and jealousy at this unknown woman's wealth.

'No wonder people wanted the Jews out of Vienna if that's how they behaved,' she said bitterly.

Poldi started back and pulled the photograph away from Ellie. 'How could you say that!' she exclaimed angrily.

'No, no, I don't mean what you think,' Ellie protested, 'I just thought…seeing that picture…'

'How can you understand what things were like here? The Kremenezkys were kind to me as a young girl. I grew up with their children. It is terrible what happened to them, terrible. It is not their fault that they had money.'

Poldi was being unfair, Ellie thought, allowing herself to criticise her employer but then defending them when Ellie joined in. Lots of people were like that, she had noticed.

But then Poldi explained to her that the Kremenezkys had been driven out of the country after the Germans had come and Ellie remembered Kurt Steinhauser's story about the same thing happening to his family in Vienna.

'That's why I was so upset on the park bench today,' said Poldi. 'I swore I would never sit down on one of those things with that filthy sign, but I just had to, I felt so weak.'

She seemed to calm down and accept that Ellie had meant nothing by her shocked exclamation at the fantastic fancy dress image. Ellie in turn told her of her friendship with Kurt Steinhauser, her anxieties about what had happened to him and his wife.

Then Poldi showed her another photo of Mrs Kremenezky. This time, it was a more naturalistic shot, a studio close-up. She was dark haired with high cheekbones and fine skin, looking out at them with a penetrating gaze that was extraordinarily intimate.

'I can see why men liked her,' said Ellie.

'But can't you see the likeness too? That's why I noticed you on the tram that day. Fate meant us to meet each other like this, I am sure.'

Ellie looked again at the photo. She could see what Poldi meant, she supposed. The woman had similar features to herself, but what did that mean? Poldi was a bit cracked, she thought, all these months cooped up in this little room. She was probably just lonely and had latched on to her because Ellie reminded her of her former employer. She must have made sure they crossed paths somehow. The weak heart was just a story. But the woman was clearly harmless.

Poldi poured them both another barack and Ellie enjoyed the sensation as the alcohol went to her head.

After kicking the Kremenezkys out, Poldi told her, the Germans had moved into the palace. Poldi was told by the Gestapo to pack up the silver, the porcelain, the clocks, jewellery, books, statuettes. She was to make herself useful, atone for a lifetime of service to the Jews by helping strip the place. In exchange she would be allowed to stay in the two basement rooms. The rest was to become administrative office space.

'But they didn't notice these,' she said finally. And she showed Ellie an old cloth bag which she took out from under the mattress in her bedroom.

It contained old coins, perhaps a couple of hundred, which Poldi tipped out onto the table between them.

'The children used to play with them,' she said. 'They used to line up their toy soldiers at each end of the room and roll the coins at the other army.'

Ellie looked at them. 'None of them are gold,' she remarked, 'but they look old. Are you sure they're not worth something?' She looked at one coin, a large one. On one side was a woman with long braided hair, on the other a man with hair descending in ringlets to his shoulders, a band around his crown. She could see 'Maximilianus' written around the edge.

'I slipped them into my apron pockets, a few at a time, when they weren't looking. Here, have one, why don't you? I've been swapping them for food down at the market.' The coin had an image of a woman on one side, an Austrian coat of arms with wings on the other.

'Oh no, you must keep it,' said Ellie, embarrassed at Poldi's impulsive generosity.

'No, you have it. It is something a bit unusual for you to keep. Something to remind you to come and see me again I hope!'

Ellie accepted the coin as Poldi gathered up the others from the table and put them in the bag. Both of them were a bit drunk from the barack and, as Poldi went to the bedroom to return the coins to their hiding place, Ellie saw that there were three more coins lying behind the bottle. Picking them up, she was about to take them through to Poldi, but then she thought better of it. Quickly and quietly, she slipped them into her bag.

After that they said their goodbyes and promised to meet again.

Around that time American planes came over Vienna for the first time, aiming their bombs at oil refineries in Floridsdorf. At first everyone thought it was another isolated raid, but a few days later there was another one over Kagran on the Eastern bank of the Danube and on the same day they struck in the South, past Simmering at the huge oil depot in Lobau. After that there were regular air raid warnings so that most weeks there was a time when Ellie had to stop whatever it was she was doing and run down to the nearest shelter. If she was in the cellar of her apartment block she would head for her own nest of pillows and blankets on the rough brick floor.

Most of the time the bombs were falling a few miles away,

but they could hear the rumble of the explosions and the next day could read about the bomb damage in the papers. Once Ellie went over the bridge to Floridsdorf to see things for herself. She got close enough to see some smoking ruins although the police turned sightseers back before you could get a good look. She was glad the refineries were on that side of the river. She, like most people, thought there would be no point in the Americans smashing up the old city, where there was no industry. All they had to worry about was a few stray bombs, although that thought was unpleasant enough.

She was beginning to think she might be able to afford a better place, perhaps further west where bombs seemed less likely. The income from the language school had improved since Mayer and his colleagues had started there and she was also paid more by the Academy now that she had lost her inhibitions about nude modelling. She'd been able to give up the last of her cleaning jobs.

Another factor was Frau Steiner, the caretaker at Biberstrasse, who knew she was a foreigner and had somehow found out that she was a divorcee. After being sent to work in some terrible places by Arbeitsamt officials in the past, Ellie hadn't registered with her local one in Vienna, which she knew was an offence. If Frau Steiner got to hear about that, who knew what might happen. The woman snooped on everyone and probably made regular reports to the local Party office.

As the weather grew warmer she began to think about making a trip to Zell am See again. Poldi, who had become a friend, encouraged her in this plan, saying that she needed to resolve the situation with Anna who must miss her mother. But Ellie wasn't sure what to do. She liked her life in Vienna. How would Anna fit into that?

Then Carl Mayer asked her to the Opera. They were putting on a piece by Dvořák, a Czech composer, which was quite controversial, he said. He thought she would like it.

This invitation gave her pause for thought. She still wasn't sure where Mayer stood, in spite of his Jewish girlfriend. After all, he was an officer in the Army and apparently had been for a long time. She also didn't know that she wanted to deepen her relationship with him as a man. He was young and strong looking enough, but there was a clean hardness to his appearance that was somehow off-putting. And she hadn't got a dress for something like that. She told him this.

'Oh I thought of that, don't worry about it,' he said. 'I'll bring over one or two of Miriam's evening dresses. She left them at my place. You're about the same size as her.'

This was reassuring to Ellie, both about her shortage of a dress and because it meant he hadn't got his mysterious fiancée off his mind – he was probably just missing her and wanted her to dress up like Miriam and go out with him for the evening. She agreed.

He turned up at the language school the following week with two gorgeous dresses. One, in red silk, was not quite the right fit somehow and she preferred the one in delphinium-blue with a sequined bodice. Carl had also brought an expensive-looking fox fur for her shoulders and she had a brooch and shoes that could match the outfit at a pinch, even if they weren't up to the standard of the rest of the outfit.

'I'll have to get an opera box if I'm going to live up to this!' he said admiringly when she came through into the conversation room with a flourish, dressed in this ensemble. She was delighted with these beautiful things and with the effect she was having on all the men in the room, who had turned their heads to look, and she only reluctantly went back out to change into her everyday working clothes.

When the evening came, Mayer drew up in a large black car with an army driver, which was quite a surprise. Frau Steiner's curtains gave an extra big twitch as she stepped out of the building and into the luxurious vehicle, door held open with a grin by a cheerful army driver who was clearly putting on a bit of an act. She sank into the comfortable leather seat at the back. It was wide enough so that they could sit next to each other without touching. He was dressed in his Wehrmacht uniform, which she now saw emphasised his somewhat sharp features. This wasn't how he usually travelled, Mayer explained, but he had begged a special favour from his Colonel just for tonight. It was only a one way service – they would have to get a taxi back.

The powerful car sped smoothly around the Ring and joined the queue of limousines pulling up at the main entrance, disgorging a procession of the wealthy, the powerful and the privileged. Inside, the staircase stretched seemingly to the heavens between ornate pillars. Vases of flowers – carnations, azaleas and lilies – stood in alcoves around the foyer and at intervals on the main staircase. All around them were men and women in finery. Men in dress uniform, cleanly cut black tunics pinned with military decorations and badges, women's hands and arms flashing with diamonds, silver and gold rings, bracelets and necklaces reflecting the brilliant lights. One slim, Nordic looking beauty wore a silver dress and pearl-drop pendant earrings, her hair piled up high with a semicircle of diamonds glittering at the back.

Ellie was both awestruck and suddenly terrified. This was not her world – what was she doing here? She clutched at Carl's arm in panic and he turned to look at her.

'Don't worry,' he whispered, 'they're not all like this at the Opera. I just thought it would be fun for you to see this side of Vienna. I think it's pretty ghastly actually.'

He guided her to the side of the foyer and along a bar where more of the dazzling people were quaffing champagne from fluted glasses and preening themselves in the numerous mirrors.

'Our stairs are here. I am afraid I couldn't afford a box, but I expect you will be relieved by that, seeing the look on your face back there.' He laughed and squeezed her arm, which was threaded through his as they climbed the stairs to an upper gallery. 'Don't worry, I didn't sink as low as standing room. We'll be comfortable enough.'

She was reassured now that they had got away from the lobby and as they went higher up the stairs she saw that the audience were in somewhat less glamorous dress. Some soldiers who were there with their girlfriends stood up to let them in and one of them tried to salute Carl as they edged past. He waved his hand airily in acknowledgement and they sat down.

The opera was Rusalka. Carl whispered to her that because it was by a Czech composer there had been objections from some quarters, but someone knew someone who knew von Schirach and he had given it his personal stamp of approval. 'Not that that counts for much in Berlin these days,' he added.

Ellie didn't really know what he was talking about, but couldn't ask because the conductor was coming on to take his bow and she soon found herself gripped by the performance. Near the start the main character, Rusalka, a woman dressed in diaphanous blue raiments that seemed to mirror the colour of Ellie's own beautiful dress, sang a lovely song to the moon that made Ellie's heart beat faster and thrilled her spirits. Like a lot of people she had been to some orchestral performances at various venues around the city, tickets being cheap if you were willing to stand, but she thought she had never heard any music as wonderful as this.

Rusalka was a water spirit, in love with a human prince, magically turned into a human by a sorcerer who said the price of this would be to lose the power of speech. Although the prince, dressed in red like all the human characters in the story, is in love with her, in the end he finds her silence maddening and he makes love to another woman.

As the plot developed, Ellie could see that Rusalka's problem was that she was only half human. She could not join in with the human world but, as it turned out, she could not return to the world of the water spirits either, except as a spirit of death, luring human beings into the depths. For her, there was no solution. She belonged nowhere. Her lamentations about her fate, partly brought about because of her own fatal love obsession with the prince, were heart rending.

As the opera went on, Ellie found herself thinking about her own life over the past few years and realising that in many ways she, too, really belonged amongst no-one. She had certainly made many friends in the places where she had been, but she had always moved on and never really felt any sense of belonging anywhere as she wandered from place to place. In Zell am See she had been an outsider, a representative of a hostile foreign country. Ilse had hated her for that, she was convinced, and she felt this had led to the breakdown of her marriage.

Then there was her time in Kufstein – she had had to flee across the border to get away from the people there after they heard about her divorce. The Luftwaffe episode was bizarre. She had never thought she belonged in the German armed forces, yet events – or rather a lazy Arbeitsamt official who had passed her on to the recruiting officer who hadn't bothered to check her papers properly – had led her into that. To her surprise, in the Munich barracks she had found a kind of comradeship with the young women, shipped there from all over the place, far from their own families, to learn the telephone operating systems.

But then, just as things were going well, she was thrown out. She wondered if Ilse Bauer had prompted Grabner to write that letter to the commandant, pointing out that she was English.

The music surged at this point – Rusalka was begging the sorcerer to make it possible for her to go back to her old life.

As the music swelled, so did Ellie's feelings. She had been thrown out of the Munich barracks and put on a train, to end up in that purgatory in the Graz chain factory. That had been the lowest point, treated like an animal, sleeping on the floor, no different from the slave labourers and prisoners.

She looked down at the expensive fur resting on her lap. Which of these many worlds was hers? Where did she belong? Nowhere it seemed. Even the bloody *Ahnenpass* episode had resulted in her being told she couldn't be classified.

The opera ended with the repentant prince seeking out Rusalka, kissing her, knowing that the kiss would end his life. Recovering her composure, Ellie reflected that it was all very beautiful and sad, but what a fool the man was. There were plenty of other fish in the sea for him, if only he had known. She gave a little laugh at this thought and Carl turned to her with a smile of pleasure as they stood up.

They caught a taxi back to Ellie's place in Biberstrasse where the Steiner curtains twitched again. She could see a pair of gimlet eyes staring from behind the glass as she invited Carl upstairs for a drink, which he readily accepted. She had developed a taste for barack since her visit to Poldi's place and that was all she had to offer her companion. They sat opposite each other, Ellie on the edge of the bed and the bottle between them.

'So you liked the opera did you?' he said, somewhat stiffly.

'Yes, it was wonderful – really wonderful. I can't say how grateful I am to you for taking me.'

Then Carl leaned forward with a sad expression on his face. 'But you were crying Ellie, you know, during the singing. I saw it. What was it? It is an unhappy story I know.'

She hadn't realised he had seen her. She explained that she was thinking about her life, that she had been feeling Rusalka's story was in some way also hers.

'Ah, that is often a case with these romantic pieces. Death and love are mixed together quite deliberately and we find ourselves caught up in it all. That is the magic of the opera.'

'No it was more than that Carl,' she corrected him. And she started then to talk about herself in a way that she had not done before with this kind but strangely distant man.

She told him about what had happened to her since she had

come to Austria and he listened sympathetically. She found herself becoming tearful again when she described her time in the factory at Graz, and he seemed to understand her distress at the memory. He moved to her side on the bed and placed an arm around her.

She reassured him that things were much better now, in her place here in Vienna, with the language school and such good friends. But she missed her daughter. She started to sob again. She missed her so much.

Carl got up to get them another drink while she blew her nose. He asked her about her life before Austria, and to her surprise that really touched a nerve. For months, if she found time to reflect at all, she had thought of more recent events in Austria, which had put such a strain on her survival skills and demanded all of her energies, so that this sudden plunge further back into her childhood seemed completely to undermine her already frail emotional state.

She found herself telling him about her mother, Billy and Papa LeBrocq, her grandmother, the sense of worthlessness she had had to overcome as a child because of her unknown parentage and the trouble that her existence had caused to her grandmother, her attempt as a teenager to leave the island and stay with her mother in Birmingham and the miserable return to Jersey. In fact, she told him everything she could think of about her life and he listened and listened on, into the early hours of the morning until, as seemed inevitable, they lay down on the bed together.

They were not good as lovers. They tried, but in bed they were awkward. Both of them felt it. He had his own demons too. In his case, as she had suspected, it was the memory of his fiancée Miriam, who he said he'd last seen in 1939. He confessed that he was still obsessed with her. She was not hurt by this, as she had sensed it already, and in the morning they parted affectionately enough.

They met occasionally after that and sometimes they slept

together. He liked to take her out into the streets, to go shopping or into the parks, or to concerts. He brought her more of the clothes that Miriam had left behind and she knew that he liked it best when she wore them for their outings, so she obliged him. But it did not help her to love him.

10

IN JULY MAYER stopped calling at her place so often and only came once to the language class. The other men said he was busy at the army command. The bombing raids on the eastern part of the city had become more frequent. Perhaps his work involved that. She knew he had something to do with organising the movement of troops but he didn't tell her much about it. This reticence was not surprising to her and she knew not to ask.

Then on the afternoon of 20th July came dramatic news which they heard at first on the radio in Julia's kitchen. The normal Vienna Radio broadcast was interrupted by an excited, near hysterical voice proclaiming, shouting that the radio station had been taken over, that Gestapo and SS units all over the city were being disarmed and that Austrian patriots should rise up to overthrow the Germans.

They couldn't believe their ears. What sounded like a shot rang out in the street outside and they ran to the window, but there was nothing but the usual peaceful street scene. Perhaps it was a car exhaust. By the time they got back the broadcast had stopped and a military march was playing. Other stations were broadcasting as normal. Julia went next door to her neighbour to see if she knew more but she did not answer, so Ellie phoned Rudofsky. He knew nothing, was absorbed in his painting, cared nothing.

Later that day they heard more news, this time from Radio Graz, whose signal could reach the city. It was an official announcement stating that traitors had made an attempt on the life of the Führer, but it had been unsuccessful and the rebels were being hunted down and arrested and would face the righteous anger of the German people. The people should all be grateful that no serious harm had come to their leader. Hitler eventually spoke himself, pointing out that the failure of the plot was a confirmation of the fate that Providence had imposed on him, that he had been preserved to accomplish his 'great task.' The women listened, appalled.

'They will be rounding people up all over the place now,' said Julia. 'The streets may not be safe – you had better stay here tonight.'

The following morning they ventured out, as all seemed quiet. Many shops were shut and there were notices saying that the theatres and concert houses would be closed until the following day. People wandered round the street with nothing to do, exchanging looks with each other, wondering if it was safe to ask for news from strangers. Here and there were huddles around the news kiosks.

Ellie went to Poldi's place. She was no more informed than anyone else but she seemed all right. They would have to wait for news from Mayer or one of his colleagues who might be able to tell them what was going on. She went home.

The next day at the language school, no-one turned up for classes. She found Walther and Julia together in the kitchen. The radio, though, said that the theatres would be opened again and shopkeepers should resume normal business. The sense of panic subsided and even the sound of the air raid siren that evening and a spell in the cellar shelter listening to rumblings in the direction of Floridsdorf felt somehow like a return to normality.

'It's as if the sea has parted for a moment, we have seen the seabed, and now the waves have come back to cover it over again,' said Ellie.

Walther commented, his usual cynicism in play, that this

was a rather poetic way of putting it, quite the French manner. But Julia was struck by the idea, saying 'Yes, we have peered briefly into a different world haven't we?'

On Saturday they expected Mayer as usual, but again, there was no-one, although the mothers and daughters had started to trickle back. The newspapers ran stories about 'nests' of plotters being smoked out, arrests and executions. Apparently some had taken their own lives. One General, it was said, had taken a train to the Eastern front and walked out in front of the Russian machine guns.

'Believe that and you'll believe anything,' muttered Rudofsky cynically when he heard that. 'Those gentlemen are better at ordering others into harm's way than doing it themselves.'

Then, after an absence of three weeks, Carl Mayer appeared again, and in a uniform with new shoulder stripes. He had been promoted to major. He refused to speak about the events surrounding the assassination attempt, or to comment on what had been going on in Vienna. As far as he was concerned, the English lessons would go on as before. He was quite grim in his manner, his skin stretched tight over his face, accentuating its sharpness, and his bearing intimidated anyone who came near him. The English lessons resumed as did the conversations in the next door room, difficult though it was to relax with the stiff uniformed figure sitting upright on the edge of his chair. He was quite impersonal and cold towards Ellie.

'Something has shaken him badly,' she confided in Julia. 'It's like he has been in an explosion or something. If he changed out of his uniform he would fall apart – it's all that is holding him together.'

Julia told her it was best to let time pass and they would see if he would return to his former self. These were difficult times, she said, not everyone could talk freely about what they had to do. We don't know enough to judge him.

But Ellie started wondering if he had played a part in

rounding up the plotters. There had been many of them in Vienna it seemed, and large numbers of red death sentence notices were posted on the bulletin boards outside police stations and the Gestapo building on the Kai. People hurried past them, eyes averted. They contributed to the climate of fear that, along with the threat of air raids, was beginning to be the dominant feeling when you went out on the streets.

But then, over time, just as Julia had anticipated, Carl began to relax. The language classes with his circle of work colleagues and friends resumed, although at first very few of them turned up. By September, though, things were back to normal on Saturday afternoons and Ellie began to enjoy the sessions again.

It had been a good move, coming to Vienna, all things considered, and she had had a good year. She had friends, work that paid pretty well, and plenty of things to interest her. She was beginning to get her life back together after the terrible time after the divorce. If only this bloody war would end. They might get some decent food then. She was sick of the endless queues at the shops to get the miserly amounts of bread, meat, potatoes, pea powder the ration cards allowed, even if you had the money to pay for more. She felt hungry far too often for comfort.

Carl took her to a café once in a while, which helped. No-one bothered to check her papers when they saw she was sitting with a man dressed in that uniform of his. Buying on the black market was possible, but that could be dangerous, especially if you were someone like her who had to keep your head down. No, the war would end soon, everyone could see that, and then maybe things would get back to normal. She would sort things out in Zell am See and get back to Jersey, perhaps for a visit. Where would she live then, she wondered? Perhaps she'd stay in Vienna. It couldn't be much longer to wait.

Later, these reflections seemed absurd in the light of what happened in the first week of November.

It was raining heavily in the morning, but Ellie knew she needed to get down to the Naschmarkt early to see if she could get some of the vegetables before they all went. There had been a few weeks when the supplies from the countryside had been generous as the farmers unloaded their excess produce from the autumn harvest. But that source was drying up now as the weather worsened and it was back to business as usual in the market.

Heavy-set women with bags and sharp elbows shoved at each other to get to the front of the crowds besieging the few stalls that had anything worth putting into the cooking pot. Ellie could give as good as she got, so succeeded in filling her bag with potatoes. They weren't too bad, only a few showing signs of mould. She headed over to Poldi's place as she knew Poldi's small frame was not up to competing in the scrum at the market, and she would appreciate some of Ellie's surplus. Ellie had a habit of taking Poldi little gifts like this, perhaps because she felt a bit guilty about having filched the coins that day. She had hidden them in the pocket of a suitcase she used to take her things down to the shelter when the air raids happened.

She got to the palace around nine o'clock that morning. Poldi thanked her for the potatoes and they had a cup of coffee together. Poldi had no beans to add to the brew, and it tasted pretty vile, but it was warm. There had been a raid that night and Poldi had spent it in the lower basement of the building, sheltering. The bombs had fallen close by. They decided to go out and take a look.

They went down Schottengasse to Palais Harrach on the Freyung first. It had taken a direct hit and the Eastern wing was smashed to bits. One of the bronze statues in the square was hanging off its plinth and some workmen were trying to lower it to the ground. Some soldiers shooed them away so they went down towards the Herrengasse, passing Café Central where

Wehrmacht soldiers were nailing wooden planks across the shattered windows. There was more devastation in Michaelerplatz and another toppled statue with workmen all around it. A fire was still burning in a nearby building but the firemen stood around doing nothing about it until a soldier came over and harangued them, gesticulating and pointing. They didn't seem to understand his German. Perhaps they didn't know how to use the equipment either.

'The statues aren't doing too well!' joked Poldi, who could be quite tough at times. She didn't seem too shaken by the sight of the ruined streets that she had known most of her life. Their feet crunched on broken glass. Other citizens had come to gawp and the soldiers tried to keep the crowds away from the edge of the damaged buildings.

'What about the horses?' asked Ellie, pointing to the Spanish Riding School, which was undamaged.

'Oh, I've heard they're going to move them out soon. You know they put the Jews there on one of the first round-ups. The place is almost empty now.'

Then they heard singing from the group of workmen manoeuvring the fallen statue, using the rhythm of the song to intensify their efforts to heave it into a truck. A man roared at them to shut their mouths and threw a stone at the men. More stones followed and the workmen, who Ellie could now see wore a large lilac-yellow P on their clothing, indicating they were Polish, sheltered behind the truck. One of them picked up a stone and threw it back and that prompted more hurling of insults and rocks at the men behind the truck. Soldiers ran to the scene with rifles which they used to push the stone throwers back.

'Let's get out of here,' said Ellie urgently to her companion, and they went up towards the Rathaus park nearby. There was a huge crater in the park and a building on the side of Ball-hausplatz was damaged so that a wall teetered dangerously. They decided to head back to Poldi's place but as they went past the Burgtheater they were diverted. A man told them there were people buried in the house at the back of the theatre. They saw that there were workmen and soldiers in a human chain, desperately shifting rubble while an ambulance stood by.

'It was a string of bombs,' said Poldi. 'You can see – they are all in a line. They drop out of the aeroplane and hit the ground in a row. I've heard there is more damage down at Dorotheergasse.'

'Well we're certainly not going there,' said Ellie. 'I've seen enough for one day.' She thought of the men in their flying machines in the night, pouring down destruction on a city of people they would never see. Michael, when she saw him that time in Metz, had explained a bit about the air defence system, a line of radar stations going across part of France, trying to intercept the bombers, but always so many of them got through. She didn't want to think about Michael right now though. They were back at the great wooden gates of the Kremenezky Palace.

'I'll be off now, Poldi,' she said. 'I've got work to do this afternoon.'

She took a roundabout way back to avoid the bombed areas, setting off along Schottengasse then heading in to cross the city centre. It was a long way but it wasn't worth trying to catch a tram. The service was patchy at best because of bomb damage to the tracks and the unpredictable route closures. It was hard to get onto them and people clung onto the open platforms, wherever they could get a space.

On the way she picked up a paper – it was a new thing called the 'Little War Paper.' She read the hate-crazed sentences: the air murderers had supposedly killed with the same mechanical ice-cold cruelty as they had over Germany. But the only result they could hope for, said the writer, was the wrath of the people, a glowing, deep-seated, silent hatred that thinks only about one thing: revenge and retribution.

She flipped over to the centre page and saw a list of

Peoples' Court judgments. An accountant had been convicted of spreading destructive rumours and quoting from the Talmud, saying it was better to be a coward for five minutes than to be dead a whole life long. He was sentenced to death.

She threw the paper onto the pavement.

The afternoon was spent in the usual way, Julia giving lessons and she and Walther running conversation groups in the next room. First, the women and children learning French and English, then the Mayer crowd. Carl wasn't there today. All the pupils left around six o' clock in the evening and Ellie felt exhausted so readily agreed to Julia's invitation to stay for an evening meal. She had somehow got hold of a chicken she said. They could roast half of it with Ellie's potatoes and Walther was going to supply a bottle of wine. He had three sugar lumps too, one for each of them, which they could have with their coffee. These were riches indeed, as Ellie had had nothing but pea soup and bread all week and there had been no sign of any meat at all. Sugar had become almost impossible to get. Once again she thanked her lucky stars she had such wonderful, generous friends.

But just as they sat down to feast, they heard the radio giving the all too familiar cuckoo sound and air raid sirens started up outside. They knew they were supposed to drop everything and get down to the basement. They couldn't believe their bad luck.

'I can't hear any flak yet,' said Ellie.

'Come on, let's eat up quickly – we can't waste this food. We'll get down to the shelter soon enough and take the wine with us. It'll be another one over in the East anyway,' said Julia, eyeing the steaming plates.

So they devoured the food as fast as they could, the sense of occasion spoiled, but getting it down anyway, satisfying their gnawing desire to fill their stomachs.

Then they heard the sound of flak guns starting up. The noise was particularly loud.

'That's coming from the Arenberg towers,' said Walther anxiously. 'We'd better shift.' He grabbed the bottle and headed for the stairs, the women following down the long winding stone staircase. Ellie kept up with Walther, who was thin and wiry and skipped down the steps two at a time, but Julia lagged behind. Her joint pains meant she always took the stairs slowly.

At the entrance to the cellar Walther turned and said to Ellie, 'You go down. I have to get my bicycle indoors.' It was crazy and she knew it, but she wasn't going to argue. He rushed for the front door and she heard Julia still descending from the first floor. She headed down into the cellar where there were other people from the building already sheltering and looked around for the bedding that belonged to the people from the language school.

Then she heard a howling sound followed by an almighty crash. Everyone in the cellar froze and there was a second of silence. Then they heard a slow roar as walls collapsed above them, loosened bricks avalanching down, glass splintering, beams cracking under intolerable weight. There were screams around her as the cellar filled with dust, a crazy pause, and then the ceiling collapsed under the burden of what lay above. Ellie was thrown to the floor, her head hitting brickwork so that for a moment she could only focus on the pain of the blow.

She did not lose consciousness, but when she regained a sense of her surroundings she found herself lying in darkness in a tiny space, her legs pinned by something so that they would not move. She put her hands to her head and felt blood in her hair.

The sound of bombing and flak guns receded and she heard groaning coming from somewhere above her in the tangled mess of bricks and beams. She tried to move her feet but although she could feel them straining against the weight, was unable to shift them. Then she became terrified at the thought of the mass of rubble and beams that lay above her. There were creaking and scraping noises and every now and again a minor tumble of bricks as the building settled. She thought the ground might tremble with the impact of more bombs which could press the weight down onto her. Dust had filled her nostrils and got into her mouth and she cleared her nose with her finger and spat. There was more groaning from above.

'Don't move!' she said to the unknown person. Her fear of being buried by a further collapse dominated her thoughts.

She lay in the darkness for longer, an hour or more perhaps, and the sounds were replaced by a deadly, tomb-like silence. After a while she heard no more groans. Her panic about a further collapse began to recede but was replaced with an even greater fear that this space was where she was going to die. She felt cold.

On the second day, she began to feel thirst. Her bowels and bladder also needed relief, and they emptied where she lay. As time wore on, her thirst increased. She heard no human sounds and when she spoke or shouted there were no replies from the other people she had momentarily seen in the cellar before the roof had collapsed.

Was this how she was going to die? How long could you last without water?

Then she started to think of rescue. Surely they would start looking for her, for the others who had been in the cellar? How much time had passed since the bomb had dropped? She had no way of knowing. She thought again about the scenes she had seen with Poldi, the men digging through the rubble at the back of the Burgtheater. She could be reached if they were determined enough. She began to shout and struggle against the load that was pinning her down, no longer cautious about bringing on a further collapse. There was only silence and one of her legs started to ache. If only there was some light, she thought.

Then she fell asleep. Time passed but she lost track of any sense of days passing. Once when she awoke, water was dripping onto her cheek. She turned her head to catch it in her mouth. The liquid tasted of urine and she remembered the groaning there had been above her, but she continued to take in the fluid.

Then there were sounds. Scraping sounds, rasping, scratching. A brick tumbled down next to her head, renewing her terror of being buried under the rubble. Then she heard voices. She shouted again. More scraping and then silence. She shouted a second time. 'I'm here!' with all the energy she could muster. This time there was a shout in reply, a man's voice, although she couldn't hear what he said.

As the rescuers drew closer more bricks fell onto her and dust came into her throat, making her cough. But by then, she knew she would be rescued and her feelings changed from terror to elation. 'I'm here!' she called, in English, in German, in French. 'I am here. Please get me out of here. Be careful, the bricks are falling.'

Finally, there was a rush of clear night air as a final tumble of dirt fell down around her head and she was looking into a man's face above her. They dug out the rest of her body and helped her gently out of the hole in which she had been entombed, three men carrying her up across a mound of rubble and then down the other side, onto the street where they laid her on a blanket.

'Ellie!' she heard. It was Walther, his faded film-star face looming into her vision. 'I told them you were there. But where is Julia?' He was quite desperate. She couldn't reply as her throat was too dry to speak. He held her head and gave her water. She knew nothing of Julia and he soon knew it too. He fed her with three sugar lumps he brought from his pocket wrapped in a handkerchief, telling her they would give her energy.

She spent just two days in the hospital. They cleaned her up and let her rest in bed. Poldi came to see her and so did Josef and Alma Rudofsky, who said she could come home with them. She wasn't physically very badly hurt. Her leg was very sore, but she could stand and walk about and she was weak. Walther came to tell her that Julia hadn't been found. She was never found.

She went to stay at the Rudofskys' place. Alma went over to Biberstrasse, got past Frau Steiner, who wanted to know everything, and brought some clothes back. The things she was wearing in the ruins of the cellar had been thrown away at the hospital. The couple made a fuss over her, bringing her food and drink, Alma accompanying her on her first expedition out of their building. She walked around a bit in the Esterhazy Park, looked up at the flak tower and asked to be taken back.

Then there was another air raid warning. Alma and Josef Rudofsky wearily prepared to go down to the cellar expecting her to come with them, but she wouldn't go. A sense of terror gripped her and her hands started to tremble. Josef stayed with her, against Alma's wishes, saying it was probably a false alarm, which it was. The next time this happened – air raids were frequent now – she managed to get down into the cellar but sat there rocking backwards and forwards, her arms wrapped around her knees, trembling and crying until it was safe to go upstairs.

After two weeks at the Rudofskys she announced that she was leaving to go and stay at Poldi's for a while. She thanked the couple for their kindness. She told them she couldn't go home yet, but she felt like a change of scene. She needed to get back on her feet. She wasn't unique, she said, there were lots of people who went through this now, dug out of ruined buildings. She couldn't afford to dwell on it.

And all the time she was saying this she was thinking about the groaning she had heard above her as she lay trapped underground. She couldn't get it out of her head that it might have been Julia.

11

At Poldi's place she slept on a mattress on the floor of the living room. The weather was freezing but the skies were clear so the bombing went on unabated. They were coming in the day now and although the targets were still mostly the oil and industrial installations in the East, there were many explosions in the city too. The Westbahnhof was damaged and train travel became difficult for those wanting to leave the city. They heard that American bombers had been flying low to strafe the trains with machine gun fire.

Nevertheless, Ellie started thinking about getting out of Vienna. She wrote a letter to her old friend Susan Zainzinger asking for help. Could she put her up in Kaprun for a while? She received no reply.

During this time at Poldi's place, sadness began to overwhelm her. In spite of Poldi's almost constant presence, she felt very lonely. Her thoughts turned often to her past, in Jersey as a teenager, or in Zell am See as a young wife and mother. She remembered with bitterness the fine hopes for the future she and Michael had shared when they travelled with Anna to his home town. These thoughts only served to remind her of what she had lost and this, together with the grief she felt at the loss of Julia van der Lye and the destruction of her life at the language school, oppressed her very much.

Yet it was clear that she could not stay at Poldi's for ever. She had lost her ration cards and papers in the bombing and had no income, having failed so far to report for civilian relief.

147

Poldi's ration card couldn't bring in enough for the two of them to eat and they couldn't go on raiding her meagre stores. There was no more modelling work as the Academy had been shut down for the duration. She would have to try and rebuild some kind of life. She went down to the First District civilian relief office in the Rathaus annexe to see what they could offer.

The man behind the desk, grey-faced and old beyond his years, exuded generic sympathy as she told her story, the sort of response that can develop in people who have heard too many tales of suffering. He picked up his pen and explained the forms she would now need to fill in, the checks that would need to be made.

'You can help speed up the process by telling me all you can about yourself here and now, as honestly as possible. It will all be checked in due course, but if you just give me all the facts now that will save a lot of time in you getting to the right people and sorting out your affairs.'

She gave him her name, her place of residence and, resignedly, told him that she had worked at the language school, but had never registered with the Arbeitsamt. She knew this was punishable, no doubt, by this and that, but she felt so demoralised that she didn't care. Let someone else make the decisions for a change, she thought, I just can't be bothered any more.

The official did not seem perturbed by the news of her non-registration with the labour office. As Ellie well knew, there were hordes of female domestic workers who avoided compulsory allocation to war work by serving the needs of the wealthier classes who encouraged their servants in this deception. Many of the people in the poorer districts – Ottakring, Simmering – complained about this, as they themselves were obliged to work in armament factories ten or even twelve hour days for less than a mark an hour. But it was hard to corral everyone, particularly when their determined employers protected them. When they were bombed out, or when their employers fled the city for their country retreats, such people were left high and dry. No doubt they ended up seeking civilian relief, just like her. She was just another case in a long line.

The man put on a sympathetic look and clasped his hands together as he leaned forward, elbows on the desk. 'And I suppose you will need a place to live now,' he started.

Ellie was demoralised, but she was not stupid. He clearly thought it was her place in Biberstrasse that had been destroyed – she hadn't actually told him where she was when the bomb fell. She'd see where this one went and play him along.

'Yes I will – I've been staying with friends but they can't put me up for ever. What have you got?'

'Well, there's a place in Rechte Bahngasse that's next on my list. It's a bit big for a single person like yourself, but it's too small for a family as well, so I could give you that if you like.'

She jumped at the chance. She remembered that in her past life – the life before the bomb fell – she had been thinking of moving to a better place.

'What's it cost?' she asked.

He mentioned a sum that was no more than she was already paying. Rechte Bahngasse wasn't a great spot, but a bigger place...

'Yes, I'll go there,' she said. She could always go back to Biberstrasse if she didn't like it.

'It's only for a few months mind. And we'll probably need to send some other people there to share the space with you eventually – it's a big place. The owners left in the summer and haven't been back for over a month, so the block warden says, so they come under the war requisitioning regulations. We can't have people leaving places empty when there's people being bombed out.'

This sounded good to Ellie. A few months – that was a lifetime as far as she was concerned. And who knows when the owners would be back? He wrote the address on a piece of paper and gave her some keys. She stood up to go.

'Not so fast now, please sit down. There are a few more things still. What about work? You will need to register.'

So, Ellie reflected, it was good news and bad news all at the same time. She wasn't going to get away with not registering for work as a single woman whose address was now known to the authorities. Anyway, she reflected, she needed a job otherwise she wouldn't eat. She'd have to register.

At the Arbeitsamt they told her to report the following Monday at the Siemens-Halske factory in Floridsdorf where she would be told what to do. This didn't sound too good, but Ellie could see no way out of it. The Arbeitsamt people warned her that penalties for disobedience were very severe and she believed them. She headed over to Biberstrasse to get the rest of her things which she put into two cases and struggled over to Recht Bahngasse where she entered the new building.

There were a lot of stairs – the place was on the fourth floor – but when she entered the apartment she was delighted by what she saw. It was a proper home, with two bedrooms, sitting room, kitchen and – joy upon joy – a bathroom. No more shared washing, as long as the water was running. And it was furnished. The people who had lived in the place had left many of their things. There were books on shelves, some clothes left hanging in a wardrobe and even fresh bed linen in the chest of drawers. She dumped the suitcases on the bed, and then heard a knock on the door.

An older man, cropped white hair, stood glaring at her.

'What are you doing here?' he asked aggressively. 'This isn't your place. It's the Lehmann's. I'm looking after it for them.'

'Well it's my place now,' said Ellie, knowing that to back down could be fatal. Some of her old energy was coming back when she faced everyday difficulties like this. 'I've got the papers to prove it too.'

'Show me them.'

She showed him the papers from the civil affairs people, granting her the right of residence for six months at the address, making sure she kept hold of them while he looked, so he couldn't snatch them away.

'Well that's a turn-up,' grumbled the man, who said his name was Mr Kaestner. He looked as if he hadn't shaved for days. His cheeks were red against his pale skin, giving him a feverish appearance, as if he were permanently angry which, Ellie reflected, he probably was. 'The Lehmanns won't be happy when I tell them. They've been here for thirty years.'

'Well they're not here now are they? And they'll be sending more people I was told – the place is big enough.'

'You'd better look after their things then. I'll have to check up on this you know,' he said, but it was a parting shot and he left her alone in the apartment again, muttering under his breath as he shuffled off.

She spread out on the bed, which was a double one. She couldn't believe her luck. The depression she had felt while staying at Poldi's was brushed away, at least for the moment, by her elation and renewed hopes for the future.

The factory job wasn't as bad as she had feared either, although it wasn't what she would have chosen for herself. The Siemens plant was another one making aircraft instruments, located in a vast underground hangar space that had been dug out by prisoners from Mauthausen the previous year to protect the plant from bombing. She had to get up early to get the tram out to Floridsdorf, but it was a journey that involved no changes, straight across the bridge, and as she was one of the first stops on the route she could always count on a seat. The day was long, packing instruments into boxes in greased paper, standing in a line with other women, for despatch to other assembly factories that made the planes, she supposed. But it wasn't slave labour in the way it had been in Graz – or at least, not in her section.

One of the girls, Lilli, was a real character. She made pigtails out of twists of cardboard and attached them somehow to the back of her head – wore them all day long, making a new set as soon as she came in each morning. Why was everyone so interested in pigtails in this country? Ellie wondered, remembering Marianne Streubel's false hair piece.

Lilli would go crazy to pack the boxes as fast as she could when a supervisor came round, spooning a dollop of grease onto the metal dials and devices and scrunching them into the coarse paper, one, two or three a minute. She made a real mess of the bench, but her show of enthusiasm was hard to fault so the supervisor couldn't say much. As soon as the man was out of the area, she'd collapse theatrically onto a stool, announcing her day's work was now done, prompting a chorus of friendly cat calls and abuse from her fellow workers. Then she'd get up to general laughter and unpack the stuff again, taking her time to clean up, then re-pack it, making the whole thing into a show.

Generally they went very slowly at their work and Ellie once noticed an older woman slipping some grit from her apron pocket into the greased packages, which were supposed to be kept clean so the bearings could run smoothly on the instruments that had moving parts. When she saw that nothing happened to the woman, she tried it herself. It gave her a thrill.

An orchestra came to play in the factory – members of the Vienna Philharmonic come to cheer them up, it seemed. All the theatres, operas and concert halls had been shut in September and this is what the musicians did instead. The players looked glum as they scratched away at their instruments at one end of the packing shed. The assembled workers clapped politely and then had to endure an inspirational speech from one of the managers, urging them on to greater efforts.

Hammer-and-sickle graffiti appeared in the toilets, generating a huge fuss. Work stopped while a manager came and gave them a talking to, yelling at them about treason, about punishment, the Gestapo, shouting that if they thought they'd get a better deal under communism they had another think coming. Then, deflated as he saw the row of blank, silent faces, he said any one of them could come and see him privately if they thought they knew who it was and there would be no consequences, he promised, as long as it didn't happen again. When it happened again, and then a third time, he didn't come back. After a while they didn't bother to whitewash the marks off the toilet wall.

You didn't have to show up every day either. There was always some excuse you could produce: the tram lines were down again, or you had some sickness. Everyone knew it was only a matter of time before the Russians came.

All in all, the job would have been all right. The comradeship with her fellow workers made a welcome contrast to the indolent mothers whose houses she had cleaned, or whose children she had taught at the language school in her past life. But she missed Julia and she felt hungry all the time. They fed them hot food at mid-day in the works canteen, but there wasn't much of it and it tasted bad. It was cold at home – it had become impossible to get coal for the stove – and as the winter deepened she got into bed and wrapped herself in blankets almost as soon as she got in. She had recurrent nightmares about being trapped in an airless box that woke her up sweating in the night. The electricity only worked intermittently so she often sat in bed staring out of the window at the night sky. She couldn't read anything if the electricity was off. She needed to save her candles for the air raids.

On the bright side, there were very few air raids at night nowadays. The bombers came over in the day, often late morning or mid-day. If she was at work she knew she was safe as the underground shelters there were deep enough to be out of reach of any of the bombs. If she was in the city she would push her way into a public shelter at the nearby Esterhazy flak tower. She preferred that to the cellar of Rechte Bahngasse which reminded her too much of her time buried under the language school building. A couple of times she was with Poldi, wandering up and down the bombed streets looking for shops that were still open. There were a lot of people about in the old centre, with some even coming in from the outer suburbs to seek shelter in the catacombs which were said to be the safest refuges of all. When the sirens went, everyone would rush to the entrances, shoving and pushing to get in. Down there, they stood in whatever space they could find, listening to the distant and not so distant explosions – like giant footsteps crashing around above their heads.

One day in January she was on the tram back from work when it stopped and everyone was told to get off or face returning to the terminus in the east. The driver was abandoning the rest of the route. There was some kind of disturbance up ahead.

Ellie pulled her coat around her, picked up her bag and trudged wearily down a diversion street thinking she might get back across the river via Kagran. It would be a long walk. As she went along some men and women ran across the street onto her side of the road, standing and looking back at where they had come from and talking excitedly. She asked one of the women what was going on.

'Oh, the police came to make arrests. They were after a bunch of women who've refused to let their sons get dragged into the *Volkssturm*. But we stoned the bastards out, back across the bridge.' The woman was young, breathing fast, excited, elated. 'The cops'll think twice about coming back here. Bloodsucking shits they are. They're the ones who ought to be hanged.'

She got home late that night. The raids were very frequent now and the gangs of workers had trouble keeping up with clearing rubble off the main highways. She had heard that water was cut off in some districts and people had to fill pails at standpipes in the street. The Russians were coming, everyone said, some of them excited by the thought, but most of them also fearful and agitated. Refugees from Budapest had begun to arrive in the city, spreading fearful stories that were whispered from one person to another in the shelters. The Russians were savages, the radio said, barbarian hordes. They were killing and raping their way across Hungary. But with the heroic efforts of the people they would be repulsed, for sure. No-one believed that, at least not anyone that Ellie knew. It seemed the city was falling apart.

When she opened the door of her apartment the room was unusually warm and Carl Mayer was sitting waiting, smoking a cigarette. He got up with a smile.

'How did you get in?' she asked. 'How did you find me?'

'Aren't you pleased to see me Ellie?'

'No, well, it's a bit of a shock that's all. Of course I'm pleased. Why's it so warm in here,' she asked, talking off her coat.

'I brought you some briquettes,' he said, pointing to some bags over by the stove bulging with brown shapes. 'I thought you could use them.'

'Well certainly, yes, thanks Carl, but tell me. How did you find me?'

'I'm an army officer, remember? I just asked around. I knew what had happened at the language school so the relief office was the obvious place to ask. The caretaker let me in when he saw my uniform. It's good to see you back on your feet.'

Ellie wasn't sure how she felt about this invasion of her place, but part of her was pleased to see Carl and it was certainly good to have some warmth. The stuff he had brought would last her a while. She went over to the stove and warmed her hands. She knew she should embrace Carl, but something in her held back from that.

'I brought something to drink too!' he said, bringing out a bottle. It was brandy, which they drank, with cigarettes to smoke too.

She told him about what had happened to her since the bomb dropped on the language school. He listened, offering sympathy and concern. It felt nice to have someone strong near her, concerned about her welfare. She told Carl she didn't know where Walther Günth was, or how to find him.

'Oh, I located him too,' said Carl. 'He's all right, living out in Mödling. He's safe enough there. He was devastated by Julia's death though, destroyed by it. I think he loved her a great deal, no?'

Ellie said she didn't know, though she supposed now that must have been their story.

Carl had told her nothing about himself and when she asked he was evasive. He said things were busy of course, and he was dashing about a lot, involved in preparations for the defence of the city. They were putting children into the front line now he said, screwing his face in a gesture of abhorrence.

'Will they come, the Russians?' she asked, suddenly anxious. 'Will they really get here? Can they really break through?'

'Well, you know the answer I should give to that. Of course they will be stopped in their tracks by our valiant forces making superhuman efforts under the magnificent leadership of…' And he stopped speaking with a laugh and a wave of his hand. 'Put it this way Ellie, I don't think I'll be wearing this for many more months,' and he indicated his uniform.

They took another drink. Ellie had a lot of questions for him about the Russians, their behaviour, what it could be like if they came to the city, but he didn't have many answers. Then he leaned back, resting his neck on the back of the couch, holding his glass up to the light between two fingers.

'And now I must ask you something Ellie. I want to start our meetings again.'

Ellie was surprised at this request, and puzzled.

'Meetings? Do you mean the English classes? What on earth do you want to start that for, at a time like this?'

He thought for a bit and then seemed to make a decision.

'Yes, you are right of course. Why learn English at a time like this? It is ridiculous.'

He paused again, but then leaned forward and looked her

straight in the face.

'I want to meet some people here every now and then. You don't need to know why. As far as you are concerned, and as far as that caretaker must know, it is a simple English lesson, as before. All right? You will be paid, I promise you, and you must be here when the people come, but you do not need to take part in our discussions.'

She thought about this. It was clearly something dangerous and it shed a new light on some of the behaviour she had witnessed during the meetings at Julia's place. The people who came were often different each week and after that business in July some of them did not come back. They had always wanted time after the English conversations to talk amongst themselves once she finished and went to the kitchen. She remembered seeing papers being passed between people, men who had stayed largely silent during the English conversations but whose voices she heard talking quietly and urgently from the kitchen. She felt a bit foolish for not realising that there was an underlying purpose to these meetings at the language school.

Carl was waiting for an answer.

'You say that these will be like English classes again, just like before?' she asked.

'Yes, that's right, and that is all you really need to think about. You will be quite safe if anyone asks you about it – they are just English classes as before. In my experience it is quite surprising how people will believe you if you stick to a simple story.'

She thought again. She had seen enough to know that the war had smashed apart millions of lives of people who were not very different from her. She wasn't the only person who felt like they were an outsider. Then for some reason she thought of Lilli and her crazy, rebellious cardboard pigtails. The thought made her smile and she looked back at Carl.

'Yes, I'll do it,' she said.

*

After that, the 'English classes' resumed and through January and February new people visited the apartment, though the meetings were at irregular times. Most of them were new to her. Berger and Von Weyr, who had come when the sessions at the Rennweg building started, came once, but not again. A new man called Hans Koppel who had a shock of thick, wavy hair and a lined face dropped in from time to time. A young woman called Margarethe came every time and chain-smoked her way through the meetings. She was clearly wealthy, judging by her clothes and the rings on her fingers, so wasn't like the rest of them. A young fellow with thick black hair and round glasses who doted on Margarethe followed her in and out. He was called Walther and Carl said he was a chemist. Carl didn't tell her much about the visitors and she didn't even learn the names of the rest of them. He explained it was probably best if she didn't know too much about them.

She explained to Mr Kaestner that this was her part-time work, a private arrangement. He grumbled about breaking some rule about running a business from a residential property and then asked her, rather lewdly, why so many of her visitors seemed to be young men. Did she think consorting in this way with soldiers and the like was something a respectable woman would do? He more or less told her he thought the tale about English lessons was a cover story, but she ignored him. If that's what Kaestner thought then it was fine – as long as he didn't guess at any other purpose for the meetings. For herself, she tried to block her ears when the visitors came and once or twice came out of the bedroom, where she lay on the bed reading, to tell them to keep it down.

Carl brought her presents – food, alcohol, more fuel, some leather which she had made into shoes, cigarettes she could either smoke or swap at the Naschmarkt. It was payment for her services, she reasoned. This meant she didn't need the money from her factory work so much now. Anyway, money was no good when there was nothing to buy. So she stopped bothering with work for days on end, going over to Poldi's if she could, or visiting Rudofsky. Out where he lived the bombing hadn't been so bad after the big raid just before Christmas that had destroyed most of the Westbahnhof. In February the zoo out at Schönbrunn was hit by bombs and many of the animals were killed. Exotic birds flew out of their cages and escaped from the war-torn city.

And she started sleeping with Carl again, which seemed to bring them both some comfort.

12

ONE AFTERNOON THERE was a new notice on the wall of the apartment building, which was becoming quite a message board. It had been put there since she had gone out that morning

Notice
Vienna has been declared as the defence sector.
Women and children are advised to leave the city.

This was ridiculous, she thought. How were they all supposed to leave? Where would they go? Much more sobering was the red announcement next to it which had been there since early March:

Notice
For high treason the People's Court
have condemned to death and permanent loss of civil rights
32 year old Laura Gadoll
who was executed today.
The senior prosecutor, People's Court.

Ellie remembered Laura Gadoll. She had come to the language classes a few times in the early days. She had been dark-haired, not much older than Ellie, with a penetrating gaze so that it had been hard to look into her eyes. She regretted now, that they'd never exchanged more than a nod.

Next to the notice 'O5' had been deeply scored into the stone. Yesterday Mr Kaestner had been scratching over it to obscure the letters, saying it would get them into trouble. She touched the rough stone, running her fingertips over the marks.

Yesterday, too, a letter had arrived for her, from Morzinplatz, the Gestapo building. She had been told to report there to explain her absences from work. She had torn it up, flushed it down the toilet, considered going to stay over at Poldi's in case the letter was followed by a knock on the door. But things were falling apart, she knew. Lots of people were getting letters like that and nothing much seemed to happen to them. She had persuaded herself she would be all right, would plead ignorance if they came looking for her, say no letter had ever arrived, spin a story about sickness. Perhaps she'd better go over to the factory and do another day there to show willing.

Carl Mayer and his friends hadn't visited recently. A woman and her four year old child had been moved in by the civilian affairs office and had taken the other bedroom. Perhaps Carl was worried about having the meetings there after that, although she didn't see that there was much risk.

The new woman's name was Hannah Weyr, a short, dark-haired woman in her thirties. She looked worn out, flopped on the bed as she explained herself. She said her husband had been reported missing in the East and she'd been bombed out of her place on the main road in Landstrasse so, like Ellie, she had been allocated to the apartment as a temporary measure. She turned out to be pretty quiet, focusing mostly on her little boy and, Ellie guessed, ruminating miserably about her personal troubles, but it was nice to have some company all the same. It was a big place to be all alone in.

Food was short and with Carl not replenishing her supplies her stomach was really starting to feel the pinch. Today she had been over to the Naschmarkt to see what she could find. There was nothing really. Most of the stall holders didn't bother opening any more and those that did sold out within minutes. The half-rotten stuff that used lie on the street at the end of the day was now few and far between. Anything that hit the floor didn't stay there long. She came away with nothing and walked back across the Resselpark. She knew she'd get something there with what she had to trade. The Lehmann's stuff had proved useful at the black market. Today she had some of their linen handkerchiefs.

In the Resselpark men and women stood about, apparently enjoying the early sunshine, but in reality casting furtive glances around them, checking for customers, keeping an eye out for police who sometimes raided the park openly. The police sometimes masqueraded as customers, though the traders could usually keep themselves safe by only doing business with women, who were less likely to be working for the police. There were heavy penalties for black market trading.

Ellie saw a familiar character standing near a bench, a small man shaded by a large hat, a bag over his shoulder, shifting from one foot to another and looking around him.

'Have you got anything today?' she asked.

The man nodded in recognition. 'Butter,' he said. 'I've got some left. Fresh from the country.'

She took a handkerchief out and showed it to him. 'How much for one of these?'

'No good to me, that.'

'What about five of them, all nice and clean, embroidered edge – luxury items.'

'Let's have a look.'

She showed him.

'No, what could I do with them? Got anything else?'

Ellie hadn't brought anything else, but knew the man was bluffing.

'You can have all five for five hundred grams,' she offered. His eyelids flickered.

'Two hundred and it's a deal.'

They settled on three hundred. He had the butter wrapped in hundred gram parcels in newspaper, which passed between them. There was some bread in the apartment from yesterday still.

'You here tomorrow?' she asked. She was saving up Mr Lehmann's shoes for a big splash.

'Who knows?' said the trader.

They parted and she had gone on across the park to home. The thought of all that butter and bread made her salivate as she opened the door to the apartment.

Poldi was there, sitting with Mrs Weyr and her boy who was playing with some wooden blocks on the floor.

'I came over here to stay with you for a while,' she announced, though there was a pleading look on her face. 'I can't be on my own any more with what's going on. Have you seen the notices? There's going to be fighting in the city. I just can't live on my own any more. I can't leave. How can I leave? Where would I go? There are no trains anyway.' She was shaking now and looked as if she might cry. Ellie glanced at Mrs Weyr, who shrugged resignedly.

'I brought things with me. Look.'

She had brought luggage with her, suitcases and bags and a large box.

'How did you get those over here?' asked Ellie.

'A trolley cart,' said Mrs Weyr. 'I helped her get the things up the stairs.'

'Yes,' said Poldi eager to explain, 'I made a little cart out of a pram and pulled it along behind me. Look what I've brought you!' and she went to one of the suitcases to open it.

'No no Poldi, don't do that now,' said Ellie laughing and putting her hands on Poldi's shoulders to guide her back to the chair, 'no need for all that.' She didn't think it was a good idea for Hannah Weyr to see whatever Poldi had brought. 'Of course you can stay Poldi. That's what friends are for.'

'Oh that's such a relief! It's only for a while. None of us know…' She sat back in the chair.

'Look what I've got us!' said Ellie brightly, bringing out her butter. She figured this might deflect any curiosity from Hannah Weyr about Poldi's horde. 'I've got some bread too.'

The little boy looked up, suddenly losing interest in his toys. His mother stroked his head and smiled for the first time Ellie had seen. Mrs Weyr then made an offer.

'I've got some dried peas. We can cook up a stew.'

The sharing of food overcame some of the barriers between them. They heated up the peas and water over a tiny gas flame, with a few bits of potato and salt, talking about their fears and expectations of the coming weeks. They knew the end was coming soon, but how would it happen? Were the stories about the Russians true?

'They can't rape all the women in Vienna,' said Poldi, munching on her bread and dipping it into the warm liquid. The boy had eaten his fill and lay on a blanket, sleeping.

'They'll go for the young ones. You and I had better be careful,' said Ellie to Mrs Weyr.

Poldi laughed. 'Thank you very much!'

Hannah Weyr gave a sad little smile. 'Don't worry. I've heard they don't care much about things like that. The newspaper said an old nun was raped twenty six times somewhere over the border. They are devils.'

'She kept a tally then?' asked Poldi, still laughing.

'Oh God, what are they going to do to us,' exclaimed Ellie, suddenly serious, her head in her hands.

'There's not much we can do about it now,' said Poldi. 'We must put our faith in the Lord to protect us.'

The other two women looked disbelievingly at Poldi, but said nothing.

'We can pretend to be old, at any rate. It might help,' said Mrs Weyr. 'And there's Gerd here,' she said pointing to her son. 'Surely they'll respect the mother of a child.'

Again, the other two didn't comment.

'How do we make ourselves look old?' asked Ellie.

'There are ashes in the stove. They'll make our hair grey,' said Mrs Weyr. 'We can draw lines on our face with this.' She held up a make-up pen. 'If we dress right, too – black stockings, you know, some of the stuff in the cupboard.' The Lehmann's clothes included some drab, old-fashioned women's things.

'God almighty,' said Ellie. 'It'll be like a ghastly fancy dress. Those clothes in the cupboard…'

She was about to say 'I'll look like my mother,' but stopped herself. Her memories of the past had an annoying habit of surprising her these days. Sometimes she found herself staring into space, thinking, seeing images of people she had known, her feelings pulled this way and that as she remembered events in her childhood, her marriage, her own motherhood, her children. Best not to have thoughts like that, she decided, and forced herself to focus on the present.

'Come on, let's get your stuff into my room,' she said to Poldi.

Poldi had brought a treasure trove with her. Bottles of pickled vegetables, tins of meat, several bottles of schnapps, her whole larder in fact. And she had brought the silver coins.

'These could be useful in the Resselpark,' said Poldi. 'They are real silver. We can get something for them I'm sure.'

Ellie thought of the handful of coins she had pocketed the first time she had met Poldi. Was this the moment to give them back, to confess her theft? Or perhaps she could surreptitiously just return them to the bag?

'Look Poldi,' she began, 'about those coins. I think I should tell you …'

'Don't worry,' said her friend, 'I know. Always knew. I count the coins.'

Ellie's eyes welled up as she realised what Poldi was saying. 'I'm sorry,' was all she could say.

But, ominously, Poldi made no response.

They put the food into the suitcases and pushed them under the bed. Later, while Poldi was asleep, Ellie spoke with Hannah Weyr again, who was still worrying about how the Russians would treat them.

'Neither of us are virgins,' said Ellie, trying to convey a hard front to the other woman, 'so whatever happens to us, we've done it all before.'

When there were raids a lot of people had to pack into the cellar at Rechte Bahngasse. There were sixteen apartments and although some had been abandoned by their owners when they fled the city, most of these had been requisitioned by the civil affairs people and filled with refugees from the bombing. Ellie and Poldi stuck together, making a 'nest' at the back of the second cellar room, far away from the entrance. They left blankets and cushions from the apartment there permanently, a chamber pot with ash from the stove in case Ellie needed it to carry out their disguise plan, and some bottles of water, but nothing else as it would have been stolen. When they went down there they carried food, candles and other supplies with them in a suitcase, bringing it back up the stairs when they left. Mrs Weyr and her son had made friends with an old lady and her teenage granddaughter from a flat below and stayed in the other cellar room with them.

But then, in mid-March, it seemed the bombing had stopped, which had an eerie effect. It was unusually warm weather and people went out in the street in vast hordes, wandering around the city looking at the damaged buildings and piles of rubble. At the Philipphof, behind the Opera, there were said to be hundreds of bodies under the rubble. There simply wasn't the energy or the will to dig them out for a proper burial. As a result, there were bad smells in the area. Ellie and Poldi came to recognise the smell when they sniffed it elsewhere near bombed buildings.

Water was going to be the next problem, people were saying. There had been a lot of underground damage and there were concerns about the water supplies becoming contaminated. A standpipe was installed in the street outside their apartment building. There were long queues and people filling their buckets from the dribbling tap were pressurised by those behind them only to take what was needed for drinking. Keeping clean became a problem and Ellie found herself scratching her skin through her clothes.

They went back to Poldi's rooms in the Kremenezky Palace and picked up whatever Poldi hadn't been able to carry with her on her first trip to Rechte Bahngasse. This included a cardboard box filled with dry biscuits. The insects had got at them, but they took the biscuits out and brushed them off. There was no point any more going to shops that accepted ration cards as there was nothing on the shelves. The Resselpark traders weren't very interested in the silver coins, or at least they pretended not to be – they wanted cigarettes – but Poldi and Ellie found that nevertheless they could exchange them for bread, ersatz coffee, salt, flour and pearl barley. They had quite a larder of supplies what with one thing and another. But it was hard to cook anything as the gas was off so much.

At night they began to hear a low rumbling sound, like thunder in the distance and knew that this was the sound of distant artillery. It came nearer until finally they could hear it even in the daytime above the sounds of the street. A notice appeared on the wall outside saying that although the enemy was pushing forward, reinforcements were on their way to hold them back. Another notice, this time handwritten, warned against foreigners who were spreading rumours and urged all men to fight for the defence of the city in the name of the Reich. It was said that two deserters from the *Volkssturm* had been left hanging in the Stadtpark. Neither Ellie nor Poldi went into the park after that.

On an afternoon in early April they heard the sound of many feet in the street outside. It was a string of soldiers, carrying heavy packs, a horse and cart with men lying wounded in it. Some of the men limped, staring ahead, seeming sightless, with haggard, unshaven faces, exhausted. Others were young boys in uniforms that were too big for them. Poldi shouted out of the window at them:

'What's happening? Tell us where they are. Where have you come from?'

None of the men looked up or replied.

That night, most of the inhabitants of the building went down to the cellar. The procession of defeated men had shaken any remaining faith anyone had that the city would be defended. The guns had grown steadily louder and there were reports of shells falling in Favoriten a bit further South.

'Which direction do you think they'll come from?' Ellie asked Mr Kaestner who sat in a makeshift deckchair opposite them in the cellar, his bony frame obviously uncomfortable in the position he was forced to adopt.

'How do I know?' replied Kaestner, suspicious as ever. 'I'm not a clairvoyant.'

Mr Kaestner was one of the few original inhabitants of the building who had remained, sharing that honour with the old lady and her granddaughter with whom Hannah Weyr had made friends and an elderly couple from the second floor who sat close together on a bench in the second cellar room. It was said that a family in number five had remained in their apartment rather than using the cellar, but no-one really knew the truth of this. Ellie had never seen anyone go in or out of that door, which remained resolutely locked.

In the second cellar room with Poldi and Ellie were the elderly couple, Mr Kaestner and an assortment of the bombed-out. A woman in her thirties had moved there with her mother when their house in Hietzing had been destroyed. An elderly gentleman sat wrapped in blankets on the floor in the middle of the cellar space, propping himself up on a brick support going up to the ceiling. He had been the owner of a jewellery store on the Karntnerstrasse, the sort of person one might have expected to leave the city once the bombing started up, but he hadn't wanted to leave his business to the looters and now it was too late to go.

The landlord of the building, who owned most of the first floor, had long since departed the city but his housekeeper, a thin woman with grey hair and a stern expression on her lined face, had stayed behind to look after the place. Anyway, she had nowhere else to go. Her employer hadn't invited her along when he fled.

It was hard to sleep in the cellar, not knowing what was going on in the streets above, or what the next few days held in store. In the early hours of the morning Ellie was jerked awake from a half-sleep by the sound of an explosion nearby, or so she thought, but then there was nothing. Ellie's skin itched and the cellar stank as the smell from the toilet buckets filled the place. A lot of the time the cellar inhabitants lay in darkness because candles were in short supply.

In the morning, Poldi and Ellie decided to venture out for water. It was early and the dawn was still breaking as they emerged onto the silent street, each carrying a bucket. There was a thick mist, moisture tinged with orange dust, with sunshine trying to break through, and they heard the sound of birds. Otherwise it was quite silent – no guns, no voices, no people. They were the first to come out for water it seemed – no-one else was at the stand pipe and they filled their buckets, watching the air slowly clear. They said nothing to each other. Their side of the street had been untouched by bombing and the procession of apartment buildings stretched off into the middle distance. The scene reminded Ellie of a painting.

The idea that this would soon all be over filled her mind and she thought of the mountains near Zell am See and then the sandy beaches of Jersey. She told Poldi what was on her mind and Poldi's face lit up. Whatever the dangers that faced them as the Russians drew nearer, the war was finally coming to an end. A new life would begin.

They struggled back, trying not to spill the water from the heavy buckets, heaving them up the stairs to the apartment.

'I'll go down and get our things,' said Ellie. 'It's pretty quiet out there and I'm sure it's safe to be upstairs for a while.'

She went down and back into the cellar. The people there were relieved to hear that things were quiet outside and began to rustle around picking up their belongings. Ellie grabbed theirs and was first out.

Coming up the basement stairs she saw Carl Mayer in the hallway, in Wehrmacht uniform.

'Quick!' he said, 'upstairs.' He looked nervously down the cellar stairs where a head was beginning to emerge behind Ellie. 'Here, I'll take that.'

Before she could react he had taken the suitcase from her and was bounding up the stairs two at a time, with Ellie following. His energy, even with the suitcase, was astonishing.

When she caught up with him in the apartment she found him collapsed in a chair in the front room with Poldi standing over him. He was in uniform. Poldi was aghast.

'He just barged in here,' she cried anxiously, 'I don't know who he is. What do you want from us? There is nothing here for you.'

'It's all right Poldi, he's a friend,' said Ellie trying to calm her down.

'A friend? A dangerous one in my opinion. We don't want soldiers in here. Look at him!'

Carl stood up.

'I need to get out of these things Ellie. Is there something I could wear here?'

'We can't hide him here,' shouted Poldi. 'He'll get us all

killed.'

'Shut up Poldi. You don't understand. This is Carl. He's a friend. Look, I'll explain everything in a minute. Just calm down and trust me. Mrs Weyr will be up here soon and you mustn't tell her. Here Carl, come in here.' She gestured him into her bedroom.

In the room she went to the cupboard and got out one of Mr Lehmann's suits.

'Here, try this on – it will probably fit you.'

He tore off his boots and uniform and stood there in his underwear, hurriedly putting on a shirt and trousers.

'Have you got any shoes? I can't wear these boots – they're a give-away.'

It was lucky she hadn't traded the shoes in the Resselpark last week, she reflected. They were a size too big for Carl, but that was all right. He stood there, transformed into a civilian.

'You don't look like a *Volkssturm* reject Carl: too much like a soldier. Come next door and we'll do something about that.'

Next door, they tried out the trick with stove ash on his hair and Ellie painted some lines on his face, which she smudged for a more natural appearance. The clothes were good quality, so she rubbed ash on them too, and scuffed the shoes while Poldi looked on. By the time they were finished, Carl looked passable as an older man who might have spent some time in a cellar. They told Hannah Weyr he was someone they knew who they'd met at the water tap. She seemed to accept this and went off to her own room.

As Ellie told Poldi about Carl, the English classes, the meetings at the language school and the apartment she had an incredible feeling of lightness that she was free to speak so openly, without fear of repercussions. But she also realised how little she really knew about him.

'All right Carl, explain,' said Ellie. 'Anything you tell me you can tell Poldi, don't worry.'

Carl said that he needed to stay out of sight for a while, and to spend the night at their place if he could. After that, he would leave as he had more to do. He told them that his plan had been discovered.

'What are you talking about Carl?' asked Ellie.

'I've been involved in the defence of the city,' he said. 'We had a plan to let the Russians in without a fight, but we were betrayed. I got away, but the others...' he looked down at the floor, apparently in despair. He looked up again.

'I can't tell you all of it, but believe me we were trying to do the right thing for the Viennese and for Austria. The Germans want to pulverise the city. They will make it uninhabitable. So many people will die. We need to put a stop to their plans. They are going to blow up all the bridges.'

'The river, you mean?' said Poldi.

'No, the canal too – everything. The plans were for a massive destruction. They don't care about the people here. In Rome they left without a fight and the city was saved. Why could they not do it here?'

'What do you mean, betrayed Carl? What kind of danger are you in?'

'I don't want him staying here Ellie,' said Poldi standing up. 'We don't want that kind of thing here.'

'Sit down Poldi. It's all right. Just listen to what he has to say.'

Carl explained a bit more. The language classes and the meetings, as Ellie knew, had been a cover for meetings between himself and other disaffected officers, as well as significant people in the emerging resistance movement – O5 people, communists.

'What happened to Laura Gadoll? How did they catch her?' asked Ellie.

Carl gave her a despairing look. 'There have been too many like that, too many. After the events last July too. They found out about us. There were so many they took. I don't know how they knew … and now…' A look of hopelessness briefly crossed his face.

'Look, it's not over yet. I can't tell you any more about all of this. Believe me, I will only be here until tomorrow and then I will leave. I have to get over to the Palais Auersperg to meet some people. No-one knows I am here so you are safe.'

Poldi reluctantly agreed to this plan and they got some food together. Carl hadn't eaten for a long time and said he had been moving around a great deal. He was very hungry and Poldi watched aghast as he ate his way through two plates of their potato stew. After that, he fell into Ellie's bed and slept for most of the day.

During the afternoon, as Carl slept, the sound of artillery fire came nearer and in the evening they began to hear a different sound, a kind of crackling and popping in the distance. Then Carl was awake. He told them this was small arms fire – machine guns and rifles. The Russians couldn't be more than a mile or two away. He advised them to go down to the cellar for the night. He would stay here and depart in the early hours of the morning when things were quieter. The Russians didn't like to fight at night.

'I'll return when all this is over, Ellie,' he said, as she prepared to go down the stairs, 'and I promise you I will tell you all of it, everything. There is so much more but this is not the time. Thank you for what you have done.' He held both her hands tightly in his and looked her intensely in the eyes as he spoke these words.

They embraced and as she went down she looked back, seeing him for the last time at the top of the stairs.

The cellar was full. All of the inhabitants of the building had heard the small arms fire and had drawn the same conclusion: it was better to be underground. Perhaps there was also a feeling of safety in numbers. They slept fitfully again through the night.

The next morning it was silent again outside, but this time Ellie and Poldi were not the first to rise. A middle-aged couple from the other room ventured out of the cellar. When they came back, there was a babble of anxious voices whispering to each other which alerted the people in the second room that something was going on. A young woman came in, excited and told them.

'Ivan is here. They're outside in the street. The Langers saw them from their window. '

The news created a further buzz of talk amongst the inhabitants of the cellar as people awoke and were told. No-one knew what to do and the talk was agitated, but quiet. There was an instinctive fear of making too much noise in case the Russians heard them.

Ellie and Poldi decided to go up. There was a thick door that barred entry from the street and there was no sign or sound of it being breached. Once upstairs in the apartment they saw that Carl had gone. They went cautiously up to the window and looked out at the street below.

The mist was there, just as it had been the previous morning, but it was less thick than before. There had been a lot of orange dust in the air, mixed with the moisture, but now it seemed more like a normal morning fog, through which they could easily see what was going on down below.

Men in strange green-brown uniforms were in the streets, sitting, standing about, cooking on fires, one or two lying as if asleep. An artillery piece attached to a vehicle was nearby and several horses and carts with bags, blankets and boxes in the carts. The men had guns slung over their shoulders and were talking and laughing in a relaxed way, smoking, eating. Three sat on blocks of stone eating soup out of their helmets. One was at the stand pipe, filling a silver coloured bucket. Another had a fur hat and a sword thrust underneath his belt. Many of them looked very young.

Ellie became conscious of Hannah Weyr standing next to

them at the window.

Then one of the men looked up and saw them. He raised his hand cheerfully and shouted something, a word of greeting. Other soldiers looked up and shouted too, waving at them, blowing kisses and laughing. They drew back from the window without responding.

'Well they're friendly enough anyway,' said Poldi.

Then they heard the bell pull. The Russians were hammering at the front door.

'We should have stayed away from the window!' exclaimed Hannah Weyr.

'I'm going down to meet them,' said Ellie firmly. 'Come with me.'

But Hannah Weyr wasn't having any of that and her little boy clung to her, sensing his mother's fear.

'Here, let's get a white flag out to show them,' said Ellie and she took one of the Lehmann's tablecloths and went to the window again with it. She unfurled it out of the window and poked her head out. By now the Russians were all looking up and they gave a cheer as they saw the white cloth.

'They're friendly,' she said to Poldi. 'Come on, they won't hurt us.'

The two of them went down the stairs. Mr Kaestner was in the hallway with another man, brought there by the knocking and ringing.

'What are you doing?' he shouted as they approached the front door.

'Don't worry,' said Ellie, 'they're just boys. They don't mean us any harm. Come on. The war is over! No more bombing, no more Gestapo, no more Heil Hitler.'

'You're mad,' said Kaestner, attempting to bar her way to the door, but she shoved him aside. He was a weak, thin old fellow and it wasn't hard to push past him.

Confidently, Ellie opened the door and went out into the street with Poldi beside her. They were surrounded by a group of soldiers who embraced them, ruffled Ellie's hair, slapped Poldi on the back and showed rows of blackened and missing teeth in wide grins. They spoke rapidly and loudly in their language. Eventually, the soldiers resorted to gesture and phrases like 'Woina kaput', 'Gitler durak!' and other strange phrases.

But it didn't matter. The feelings were good and the women were welcome. Seeing this from the door, Kaestner too emerged and gradually a trickle of cellar dwellers emerged into the street to meet the Russians. The doors of neighbouring buildings began to open and soon the street was filled with Austrian civilians mixing with the Russians. White sheets appeared at window openings, some red and white flags, too, the swastikas removed.

'Someone's had their scissors out,' laughed Poldi.

A pair of little boys went from one soldier to the next, receiving kisses and friendly pats on the cheek, their mothers in tow. Some women offered the Russians cigarettes. Ellie heard a Russian officer asking one of the women if there were any Germans in the houses. The woman replied proudly, 'Only Austrians!' A middle aged man ventured out to join his wife, wearing a Styrian hat with a feather stuck in the hat band and a strip of white cloth pinned around his upper arm.

After a while, Poldi and Ellie extracted themselves from the embraces of the enthusiastic young men and got back into their apartment. Most of that day they spent there, looking out of the window at the scenes below. It was a good day.

The evening came and the Russians lit fires outside. Laughing and singing started up and it was clear that the soldiers had got hold of some alcohol. A harmonica player started up a tune and there was dancing. The women in the apartment were relieved. The Russians were a fine, friendly lot. Their worries, at least for now, were over. The war was over.

As the darkness fell they realised they had left their suitcases and belongings in the cellar so all three of them went down the stairs to collect them. There were a couple of other women there too, sorting out blankets and bedding. It seemed they wouldn't need to use that place any more and it was time to retrieve what they could and try to give it a clean, return the bedding to the apartments above.

So there were five women in the cellar when the Russians arrived, Poldi, Hannah Weyr, Ellie and two others. One of them was the teenager come to collect the things that belonged to her and her grandmother. Her name was Eva Kopecky and she had blonde hair. Ellie didn't know the other woman's name.

The four soldiers appeared in the doorway, laughing and pushing at each other, speaking in their strange-sounding language. One of them had his gun off his shoulder. He pointed it at the women and a couple of the others shone their torches into the women's faces. Eva Kopecky put her hand up over her eyes to shield them from the bright light, but one of the soldiers grabbed her wrist and pushed her hand away, staring into her face. Ellie and Poldi hadn't bothered with their plan to put ashes in their hair, but they were filthy with dirt anyway.

Then they lined the women up against the wall and, one by one, tore the clothes off them to expose their breasts.

Only Poldi was spared.

13

THE GERMANS HAD been chased back over the Po in April and by the end of the month it was all over. The Field Security men were ordered to observe the surrender of German soldiers in the mountains beyond Padua, who would then be shepherded back to holding camps in the Po valley.

'Our job is to watch out for SS masquerading as Wehrmacht. We need to pick them out if we can – they get special treatment,' said Ken Gillett, CO of the unit.

'How are we going to do that – give us a clue,' asked Elliott, piping up cheekily from the ranks of men sat on folding chairs in the briefing tent.

Gillett looked exasperated. 'Use your intelligence and keep your eyes and ears open,' said the captain. 'They're not going to tell you who they are, are they?'

A ripple of laughter ran around the tent. Gillett continued.

'Look for suspicious behaviour,' he said. 'Look out for any signs that someone is behaving differently from the rest of them – look out for anyone other Germans treat differently. Could be giving someone too much respect, or the opposite – hostility even. You'll know it when you see it. Nicholson here will set up a desk with me and we'll be having a jolly good chat with anyone you send across.'

By now they were used to interpreting vague orders. The FSS were famous for it amongst the regular troops – wasn't that why they had all that brain power? Gillett himself probably didn't have a clue what they were looking for and he was known to be a blusterer. Elliott whispered to Dashwood that the old man was on a hiding to nothing, but only got a shove in the ribs.

They got to the location later that afternoon, where the Welsh Guards were supervising the surrender. It was an open field high up in a valley, surrounded by pine forest. The road wound down into it at the top end, and away at the other end to more open regions. Germans came in groups down from the mountains throughout the afternoon, most seeming relieved that it was all over. The Guards had spread out over the field, a couple of Shermans with turrets pointing up at the higher road, just in case, although none of the surrendering soldiers showed any sign of fight. It was hard to believe these weary, unshaven, mud-splattered men, most of them in soft caps after ditching their hard helmets, had held up the Allied advance for so long. They were quiet as they filed down the road into the field, with hands on heads or held up at shoulder height as they approached the British, submitted to a search, and then were sent trudging on further down the valley. A medical team examined the casualties – the walking wounded and those carried down by their comrades – and assessed whether they should be put on a hospital truck for the rest of their journey. Tommies stood around gazing at their former enemies. They didn't say much to the Germans and the Germans didn't say much to them.

Mid-afternoon, a company of German paratroopers appeared, marching in formation down the road towards the open space. The Tommies stiffened and instinctively lifted their rifles to their waists. The paratroopers were led by a blond, Nazi-looking officer who marched up to a Guards officer and started telling him, in perfect English, how his men were to be treated and what food they were to be given. He was a paratrooper, he said, and he had only agreed to surrender if this was to the Guards.

'We might have one here,' muttered Gillett under his breath. So far, they hadn't had a bite.

'He's putting on a bloody good show,' replied Nicholson.

The Guards officer, a thin man with a pencil moustache, was deflecting the German's commands with a languid ease, born of a lifetime's knowledge of superiority to foreigners, but the German was persistent. Elliott went over and pointed to the tent where Nicholson and Gillett sat.

They ran the blond German rapidly through his service history, which he answered by rattling off a chronological list of campaigns in which he had served. Nicholson and Gillett knew enough about the German military actions of the past few years to recognise this as probably authentic. The paratroop officer continued, now grinning proudly.

'And I caught three men of your regiment last year in Florence last August, did you know? They came into the city in a jeep like tourists, but we had not quite left you see, and they fell straight into our arms like babies – it was absolutely a bad surprise for them.'

This had been a famous incident amongst the Guards, who had taken the city the previous summer, and it set the seal on the German's claim to be a genuine paratrooper, since it was known that a division of those men had been the last to leave. Three British officers had decided to go up ahead of the main force entering the city to claim it for themselves. Their abandoned jeep had been found near the Duomo, a message written in English by the Germans on a piece of cardboard: 'We will return.'

'Well, you didn't keep your promise,' said Nicholson. The German shrugged. Gillett and Nicholson dismissed him and he rejoined his men who were filing down the valley.

'Arrogant bastard,' muttered Gillett.

An hour later, as the light lowered and the stream of Germans dried to a trickle, there was another incident. This time, a German staff major, a fat fellow clutching a leather suitcase, was sent over to the FSS desk by the Guards. Six or seven of his men came with him, one of whom was a boy with striking good looks – hair down to his collar and long black eyelashes. The major was very upset and spoke in rapid German, gesticulating, hot in the face, grabbing at the shoulder of the pretty boy soldier. The other Germans stood around sniggering, clearly amused by the scene. Gillett's German was better than Nicholson's, so he translated.

'He's saying he can't be separated from his servant, this boy here. He seems quite worked up about it.'

The Guards were telling the Germans to go on down the valley where officers would be separated from ordinary ranks.

'He doesn't like the idea.'

'I think I can guess why,' said Nicholson, looking at the laughing faces of the German soldiers and the embarrassment on the face of the young boy soldier.

At this point, the German major, who by this time actually had tears flowing down his cheeks, put his suitcase on the desk between them. He scrabbled to open the catch and started fumbling around in a mess of clothes and papers. Nicholson stood up and looked in.

'Watch out sir, there's a gun there,' he said urgently, seizing the German's wrist. He could see a tiny automatic pistol lying at the bottom of the case. When he took a closer look he saw it was the sort of toy pistol ladies put into evening bags.

'I don't think it's anything to worry about though,' he said laughing. But at that point the German used his left hand to seize the weapon and it went off with a pop. Soldiers came running over and knocked him to the ground while the rest of the Germans stood well back, protesting their non-involvement to the threatening Tommies all around them. The German was hauled to his feet and marched off towards the forest.

'I think that bloody thing nicked me,' said Gillett, clutching his wrist, evidently in some pain. Nicholson looked as Gillett revealed what was underneath and could see a bloody mess. 'I think my wrist is broken,' he said.

A doctor was called over, a temporary bandage applied and Gillett was bundled into an army ambulance which rode off down the valley. As it left, a shot rang out in the forest.

After that, Nicholson was appointed acting lieutenant heading his FSS unit and they spent a couple more days in the mountains with the Guards until the flow of surrendering soldiers dried up. They heard that Gillett had a wound to the metacarpals on his right hand and would need a month or two to get his grip back to normal ('Shot by a bloody fat pansy,' laughed Dashwood). Nicholson would therefore need to stay as unit leader until further notice.

With the German surrender, the occupation of Austrian territory was an urgent priority. They were ordered to proceed to Villach in Carinthia, across the border, and they spent three days journeying by jeep and motorbike as part of a long convoy of vehicles, winding up along roads that passed through mountain villages and between huge Alpine peaks. They reached the Austrian frontier at Tarvisio at the head of the Predil Pass.

Austrian customs men were still in their posts as the British forces crossed the frontier. A railway ran close to the customs hut and a long train of flat-cars passed in the opposite direction, making its way towards Italy. Thousands of men rode on it, Italians and others going home. They yelled abuse at the customs men and cheered the British soldiers, who waved back.

So this is what it's like to be part of a conquering army, thought Louis Nicholson.

14

TWO WEEKS AFTER the incident in the cellar Poldi and Ellie crossed the Stadtpark on their way to the canal. They had heard that the Gestapo building had burned down and, like a lot of people, they wanted to see for themselves. In the park there were fresh graves of fallen Russian soldiers, flowers festooned over one of them, plaques with Russian script recording the names of the dead on red wooden posts stuck into the piled earth. Sometimes there were just numbers.

The Kai was devastated – by far the worst damage they had seen. Every building from the Biberstrasse entrance up to the end of Morzinplatz was smashed up and most had collapsed completely. Rubble spread out over the road between the buildings and the canal where there were some half sunk barges. Schwedenbrücke had crumpled into the water and, ahead and behind, the other bridges were in a similar state.

'How did this happen?' asked Poldi. 'It can't have been the bombs. I was up here three weeks ago and it wasn't like this.'

They clambered over a pile of bricks and got a sight of the collapsed Metropole where the Gestapo building had been. A crowd of people had come to look and there were a couple of Russian soldiers and some policemen preventing people from getting access to the ruins themselves. It was as if the people of Vienna couldn't believe the Gestapo had been finished off unless they could see it, touch it for themselves, get hold of some piece of the dreaded building. There were some flowers on the ground, some wooden crosses stuck in between bricks. A woman was on her knees praying. People stood around her, hands clutched to their chests. A man was weeping.

'They used to kill prisoners in there you know,' said Poldi in a flat voice. 'I was out visiting my aunt's grave in the cemetery out at Simmering and I saw the results. It was horrible.'

'What do you mean?'

'Last year. I was out there in the evening. It was getting dark and a truck pulled up and I watched from behind a tree. Some men unloaded sacks onto the ground and pushed them over into one of the graves. I could see heads rolling on the ground. The Gestapo had a guillotine in the basement.'

'Come on, let's go,' said Ellie, instantly wanting to suppress this terrible image. 'I've had enough of this.'

They headed on past Morzinplatz to a park where the surrounding buildings were undamaged and then towards the inner city up some steps past a church. They stayed on the wider streets where the crowds were, stepping over piles of rubble, skirting round heaps of rubbish. A broken tramline stuck up in the air near Stephansplatz where an artillery shell had fallen. Apparently the defenders had shelled the centre from the Augarten flak towers. The shops on Karntnerstrasse were all shut, boarded up for the most part with 'Empty' painted on the shutters. They turned right to get up to Schottengasse, heading for Poldi's place. She wanted to check it out to see if she could return there.

At the Palace they saw a group of policemen on the corner. They weren't the usual bunch of old men brought back from retirement who had tried to keep order during the bombing. These were fierce looking characters with guns stuck in their uniform belts. God knew where they had come from or how they had wheedled their way into police uniforms. They weren't Russians, for sure, yet they were allowed to carry guns. It was best to give them a wide berth, so Ellie and her friend stayed on the other side of the road and went around the back, past the university and up a side street.

They found the side door was intact, got into Poldi's rooms which were untouched. Then they decided to explore the rest of the building. Before the Russians came the Palace had been turned into offices by the German administration. Anything might have happened upstairs after they left, said Poldi, they had better take a look round.

They went up the steps to the ground floor and headed for the main entrance hall. Ellie hadn't seen this part of the building before. It was completely undamaged by bombs and the fighting seemed to have passed it by as well. Even the window glass was intact. It was as stunning inside as it was outside. The huge main doors onto the street, studded with brass, were locked and apparently unopened. The ceiling was covered in painting and around the walls were alcoves with statues and great vases still in them, electric lamps in brass wall brackets in rows along the walls, a chandelier dropping majestically from the central ceiling boss. A grand staircase carpeted in red led upstairs to huge reception rooms. Poldi led Ellie through the rooms, describing things as they used to be, exclaiming in surprise and disapproval at how they were now, at how many familiar furnishings were missing, replaced by rows of desks and chairs, filing cabinets, paper strewn around, much of it on the floor, desk drawers pulled out and emptied, an overturned chair in one great ballroom, notice boards on walls. It had been a centre for the organisation of industrial production under the German authorities and the offices had clearly been abandoned, in some cases in a hurry. Poldi went about tutting about the holes made in the walls, as if the place was her own.

There were pictures of Hitler on the walls of some of the rooms. They removed these, prised the paper images out from behind the picture glass, and carefully tore them into tiny pieces. There was no point in inflaming the Russians once they got round to exploring the building.

'I suppose the Kremenezkys will be back one of these days,' Poldi said. 'I'll need to look after the place for them so that it is ready for their return.'

Ellie thought she was being rather optimistic, but said nothing. She was impressed by the transformation in Poldi's manner, her proprietorial approach to the building where she had been housekeeper and servant for so many years, the return of her confidence.

'I don't suppose the Russians will stay out of here for much longer,' she said to Poldi. 'I wouldn't tangle with them if I were you.'

'Pooh, the Russians. Barbarians most of them. They wouldn't know what to do with a place like this,' said Poldi dismissively.

Ellie wondered at this. Images of the cellar came back to her, the soldiers holding down the women who, screaming and struggling at first, were then terrified into silence by the soldier with the gun. In the darkness she hadn't seen Poldi, just torch-lights flashing around the walls and the tangled bodies on the floor, until her own turn had come.

They went up the stairs again, reaching the third floor of the palace, where things were a bit different. Clearly the Russians, or someone with some military purpose, had been up there. They noticed some damage on the ceiling – holes in the plas-terwork, and one of the windows was smashed. On the floor there were shell casings from a gun. The room smelled and in the corner was a pile of dried faeces.

'Some of them must have been up here, firing from the window,' said Ellie while Poldi poked around looking for more damage.

'I need to get back here as soon as possible,' said Poldi. 'You're right, the Russians will want to get their hands on this place. I'm surprised they haven't been here already.'

'They've only been here three weeks,' said Ellie.

'Well someone needs to be here to tell them what's what

when they get round to knocking on those doors.'

Knocking them down more like, thought Ellie, but again kept her thoughts to herself.

'Are you sure you want to be here on your own again?' she asked. 'You know what they're like.'

As she spoke, the assault in the cellar came into her mind again. The man who had attacked Ellie wasn't a man, just a young boy soldier, egged on by his drunken comrades once they had finished with the other women. The boy had been nervous, had taken less than a minute. She told herself that she hadn't felt anything, nothing really, nothing to feel. Just a boy. A pathetic boy who didn't know what he was doing.

Hannah Weyr, on the other hand, had had a much harder time of it. She tried her best when her son was with her, but too often since the rape Ellie had found her huddled up in bed, crying her eyes out. She couldn't be comforted and her grief incorporated not just her traumatic encounter with the soldiers in the cellar, but the loss of her husband and her home and the whole fabric of her life during the previous year.

'Don't worry about me,' said Poldi, 'they won't hurt me. I'll be able to help them I expect – show them where everything is.' She looked around another room and turned back to Ellie. 'Let's go down to the kitchens. Perhaps we'll find something there.'

They went down the grand staircase again, into another subterranean area. The kitchens were a suite of underground rooms with steel surfaces, copper pots and pans, black kitchen ranges and stoves. They went to the larder area hopefully, but there was nothing on the shelves except a sack of rice, spilling out. The Germans, or somebody, had cleaned the place out of food and drink.

'This rice will come in handy,' said Ellie. 'There must be five kilos of the stuff here.'

They took it back to Poldi's room and divided it in half between them. The plan was to go back to Rechte Bahngasse to get Poldi's things so she could get set up again here.

They went out into the street again. It was late afternoon. 'We'd better get back before it gets dark,' said Poldi. 'It's not safe with all the foreigners wandering round the streets.'

Vienna was filled with all kinds of displaced people, apart from the normally resident Viennese. There were Reich Germans who were now uncertain of their place in the city, some having gone back to Germany but many still in Vienna, there being no homes left standing in the cities and towns from whence they had come. There were Czechs, Russians, Polish, French, Greeks and Italians who had until then lived in labour camps, working in the industrial plants in the East of the city, who now had no work and no food supply. They queued up when Russian soup kitchens appeared in the streets, but in the day and through most of the night they wandered around looking for opportunities to loot. You sometimes saw groups of them in the cafes, taking over the places, singing, playing accordions, guitars, drinking bottles of anything they could find. It was a wonder that none of them had got into the Kremenezky Palace yet. There were even some ragged, emaciated Jewish survivors of who knows what horrors, who had found their way back to the Leopoldstadt area and were trying to get back into the places they had once lived in, reclaim their possessions if any could still be found. No one knew what to do with them. There were also new arrivals from the East, German speaking refugees. All of them clamoured for food and shelter. It was lucky that it was a warm spring, because so many slept on the streets.

On May 1st there was a May Day celebration along the Ringstrasse. The Russians put on a military parade, marching behind tanks, artillery, troop carriers while Viennese stood and cheered, as they knew they must. At the Parliament building there were speeches from Renner, the new man in charge, and

Marshal Tolbukhin. Music played through loudspeakers and Russian soldiers danced with Austrian women, spinning round in waltz circles. Some women danced with each other. There were film cameras to record the occasion.

Then ration cards were issued again. People released from concentration camps got them first, then Austrian citizens. Kaestner said to Ellie that it was all very fine to prioritise camp inmates, but what the Russians didn't realise was that many of them were simply criminals. In fact some of the new police force were that sort themselves, pretending to have been freedom fighters.

Ellie's ration card said she had a right to a kilo of bread a week and a few grams of sugar and fat per day. But the challenge was where to find such things, as supplies were intermittent to say the least. What was left of the food Poldi had brought over to Rechte Bahngasse had been repatriated to the Kremenezky Palace and the rice wasn't much good to eat unless you soaked it overnight in cold water – there was no gas to cook on. Ellie felt constant hunger pangs.

The water wasn't switched on either, so the standpipes were still the only source for the people living in Rechte Bahngasse. You had to be careful about going to the water taps too late in the day, as Ellie learned to her cost. She went to fill her bucket just as dusk was falling and there were no other women there, thinking it would save her the bore of queuing in line. When the bucket was half full she felt a hand round her mouth and she was dragged backwards off her feet. Alcoholic breath filled her nostrils as she was carried away across the bridge, over the rail track running down the centre of the street and then dumped on her back behind a wall. Terror filled her mind and body as she realised what was happening. This wasn't going to be like that pathetic boy in the cellar. Her attacker was a stocky, muscular Russian soldier with a wild look in his eyes.

He bent down towards her but she put her hand down between her legs shouting out 'Nein, blut, blut!' to him, holding her fingers up stained with blood. He went white, spat on the ground in angry frustration and left her lying there. Ellie had been told this sometimes worked with the Russians who were said to be revolted by menstrual blood.

After that she made sure she went to the water tap at busier times and stood in line for her turn.

At the end of May there was a Corpus Christi procession by the Catholics. Ellie went to look. Cardinal Innitzer led the procession winding through the inner city streets to the ruined Stephansdom, looking old and thin. Politicians walked behind. The crowd was mostly silent. People received communion on the steps of the cathedral as a steady rain fell.

Ellie had been in the Resselpark. The time had come to trade the other pair of leather shoes left by the Lehmanns and she had obtained a fine cut of ham for them – nearly 400 grams of the stuff, sliced. It really was quite exceptional. The packet of meat was closely guarded in her bag which she had put under her coat, so there was no chance of some marauder sensing she had such precious booty as she walked back to the apartment. They were good shoes, worth more than a few slices of ham under normal circumstances. She wondered what had happened to Carl, who had taken the other pair of shoes, as she went up the stairs to the apartment.

Mr Kaestner was standing across from her entrance door, a triumphant smile on his face.

'You've got a shock coming now,' he said, looking pleased with himself. 'Best if you know before you go in I thought. I saw you coming back. What have you got there?' He pointed to the bulge under her coat.

She avoided him and turned the key in the door to go in, but it was pulled open as she turned the lock and another man stood in the entrance blocking the way. He quickly whipped Ellie's keys out of the door and pocketed them. He was younger than Kaestner, his grey hair cropped short, his face and eyes cold.

'Ah, so you've come back finally. I have got your things ready. My name is Lehmann and we have returned. I told the other woman and she has left with her son. It is time for you to go elsewhere.'

With Kaestner behind her and Lehmann in front Ellie didn't know which way to face. Lehmann slid a pile of her belongings and her suitcase across the floor with his foot, pushing them across the threshold into the corridor, making sure he held onto the door with both hands.

'Can I just come in for a minute to look round?' was all she could think of saying, and then, desperately, when there was no movement, 'What about my food, the food in the kitchen?'

'We'll call that a fair exchange shall we?' said Lehmann. 'I can see you have had a comfortable time here. I won't ask what has happened to my clothes and shoes.'

'But I still have three months to run on my...'

Lehmann laughed at this. 'Three months, yes I'm sure, three months. And no doubt you have papers and everything like that, just like your friend. Look, I am sorry but that really won't do. This is our place, we are back and it is time for you to leave. That is all there is to it, papers or not. Complain to the Russians if you like and you will see where that gets you.'

And he closed the door against her face, leaving her with her pile of belongings and Kaestner standing behind her in his doorway, his arms folded, looking at the scene before him with shining, victorious eyes.

She looked up at him and said nothing. This particular game was up, she could see. She would have to leave and as it was already approaching the late afternoon hour when the streets became unsafe, she would need to get over to Poldi's double quick. It was all she could think of doing as she picked up her things and struggled down the stairs, always aware of Kaestner's baleful gaze. Then she was out on the street.

The thought occurred to her to go back to the room in Biberstrasse, but she dismissed it. Who knows what she would find there and, anyway, she'd lost the key in the rubble of the language school. The Rudofskys were too far away. No, Poldi was the best option now. She lifted up her belongings and trudged off.

But at Poldi's place she couldn't raise anyone. She banged on the side entrance and pressed the bell push but it must have been broken because she heard no ringing. If Poldi was in she wouldn't hear her. She went round to the front of the building. At the main entrance there was a Russian sentry. Clearly there had been some changes since she had last been there. She went back to the side entrance. It was recessed from the street and she put down her suitcase and sat against it. There were a lot of people sleeping on the streets these days. If she stayed where she was, she'd just be another one who had found a quiet corner to settle down. She would just have to wait. If this didn't work out, there was always Rudofsky.

The side street wasn't much frequented by passers-by, so she was undisturbed as dusk turned to darkness. The night was warm and she had plenty of clothes to put on under her coat. She'd face the problem of what to do when tomorrow came.

Poldi emerged from the side door in the morning to find her friend there asleep on the pavement, her head on the suitcase. She hadn't heard the banging at the door the previous day and, yes, the bell was broken now. Yes, things had changed. The Russians were occupying the place, but that was all right, she said, they were friendly enough, left her alone and let her stay. Just like the Germans, they had set it up as an office – something to do with industry again, Poldi didn't really know. They went in together and Ellie showed her the ham, which was a fantastic and welcome surprise for Poldi. It was all they could do not to wolf it all down in one go.

'You wouldn't believe how ignorant some of those Russian boys are,' she told Ellie. 'When they first came to the palace they managed to get the water running again and the toilets started flushing. A great relief I can tell you. But some of them didn't know what to make of them – they'd never used a toilet before. I think in their villages they just go outside. And do you know when they got the electricity working again the soldiers took all the light bulbs they could find too. The officers had to stop them from posting them back home. Apparently they thought the bulbs would work back in Russia just by getting electricity from the air or something. They didn't realise about wires…'

Ellie had seen Russian soldiers trying out bicycles in the street, obviously new to them, wobbling around. They were obsessed with gadgets – watches, cigarette lighters, cameras – and would pay a lot in the Resselpark for such things. Or they would simply take them off people if they could. There had been some shootings when people had resisted. There was clearly a shortage of such things in Russia, Ellie had concluded. It didn't sound like a great country to live in.

'They're like big children with guns,' she said to Poldi.

So she stayed at Poldi's after that. She considered walking out to see the Rudofskys but the thought made her feel tired. No doubt they'd help her again, but why bother? The weather was warm and there was plenty of space here. She and Poldi liked being together. The older woman had turned out to be quite a character, tougher than she had seemed when she first found her on the park bench. Their only problem was that after a week or so they were running out of food. The ration cards gave them hardly anything and both women began to feel very hungry. Ellie knew she could get paid in potatoes if she joined the ranks of the rubble clearers, women who stood in line all day passing buckets of stones to each other, clearing away the remains of destroyed buildings, but she wondered whether there was a better solution.

Eventually the idea came to them that they might find mushrooms in the Vienna woods north of the city. Poldi had been mushroom collecting up there before the war, and she knew which ones were edible. It was the right time of year for it too. Other people were doing it, she'd heard. And it would get them out of the city, which was claustrophobic and depressing.

'There are pools up there too where you can get crayfish sometimes. They are good to eat. Why don't we try it?' she said.

The two of them got kitted out for an expedition. They'd have to stay in the woods overnight, so they took blankets and coats. They didn't have proper rucksacks but they made some out of bags and strips of cloth so they could carry things easily on their backs. One morning in July they set off walking northwards, through Grinzing and up into the Kierlinger forest by the afternoon. There they hunted around, filling their bags with the wild mushrooms that Poldi said were good to eat. They joined a group who had lit a fire, a woman, her sister and two young boys who had come up from Ottakring. They told them there were crayfish to be found in a pond over the brow of a nearby hill and they resolved to head over there the following morning. Meanwhile, they cooked some of the mushrooms, toasting them on sticks over the fire. They tasted earthy but good.

The next day, after a fruitless excursion to find the crayfish, Poldi said she was ready to head back, but Ellie was enjoying herself. The woods felt fresh and clean after the city streets. They agreed to split up. Ellie headed further west through the trees and came out of the forest, walking through villages on the banks of the Danube. She thought she'd see if she could hitch a lift back along the main road through Penzing into the city. She'd been up here before with Walther Günth in better days and knew her way around. There were plenty of others on the road to ask for directions anyway.

It was clear that food was more plentiful here than in the city. The people had gardens and livestock and the ground was fertile. There were chickens in some of the yards and she could see the kitchen gardens over some of the walls, although she didn't look too hard after she was shooed away by a man who threw a stone in her direction. The locals were not friendly. There were too many people coming out of the city hunting for food. But it was good to be out on the open road in the summer air, munching on a mushroom every now and again if she got hungry. She fell in with a couple, also from Ottakring, and together they marched along, now heading back into the city.

The couple turned out to be in possession of a large sack of potatoes and they offered to sell her some. They had got it from the man's sister who lived out in Ravelsbach quite some way away. He could always go out there and get some more and the money would help with other things. They did a deal and some of the potatoes transferred into Ellie's bag. Then they were lucky with a lift and a horse and cart brought them back into the city in the late afternoon.

Poldi was sitting with a Russian officer when she got back, a broad-shouldered fellow looking relaxed as he sat back in his chair. She explained that he was from the offices that had been set up in the building. He had brought some presents – a bottle of barack, some butter and flour. Maybe they didn't need to slog out into the countryside to get food after all, although Ellie felt happy that she had made the effort.

The man obviously wasn't expecting Ellie to turn up and he got up, seeming embarrassed. He spoke to her in a halting German.

'You Poldi friend,' he said, 'I too. Friend.' He put out his hand to her and she shook it. Russians were clearly not all the same, she thought.

Poldi indicated to him to sit down again and she poured them all some of the barack. Knowing the effects of alcohol on other Russians, Ellie felt apprehensive about this but Poldi was reassuring. This Ivan was a bit different, she said. He was an officer, an educated man. He had been kind to her, had got the other officers to agree she could live in her rooms in the basement once he understood her position. And look, now he had brought them this food and drink.

'I Major Anatol Shevchenko,' said the Russian, his mouth parting in a warm smile, revealing perfect white teeth. 'Anatol.'

Ellie told him her name. Conversation was clearly going to be difficult, but the man was friendly and clean, had brought them things they needed and didn't seem to have any underlying agenda, so a warm welcome for him was definitely what was required.

'I've agreed to do some laundry for him,' said Poldi. 'He needs his uniform cleaned and ironed.'

So there was an agenda after all, though one that was innocuous.

'That's nice Poldi, you've found a friend!' said Ellie laughing. As she laughed, Anatol joined in, though he probably didn't know what he was laughing about. Perhaps he just liked laughing. They were going to get on.

As the evening developed the bottle went down, their stomachs filled with the food he had brought and they found out more about him. He came from Moscow it seemed, and had been at Stalingrad towards the end. He tried to describe what he and his men had done when they got to Vienna, but the language was too difficult. He traced a map on the table though, drawing with a pencil on a newspaper, and it was clear that he had entered the city from the west.

'I thought the Russians had come in through Favoriten,' said Ellie to Poldi.

Anatol contradicted her. 'Niet, niet,' he said, 'niet Favoriten.' He clearly understood more than he could speak. He showed them again on the map.

Poldi said 'Schönbrunn?'

He answered. 'Yes, yes, Schönbrunn, big place, yes. Austrians help, show us the way.' He smiled. 'Good Austrians, not bad, help us.'

'I think he's saying they had some local guides and came past the Schönbrunn Palace,' said Ellie. 'Zoo, animals,' she said to him. There was a zoo there and she thought he might remember it. He didn't know what she was talking about though.

It was frustrating with the lack of a mutual language, but they did their best and Ellie could see that he was a gentle, intelligent man. They talked on, Ellie telling Poldi about her further explorations of the countryside while Anatol sat back. Finally he said, 'You bed sleep now. I go. I come back see you again,' he said, looking at Ellie. She sensed immediately what was on his mind. He wasn't so different then, but she liked him all the same and gave him her hand as he left.

Ellie lived with Poldi throughout July and eventually made contact with the Rudofskys again. Rudofsky had a plaster cast on his arm which at first worried her, but he explained his arm was perfectly all right, taking the cast off with a laugh. It was just a way of avoiding getting press-ganged by the Russians. Lots of people were getting accosted in the street and told they had to clear rubble. Some of them were getting sent over to the factories in Floridsdorf that had survived the bombing to help dismantle the machinery and pack it up for transport. He didn't want that, so he waved his plastered arm in a sling if a Russian came near him in the street and they left him alone.

During the fighting they hadn't gone down into the cellar but had watched events in the street from an upstairs window. They had seen bands of Russian soldiers led by civilians wearing red and white armbands, creeping, crouching and running from one doorway to the next. Some of the civilians had been carrying rifles. There had been no gunfire in their street, though they had heard some nearby. When the first wave of assault troops had passed, a more relaxed bunch of

Russians appeared, or perhaps it was some of the advanced wave falling back for the evening, and they set up the usual cooking pot outside. The Rudofskys had descended and gone out to greet them. There was no trouble. Rudofsky had drawn some pencil sketches of the Russians who were delighted with them.

Alma Rudofsky said she knew of a place in Schönbrunner-strasse where Ellie could stay, so she left Poldi again. It was small place, not as posh as the apartment in Rechte Bahngasse, but it had furniture and the gas and water worked. Even the electricity came on once in a while so there was sometimes light in the evenings. Anatol, who was by now a devotee, came to visit her there, bringing the usual presents of food and drink. With her rations and these supplies, she managed to keep hunger at bay.

Of course, Anatol expected a return on his investment but that was acceptable to her she decided: the alternative was to live in a state of semi-starvation. Who else was she supposed to get help from anyway? Every couple of days he would turn up and spend the night with her. She had no idea of what he did during the day or what his position was, or really very much about him at all. His German was so limited that their communication was largely about the most basic matters. But they both knew what they needed, so what was the point of talk?

The musical life of the city was starting up again. Theatre and cinemas opened up and people flocked to them. She heard that opera singers got extra rations after one of them had collapsed on the stage, complaining of hunger. For some reason the Russians thought such cultural things were important. She couldn't understand why they didn't put the same priority into feeding ordinary people, but she was happy enough with it. Music was food for the soul perhaps. But, she wondered, did she have a soul any more? Perhaps the thing she had with Anatol showed she hadn't got one.

Yet when she got standing room at a concert and heard Schubert's Unfinished, some Beethoven and Tchaikowsky, she was tempted into the belief that her soul had not expired quite yet. The music transported her into another world. She remembered some similar moments she had spent with Carl Mayer listening to music. She and Carl had shared a lot together, even if there were things he hadn't wanted to talk about. Perhaps that was as close as she would get now to feeling passion for a man. Maybe you only fall in love once in your life, as she thought she must have had done with Michael. After that, love becomes more like one of the deals done in the Resselpark.

People crowded into the public places of the city during the day, aimless as they wandered in the streets, parks and market, hoping for food. Rumours flew about all the time. On everyone's mind was the issue of when the Americans and the British would get to Vienna. Germany had capitulated weeks ago and it was known that the armies of these nations had entered Austria some time after the Russians, from the South and from the West. Everyone knew that since July the French had controlled the Vorarlberg, the Americans the area around Salzburg, the British the south of the country around Klagenfurt and Graz. But Vienna itself was surrounded by Russian areas and, for the moment, was governed by them, if government it could be called.

The Russians were chaotic. On the one hand they provided music and soup kitchens which cropped up randomly on street corners for the day, no-one being able to say if they would be there again a day later. On the other hand, truckloads of potatoes destined for the city were hijacked and diverted to be turned into vodka by gangs of soldiers. Some cows were driven into the middle of the city and slaughtered in the street, providing a glut of meat for a week, followed by weeks with no meat at all. Their soldiers seemed at times to be uncontrollable by the officers, looting, raping and sometimes shooting

Austrians who tried to stop them in spite of the most terrible penalties for these crimes if they were caught. Their own security people were notoriously harsh, but their justice only reached a few of the offenders. As a result, the Viennese both feared and began to hate the Russians.

In June it was known that some British and Americans had come to Vienna, but Ellie couldn't find anyone who had actually seen them. Then, in late July, Ellie was on Mariahilferstrasse coming back from the Rudofskys. She was about to turn down past Esterhazy Park to get home when she heard the sound of engines and a procession of olive-green military vehicles came along the road. The first few were Russian but then there were nine or ten American open jeeps flying the Stars and Stripes. The men inside looked straight ahead as the people in the street stared.

Finally, four jeeps with Union Jacks brought up the rear. Ellie saw British army uniforms. A tall officer was looking round at the crowds on the pavement who had started waving and shouting to the men in the cars, who did not respond. The cars stopped, the convoy briefly stalled. Ellie stepped forward to within a few feet of the leading British vehicle, a sudden surge of feeling building up in her at the sight of her fellow countrymen. She shouted out in English:

'Are you British?'

It was a silly question, she realised, because of course they had to be British, but it caught the tall officer's attention. He looked at her surprised and opened his mouth, but then the jeep lurched forward, his head jerked back with the sudden acceleration, and he was gone. She had a powerful sense of missed opportunity, of lost connection. Here she was, drowning, she thought, and someone had thrown a life belt to her, but it had fallen just out of her reach.

There were other kinds of military procession for the population to goggle at too. Throughout July the Russians had been building a grand war memorial in Schwarzenbergplatz. Or at least, a collection of prisoners of war and Austrian civilians had been building it, under the direction of Russian engineers. Its centre piece was a column, on top of which stood a statue of a soldier, a golden shield resting on the ground near his feet, a golden helmet on his head, his hand holding a flag pole that pointed to the sky. It was very impressive and many people went to look at it being built, although she did hear one wit in the street muttering, 'Tomb of the unknown rapist' to his companions, to which one of them laughed and said back, 'No, looter's memorial, more like.'

In August it was finished and Anatol invited her to the unveiling ceremony. He was required to be in the formal parade, but he could get her a good place to see the march past and speeches. She agreed to go. They would meet up afterwards.

She stood in a section corralled off for people with tickets and she had a good view of the monument. It was a hot day and it was a long wait in the sun. She wished she had some water. Around two o' clock a military band struck up and then a procession of Russian vehicles and soldiers began to march past and into the square. There were too many to fit into the space, so the vehicles – military hardware, artillery pieces, rocket launchers – moved on down the Rennweg and away while soldiers marching in tight rows into the square lined up in front of the monument, red flags unfurled, medals on chests, eyes narrowing to screen out the sun as they held their heads up firmly to the front.

Anatol had told her that the units staying in the square would contain troops from the battalions that had taken part in the assault on the city – a special honour. A line of men held captured Nazi flags, metal swastikas and eagles stuck on the end of the poles, pointing down at the ground. The speeches started.

A big man with an enormous hat and row upon row of medals across his chest started speaking in Russian, his words amplified. Behind him was a huge image of Stalin. As he spoke, his voice intensified with emotion and loudened. Ellie saw that some of the soldiers near her began to weep even as they stood with eyes facing forward. Then the speech was read out again, this time in German, by another man in Soviet uniform. He spoke of this being a day for which they had waited for so long, which had now finally come. The monument was a tribute and everlasting memorial to the twenty thousand men who had paid the ultimate sacrifice in liberating the city. She looked up at the statue of a soldier at the top of the monumental column, his gold shield emblazoned with a hammer and sickle shining bright in the sunshine. She remembered the hammer and sickles scrawled on the walls of the armament factory in Floridsdorf and began to feel tears in her own eyes.

The man continued his speech. The people who died had mothers, fathers, wives and children, he said. They served because they believed in the fight against fascism and for the people of Europe to throw off the dictator's yoke. The men who lost their lives liberating the city had made a tremendous sacrifice.

As the speech went on, Ellie found that she too was sobbing, thinking of all those young men who had died in a strange land. When, at the end, the man said something about our victorious allies and their heroic contribution to the effort to defeat Germany she found her heart surging with hope and longing.

Then a great shouting and cheering arose from the soldiers in the parade. It was controlled and orchestrated by their officers, the men staying in their ranks and standing stiffly as they voiced their great human noise. Some of the civilians in the crowd stayed silent but others joined in, Ellie with them, carried away in the moment. A military band struck up with the Russian national anthem, to which every soldier in the square knew the words, so that a mass of voices arose to sing the strangely beautiful tune.

That evening Anatol came to Schönbrunnerstrasse bearing

gifts – a fish and a bottle of red wine. He was in his dress uniform still and looked very handsome. She cooked the fish and they ate it, pouring glasses of drink. Ellie tried to tell him about her feelings during the parade.

'I was crying my eyes out Anatol, thinking of all those brave men who died. So young and so far from home. When they started talking about their families I just couldn't hold myself together.'

'Yes Ellie, brave. Brave men surely,' said Anatol somewhat gloomily. 'Families, yes yes.'

'I am longing for the British to come to Vienna,' she exclaimed.

'Yes British they come, they come soon.'

'It will be so good to speak English again,' she said.

'Speak English, yes.' He had a habit of repeating her words, as if it helped him understand. 'You speak English.' Then he seemed to pause for thought. 'Why you speak English?'

'It is my language Anatol, my country!' she beamed at him, her face alight with the thought.

'You English country. English?' he said, evidently surprised by this. 'How is that you English?'

She tried to explain to him, but it was hard to get very much across. She had never really talked to him about herself, nor he to her. Their relationship was not based on conversation. She realised that she knew very little about him. Did he have a family? Who had he left behind?

He seemed at first worried by the news that she was not Austrian, then curious, and then tried hard to learn more, but after a while the effort of trying to communicate was too much for them. It had been a long day standing in the sun and the wine was taking effect so that they were soon ready for bed.

After that Anatol visited only once more. He didn't stay the night but took her out to the little park opposite the apartment block and asked her many questions about her life in Austria, her marriage, her children, what had happened to her to bring her to Vienna. She answered as best she could, missing out her time in Munich with the Luftwaffe telephonists, suddenly cautious about how much she revealed to him. He promised he would return soon and that she shouldn't worry.

Her cautious approach to Anatol's questions was not enough to protect her. One morning in late August as she came out of the apartment building a car was waiting outside the building, the engine running and a door open, a man at the steering wheel. Two other men in grey raincoats came next to her and silently took her arms as she stepped out onto the pavement, forcing her towards the car and pushing her down into the rear seat. They sat either side of her as the car drove away from the building towards the southern suburbs.

15

Louis Nicholson to his wife, Ruth
May 15th 1945
Klagenfurt

Dearest Ruth,

We are in Austria now, in a place called Klagenfurt. It's been a hectic time but I've finally got a moment to write. I long to see you my darling but there is not much chance of any home leave until things settle down here. I live in hope!

Conditions here are not at all like Naples when we first arrived there. I think I will never forget the dreadful situation of those people – living like wild beasts, medieval. It's hard to get it out of my mind.

Klagenfurt – Carinthia I should say, as that is the name of the region – is a lovely part of the world. Perhaps when times are different you will come here with me and see for yourself. The town got a bit of a pasting at some point, but there is a lake where people bathe and sail, tourist hotels and so on, luxury villas. We had to turn out a few Nazis and their girlfriends who had holed up in them, hoping to keep their heads down for the duration. A lot of the hotels were used as convalescent homes for their officers and men wounded in the East. They are being moved out to make room for our people.

There are thousands of people flooding into the area and they all need sorting and feeding. Luckily that's not my

205

job – all kinds of military refugees and their followers running away from the Soviets and the Yugoslavs. The local population are a pretty varied lot already, what with the foreigners and POWs who the Germans put to work. They've opened up all the camps where these people were housed and they wander in and out, mostly looking for food. Some of them are in a bad way.

We've also got Cossacks who fought on the German side and Yugoslavs who didn't agree with Tito. Half the original people here seem to have been Slovenians, not Austrians and they have their own ideas about what they deserve, which our chaps don't always agree with. The Yugos have been causing a lot of trouble, running up flags and making proclamations here and there. They've been chased out of the towns by our men. We will just have to hope it doesn't get too nasty.

I've got to go over to Graz tomorrow for a meeting with the Russians – I'm not sure what about. I haven't met a Russian yet. I'll let you know what they're like.

My German isn't as good as it might be. I was fine in Italy but now our dear friend Dashwood has the upper hand as that's his speciality, so he'll be coming with me to Graz. I must get the language sorted out so I don't have to drag him along to everything. He has been making himself at home here. He and a couple of others are billeted in a gasthaus on the southern shore of the lake while the rest of us are here in the town. By all accounts it is a very comfortable berth and he has been waxing lyrical about the charms of the daughter of the house, who apparently is blonde, beautiful and friendly, a disastrous combination for poor old Dashwood. We are not supposed to get too friendly with the Austrian civilians but it's hard to know how the dear fellow will be restrained from making a fool of himself again. I just hope she treats him better than his 'contessa' did in Naples.

Enough of him. I will be putting ideas into your head my darling, with all this talk of beautiful young women. You need have no fears for me on that front (ha ha!). Naples has made me cynical I'm afraid. Oh I don't know what I am saying – you must scratch that bit out.

I miss you a great deal my darling and I want so much to be with you. Write and tell me your news. How are things in London? The post is much better these days, thank God.

I will write again soon,

Your loving husband, Louis.

May 30th 1945

Dearest,

I am sad and troubled this evening, not for personal reasons but because (a) I have not heard from you since my last letter (don't worry, I forgive you, the post is erratic no doubt) and (b) because of some things that have happened here.

First I should perhaps tell you some brighter things, relating to our friend Dashwood, who continues to provide amusement for all of us. Do you remember I told you about his new lady love? It turns out that she is just 15. Yes, fifteen! She really is quite extraordinarily beautiful in a blonde, Germanic kind of way. She is supposed to provide waitress service to guests but it seems she likes to sit on the men's laps and sing songs with them. I found out because the parents came to see me to complain and they asked me to have a word with my fellows.

I therefore went there yesterday evening and spoke to them all. As well as our people there are five or six Welsh Guards there, assigned to the POW camp over at St Ruprecht. It was hard for them (and me!) not to laugh I am sorry to say. Do you know what Dashwood said afterwards?

'You can't put the toothpaste back into the tube.' The man really is quite repulsive. He seemed offended when I told him to leave the girl alone. I told him I was his commanding officer now and he made some stupid remark about absent friends or something.

I am sorry Ruth, I suppose it is not such a funny story. It annoyed me to see him blustering about like that, thinking he owns the country and every woman in it. I ought to know better I suppose.

More seriously, I'm afraid something vile has happened to some of the displaced people I mentioned in my last letter, although of course they are no doubt not blameless themselves. There were many Cossacks who fought on the German side in camps at Spittal and Judenburg. The Welsh Guards had to force them onto trains last week to send them back to the Soviets. I wasn't there but apparently there were appalling scenes once they realised what was going on. Some of their women tried to jump off a bridge with their babies saying they'd rather die than go back to Russia. Of course it's hard to know what to make of that but they can't have been anticipating a very warm welcome. Amazingly, some of their German officers chose to go with them.

Then we were asked to help out with another operation and that's the one that has really upset me because now I know what happened to the people, Jugoslavs this time. Apparently an agreement was made that involved sending the lot of them back to where they came from, whatever side they had been on. They were all told they were off to Italy, otherwise they wouldn't have got into the carriages. Then they chugged off through the mountains and we poor fools thought nothing more of it.

Then a couple of days ago a man was brought in to our office. He was in a terrible condition, wild eyed, crazy looking, gabbling away so even when we found an interpreter we could hardly get any sense out of him. His teeth had been bashed in and I think some kind of injury to his tongue meant he could hardly speak. He turned out to be one of the Chetniks who had escaped from the rest after the train was stopped on the other side of the border. They fought against Tito you know. But it seems the men on the trains were taken out and shot down as soon as they got over the border by the Yugolavs, the whole lot of them. He was covered in their bodies and played dead and somehow got away. I can't tell you how sickened I feel, knowing I played a part in it. I thought I had seen it all in Naples, but it seems there is no end to it, even after 'peace' is supposed to have broken out.

So there you are my darling. I am sorry to burden you with my troubles and worries. There is so much to do here, not all of it as dreadful as the things I have described. Perhaps there is some good that we can do, putting things back together for the people here. Not all of them were Nazis.

Dashwood, as you can imagine, is relatively unmoved by these events. That is to say, he was as shaken as the rest of us when he heard about the Chetniks – he is not inhuman – but I can't help remembering his comment about the Cossacks. He said so many people have died, what would another thirty thousand matter? I suppose he's just trying to laugh things off. Perhaps he is better at dealing with these things than I am, but I find it hard to forgive someone saying that. There has to be some kind of moral screw loose in the man.

I wonder if I am letting him get under my skin too much. Should I take things less seriously Ruth? It does me no good to agonise over these things I know. I have no power to control such events after all. Write to me soon please. I need to hear from you so much.

Your loving husband, Louis.

June 1945

Dear Ruth

Your letter, received last week, concerned me as you may imagine. The war has split us apart for a long time of course, far too long, so I can see why you are thinking in this way. I am doing what I can to arrange for a period of leave but it is difficult at such a distance to discuss the issues you raise. You are of course free to do as you please. As you know, I have never imagined that the fact of our marriage meant that I would possess you exclusively; that has always struck me as a desperately wrongheaded way to look upon relations between men and women. I was just hoping you would bear our separation with more fortitude. I suppose I was being unrealistic.

It is damnable that I cannot speak with you. I will do my best to find a telephone link.

Can I propose something? It is that we put these matters to one side for a while and write our letters in the old way. You must live your life in England but please don't tell me the details and I will try not to ask. Try to look at my photograph from time to time and remember all of the wonderful things that once brought us together. I will do the same.

In this spirit, I offer you my news of the past week or so.

I don't think I told you about the visit to Graz did I? It was informative about a range of things. The Russians seemed friendly at first and they plied us with drinks and good food, making little speeches about comradeship etc etc with lots of singing and general bonhomie. But it all seemed like a great cover-up when we found out some of the things they'd been doing. Apparently as soon as they got established in the country they got hold of a plan of all the railway lines and rolling stock in Austria. They have been taking the factory equipment out and using the trains to send it back to Russia for their own industry. There is going to be nothing left. So there are no spare parts for trucks and we can't move supplies about. The food situation is bound to go downhill as a result. Most of the time was spent talking about that and trying to get through the Russians' blustering on the subject.

Then there is their behaviour in the towns and villages where they have control. I heard of a place near the border where they installed some commissar or whatever they call them who promptly invited all his friends over to the local schloss which he had requisitioned and spent weeks on end in a kind of extended orgy, drinking their way through the wine cellar and harassing local girls. One of the women jumped out of a bathroom window to get away and broke her neck. It seems the NKVD eventually caught up with him and he was sent to face whatever sort of justice they have in Moscow for such people, but the damage was done. How they're going to get the Austrians on their side in these elections they're promising, after that sort of behaviour, is beyond me.

I don't really know what you want from me at this distance Ruth. It is as if we are communicating through a mist, our faces that were once so clear, obscure to one another. We must try to hold on to our memories.

My letter would not, of course, be complete without an update on the Dashwood saga. I fear that things continue to go downhill between us, even as we are thrust together more often because of the language issue. His German really is excellent and he has made great strides in befriending the natives as a result. By that I mean the Austrians, with whom he gets on like a house on fire.

We were called up to Mallnitz after Graz, Dashwood, myself and Lofty Elliott, to join up with some people from Villach FSS. A supply train on its way to Klagenfurt had been derailed on the other side of the tunnel that goes through a mountain into an area controlled by the Americans. There was a chap there who everyone thought had done it, or at least somehow been involved, a Polish Jew, no doubt holding a flag for the Jews against our people in Palestine. The Austrian police found him, a young fellow wandering around in the forest with a pistol. If he and his friends had done it, they weren't very clever because the explosives they had laid just turned the train over onto its side against an embankment.

Anyway, I tell you this just to show you how Dashwood excelled himself once again. The fellow with the pistol was due to be sent back through the tunnel into American custody, since he had come out of an American DP camp near Bad Gastein, but we had him for a bit and I left him alone under guard. When I got back the chap had a bloody nose and had been knocked about and I was pretty annoyed about it. Of course it was ruddy Dashwood again – 'he fell down the stairs' was the claim. Once again I had to give him a good telling off.

I'll stop these foolish stories now Ruth. It must be very dull for you to hear these tales of young men gallivanting around in a foreign land. I am trying to keep my chin up. You do the same and write soon.

Your affectionate husband, Louis.

August 1945

Dearest Ruth,
Still no letter from you. Please write. My news: these are interesting times as the zone borders have now been agreed. We British will have East Tyrol, Styria and Carinthia and parts of Vienna. We are already moving into our areas, except Vienna where there are delays but that will come soon.

Last month I was in Vienna to establish our future accommodation and meet our American, French and Russian colleagues. I'll be up there again in September I expect – they want me to act as liaison between the Vienna FSS, when it gets set up, and the main British zone in the South. The delay in our getting to the capital is due to some kind of political wrangle with the Russians about the people they have installed as a government. I met some of them, government members that is, Austrians who in some cases had spent the war in Moscow, or in Dachau. Their chief is an old fellow called Renner who apparently ran something in one of the pre-war governments. He is no fool and certainly no stooge of the Russians.

Anyway, our hosts were their usual genial selves, plenty of food, drink, dancing and kissing. They got on better with the Americans than us I think. Our chaps object to being kissed but the Americans seem to put up with that kind of thing much better. It seems the Russians are tired of feeding the Viennese and they've set a deadline for their withdrawal, after which anyone left outside their zone will starve unless we start supplying them.

We were taken to the Sacher Hotel in the old city in the evening and had a visit from a man called Mayer who was complaining mightily and thought we might help. Evidently he feels he was part of what he called the 'Austrian re-sistance' and he told a complicated tale of how his people had guided the Russians into the city when they were fighting their way in. He is annoyed that the Russians are now arresting some of his friends on suspicion of this or that. But we are not yet in a position to do much about it, even if his story proves true. He left, somewhat disap-pointed with the response I think.

We had a day to take a look round with Russian 'guides' whose job it was, I think, to keep a close eye on us. The destruction is nothing like as bad as Naples. The people in the streets are very numerous, on foot largely as there are very few vehicles. We made quite a sight and sound I imagine as our convoy drove in. The Viennese seemed excited about us being there. I think they are pretty sick of the Russians.

Driving down the main street into the centre I heard an odd thing – a woman's voice shouting out to me from the crowd on the pavement. She shouted something in English, I'm quite sure, but I didn't have time to answer before we moved off. I am sure it was an English voice though. Perhaps there are British people amongst them. I suppose nothing should surprise me any more about this war. A woman though? Perhaps I was hearing things. I am very tired.

I send my love to you Ruth, and hope to hear from you soon. Don't leave it too long.

Your Louis.

PS: I have no Dashwood stories to report this time. He has been behaving himself recently, I am sorry to say.

PPS: here is a sight to remember: the Americans brought some GIs with them, one of whom was a Red Indian I think – narrow, Mongolian looking eyes and high cheekbones. I saw him standing guard next to the entrance of the hotel, making eyes at a Russian soldier who must have actually been from Mongolia itself, same eyes and cheekbones, wrap-leggings such as the Chinese wear. The two of them looked like brothers.

16

AFTER SHE HAD been bundled into the car Ellie was driven down to Favoriten. The two men who had picked her up seemed impervious to her questions about what was going on and muttered to each other in Russian. They turned into Hardmuthgasse and she saw a large white building with barred windows – a prison. Panic overwhelmed her, but there was nothing she could do.

At the main entrance the men spoke to a uniformed woman at a reception desk. She heard her name spoken and she tried to say something, desperate to influence things, but it was no use. None of them seemed able to understand German. The part of her that was still rational sensed that it would be unwise to try any other languages. This business must have something to do with Anatol finding out she was British.

She was then taken through some corridors to the other end of the building and put into a cell on her own. A bed with a thin mattress ran along one side and there was a bucket. She sat down on the edge of the bed, her feelings in turmoil. She could not think what they wanted or understand why she was there.

She was left entirely on her own for two days and nights, apart from supervised visits to the toilet area to slop out her bucket, and trays with soup, bread and water which appeared twice a day, brought by an impassive female guard who said nothing.

Her fears about what would happen to her grew uncontrollably, so that by the time she was led out of the cell to meet her interrogator she was desperate to communicate.

She did not hear the man's name, only that he was Commissioner something. He had a white, rounded face with eyebrows that seemed permanently raised in surprise. When he spoke, the pitch of his voice rose at the end of the sentence, so that she had the impression of always being asked questions, even on the rare occasions where this was not the case. He smoked continuously. She felt afraid to ask anything of him.

'You are Mrs Eloise Bauer?'

She affirmed this in a small voice.

'And you are English?'

Again she affirmed.

'What are you doing in this country Mrs Bauer?'

She began to tell her story, at first hesitant, then more confidently, experiencing feelings of release, of self-justification against some mysterious accusatory power that came as much from within herself as from the man across the desk who, in fact, had made no charges against her. He said nothing, wrote nothing, just listened and smoked and, if she ran out of things to say, said 'Go on' or 'Continue' until she reached the end.

Then he offered her a cigarette, which she took and smoked with unsteady hands, and asked her to repeat parts of the story. He listened again impassively, saying almost nothing. As she spoke she began to notice his silence and wonder what lay behind it.

Then he said she must now go back to her cell. He would see her again soon.

Her panic again took over and she stood up, trembling, with tears streaming down her face.

'But why am I here? You must tell me. What do you want with me? I have done nothing wrong. Please tell me why you have brought me here.'

He stared back at her with eyes that looked quite blank

behind the wreaths of smoke.

'Do not worry,' he said eventually. 'I will see you again.'

But days went by without any word of when she might be given another chance to explain herself. The waiting took its toll. On one day she found that she could not stand up in her cell for more than a moment. Her legs kept giving way when she tried. The next day she found herself infused with a ferocious energy and in desperation she banged on the door of the cell, screaming out 'Why am I here?' The sound of her hammering echoed down what seemed to be an empty corridor. Eventually the female guard came, pushed her down on the bed, said something she could not understand, and left.

After passing violently through these stages of frustration and terror, she then found these feelings subside, her body at first relaxing into a deep exhaustion. One day she slept through two mealtimes and woke in the night, hungry for the meagre ration of soup and bread that she had missed. And then, in a calmer state, she began to think. What could have led them to arrest her?

The obvious explanation was that it had something to do with Anatol. When he had found out she was British he had behaved oddly. Had he told his superiors? Why would he do that though? He would get into as much trouble as her if he said anything about them.

Then she found herself thinking more and more about Poldi. Perhaps she had said something to someone. That was all it took. How well did she really know Poldi anyway? Had she really been forgiven for taking the coins? She remembered the story Poldi had told about helping the Gestapo clear out the Kremenezky Palace, in exchange for them allowing her to continue living there. Surely she'd be thinking of doing the same kind of deal with the Russians, about to move into the building themselves. Telling them about a British woman mixed up in plots with German soldiers, carrying on a relationship with a Russian officer, would be a perfect offering.

It was another week before she met her interrogator. He asked her many questions. Why had she joined the Luftwaffe? What had she done for them? Whose telephone numbers had she been asked to memorise? What were the numbers? Why had she gone to Graz and what had she done there? What were her relations with her husband? Please describe the so-called language school that according to her had been bombed. Where was it again? Who was this Mrs van der Lye and where was she now? Tell him, please, about Major Shevchenko. What was the nature of their relationship and what had they discussed? Did she know that he was in trouble now?

The questions came rapidly and she tried to answer them as best she could, but at some level it felt like a child's game, testing her memory perhaps? Her consistency? Then he got onto the topic of Carl Mayer and at this point she sensed that it was no longer a game but something he really wanted to know about. How many times had she met him? Describe what he said on this occasion, on that occasion. Where had she last seen him? Did she know where he was now? What did she know about the other people who had come to the language school? What had her involvement been in O5?

She answered the questions as best she could, although it seemed clear that there was a lot that she could not answer, or at least not in the way that the Commissioner seemed to expect. Finally, after an hour going round the same topics, he shrugged his shoulders and murmured something to himself in Russian. She was returned to her cell. Another couple of days passed.

On the morning of the tenth day, the door opened and a soldier said in German that she was to come with him and to bring any belongings. She picked up her coat and bag and was led down the corridor. The thought flashed into her mind that she could be going to her death. This must be how these things were done. Take the unsuspecting victim for a walk, and then… She dropped her things in the corridor and her legs weakened again with fear. But the guard took her coat, picked up her bag, shoved it into her hands again and pressed her to go on.

In the entrance hall, the soldier stopped at the reception desk and said her name to the same woman who had been there before. He then pointed to a door, indicating that she should go through, which she did, terrified of what would be on the other side.

She was in a room with many desks. A man in British uniform looked up, smiled and stood up to greet her.

'Hello Mrs Bauer,' he said, taking her hand in his. 'You are her aren't you? You are British I think?'

She collapsed into his arms.

They drove out of Hardmuthgasse and she took in deep breaths as she smelled the odour of freshly baked bread coming from the Favoriten bakery. Her tears of relief had stopped flowing and she had begun to take in the miraculous news that she was being released into his custody.

'I am here for a couple more days now, but in the meantime we'll get you back to your place and you can get your things ready for a move. It's high time you got out of here I think,' said Louis cheerfully as he spun the wheel to turn into the main road.

'How did you find out I was here?' she said in English, amazed at how strange the sound of the language felt on her own tongue.

'Oh, the Russians told us they picked up a British woman and they didn't know what to do with her. They don't send everyone they pick up to Siberia you know.'

'They didn't tell me that,' said Ellie. He looked over at her as he drove.

'I thought I'd have to carry you to the car back there.'

'I'm sorry. I was just, just so…'

'Hey, don't,' he said, putting a hand on her arm. 'Don't start that again. You'll be all right now. We've got you.'

'What happened to Anatol?' she said, suddenly gripped by anxiety again.

'Anatol? Oh, you mean Schevchenko. He got you into this mess. I wouldn't worry too much about him. No doubt he'll face a bit of criticism from his superiors for getting involved with… I mean,' Louis hesitated as he realised what he was about to say.

'No, that's all right. You mean he was involved with me. Yes, he was, but…'

'Don't think about it,' said Louis. 'I am afraid that part of your life is over now. We will get you out of here and down to our zone in a couple of days' time. You'll be much better off down there, you'll see.'

They had reached the apartment building.

'Off you go then,' said Louis. 'I need to get back to the centre, but I'll come and see you this evening to make sure everything is all right, OK?'

She hesitated, half out of the car.

'Oh, perhaps some money for food? You must be starving,' he said, bringing out his wallet.

'No no, that's not it. I just wanted to say thank you. Thank you so much. You don't know – you can't know…'

Louis smiled warmly at her. 'That's all right Mrs Bauer. We will see you are all right. I will make sure of it. I'll see you this evening – I'll be along about six o' clock.' He drove off before she could dissolve again.

The apartment was as she had left it. She was indeed hungry, but above all she felt filthy, not having had a wash or a change of clothes for two weeks. When she looked in the mirror she was appalled at her appearance, her hair tangled, tear streaks down her cheeks. The Englishman must have thought she was a wild beast. She must get herself cleaned up, she thought, and was pleased to see that water came out of the tap into the kitchen sink. She would try to wash her hair before he came back.

Louis headed for the Schönbrunn Palace where the British headquarters was getting established, thinking about his encounter. He hadn't been shocked by her appearance. In Naples he had got used to dealing with people who had been forced to live like animals, scavenging for food. In that devastated city he had also seen the women who threw themselves in the paths of British soldiers. Three cigarettes would buy one for as long as you liked. You could see Austrian equivalents near the railway stations in Vienna.

He could see that Eloise Bauer was not one of those women. He recalled the moment he had first seen her in the prison. She was a ragged sight, in a desperate state of fear and anxiety, suddenly released by his presence. He thought he had spoken to her before she cried out and fell, so that he had needed to enfold her in his arms. He remembered the feel of her thin body against his and under his hands as he lowered her into a seat.

The situation with the Russian Major – Schevchenko – then occupied his thoughts. The man had come to them in the Schönbrunn, probably breaking all kinds of protocols, to tell them that there was an English woman in trouble in the lock-up at Hardmuthgasse. This had triggered a predictable response from the military-diplomatic hierarchy and there had been contact with the Russian administration over the matter, making representations about a 'British national.' The Russians were still on their best behaviour with the British, who had just arrived and had to be kept sweet for a time while they finished stripping out the factories east of the river. They agreed to an FSS man coming down to pick her up. Louis reflected that they had probably concluded that she had no useful information. Schevchenko hadn't been seen again.

He wondered what her relationship had been with the Russian major. Why were the Russians so interested in her anyway? He thought of her sitting next to him in the car as they drove across the city. Now she was probably worried about whether he would come back. Or perhaps she really was up to something and would disappear before he returned to pick her up. He decided that he had better change his plans for her and he lifted the phone to make a call to the accommodation section.

By six o'clock her hair was still wet. There was no soap but she had been able to get the worst of the matted tangles combed out and the water she splashed onto her body had made her feel less like a creature emerging from a grimy cave. She had put on the only clean dress she now had, a light blue one that she had kept for Anatol's visits. She stood at the window, looking out into the street below, watching and waiting.

Captain Nicholson had been kind to her, she thought. She had come across upper class Englishmen before, when she had worked in the hotel in Jersey. They had been with their wives on tourist breaks. Some of them liked to remind her of their superiority, complaining when faced with some lapse in perfect service. Even the nice ones, who tried to talk to her like a human being, seemed be making an effort, expecting her to be grateful for their consideration.

This English officer was different though. Perhaps it was just the situation; after all she was not serving him as a guest in a hotel. But she sensed that he had an instinctive knowledge of who she was and what she had been through. Even when she was collapsing, with his arms around her, she could feel this sympathetic intelligence in him. And when he spoke with her, it seemed like he was making no effort at all.

Then there was a knock on the door and he was there.

'Sorry, I rang the bell but it must be broken and the front door was open. There's been a change of plan – I don't think you should stay here. The Russians know where you live. We wouldn't want them to change their minds.'

Fear went through her body. 'Where can I go?' she asked, her voice trembling.

'Don't worry. Get your things together. I've got you a room at Sacher's. It's where we put our guests.'

'Sacher's? You mean the hotel?'

'Yes, that's it. We can put you up there for the night and get you away in the morning. I'm due to go back to Klagenfurt tomorrow. You can come with me.'

She couldn't believe what she was hearing. Sacher's itself was hallowed territory, a place where the Gestapo and the rest of the Nazi hierarchy had entertained the most prestigious of their coterie, a place of legendary indulgence. She had never crossed the threshold. But more important than that was the news that this man was going to get her out of Vienna and away from the encircling danger of the Russians.

Her coat was soon draped over a suitcase containing the rest of her belongings. Louis checked around to see if she had missed anything. The place was very bare, nothing in the kitchen cupboards.

'Have you eaten?' he said suddenly.

'No. I have nothing here,' she said weakly, abruptly feeling hunger pangs in her stomach. 'Have you got anything with you I could have?'

'Nothing here or in the car I'm afraid, but let's see what we can rustle up at Sacher's shall we? We must get some food into you. Come on, let's go.'

They went out and down the stairs, Ellie closing the door on yet another apartment building. She wondered as they walked to the car how many of these places she had lived in. It felt like she had been shifting from one disaster to another for years. The tiny room in Biberstrasse and the succession of rooms before that; the Lehmanns kicking her out of Rechtbahngasse. She suppressed other thoughts – the bombing, the cellar, Anna, trying to focus on what might be coming next.

They drove the mile or so to the centre. British military vehicles and a few civilian cars were parked in the street outside
the hotel. The hotel itself had been untouched by the destruction and the place reminded her of the opera foyer when she
had gone to see Rusalka with Carl, red and gold furnishings
and fittings, deep carpets. This time, though, she found the
flamboyant luxury cloying, like an over-rich cream cake.

They went to the reception counter where Louis produced
some papers and signed for her. She was given a key and a
ticket with a room number on it.

'You go upstairs and I'll get us some food organised double
quick,' he said with a smile.

The lift was working, as were all the electric lights and she
went up to her room on the third floor. Inside, she headed
straight for the bathroom and looked into the mirror. She was
very conscious of her appearance in this place of luxury, her
hair still drying from her attempts to clean up. Her battered
suitcase, coat and bag in the entrance lobby had made her look
like a refugee from the street, which indeed she supposed she
was.

The biggest surprise came when she turned on the bath tap.
She couldn't believe her luck: hot water. She hadn't experienced that for months. She left it running, and then noticed
soap, of all things, next to the sink. Looking around the cupboards and drawers in the room, she found a dressing gown
and, to her continued delight and amazement, an electric trouser press with 'John Corby, Windsor' stamped on a little metal
plaque on one of the arms. She recognised what it was from
her days in hotel service. She plugged it in and it began to heat
up.

She took off her dress and examined its creases. It would
have been nice to have an iron, but the trouser press would
help.

*

An hour later, she came down to the lobby and looked around for Louis who she found seated in a leather sofa reading a newspaper and smoking. He was dressed in uniform but wore it loosely, as if it was casual dress. His whole manner was casual in fact. He offered her a cigarette which he lit with a silver lighter, the flame steady in his hand. She looked into his eyes once the cigarette was lit and saw that they were a deep blue.

'I was just about to get them to call up to your room,' he said. 'They're serving dinner.'

As he spoke, his eyes ran over her figure.

'I wouldn't have recognised you!' he said admiringly. 'How did you do that?'

'You have no idea how wonderful a hot bath felt Captain Nicholson.'

'Oh, call me Louis. Is it all right if I use your first name? Is it Eloise or Ellie?'

'Most people call me Ellie. You can if you like,' she said graciously, and they went into the dining room where men in uniform sat in small groups or pairs at the tables, talking in low voices. A waiter led them to a table and men looked up as Ellie passed by with her tall companion. Apart from a couple of uniformed older women seated in a corner together, she was the only woman in the room.

They were brought bread rolls and soup to start with and were told pork chops would follow. Louis watched her devour both rolls and then apologised for the restricted menu.

'You must be joking! I haven't eaten like this in ages,' said Ellie, and then, 'I'm sorry, I've eaten them both.'

'Don't worry, I can always ask for more,' he said, laughing. 'It's good to see you filling up. But perhaps you had better save yourself for the main course?'

This duly arrived and, belatedly, Louis asked for a bottle of wine, which turned out to be remarkably good. It was from France.

'The French are selling us all their best stuff,' said Louis.

'Their market for wine has collapsed.'

The wine started to go to Ellie's head as he spoke. She had not taken drink for a long time.

'What do you think they wanted me for?' she suddenly asked him. 'The Russians I mean.'

'It's hard to be sure. I have some ideas but it may help if you tell me what they asked you about,' he replied.

A hint of suspicion ran through her mind and she said to him, a wry smile on her face, 'So is this how a British interrogation works then? You take your victim to dinner and ply them with French wine. I must say I prefer it to the Russian approach.'

He grinned back at her. 'No, it's nothing like that. You don't have to tell me anything now. I should warn you, though, that when we get to Klagenfurt our people are likely to want to ask you a few questions. They have to I'm afraid.'

She thought a bit about that. 'I've got nothing to hide,' she said eventually. 'Ask me what you like and I'll tell you. It's not that interesting I'm afraid.'

'Oh no, let's not spoil our dinner. I'm not acting in an official capacity now. Leave it until Klagenfurt. You might like to know how we heard about you.'

He told her the story of Anatol's visit to the Schönbrunn HQ and the subsequent events. She wasn't sure what to make of this. Until now she had thought it was Anatol who had got her into this trouble. Now it seemed he had gone to the British to help get her out of the prison. Whose side was he on? What had happened to him now?

Louis continued. 'When we heard the Russians had got hold of an Englishwoman I suppose it was just an instinctive thing to try to get you out of their hands.'

'Oh, but I'm not really English any more,' she interrupted. 'If I could find my passport it would be Austrian. I was married you see.'

'Well I've got you in here under false pretences then,' he

said laughing again. 'We're not supposed to fraternise with Austrian women.'

'I'm not so sure I feel like an Austrian woman,' she said. 'I suppose I'm not really sure what I am,' she reflected more seriously.

'There are a lot of people in that position these days,' he remarked.

Then they began to talk about the Russians. She told him about their questions.

'And then they asked me about my relationship with Carl Mayer,' she said.

'Mayer,' he said, instantly alert. 'You know him?'

'Knew him,' she corrected. 'Haven't seen him since a day in April when he came to my place for a night. He was on the run. I don't know where he is now.'

'Oh, he's all right,' said Louis. 'I saw him only last week. He came over to Schönbrunn. He is going round all the Allied HQs I think.'

'He's alive!' said Ellie, excited and shocked by this news. 'I can't believe it. How is he? What did he say?'

Louis answered her questions with one of his own: 'What do you know about him?'

This made Ellie suddenly cautious again. Both of them fell silent and she wondered what might be going on in his mind, aware that further talk could take her into territory that would do her no good. He seemed similarly reluctant to continue.

But she was burning to know more and was the first to break the silence, taking a swig of wine and announcing with bravado, 'In for a penny in for a pound, I always say! I'll tell you what I know then. I hope you'll give me some news about Carl after that. I am so glad to know he is alive and well.'

Then she told him about Carl Mayer, from his initial visit to the language school, the meetings there with his circle, the time after the July plot the previous year, his renewal of contact with her after the language school was destroyed and the gradual revelation that he was involved in meetings with Austrians who wanted to help the Russians enter the city.

'I didn't know everything he was involved with. He wanted to protect me I think, by keeping as much as he could to himself, until he had to tell me. And then that last night I saw him, just before the Russians came, he was free to talk and he told me more, but not everything I think.'

'He told us he was involved in defending the city,' Louis replied. 'I probably shouldn't tell you too much about him, but it seems you know a lot of it already. I am getting the impression this Mayer is a very lucky but also very brave man. His wife must be proud of him.'

'His wife?' said Ellie, 'What do you mean?'

'His wife, yes. He spoke about her when he came to see us. It's quite a story.'

She realised that this was another little secret that Carl had been keeping from her. She was shocked by the news, angry at some level, but oddly enough, not disappointed.

'I can see this has a personal side to it,' said Louis.

'Yes,' she admitted, looking up into his eyes, her own suddenly filled with sadness. 'Tell me more about his wife, won't you?' She remembered the clothes that he said belonged to his fiancée in England, his pleasure at seeing her in them, going out with him to concerts and the opera.

Louis then told her some surprising news. Carl Mayer's wife was indeed Jewish. But she had not been in England during the war. She had been here, in Vienna, hiding in a friend's apartment. She had spent the years of occupation there, visited occasionally by Carl, a 'submarine,' one of the few who had survived.

'He brought me some of her clothes,' said Ellie. 'This dress, for instance.' It was an expensive item in blue silk. Its creases freshly ironed out, she knew it looked gorgeous on her slim figure.

'Look,' said Louis, leaning forward. 'It's not necessarily

going to be that easy getting you through the Russian zone. We have to drive south. It's a good couple of hundred miles. We've got all the papers related to your release from their custody, but we told the Russians we'd keep you in Vienna. They don't know about our plan to get you out. There will be checkpoints and there will be another man with me, but we may have to engage in a bit of skulduggery.'

She felt her anxiety levels rising again and it showed on her face.

'Don't worry. We've done it before with one or two people we wanted to spirit away down south. I just wanted to warn you that's all. I'll explain what's involved in the morning.'

Standing in the hotel lobby area, Ellie thanked him profusely for all he had done.

He said, of course, that it was 'nothing' in the way that is common amongst the British when faced with gratitude, but in fact he went away feeling very pleased with himself. She was an attractive, even glamorous woman, for whom he had warm feelings of appreciation, and he knew that no man could be unhappy to have someone like that in their debt.

He had known not to ask her more about her personal relationship with Mayer. There would be time enough for questions and, anyway, he wasn't sure he wanted to think about her with yet another man. How many men did she have in tow anyway?

Then he thought of more practical, professional matters. Her revelations about Mayer would interest his colleagues – he was sure now that this was why the Russians had picked her up. Mayer had visited both the Americans and the British as soon as they had established a presence in the city and, for all he knew, the French, telling a tale that seemed largely about proving his own credentials as a resistance leader and complaining of the Russian attitude towards him and his friends. He said the Russians had even had him in custody for a while. The British had not known how much of Mayer's story to believe. It was going to be very helpful to have independent corroboration.

The next morning he and Dashwood turned up in a new car, a black Fiat with beautiful red leather upholstery. Dashwood had found it in the woods near Villach where it had been abandoned, along with hundreds of others, by Germans who had driven them into Austria from northern Italy before the surrender. The officers bagged the best ones. Dashwood was only a sergeant so the Fiat was small, but it was beautifully formed, unlike Dashwood who was thickset and florid of face.

Louis went into the hotel and fetched Ellie out onto the street. His colleague put on a bit of an act, holding the passenger door open as if he were a chauffeur. As she came towards him he took her hand and bowed low, kissing it.

'Honoured to be your servant madam,' he said with a flourish, holding onto her hand just a little longer than the joke lasted. She smiled graciously nevertheless before withdrawing her hand. Louis put her suitcase into the boot and helped her climb into the back seat.

'Don't worry about Sergeant Dashwood, he's always like this,' he said to her. 'You'll get used to him soon enough.' Then he added, 'Look, this is just for now: we're going to have to stop in a little while and re-arrange things.'

'Off we go then,' announced Dashwood. 'Wave goodbye to Vienna!' and he started up the motor, setting off down the street at some speed.

'Steady on Peter,' said Louis. 'There's a speed limit you know.' Many of the vehicles in the city these days were horse-drawn carts of one sort or another and a car rushing about the place was dangerous.

Dashwood shouted, 'Certainly Nicko!' over the engine noise, but ignored his advice. They rapidly made their way across the Ring and then Dashwood twisted the steering wheel over to the right and came to an abrupt halt in a quiet side road. 'Right, now we can switch over!' he announced breezily.

Louis explained to her that they were going to have to adopt a subterfuge to get them past the Russian checkpoints. One was coming up a bit further down the road, and there would be another one as they exited the city, but after that they would be clear of them for a very large part of their journey, before a final one as they entered the British zone in the south.

'They'll check our papers, but it will be better if they just see the two of us. There could be trouble if they see you.'

'Where will I hide?' said Ellie.

'Try not to worry,' said Louis, immediately seeing the concern on her face. 'We've done this before. They don't search the car. If you won't mind, you'll need to get in the boot.'

She got out of the car and the luggage was transferred to the back seat. There was a blanket and a pillow in the boot.

'You'll be all right in there. Just keep quiet when we stop. They never search.'

She hesitated. 'Are you sure?'

The two men chorused, 'Yes, don't worry, you'll be fine, out of here in a jiffy' and other such cheerful, reassuring messages. Realising she had no choice she decided she must put her faith in her two fellow countrymen. She got in, lay down on her side, and the boot was closed on her so that she was in the dark. Immediately, she began to shiver. She found herself wondering whether she could trust them to let her out and she struggled within herself to try to suppress this thought.

She felt the car moving off and after about five minutes, draw to a halt again. This must be the first checkpoint. Voices spoke around her, Russian, German, English, and the car moved off again. She smelled bread in the air, and realised they were driving through the Russian zone near Favoriten. Another five minutes, in which the car went over several potholes that threw her about in the back, and then they drew up at the second checkpoint where the same thing happened. This time, there was a bang on the boot as the car pulled away which gave her a fright, but she managed to stay silent in spite of her rising sense of panic. The car drove on for a further ten minutes and then she felt it swerve sharply to the right and stop.

Louis opened the boot and saw her trembling un-controllably, although the day was not cold, and she was biting her knuckles.

'What's the matter?' he asked. 'Don't be so frightened. We're past the worst of it! The guard just slapped the car on its way as we moved off, cheeky sod.'

'It's not that,' she said. 'It's just the feeling of being in this darkness all cramped up.'

'Well you're all right now,' he replied. 'You can get out and join us.' He helped her out of the boot and they transferred the luggage back so that she had a space on the back seat. He offered her a drink of coffee from a thermos. Her hands shivered as she took the drink. 'You're shaken up by all this, I can see,' he said as Dashwood got into the driver's seat again.

'I don't like being cooped up in dark places,' she said, her hands gradually losing their tremor. 'It makes me nervous. I'm sorry.' She was recovering her equilibrium now. 'How long have we got before the next checkpoint?' she asked.

'Oh, a while yet,' said Dashwood, turning round in the seat. 'It's about a hundred kilometres to Semmering where our zone starts. Then we'll be up in the mountains and down the other side if this little Italian beauty treats us right,' and he slapped the side of the car. 'Do you want the hood down for a bit of fresh air?' he boomed, his face filled with enthusiasm at the idea. He was like a child with a new toy. The other two felt obliged to agree, even though the air as they rattled along the sometimes uneven roads was really too cold.

She kept her head down in the back to avoid the chance of passing Russians seeing her, but there was nothing much on the roads. They skirted round Wiener Neustadt. Ellie had never been there. 'It's been bombed to bits,' commented Louis as they looked over towards the town.

'Yes, we were bombed too. I mean, I was bombed,' and she told him about the destruction of the language school, her time underground, her rescue by the men who had dug her out. He turned round to listen as she spoke to him above the sound of the engine and she could see that there was kindness in his eyes.

They made their way across the flat countryside, passing vineyards and maize fields, before rising up through low hills and a forested area towards the steep climb that would take them up towards Semmering. Before they started up the winding ascent they stopped the car for her, once again, to take up her hiding position. Louis noticed that her hands no longer shook. She saw him looking at them and touched his arm with a warm hand. 'I'll be all right now, I think. It helped to tell you about it.'

But in Semmering, laying in the darkness, new fears assailed her as the inspection seemed to go on for ever. She heard Russian voices and then those of the two British men answering them. She started wondering if they were going to search the car. What would happen if they found her? She imagined being taken back to the prison cell in Hardmuthgasse and the thought brought a tightness to her throat so that she started to feel like coughing, which she knew would be disastrous. She held her hand tightly over her mouth to suppress any sounds that might come out.

Eventually, though, the barrier was lifted to allow them down the road to the British end of the checkpoint. Driving through, Dashwood cheerily shouted out to the guard, 'Bringing home our booty!' and accelerated away. As soon as they were out of sight, Dashwood braked, bringing the car to a sudden halt which flung Ellie against the edge of the boot.

'Welcome to English territory Mrs B!' said Dashwood extravagantly, taking her hand to help her out. He took a step back and bowed, putting on the same chevalier act he had done when he had first met her, producing the same raised eyebrows in Louis and another gracious acceptance of his clowning from Ellie, who thought she might as well play along. Dashwood was a nervous man, it seemed, rather too keen to impress.

On they went then, down the valley towards Judenburg, turning up a narrow road that took them higher up and over towards Wolfsberg. They stopped at a point that Louis said marked the border between Styria and Carinthia and looked out down the valley to the south. The men went to relieve themselves in a patch of forest by the side of the road. As they stood together, Dashwood remarked:

'You've found yourself a good-looking girlfriend there, Nicko.'

Louis knew better than to respond to this and just grunted as he did up his fly.

'Have it your own way then, and I'll have it mine,' said Dashwood, walking back to the car. Louis was left looking out at the view.

There was no hurry now, he reflected. In the British zone they were safe. If it were not for the presence of Dashwood he would be enjoying this drive through the beautiful green Austrian countryside with this interesting female companion. For two years now he had been away from England on active service, with only a couple of week's home leave in all that time. He had interrupted his university studies to join up in 1943 and had then been posted to Italy. He had no doubt his war experiences had changed him and he sometimes wondered if he could really just go home when it was all over and take up where he left off. Other people would be different too, their lives also having moved on. There was no doubt that this foreign adventure would come to an end, perhaps as soon as next year. He had no intention of staying in the army as a professional soldier. He would need at some point to join up the present with his past.

Ruth, though often in his thoughts, at the same time felt like a fading memory of a previous life. Unlike some of the other officers who had wives at home, he had not taken any of the numerous opportunities offered him for romantic liaisons with local girls. The thought of the hurried sexual encounters enjoyed by rank and file soldiers in the brothels of Naples filled him with loathing and also, he had to admit, a kind of fear which had nothing to do with the dire official warnings about venereal disease.

He started off back to the car and as he came through the trees saw Dashwood approaching Ellie, who was sitting on a rock looking at the view, from behind. Before she could turn round, the man slid his hands around her shoulders and, laughing, bent his head to bury his face in her neck, at which Ellie immediately sprang up, swivelled round and delivered a resounding smack to Dashwood's cheek. His hand went up to his face and Louis heard the idiot remonstrating with her, saying it was just a joke, a bit of fun, she shouldn't take offence.

Louis decided not to get involved. It seemed this woman could look after her own interests when she needed to. She must have worked out that Dashwood was one of life's prize idiots.

The three of them motored on in silence, the two men in the front and Ellie eventually falling asleep on the back seat, the nervous tension of the day now dissipating through her body, so that around three in the afternoon they rolled up in Klagenfurt, the tyres rumbling over the cobbled streets outside the railway station.

17

A SNOWFALL IN NOVEMBER was the start of what became the coldest winter that anyone could remember. Louis initially arranged for her to be lodged with a local farmer and his wife in Pischeldorf, a few miles out of Klagenfurt. He knew, though, that if she was to find work over the winter it would have to be in Klagenfurt itself, so she would need to move there, as the road was often impassable and there was no public transport, so he approached the accommodation section for a place in one of the requisitioned houses in the centre of town. It would be easy to find Ellie work in the British administration; they needed someone who could interpret and translate documents in the Labour section. But she would need to be screened, even if only superficially. He went up to Pischeldorf to help her fill in the necessary paperwork.

'What am I supposed to put here?' she said, pointing to something on the form she was filling in. 'I did have to sign a document once.'

He leaned over her shoulder and saw that the question asked, 'Have you ever sworn an oath of secrecy to any organisation?'

'Which organisation was that?'

'It was when I was in Munich training to be a telephone operator. They made me sign something, promising never to reveal these phone numbers I was supposed to memorise.'

He knew about her time in Munich, but not about this.

'What phone numbers?'

'Oh, we were supposed to know the numbers of various offices – command centres they called them – so we wouldn't have to waste time looking them up. To be honest, I've forgotten them all now.'

'Best to answer no to that,' he advised. 'I don't think signing a sheet of paper counts as an oath. This form is something we use to identify Nazis. No point in you setting up a false alarm by filling it in the wrong way.'

'But surely anyone who wants to lie about their past can just put down what they want?' she said.

He laughed. 'There you have it in a nutshell! Perhaps you should join us in the Section.' He picked up the form and looked through it. She had answered most of the questions with a 'no' or 'does not apply'.

'This looks fine,' he concluded. He knew that if he, as a Field Security officer, approved her application she would have no problems.

She then had to provide information about her skills and qualifications for the position he had lined up for her, supply the names of people who could write references and so on. She pointed out that it might be hard to find any of the people for whom she had worked over the years. Again, Louis was helpful, talking her through the different jobs she had done, reassuring her that a reference from him would be all that was needed. In fact he found himself falling over himself to be helpful to her, and was so taken with this task and the pleasure that it brought him that he hardly paused to think about why he was feeling this way.

She, for her part, could easily see what was happening with him. He could have delegated others to deal with her bureaucratic problems, but he had made time in his day to come out to Pischeldorf himself. As a displaced person she could have been put in some camp, mixed in with the people of different nationalities who were being slowly sorted and screened by the occupation authorities, kept in limbo while their fate was decided. Yet he had singled her out for preferential treatment. No doubt he would say, if challenged, that this was because she was a British woman, but she knew better than to force him into this deception. She liked his attention. And she sensed that as an FSS officer – albeit newly promoted to his captain's rank – he had the power to help her a great deal.

She asked herself how she felt about him as a man and came up with a mixture of things. He was kind to her and sensitive to her needs, something she had not experienced in a man for a long time. Carl had come close, but his secret life, which she had always wondered about, explained why he always held back from her. For him she had been a substitute for the woman he really wanted. She thought of Carl with a mixture of affection and lingering annoyance at his deception.

The picture with Anatol had been much simpler. He remained, fundamentally, a stranger to her; a useful relationship when survival was the main aim. And when he made love to her she had too often found herself thinking of the scene in the cellar at Rechte Bahngasse with the young Russian soldier. She shuddered as she thought of the boy's nervous fumbling, and the screams and the crying of the other women who had been with her in that dark, subterranean place.

'Are you cold Eloise?' asked Louis, putting his hand on her shoulder. Brought back into the present, she looked up at him and smiled, briefly placing her hand over his.

'No, I was just thinking.'

He withdrew his hand from under hers. 'Well that's fine then. I think we've done all the paperwork now. I'll take it into town and come back once I know the outcome – a few days, I should think. You'll be all right. They need someone who can speak good German, especially this country dialect.'

He found German a strangely difficult language. Italian had come easy to him – he could relate it to the French and Latin he had learned at school – but with German it wasn't just the peasant dialect that was the problem. He simply didn't have an ear for the language. Fluency in German was something that Ellie and Dashwood had in common, if nothing else.

Dashwood's contacts with the local people were proving useful for the work of the unit and Louis increasingly relied on him when inquiries had to be made from Austrians. There had been some trouble at the refugee camp outside Klagenfurt – an Austrian from the town had been found dead in a ditch and the Jewish DPs were blamed. They got better rations than the townspeople, sold the surplus on the black market and didn't have to work to earn these supplies, so this provoked resentment. The situation had to be defused and Field Security were brought in so that people could see that a proper criminal investigation was being carried out. It led nowhere; there were no witnesses and precious little to go on, but the process had calmed things down and Dashwood was a hit with the Austrians as they could see that he was on their side. He was more popular with their men than their women though.

'We'll get you established in town and see how things go. We could do with a female interpreter ourselves sometimes, in my unit. There's plenty of work for someone with your kind of background. You should be happy; you're in demand!'

She smiled slightly sadly at this thought and after a few more pleasantries, since she could see Louis was trying to cheer her up, he departed.

Later that month she moved into a small house in town where she had the upper floor and share of a kitchen downstairs. It had belonged to a German family who had now been obliged to return to Hamburg. There were rabbits in hutches along the side of the garden wall and Ellie enjoyed clearing out their cages, feeding and stroking them, although she knew they were destined for the pot.

The work of the Labour section involved the organisation of all matters pertaining to the employment of Austrian civilians in the service of the military administration. Work parties led by soldiers were sent to the forests around Leoben to cut firewood that was shipped to Vienna; these had to be kitted out with warm clothes and equipment, and the men's payments organised. Others were set to work clearing bomb damage in preparation for the spring, when new building could begin. Cooks, valets and servants had to be found for the officers' mess. A range of transport services to add to those run by the military were being set up to supply the numerous POW and displaced person's camps outside Villach and Klagenfurt and other points in the countryside. All of the people involved in these operations had to be screened, registered, equipped and paid.

Ellie found herself in the midst of all of these activities and soon made a name for herself in the Labour office as a reliable and intelligent interpreter, prepared to work all of the hours that it took and more. At the end of the day, when others were flagging she was annoyed to have to stop work and return to her rooms in town. Work was an anaesthetic which stifled her tendency to think about the past or to dwell too much on her feelings. All the same, now that things were on a more even keel she began to think about Anna more. Zell am See was in the American sector and travel for someone like her was difficult. She would have to see if she could arrange something.

The Austrians were desperate to get work with the occupying power. Many of the men had undergone extreme privations as a result of their war service and subsequent captivity, in some cases under the Russians who had treated them very badly, so that finding a source of nourishment to get their depleted bodies through the winter became an urgent, life or death priority for some. Conditions for other civilians were also extremely difficult, chiefly because food was in such short supply and fuel for heating also hard to obtain. People who were too old or too young to work and whose sons and fathers had failed to come home from the front or from Russian POW camps – and there were many of these families – had it the worst, with many deaths from starvation and cold that winter.

The money that could be earned by working for the British, and the informal access to Army stores that such work allowed, meant that there were all kinds of opportunities for the lucky ones to obtain supplies. A black market developed, trading in food but also such essentials as tyres, car parts, petrol, seed for the coming spring sowing and other necessities of a rural economy. The black market in turn kept the men of the FSS busy, in addition to their other tasks: hunting out people on their arrest lists, the detection and frustration of the activities of Jugoslav partisans and smugglers on the border, and the myriad of screenings, investigations, interrogations and inquiries into nefarious activities of all kinds in the locality.

Some of the people released from concentration camps and now in camps for displaced persons were actually common criminals, claiming to have been incarcerated for political reasons; some were even SS, imprisoned by the Nazis for a variety of misdemeanours. These complexities all had to be looked into and final judgements made, under the banner of denazification, which Louis increasingly came to feel was more a propaganda slogan than a real movement towards restorative justice.

He felt overwhelmed at times by the amount of sin that he and his men were expected to detect and frustrate, but at the same time felt a cynical amusement at the idea that this flood of wrongdoing could be halted by the concerted actions of the authority that he represented. His experiences in Italy had shown him that what he was dealing with was the normal state of humanity, resurgent in the wake of the great conflict that had passed across the land.

And periodically, as Ellie and Louis engaged in their separate whirlwinds of activity, their thoughts returned to the subject of each other. They saw each other occasionally at work as Ellie was sometimes called to interpret for his unit. If they did not see each other, she saw the men who worked under him, understanding that they spoke of his leadership with liking and respect, which pleased her. Or she was simply reminded of him when a document came across her desk to translate, with a space for his signature.

She particularly liked the fact that he chose to call her Eloise. It felt like a serious name, one that spoke to something that was at the core of her. Ellie, the name by which everyone else knew her, felt more superficial, part of a cheery, outward-facing self that was not always in tune with how she felt inside.

Then, on a cold day in January, he called by her office and invited her to go with him to a winter sports day at the weekend, organised by the services. It was for officers and NCOs only. There would be ice-skating and a bit of mild skiing on a slope overlooking the lake as well as a variety of other events. Afterwards they might go to the officer's club at Maria Wörth.

'The skiing won't be up to much I'm afraid. It's just a little slope,' he laughed apologetically, 'but you might have a bit of fun seeing how our chaps manage, falling over and all that. I expect you're used to the proper Alpine stuff. You can have a go if you like and show us how to do it.'

She accepted his invitation without telling him she had never been on a pair of skis in her life. There hadn't been op-portunities for her to learn that kind of thing in Zell am See; skiing was for wealthy tourists. It was a sign of how little this man really knew of her. A part of her wanted to keep it that way.

Dear Ruth,
This is a letter I never thought I would write, but I think it is only fair that I should tell you what is on my mind and in my heart, just as you have been honest, some might say brutally so, with me.

In recent weeks I have found myself becoming involved in the life of a British woman here, who has seen the war out in this country. Hers is a long and tragic story and I think I do not know it all as yet. But I am convinced that she is a person who, in other circumstances, you might be pleased to call a friend. I have assisted her in relocating here from Vienna where she was in difficulties and have ensured that she is provided with the necessities of life.

I write now to tell you that this woman has become increasingly dear to me. I cannot say more than this as I do not want to hurt you unnecessarily. Nor do I know what the future holds. In my defence, for I feel I must defend myself, although I know that I am not the first to break our vows, I have not gone down the road that many men here have done. You perhaps know that it is common for soldiers to take up with women here, married men with wives at home as well as others. Many of them would no doubt claim that their secrecy about these illicit affairs protects the women they have left behind in England. When they return they hope to be able to preserve their families' happiness without facing jealous accusations. I know, however, from your own example, that we aspire to be better than this in our relations with each other.

I will not write again until I hear from you. If you want to know more, I will tell you, or you can choose to keep things as they are. I think I shall have some home leave in the summer. I shall hope to see you then.

Your husband, Louis.

The next morning, he came and picked up Ellie and they drove out to the lakeside. On the northern shore opposite Maria Wörth there was a flattish expanse where trucks and jeeps of various sorts had pulled up. The snow had been cleared from a large area near the vehicles and a playing pitch had been marked out.

'Some of the drivers have organised a game of football,' Louis explained. 'The ground's not too hard under the snow.'

They went down to the frozen lakeside where men and some women were standing about chatting and laughing in the cold. There was a tea urn on a portable gas stove and they got themselves a drink.

'Here, come and say hello to my chaps,' said Louis, pointing out a group of FSS men who were strapping on some ice skates. 'You probably know them all already.'

She did indeed know most of them from her work. Dashwood, of course, who was in the middle of the group, was only too well known to her. He hadn't given up on her after the incident on the road, although she'd done all she could to fend him off. As a result she sensed that he had grown resentful, jealous of her friendship with Louis. At one point he had even taunted her, saying, 'Are you sure you can pull off this officer's wife thing?' He seemed to have an instinct for knowing how to twist the knife.

But for the rest of them, they were a bunch of fine, healthy young men who were excited about their day off, planning to have fun larking about on the skates. There was Harris, the chief clerk of the unit who had been with Louis all the way though Italy, a small man with intelligent eyes behind large spectacles. Sergeant Elliott, who they all called 'Lofty' for obvious reasons, was struggling with skates that were too small for his huge feet. James Davies, a swarthy individual with an eccentric history that often seemed to involve Louis in covering up for his transgressions, was helping him with them.

With the exception of Dashwood, whose jealousy seemed unremitting, they were always very friendly to her and now that she saw them together as a group she felt suddenly warm towards them. They were an odd lot in the FSS, not like other soldiers. More independent, she supposed. None of them bothered to address Louis as 'Captain' unless they were in hearing distance of other officers and he never forced the issue.

It was as if he was the first amongst equals rather than a commanding officer. He had told her that they were all officer material by background and education anyway, but the army couldn't have a unit where everyone was a captain.

'Hello sergeants!' said Ellie cheerily as she strode over to the men with Louis.

They all looked up as Louis and Ellie approached them together, responding to Ellie with happy grins. Louis sensed that they had all come to the same conclusion. He had been unable to conceal his personal interest in the exotic woman who had appeared in their midst before Christmas. Now here he was with her, on a weekend outing.

'Here, put these on,' said Harris, handing her a pair of skates. 'They look small enough for you.'

'All right, I'll give it a go!' said Ellie, tying the leather straps. 'I've never done this before.'

'Do you think we have?' said Harris, and the rest of the men laughed.

They teetered towards the ice on the blades and, of course, were all over the place almost straight away, slipping and sliding sideways, taking short steps to stay upright, falling over with a thump. Further out were those who had skated before. Then Dashwood lumbered onto the ice. He was heavy man and everyone watched for him to fall over. Ellie wondered if the ice would hold his weight. But to everyone's surprise, he pushed off from the side confidently and began to glide out to the centre at speed, apparently making no effort. About fifty yards out he turned gracefully and briefly stood still, looking back to see the impression he had created. They were all agog.

'Where did you learn to do that, Dashers?' shouted one of the men.

'Croydon ice rink!' he yelled back, and began a rapid glide back to the admiring group. He'd done it since he was a boy, he explained. It was good to be on the ice again. He seemed pretty pleased with himself, weaving his way around the other skaters in elegant, curving movements for a while, before returning to the shore, breathing heavily. But as he took his skates off he looked up at Ellie and Louis watching him and scowled.

Louis caught her sleeve. 'Come on, let's head up to the slope and watch the skiing.'

Away from Dashwood's baleful presence she started to feel quite elated and gripped Louis' arm tightly, pulling him energetically along with her, towards the little ski slope, Louis pretending to resist her pace, laughing and protesting.

They watched the men and some women coming down the slope. Some of the officers were very practiced at this, and made stylish swoops in the snow, kicking up clouds of ice spray to the appreciative gasps and applause of onlookers.

'Don't you ski?' she asked Louis eagerly.

'No, not me. I wasn't brought up to afford that kind of thing. Some of these chaps ski regularly in the Cairngorms. They could even have been hereabouts before the war. This isn't a poor man's sport.'

'But you're not a poor man are you, Louis?' she said, although in truth she was only guessing.

'No, I suppose not, but my family isn't in that league,' he responded. 'Come on, let's get a drink.'

They wandered through the crowds of officers, some of whom had women with them, either from the women's army corps or the occasional Austrian girlfriend, and ended up back at the football pitch, the game now being over.

Schnapps and other drinks were now provided for the officers. The NCOs had beer in a separate tent, so none of the other FSS men were there. There were a few Austrians in the officer's marquee, mixing with the British. Louis told her that these were some local aristocrats, invited along to improve relations with the occupiers. Ellie had noticed people like this got on surprisingly well with the British upper echelons, given that they were former enemies. They found themselves next to a solid looking man in the uniform of a colonel of the Guards, who was accompanied by a blonde woman in uniform.

'Hello Nicholson,' he said, noticing Louis, 'enjoying yourself, eh?' He drawled the words out, clearly somewhat the worse for wear. 'Aren't you going to introduce me to your lady friend?'

'Oh, yes of course sir. This is Eloise Bauer. Mrs Bauer, this is Colonel Baxter' and Ellie stepped forward shyly, ready for the colonel to greet her.

'Mrs Bauer? Does that mean you're one of the Austrians then?' said Baxter, failing to take her proferred hand.

'No no,' said Louis. 'Mrs Bauer is English. From the Channel Islands actually.'

'Oh, jolly good,' said the senior officer, finally shaking her hand. 'Which one?'

Ellie explained and it became clear that the colonel knew Jersey, had holidayed there on several occasions. He said he had found it a most agreeable place. She realised he must have been one of the English types she had served in her time working at the hotel. She felt defensive as the conversation progressed, although Baxter's girlfriend, whose name was Betty, seemed nice enough.

She looked around and saw other versions of the colonel, overheard scraps of talk. Behind her someone chortled about a story he was telling about a 'very amusing fellow.' His companion countered with the opinion that the fellow was a 'thorough gentleman' nevertheless, impeccably dressed at all times. In fact the whole company were very good fellows if the truth be known.

Ellie wondered what she was doing with these people.

Her attention turned back to the colonel, who was talking about something called an Eton field game back in June last year. Apparently he, an old Harrovian, had thought of a jolly good wheeze to spoil their fun. He didn't suppose they'd ever forgive him. Half an hour after the match began he had issued a general call back to camp with one hour's notice to move, and then cancelled the order once they all got there. That would serve them right for keeping their game to themselves, the blighters. Colonel Baxter found this very amusing, his drink spilling as he chuckled about the jolly time he'd had.

He wandered off with his lady friend after that, leaving Louis and Ellie to find their way out of the marquee to the vehicle park. He drove her back into town. Without speaking about it they had decided against a visit to the officer's club on the other side of the lake.

'He's a bit of an old buffer I'm afraid,' Louis said apologetically. 'I'm sorry we had to bump into him.'

'Oh no, that's all right,' she replied. 'After all the years I've spent here I'm just not very used to people like that so I didn't have much to say. His girlfriend was nice though, wasn't she?'

They agreed on that and went inside the house and up the stairs. She decided to tell him a bit more about herself. He deserved to know, after his devotion to her welfare. So she began with Jersey, explaining how it was she had come to Austria in '38. As she spoke she was struck by how strange, in retrospect, she found her decision. Why hadn't she stayed in Jersey amongst people she knew, when anyone could have seen the world was on the verge of war? She realised it had been the very worst decision she could possibly have made.

He responded to her introspective mood by asking her more. She found herself telling him, without sentiment or tears, of the situation that had developed with Marianne Streubel. Eventually, she began telling him about Anna and then feelings really began to stir that had remained dormant during the months of struggle for her own survival.

For a moment she thought she was going to break down in tears, but then this passed and she explained, wistfully, that she felt she must see Anna again and see what sort of future, if any, they might have together as mother and daughter. She must be eight years old now. That thought hit her hard, and she fell silent.

At that point Louis got up and came over to her. He kneeled on the floor before her seat so that his head was at the same level as hers and, looking into her eyes, said, 'I'll take you to see her. I'll take you there. I'll take you wherever you want to go.'

She took his hands in hers and bent her head forward to kiss him, and for him to kiss her.

By the time the snow started to melt, Louis was spending most of his nights at Ellie's place and had moved his things over there. His lodgings had been pretty sparse anyway, and he found that she provided a home for him. He wondered, in his more self-critical moments, whether this wasn't a large part of the feeling he had for her, after so much time away from Ruth. He found himself coming back in the evening, hoping that she would be there, shouting out, 'I'm home,' as he entered the house and marvelling at the domesticity of this simple act. It was as if they were pretending to be husband and wife. She even tried to iron his clothes for him on one occasion, before he stopped her. It gave him guilty feelings about Ruth.

She on her part could not suppress, although she tried, the almost ecstatic sensations that went through her when she thought of him, and then when he touched her. The intensity of her feelings for him frightened her, at the same time as they impelled her towards him. He was like a prize she had won at the end of a long and hard journey, and also a resting place, a relief from the hardness of her life, the sensation of which soothed, comforted and excited at one and the same time.

And she couldn't believe how a man could be so independently able to manage his own domestic affairs. The Austrian men she had met, Michael for example, but also even bohemians like Rudofsky who one might have expected to be a bit different, were incapable of lifting a finger around the house.

Some of the civilians in the administration, as well as some officers, had been able to bring their wives and families out there. Other men had formed relationships with Austrian women that had resulted in children. She marvelled at the sight, increasingly common in Klagenfurt, of British men pushing babies in prams in the streets. No Austrian man would have done a thing like that.

Her work continued, as did his, and he increasingly found reasons to employ her services as an interpreter. They travelled up to a displaced person's camp outside Spittal on one occasion and, after their work there was done, spent the weekend on the Gurk river where there was a fishing lodge used by the British.

The Carinthian countryside became more beautiful as the spring progressed and whenever they could they went out into the hills, driving past chestnut trees to villages called St This and St That, their stops making a spectacle for the local inhabitants who came out of their houses at the sight of a stranger. The country people were not in as bad a state as those in the towns, as they had their land to live off and could squirrel away their food stores, out of sight. All the same, the people gathered round the car, hoping for something from a representative of the power that now claimed to regulate their affairs.

On these occasions Ellie enjoyed playing the part of an Englishwoman, responding only in English to the peasants, who then thought she could not understand them. Louis' own capacity to deal with their dialect was also soon revealed to be poor, so the country people would then sometimes say secret things to each other about the couple, which Ellie would later translate for him, much to their mutual amusement. On one occasion she told him that a woman had said that they were a fine-looking couple, a thought which pleased them both.

There was an orchestra in Klagenfurt that put on occasional concerts which they attended once or twice. An accordion band appeared one evening, surrounded the main square with coloured lights and there was dancing in the street. Then a touring company from Graz turned up to put on an open air performance of *Die Fledermaus*. Louis wasn't a music lover, but he went along and enjoyed it, with Ellie explaining the story next to him. Afterwards she told him of her music-going in Vienna, of the artists she had known there, of her friendship with Julia van der Lye. And she briefly thought about Poldi and wondered what she was doing now.

At other times they went to the shores of the Wörthersee. There was a hotel with wooden planking that ran all the way down to the water which they liked to visit. They could get a meal there, or drinks, and then brave the water which at first remained cold after the winter. As the summer progressed and the water warmed up they went to the public bathing area next to the town itself. Louis took photographs of her there, in her two-piece bathing costume, lying on the sandy beach in front of the boardwalk, or standing, smiling, reaching up into the weeping willow trees.

One evening at the hotel Louis said he wanted to take her to Italy for a weekend. He knew a number of people who had driven down the mountain road to Udine. They had come back from there with Chianti and chocolate and he had heard there was a fantastic market with all sorts of things you couldn't get anywhere else. They'd see the mountains; he could show off his Italian.

'I want to go to Zell am See first, Louis,' she responded. 'Do you remember? You said you would take me.'

It was a subject they had not discussed since that first night they had spent together. The enjoyment of each other in the past few weeks, their dream-like existence, their happiness, had depended on avoiding certain subjects. Ellie had not inquired too deeply into his life in England, apart from the occasional childhood tale that entered their conversations. He had thought of telling her about Ruth, had been on the verge of doing so several times, but the right time had somehow never come. And in spite of his initial promise to her, that he would take her anywhere she wanted, he had not really wanted to discuss Zell am See either. It brought home to him the reality of her past as a divorced woman, which discomfited him. Yet, when she reminded him of his promise, he knew he must honour it.

'Of course. We must do that now that the roads are clear. I've got some contacts up there – an American called Herz I've been meaning to meet. I can make it into an official trip with you as an interpreter. We can spend the week there, while you see your...' he hesitated.

'My daughter,' she said, completing his sentence, 'while I see my daughter.'

18

She didn't think she was recognised at the hotel, although she knew the man behind the desk. The last time she had been there she'd been helping out in the kitchens. No doubt it was too much of a leap for him to associate the woman on the arm of a British officer with a kitchen skivvy from years before. She spoke to Louis in English to complete the impression.

It had been a long drive and they were tired that evening. Herz wasn't due in town until the following day. She had told him it would be best if she first went to see her friend, Susan Zainzinger in Kaprun. He could come with her if he liked. Susan would be able to tell them the lie of the land.

The next day they drove to Kaprun, passing along the lake shore where Ellie had spent so many afternoons with Anna, through the area of new housing and over the low-lying fields to the town at the foot of the valley leading up to the great construction site, now abandoned by its workers. Approaching Susan's house, she felt a sudden reluctance to go on. She hesitated, clutching at Louis' arm.

'What's the matter?'

'Oh, I'm not sure. It's nothing, or no, it is. I mean, this is a bit harder than I expected.'

She had stopped now, looking up at the dark house-front that stood on a rise above the street level.

'If this friend of yours is as nice as you say, she will understand. Come on,' said Louis, pulling at her sleeve. He knocked on the door, but there was no answer. Ellie reflected that there

253

was probably a reason why she had asked him along – perhaps she couldn't have done this on her own. He knocked again and a woman opened a window from the house next door.

'What do you want?' she shouted.

Susan Zainzinger was out, they were told. She was shopping. She'd be back soon. They decided to wait and sat down on one of the steps leading up to the house. It was a warm day and the jeep was parked across the road. Curtains moved as people looked out at the vehicle, and surreptitiously at the pair sitting on the step. It was an uncomfortable feeling.

Then she saw a woman carrying a shopping bag coming up the hill towards them. She walked slowly, the bag seeming heavy, but as she neared them Ellie recognised her, stood and ran towards her. 'Susan!' she cried out, and she was suddenly facing her old friend.

Susan at first did not respond. She looked so much older, streaks of grey prominent in her once dark hair, her cheeks thin, her eyes tired. Yet her face widened in surprise when she eventually recognised Ellie and she dropped her bag with a shriek of recognition. They flung their arms around each other and cried and laughed.

Louis came over. 'This is Louis,' said Ellie, 'I mean Captain Nicholson. Oh never mind, this is Louis. This is Susan, my dear friend Susan who was so kind to me when I lived here.'

Louis shook her hand and found himself giving a little bow. Susan looked at him with disbelief.

'Where did he come from!' she exclaimed, and then put her hand to her mouth, embarrassed by what she had said. 'I mean, where have you come from?'

Ellie explained as Louis picked up the bag and they went up to the house. Inside it felt smaller and darker than she remembered. Susan pointed them to some chairs but Ellie stayed standing.

'You must tell me about Paul and your husband. Where are they?'

Susan's face fell at this. 'Franz is out in the fields. He'll be back this evening. But Paul...'

'Yes Paul, tell me. The last time you wrote you said something about him getting into trouble because of Josef Marcher.'

'Yes, that's right, he was in trouble,' Susan said, as if remembering something that had happened so long ago that she was unable to remember it. 'Paul is dead,' she eventually blurted out. 'He is dead, three years ago now,' and she put her hands to her face.

Ellie went to comfort her while Louis looked on unhappily. Ellie remembered Paul's kindness to her, how he had waited in the road for her in the evenings, coming back to Kaprun.

'He was a good man,' she said to Susan, and she found herself crying too.

Susan, when she could talk, told them that in 1943 Paul had been summoned back from Jersey to face a charge of spreading defeatist rumours, for which he had been convicted and sentenced to serve a prison term. This had been suspended until the cessation of hostilities and he was transferred to a punishment battalion. She had been allowed to see him before he had left for the East and they had both known that this was going to be a death sentence. Such men were used to clear minefields.

'And Josef? What became of him?' asked Ellie, remembering his last letter from Stalingrad.

'Oh, I expect he died a hero,' said Susan bitterly. 'To hear his mother talk these days you would think he must have been some kind of superman. The way she goes on about him.'

'Did he come back?' asked Ellie.

'Why should you care about that?' asked Susan, suddenly hostile.

'Me, care? About that bastard?' Ellie laughed scornfully. 'Not likely.'

'No-one's heard a thing about him since Stalingrad. He's either dead or somewhere in Siberia. I hope he never comes back,' Susan spat out.

Louis stood up, evidently feeling surplus to requirements. 'I think I'll go out for a bit,' he said. 'I can see you two have a lot to talk about.'

'Oh I'm sorry Louis,' said Ellie. Both she and Susan tried to reassure him that he could stay, but he insisted. It was better that way. He'd go for a walk up the valley – be back in an hour or two.

'He seems very nice,' said Susan after Louis had gone out.

The conversation turned to Zell am See and the situation in the town since the Americans had arrived. Apparently a bunch of young men had popped up, seemingly from nowhere, in the last few weeks of the war, saying they had been members of the Resistance, claiming to have been responsible for one or two minor acts of sabotage that, until then, nobody had noticed. Some sugar in a petrol tank perhaps, said Susan dismissively.

She then said they were lucky they didn't have the Russians running things. This prompted Ellie to talk about her own bad experiences with Russians.

'I wrote to you, Susan. You know? From Graz and then after I was bombed out and then again after the Russians came. I wanted to get away. Did you get my letters?'

Susan looked away at that point, answering lightly as she went over to the stove to boil some water, 'No, I received no letters. When did you write?'

She was apologetic; she was sure she could have helped her, if only she had known. Ellie sensed that this was not a topic that Susan was comfortable with and decided that it was time to get to the point of her visit.

'I've come to see Anna,' she announced. 'You know that, don't you?'

Susan paused as she poured the hot water. 'I thought you must have done.'

'Do you know how she is?'

'Is that why you've come to see me?' said Susan accusingly.

'It is and it isn't,' said Ellie defensively. 'Of course I wanted to see you, you know that. But I also thought it would be a good idea to see you first, before descending on them, in case you could give me any advice.'

'Are you so sure you want to see Anna?' asked Susan. 'I mean, to see her for her own sake?'

'What do you mean?' said Ellie, starting to feel aggrieved at her friend's attitude. Susan had changed since the old days. She was more suspicious of people, less friendly.

'I mean, do you really want to see Anna, or do you just want to get your revenge on Michael for taking her?'

'That's not true. She's my daughter. I haven't seen her for nearly three years.' Ellie was getting upset. 'What do you mean about me getting my revenge anyway?'

'Oh, you know, you with this English officer. He could make trouble for them.'

Ellie hadn't thought of this, although she was conscious that Susan had touched a nerve in her. But she continued protesting that she just wanted to see Anna, so that Susan eventually relaxed.

'Well, there is not much I can tell you,' she said. 'Since Michael married Marianne I don't think I've seen either of them. I heard they got one of the new places and she moved in with the children while he was in Metz. He's back now. He had an easy time of it compared with some of them. That's all I know.'

'I see,' said Ellie heavily, 'he married her. How do you mean, the children?'

'She had a little girl I think. And then I suppose there is Anna. She must be with them, unless she stayed at her grandmother's place. I'm sorry, but you're going to have to find that out for yourself. I haven't kept up with them.'

Ellie was about to ask more but at that point there was a knock, the door opened and it was Louis, back from his walk.

He had a man in American uniform with him.

'This is Martin Herz. Martin, this is Eloise. I met Martin in the main street.'

Herz explained that he had arrived earlier than expected and, having made inquiries at the hotel, had decided to drive up to Kaprun to see if he could find them. He needed a stroll anyway he said, had been up to take a look at the power station at the foot of the valley. He was a fresh, open-faced young man and his American contained a distinct German accent, which Ellie commented on.

'Oh, that. Well I have relatives in Vienna,' he said, airily. 'It's a long story.'

Susan, in a coarse brown dress and apron, stood at the door at the top of the steps listening to them talking in a language she could not understand. Louis looked up at her.

'We'd better be going,' he said to Ellie.

Ellie and Susan hugged each other goodbye, promising to see each other again before Ellie went back. As they got into the jeep and drove away Ellie sensed that the whole street was watching them.

The next morning it was agreed that Louis would accompany Ellie to the house of her ex mother-in-law. If all went well he would return to the hotel to pick up Martin Herz and they would drive up to Kaprun to take a walk in the mountains. Ellie could come with them, or stay in town for the day, depending on what developed.

She had been apprehensive about seeing Susan again but, anticipating this encounter with Ilse Bauer, she felt even more nervous. She gripped his arm tightly as they walked away from the hotel. He was grim-faced.

It was only a few streets from the hotel and they were upon the house before Ellie felt ready, yet she knew she had to go on. Louis stepped forward. 'I'll do this,' he said, and knocked loudly on the door.

After a pause, Ilse Bauer opened the door. At first she saw only Louis, who was in his uniform.

'What is it?' she said, suspiciously. She hadn't changed, Ellie thought; the woman was ageless, her hair still bound up in the same way, slightly masculine features, her eyes sunk back in dark sockets so that it was hard to tell what expression lay behind them. She seemed to be wearing the same old brown dress and blue apron she had on the very first time they had met.

'Mrs Ilse Bauer?' asked Louis, sounding like a policeman.

'Who's asking?' she answered back.

'I've brought someone to see you,' he said, and he stepped aside so that she now saw Ellie, who was frozen to the spot. Ilse gave a little, almost imperceptible start and her eyes narrowed a little, but otherwise gave no particular mark of surprise. But her voice became sharper.

'Ah, I see. I was expecting this, I suppose. What are you here for now?'

'Can we come in?' said Louis. 'I am Captain Nicholson from the British administration in Klagenfurt.'

'Yes, I can see that,' said Ilse. 'You are British of course. Just ask me your questions here if you please.'

At this point Johannes, her husband, appeared behind her. He stood silently, eyeing the couple at his door.

'So you've found yourself another soldier friend, have you?' said his wife, now looking directly at Ellie, who started as if to reply. Louis signalled to her to keep quiet.

'That's enough of that. We have come to see Anna Bauer and her father. Are they here?'

'Why, what are you hoping for?' said Ilse. 'This woman left here years ago. What is she so interested in, coming back now?'

'I want to see Anna,' said Ellie urgently. 'I simply want to see my daughter. You ought to be able to understand that. Tell us, is she here?'

'No, you will have to be disappointed this time,' said Ilse with a smirk.

Her husband spoke behind her. 'They left this place long ago. They're living over by Waibel's now.'

Ilse turned to him and angrily shooed him inside. As she did so, Louis stepped past her. 'I'll take a look round if you don't mind.'

There was nothing the old couple could do to stop him as he pushed past Ilse, who was left fuming on the doorstep, blocking the door and glaring at Ellie, who in her turn, stared back. Neither of them spoke to each other as they listened to Louis moving around in the house behind them. Ellie sensed that Ilse was frightened in spite of the tough front she was presenting. She shouted out to Louis.

'Look in the back yard, there's a shed there.'

'I told you, you won't find them here, my girl. No such luck. I don't know how you have got the cheek to come back here,' said Ilse, her self-assurance coming back.

Louis emerged, shaking his head to indicate he had found nothing. At this Ellie strode forward and shook Ilse's shoulders with both her hands. 'Tell us where they are!' she shouted furiously. The two of them struggled briefly, Ilse breaking free of Ellie's grip as Johannes came once again to the door.

'That's enough of that,' he said, his huge hands keeping the women apart. 'They are living over at Waibel's place now, like I said. That's where you'll find them like enough. Now you leave each other alone.'

Louis also pulled Ellie away, saying sharply to the old man, 'We'll need the address then. The street and the number. And make sure you get it right. You won't see the end of this if we don't find them.'

The information was readily forthcoming and they went down to the nearby lakeshore and sat on a bench. Ellie was angry and upset at the encounter. It had been as bad as she had imagined.

At the same time, though, her feelings were confused about renewing contact with Anna, who now seemed so close at hand. In Vienna, thoughts of her daughter had been few and far between, but in the past few weeks and months she had become increasingly preoccupied with seeing her again, even finding herself longing for Anna. Yet now she felt strangely reluctant to proceed.

'Come on,' said Louis, who seemed impatient to take the matter forward. 'We can't sit on this bench forever. Let's go over to this place and see if we can find them.'

They walked off in the direction of the new estate at Waibel's but were disappointed. Yes, said the neighbours, the Bauers lived there, but they had gone away for a few days. No, said the neighbours, they didn't know where. Had they tried at his parents' house? Perhaps they would be able to help?

Louis told her he had come across this routine of the disappearing act before, the 'gone away for a few days' story from smiling, seemingly helpful neighbours.

'We should have done all of this before the whole town got to know we were here,' he said. 'Word must have got around.'

Ellie nodded in agreement, feeling distraught at the roller-coaster of expectancy and disappointment. 'We'll never find them Louis, not now. I'll have to go home without seeing her.' She was about to start crying again.

'Oh don't you worry,' he said hurriedly. 'We've got a few options left yet. Come on. I suggest we make a visit to the town hall. Martin can help us a bit, I think. We'll put the fear of God up these bloody natives. You'll see.'

They headed back to the hotel. As they walked through the streets, whose familiarity gave Ellie an uneasy feeling, she averted her eyes from passers-by who she felt must be looking at her, or talking behind her back after they had passed. She wished she was somewhere else, or even someone else. She also sensed that Louis was irritated with her. She felt a vague sense of injustice at this, but since he had made no direct accusations she was unable to defend herself.

Martin Herz was in the lobby as they came in, reading a paper and smoking a pipe. He looked up with a genial expression on his face as he saw them. 'Any luck?' he asked, but soon saw from their faces that the question was unnecessary.

'Can you give us a hand old chap,' said Louis. 'We need to pay a visit to the Rathaus to try and get some information about the whereabouts of this family. It'll come better from an American. I'm afraid our inquiries haven't got us very far.'

'Of course,' said Martin. 'Anything I can do to help. How about a coffee before we go?'

They declined. Louis seemed anxious to resolve the issue and Ellie felt far too unsettled to want to pause. The three of them strode across the lobby and out of the hotel. As they passed the reception desk Ellie saw the hotel manager behind the desk, staring blankly at them, expressionless.

In the town hall they explained their business to a young woman behind the counter. She was goggle-eyed at the sight of the uniforms of two of the major occupation forces and scuttled down the corridor to get her immediate boss. This turned out to be a middle-aged woman who Ellie didn't recognise. She sat them down on a bench, saying she would find out who could see them, her heels clicking rapidly away on the hard wooden floor. When she came back they were taken upstairs to offices that Ellie recognised.

'This is the housing department,' she told them. 'I used to work here.'

Martin looked at her strangely, but before he could say anything more they were ushered in to a large, overheated room. A man who she knew to be Julius Grabner was behind the desk, his piggy eyes twinkling behind folds of fat just as Ellie remembered them. He was no longer wearing a brown shirt, she thought wryly. He stood up as they came in.

'Hello gentlemen,' he said, ignoring Ellie and shaking each man by the hand as they introduced themselves. 'My name is

Grabner, head of the housing department. I understand you are making some inquiries about the whereabouts of a local family. I hope I may be able to help. Would you care for some coffee?'

They declined, but sat down, the two men on chairs opposite him across the large desk, Ellie sinking back into a large brown leather sofa. She knew that Grabner had recognised her, though he had given out no hint of it.

'We are looking for the daughter of Mrs Bauer here,' said Martin. 'It is a personal matter, but she is a British citizen who has interests here and we are providing her with assistance. The girl's grandparents, who live in the town, have been unable to locate her.'

'Ah, I see. Yes, of course. A British citizen you say. My congratulations, Mrs Bauer,' he said, directing his gaze at her for a moment. 'And have you been unable to make any other inquiries?' Grabner placed his palms together under his chin and leaned forward, as if interested in what they might say. Behind his large desk, in his territory and in spite of their uniformed majesty, the two men briefly appeared like supplicants.

'This is a personal matter, Herr Grabner, but you should know that it is also of interest to the military administration that this matter be resolved,' said Martin. 'Your assistance is required.'

'Well yes, of course,' said Grabner, thoughtfully, 'of course, the American administration. But you must tell me how I can help. What did the grandparents say?'

'The girl normally lives with her father, a Mr Michael Bauer, at an address in Neue Heimat, but they appear to have gone,' said Louis, then adding, 'We have reason to believe that they are avoiding us.'

'Michael Bauer? Oh yes of course, I know him personally, or at least I know the father. Johannes Bauer has worked for the town for many years. It surprises me to hear that his son is mixed up in any...'

At this point Ellie leapt to her feet and before her two companions could stop her, she was shouting into Grabner's face across the desk. 'You bloody liar! You bastard! You know exactly where they are.' Her anger made the blood rush to her face and she looked like she was going to climb across the desk to him, or throw something. Louis jumped up and restrained her.

Grabner quickly recovered his equilibrium after the verbal assault. 'Don't worry,' he said to the two men, 'I understand. The lady is upset. When children are involved…'

This made Ellie even more furious so that she now turned to Louis and to Martin. 'He knows where they are. I know this man. He was one of the Nazis running this place when I was here. I don't know how he's managed to stay in charge. It's disgusting.'

Grabner said nothing to this, but managed to put an expression half-way between hurt and surprise on his face, as Louis continued to stand between Ellie and Grabner's desk. Martin now stood up and leaned over the desk towards Grabner, grabbing his collar and starting to utter threats.

'There is no need for that kind of behaviour Lieutenant Herz,' interrupted Grabner, shaking him off. 'The woman is quite unstable I am afraid. But it is true, I can of course help you. We could have managed without all this fuss. Here, let me take you into the office and we will see what we can do.'

He came around the desk, giving Ellie a wide berth, and took Martin out of the room with him.

'He is such a bastard that man,' said Ellie, collapsing on to one of the chairs, her hand to her head, 'such a bloody pig. He hasn't changed a bit. Oh, I've got such a headache.'

Louis brought her a glass of water from a carafe in the hall outside and stood behind her, his hand stroking the back of her neck. Martin came back without Grabner.

'He's given me another address,' he said, waving a bit of paper. 'Come on, we'd better get down there before someone warns them.'

They went out of the town hall without seeing Grabner again, who had made himself scarce once he had scribbled down the address. He hadn't had to look it up in any file, said Martin, so he must have known it all along. It was just a ruse to get himself out of the office and away from them.

Zell am See was a small place and the wealthier inhabitants all lived in the area behind the town hall. The address was in one of those streets and they soon found themselves outside the gate of a large, two-storey, detached building with a strongly sloping roof. 'Streubel' was etched in white letters on the gate post.

Ellie knew what this meant. Could Anna be inside the house right now? Far from filling her heart with hope, the thought unsettled her even more and her head began to throb with such pain that she could hardly see. She managed to tell the men this was the house belonging to Marianne's parents.

'Who is Marianne?' asked Martin.

Ellie was too tired and her head was too painful to explain, so Louis took on the task of updating Martin on the Bauer family, in so far as he understood it. He had begun to realise he was getting embroiled in something very complex. This sensation was familiar from his regular policing activities where he was often involved in a tangled web of accusation, counter-accusation, lies and evasions. This time, though, he was personally involved.

It was an uncomfortable realisation. The affair felt distasteful, even sordid. He respected Martin Herz as a fellow professional but he didn't know him very well. He was embarrassed about embroiling this relative stranger in what was essentially his girlfriend's family row.

Ellie was flagging quite seriously. The confrontations appeared to have taken the energy out of her, and she said her headache was getting worse. Louis therefore made a decision, saying they should strike while the iron was hot and catch the fugitives before word got to them. A visit to this house right now was essential but he didn't think Ellie could manage another confrontation. She said nothing to contradict him.

He suggested that Martin could take Ellie back to the hotel. Meanwhile, he would see who was in the house and report back to them. If they were there they wouldn't flee again. They would know that he and the Americans could bring a great deal of trouble down on them if they made a run for it.

He also thought, although he didn't say it, that he might discover what they thought they were running from. What could be so terrible about letting a mother spend some time with her daughter?

Ellie agreed to this and by the time Louis arrived back it was lunchtime. Ellie was upstairs, lying down. Martin was at his station in the lobby, reading a newspaper. The hotel manager was still at his desk, looking busy.

After checking on Ellie, who was asleep on the bed in her room, the two of them ordered up some food and drink.

'There was an old couple there,' reported Louis. 'Mr and Mrs Streubel. He's a comfortable looking fellow. They are parents of this Marianne Streubel woman who has taken up with the father. They let me take a look around, but their story rang true to me: they hadn't seen their daughter or her husband for weeks. I'm afraid we've drawn a blank. I'll have to tell Eloise at some point.'

Martin nodded sympathetically.

'I tell you what,' said Louis suddenly. 'Let's you and I get away from all this for a bit. Have you brought some boots? Good. There's the rest of the afternoon left. I fancy a walk to clear the air. There seem to be some paths up the mountain going out of town. I'll leave a note for Eloise to let her know.'

Louis found the fresh air and summer warmth invigorating as they strode along a path running up through woods overlooking the town. He liked Martin Herz and wanted to get to know him better, and also to find out more about how things were turning out in the American zone. He knew Martin's job involved investigating and writing reports on the political situation. Like the FSS, he had considerable freedom to decide where he went and with whom he talked, and Louis knew that he had met politicians large and small.

As they talked, gradually climbing higher, Louis increasingly had a sense of rising above the affairs with which he had been involved during the morning, which at some level seemed petty. They stood on a promontory overlooking the town and gazed down at the houses and streets below them – a bird's eye view. It was good to be in masculine, soldierly company. After all, that was why he was in this country, to be a soldier, and to rule these people.

'I've been spending a lot of time at Steyr,' Martin said. 'The Germans built an enormous industrial complex there. The Russians did their best to strip it bare and there's not a lot left. It's a real headache for our guys.'

'How's that?'

'Oh, well, you know. I guess your people have had something similar in Graz. In Steyr it's all on a much bigger scale. The Russians couldn't take it all and we do what we can with what's left. But on top of that there are the managers. They're a motley crew to say the least.'

'Have you got rid of the Germans?' asked Louis.

'We got rid of the worst of them at the top, but Nazis are still there, for sure. And you wouldn't believe how those guys are twisting and turning to keep their jobs, protected by the people at the top most of the time. CIC have been trying to use that goddamn questionnaire.'

Louis snorted in sympathy.

'They used a stripped-down version but the managers wouldn't hand it out. The guys on the factory floor tell you the same old Nazis are still giving them orders, but the guys at the top tell us if they got rid of them they'd never get production going again. They need the expertise.'

'It's much the same story with us,' said Louis, who was also remembering Ellie's outburst against Grabner. What kind of expertise had allowed that man to keep his job?

The two men walked on as they compared notes, climbing ever higher until they stood on a peak from which they could see over to snow-capped mountains.

'We've got nothing like this in England,' said Louis, taking in the scene.

'You should come over to the States some day,' said Martin. 'You'll see all the mountains you want there. I've been up in the Rockies a few times, hiking. When this is all over...'

'I will,' Louis replied warmly. 'Thanks. I'll remember that.'

He paused a bit, hesitating.

'And look, I just wanted to say, I'm sorry, I mean, thanks for getting involved, with Eloise and all that...'

'Hey, no, that's no problem. Anything I can do. I can see you're mixed up in something deep with your girlfriend.'

Louis fell silent again, thinking.

'She's a fine woman by the way,' said Martin, reassuringly. 'You're a lucky man,' he said and slapped Louis on the back.

Louis felt better. Talking about professional and political matters had helped. He could distance himself from the confused tangle of feelings he had experienced down below in the town.

They got back in the early evening and found Ellie waiting for them in the lobby. Her headache had gone, she said, perhaps it was time to get something to eat. The two men, hungry from their walk, readily agreed and they went to see if there was anything decent on offer in the hotel restaurant.

They finished their supper and had asked for a coffee when they heard raised voices from the hotel lobby. Then there was a clatter as the door to the eating area was pushed open and a man in a black coat, long white hair streaming behind him and over his eyes, rushed through it, followed by the hotel manager who tugged at his coat saying he couldn't go in there.

The man resisted the manager's grip and looked over at them. As he did so, Ellie stood up.

'Kurt!' she exclaimed, going over to the old man. The manager took a step back, saying he had tried to stop the intruder, who was clearly not a hotel guest. He had come in from the street. He would only trouble them.

'I know this man,' said Ellie, who had by now been joined by Martin Herz. 'Martin, this is Mr Steinhauser.' They shook hands and Ellie told the manager they would look after this. The manager retired, muttering under his breath and they sat Kurt Steinhauser down and got him a coffee.

He had changed since she last saw him. He was wrapped in a dirty old coat which he appeared not to want to remove, and his shoes, previously polished and clean, were now grimy. Paper stuck out from the soles where he had used it to patch up holes. His hair, which used to be a constant source of amused fussing by his wife to keep it under control, was now long and wild. His face was thinner and his age showed more, his eyes red-rimmed and watery, cheeks drawn in against the bone where before they had been comfortably full.

'I knew I would find you here! They told me you had returned.' He spoke eagerly, gripping both her hands in his, ignoring the coffee when it came. 'And you are with American officers. I had to see you when I heard. You can help me, you must help me.'

A story then began to fall, hesitantly at first, from his lips, then more eloquently as he saw that the two men listened attentively without interrupting. Ellie continued to hold his hands in hers, until he was pouring out his tale with great gushes of emotion, drawing in his wheezy breath to gather strength for his words, which eventually became a flood.

He told them about his deportation from the town. He had been obliged to sell his business at a knock-down price and go to Vienna where he had to live in an apartment block designated for Jews only. Irma had elected to come with him, although she was not a Jew. He was made to work in a sewage works in Simmering. They had survived because Irma did not have to wear a Jewish star and could find work to earn the money that kept them alive. He picked up many illnesses in the sewage works, skin rashes, throat infections. He thought it was the chemicals they used, from which he was given no protection.

Then they had been told that he must go to Theresienstadt. Again, Irma could have stayed behind, but she had again decided she would go with him and share his fate. They had felt they could not live without each other.

Ellie could sense what was coming next. Everyone now knew about conditions in Theresienstadt. Kurt told them that Irma had died there. After that, he could not speak for a long time.

'When they liberated us, I made my way back to Zell am See and I have been staying here ever since, living in a room at the back of town. See, they have given me this.'

He rummaged in his coat pocket and pulled out a tattered card which they passed round. Under an Austrian eagle it stated 'Victim identification' citing a welfare law decree. Below that there was a statement saying that all authorities and public bodies should note that its bearer should be given preferential treatment, should this be asked for. Kurt's photograph was stapled to the other side, his name below an authenticating stamp.

'I've never seen one of those before,' said Louis.

'Much good it has done me,' said Mr Steinhauser bitterly.

Then he addressed himself to Martin Herz, holding him in his gaze and transferring one of his thin hands from Ellie to grip Martin's sleeve as he spoke. He explained that his photography shop had been taken from him when he was sent to Vienna. The money he had received for it had been nothing, a tiny fraction of what it was worth. A man called Gruber had been the beneficiary.

Ellie remembered Gruber, and nodded to the others in support of Kurt's story.

'And now they won't give it back!' he exclaimed in fury and despair. 'They stole it from me!'

He had returned to the town and had instituted legal proceedings against Gruber, who continued to run the shop as if he owned it. In fact, it had done poorly under Gruber's management, but there was still a collection of valuable stock. When he had heard that Kurt was back in town, Gruber had proceeded to sell off the stock cheaply, so that the shop was now almost completely empty.

The legal proceedings had run their course. At this point Kurt was unable to speak as his breath began to speed up and he took great gasps to get air into him. Ellie got up to find him some water, which he drank while she bathed his head a little with a dampened napkin.

When he was able to resume, he told them the verdict of the Austrian court. He could have his shop back, but he must pay Gruber a sum of money for running it in his absence.

'This is too much to bear,' said Kurt. 'He took everything I owned, my shop, my money, my goods. The idea that I should pay him for this! It cannot be understood. The Nazis are supposed to be finished, but the whole atmosphere still stinks of them. There is no justice to be had. Everything is done the same way, everything in accordance with the law.' At this, Kurt spat, a thick gob of brown spittle that stained the carpet.

This was so unlike the polite, cultured man that Ellie had once known that she was as shocked by this action as much as by anything Kurt had told them. It was also clear that Kurt was so wrapped up in his own troubles that he was no longer curious about her, which she felt at first to be hurtful, but then realised that it marked a profound change in the man, whose kindly interest in other people had once made him such an attractive friend.

'What will you do now?' she asked him.

'It is not worth having that shop any more. I want compensation! I want to join my relatives in America, but I don't want to arrive as a poor man.' He turned to Martin. 'Major Herz,' he said pleadingly, inflating Martin's rank. 'I have come to you because I heard that an important American official was in town, helping my old friend. The whole town knows of your actions.'

Louis spluttered into his coffee at this statement. Ellie realised they must have been watched on every street corner since their arrival.

'Now that you know what has happened, you can report this to the American authorities and perhaps you can help overturn this verdict of the Austrian court. I beg you Major Herz, will you take up my case?'

Martin explained that although he was perhaps not the best person to deal with this, he would certainly find the right person once he got back to Salzburg the next day. Kurt would receive a visit from someone who could take all the details and would look into it.

Mr Steinhauser left them then, no doubt feeling that his case had been laid at the feet of those competent to act on it, kissing Ellie goodbye and sharing tears that mixed gratitude with sorrow for the past.

On their final day in Zell am See Martin bade goodbye to them and headed back to Salzburg. Louis and Ellie had decided that they were going to make one last try at Ilse's house. Ellie told him she had been thinking about her own troubles in the light of Mr Steinhauser's story. She was beginning to realise how difficult it would be to put everything together again. Anna was eight years old now. Perhaps she had forgotten her mother. Perhaps she was better off with her father and her new family.

Louis told her he didn't like the sound of this. She was too depressed about the reversals of the previous few days. He was sure she would soon change her mind.

'Anna must remember you. Wouldn't it be good for her to see you?' he asked.

Ellie sensed uncertainty in his voice. She also knew, at some level, that he was no longer her unquestioning ally.

Nevertheless their momentum carried them down to Ilse's house that morning. This time she came out to meet them before they could knock on the door.

'You can look if you want; they're not here,' she said airily, gesturing to Louis to go inside. Saying nothing, Ellie also brushed past her.

She recognised the furniture, such as it was, from years before, the kitchen where she and Ilse had cooked and the family had eaten, the room where she had slept and given birth, even the bed cover was the same. They went out into the back yard and looked in the wood shed. There was, as they had both expected, nobody there. Johannes must have been out at his work.

They went back into the main room at the front where Ilse was now standing, waiting for them to leave, her arms crossed over her chest.

'Seen enough?' she spat out at them.

Then, on a shelf, Ellie saw Anna's doll, a cloth figure, dressed in a green skirt and an embroidered blouse that Ellie had sewn herself in Jersey. Ilse followed her gaze.

'Ah, that. You can have it if you like. Anna is no longer interested in it.'

Ellie was reaching for the doll as Ilse spoke these words and they pierced her like a knife. This woman had seen Anna recently, she was sure. She knew where she was. She remembered the brief flashes of warmth that had passed between them occasionally in the past. Ilse was not a monster. Surely she could appeal to her.

'Ilse,' she said, looking into the other woman's eyes, as she stood there, arms still crossed, defiant. 'You can tell me where Anna is. I only want to see her for a few hours. I don't want to take her away from Michael if that is what you are worried about. Just tell us where she is.'

Ilse paused a bit and then replied, her eyes glittering and small as she spoke. 'I understand perfectly well. I have told you their address and you should believe me when I say that I do not know where my son and his family have gone. Perhaps they are with one of his sisters for a while. They do not keep me informed of all their movements. But I do have something for you. Wait here.'

She left the room briefly and came back with an envelope, which she thrust into Ellie's hand.

'You did not keep your copy after you signed it. It was for you, and you should have it.'

Ellie opened the envelope and drew a folded sheet of paper from within and began to read. Louis watched her as she cried out in distress, dropped the paper and sank down with her head in her hands. He went over to her while Ilse watched them.

'Take a look,' Ilse said to Louis, who picked up the paper and read it for himself. Then he put it back in the envelope and took Ellie by the waist to raise her up. They walked out of the door without looking back.

They drove East, past Sankt Johann and then over the mountains towards the south. High up, Louis pulled the car over to the side of the road and sat for a bit, looking out over the valley below.

Eventually he asked her, 'Why didn't you tell me there was another child?'

She said nothing for a while. Then she spoke. 'I suppose you wouldn't have understood. I'm not sure I could explain it to you even now.'

'Well you don't have to if you don't want to,' he replied. And then he said, 'I don't suppose I have a right to know.'

As she took that in, a statement which fell as heavily on her feelings as anything anyone had ever said to her, he added, turning now to look at her, 'and why did you sign them away, your children? Perhaps you can explain that to me?'

'They forced me to,' replied Ellie. 'I had to sign that paper or they would have done terrible things to me.'

'Like what?' he said sceptically. 'What terrible things?'

Ellie found his cold, accusatory tone almost impossible to bear.

'You don't understand. You can't understand what things were like. They told me that I was an unfit mother, that a better mother had been found for Anna and…and…'

'and Maria,' he added for her. 'Maria, I believe she is called.'

'Yes, and Maria,' she said, suddenly angry with him.

They spoke for a long time after that and she told him about the birth of her second daughter, as she insisted to him she must. She was determined to prove to him that the decision to give Maria over to the care of others had been the advice given to her by Ilse and the midwife, who were helping her with the difficulties she had in feeding the baby and in keeping it alive. Anxiously, she told him that Ilse had done the same with her own daughters, who had been sent to country families when they were very young.

Yet as she said these things she felt a question burning away in her own mind: why had she deleted the memory of Maria for all these years, and had only ever thought of Anna as her daughter?

Louis tried to listen carefully as her tone became more pleading. Perhaps it was normal in this part of the world for small children to be given away to other people? She on her part sensed this openness in him and was encouraged by it.

The paper Ilse Bauer had shown them was an official form saying that Ellie could not be trusted to bring up her children as National Socialists so she must sign away her right to be their mother. Her signature was on the form.

The vision of the signature had seared itself into Louis' mind. It seemed beyond him to understand how she could have agreed to such a thing unless – and he recoiled from this thought even as it surfaced – the separation was somehow justified. How well did he know this woman after all?

But as he listened to her desperate attempts to persuade him that she had no alternative, he came to believe that her life during the war years must have been almost unimaginably different from his own. He thought that he had known most of the tortuous forms of suffering that the Nazi regime had managed to impose upon the lives of ordinary people, but this seemed to be a new twist of that knife. He reflected that it was like the separation of Kurt Steinhauser from his assets: an Aryanisation of the human property of the Reich. And the encounter the evening before with Steinhauser had reminded him that this suffering did not necessarily end with the official defeat of the regime. He began to see in Ellie's face the same piteous look the old man's had acquired the night before.

'I want to have faith in you Eloise,' he finally said. 'Believe me, I want to understand. It's just so hard for me to grasp all of this. You've got to realize…'

He ran out of words and leaned towards her so that she put her arms around him. He eventually put his around her. They were silent then for a while, holding each other, both of them unsure of what to think, both of them trying to recover the peace and comfort that they had found before in their close- ness. Louis thought at that moment he still loved her and wanted to be with her. And she knew that she wanted him to stay.

They drove on in silence.

Shortly after their return to Klagenfurt he told her that he
had been given three weeks home leave, which he was going to
take, that it was only a brief parting and that he would return.
And she knew by then that he would never come back and
that she would be alone again.

He wrote to her from London, explaining to her that he
had been reconciled with his wife, Ruth, who she now learned
of for the first time. He only had three months left until he was
demobbed. His superiors had agreed that there was little point
in his returning to an overseas posting for so short a time. He
was sorry. He would do all he could to help her. He hoped she
would understand. Their time together would always be precious to him. She tore up the letter.

19

With Louis gone Ellie reverted to the patterns she had followed before her affair with him had begun, spending long hours at work in the Labour section, trying to bury her feelings under a pile of paperwork. She grew thinner and people in the office looked askance at her, worried by her grim demeanour as she sat at her desk working through the piles of documents needing translation. She was utterly miserable. This felt like one of the worst of the many losses she had had to contend with.

At the same time, even in the depths of her misery, a part of her knew that she was practised in dealing with disappointments and separations. When she was younger these had felt overwhelming and there were times when she had wondered whether it would have been better if her life simply ended. She remembered feeling that way as a teenager when she had run away from her mother in Birmingham, and again in Kufstein when the news of her divorce came through and her hopes of family life with Michael and Anna had been shattered. But not this time. Her grief was no less intense than it had been on those occasions, but now she was able to say to herself, at least in moments of clarity, that her heartache would eventually pass. There were some advantages to getting older, she reflected bitterly.

She was helped at this time by a kindly person working in the same office who sensed her pain and, unlike the other workers, made an effort to bring her out of herself. His name was Clifford Tarraway, a bespectacled, short man whose army uniform sat incongruously with his appearance: Clifford was no soldier. He looked as if he would be more at home in a library, dusting the books.

But he was a considerate man and she appreciated his comforting presence. They used to go for walks together in their lunch breaks, sometimes reaching the lake shore where she had spent summer evenings and weekends on the beach with Louis. She told him about why she was so sad and he listened carefully. He, in turn, told her about the village in Suffolk he came from, his mother there, his family and the people he knew. His village seemed to Ellie like a gentler, English version of Zell am See. He said he longed to return.

As far as most of their fellow workers knew she was still the glamorous girlfriend of the well-liked FSS captain, Louis Nicholson. Tarraway's timorous version of masculinity was so far below Ellie's class that the possibility of anything going on between them was unthinkable. Yet on one of their walks to the lake side, as they stood looking out at the hills in the distance, with the high mountains looming grey behind them, she allowed him to hold her hand.

In time, Ellie decided that her life in Austria was going nowhere and she must start a new life in England. She made a formal application as a displaced person to be repatriated to the country of her birth. She was told that in order for her application for a British passport to be considered she would need to be vetted by the Field Security Service. She would be asked how she came to be in Austria and what she had been doing there during the hostilities.

On the morning of her interrogation she dressed carefully in freshly laundered work clothes, a brown pleated skirt and white blouse, checked her face in the mirror as she applied a discreet amount of lipstick, then drew a deep breath as she headed out into the street. The office to which she must report was in the central square, just round the corner from the Labour section. As she walked hurriedly across the Schillerpark, the summer flowers in full bloom in the newly established beds, she wondered anxiously what she would say. She calmed down a bit when she reflected that she knew most of the FSS men in the town, so if it was one of them who questioned her she'd have an easy time of it. But then her worries returned: just because she knew all the FSS men in Klagenfurt they might decide to get some stranger in from the Villach unit to do the job.

She resolved to tell them as much of the truth as she could bear. She knew they could check up on her story; Louis had occasionally got her involved in just these kinds of inquiries, translating for him as he questioned Austrian civilians to see if the stories he had been told could be corroborated.

On the other hand, what had she got to hide? She was British, stranded in this country against her will. She'd shown her loyalty by working for them all these months. They couldn't have any doubts about her.

She knew the building and entered through a side door, passing along a plain corridor to the front desk and surprising the young woman there who Ellie didn't recognise. She must be new out of England. She felt a sudden pang of jealousy that this girl could travel so freely while she, Ellie, had to go through all this to get back to her home country.

'I've come for my interview,' she announced, rather more brusquely than she intended, causing the young woman to give another start. 'At 10 o'clock I think. I'm Eloise Bauer.'

The girl looked puzzled at this, clearly taking in Ellie's English accent. She must have been expecting an Austrian.

'I'm British,' said Ellie, sensing the confusion but also getting a thrill from asserting her nationality. The girl was very young and smiled nervously at the vigorous, mature woman in front of her, hot from her walk and pulling at her blouse to send some of the cool air of the lobby past her skin and calm her pounding heart. A brief phone call and Ellie was told to go to a room on the floor above. She headed up the stairs and knocked on the door.

'Come in,' said a voice that sent a shudder through Ellie. In the room, it was confirmed: Dashwood was sitting on the other side of the desk, a notepad in front of him. The room was bare except for two chairs, a table between them and the King's picture on the wall behind Dashwood. For a second the memory of being with Poldi, tearing up pictures of Hitler in the Kremenezky Palace flashed through her mind.

'But you can't, it can't be...' she stuttered. 'I know you.'

'Yes,' he drawled, 'they can't spare anyone from Villach and all my chaps are busy. I'm running the show now that Captain Nicholson has gone. Don't worry Mrs Bauer, I am quite capable of doing one of these,' he said with a sigh that was too loud to be convincing. He had clearly prepared for this moment.

Ellie was not reassured. She had avoided him over the past few months but she had no reason to believe that he had got over his sexual jealousy about her affair with Louis.

'Shall we begin then?' he asked as he indicated the chair opposite his. 'You know what this is about and I've only got 'til eleven. We've never really had a proper chat have we? Let's start with you telling me how it is you came to be in this country.'

She sat on the edge of the chair, straight-backed, her elbows on the desk and looked up into his broad, florid face, his wide shoulders, the frame of a rugby player or a boxer who had gone to seed. He was large-boned, coarse. How could he have imagined that she would sleep with him?

Then she took a deep breath and began her story from what she supposed was the very beginning: her meeting with Michael at the Weihnachten celebrations at the St Helier House Hotel in December 1934.

As she spoke she became wrapped up in her memories and

began to forget her surroundings and who she was talking to. She described falling in love with Michael, her marriage, the birth of Anna. She remembered her younger self and the hopes she once had for the future, hopes which now seemed so unrealistic. Everything had fallen apart for her and Michael. Her voice faltered and her eyes began to mist over, so that Dashwood shifted uneasily in his seat.

'Let's get through this part shall we? I'd like to know why you decided to come to this country in the first place. Did you think the political situation here would suit you better?' He laughed, as if he had told a joke.

'No of course not,' Ellie said hotly, suddenly jerked back into awareness of the present. She described what had made Michael want to move, his mother's letters to him, the chance of a job. Even as she spoke, though, she found herself imagining what Dashwood must be thinking: she had been a silly, naïve girl who had taken the most stupid decision possible. Hadn't it led to one disaster after another? How could she not have seen what was coming? She knew she had to persuade this man that it was purely a personal decision, nothing to do with any political beliefs.

'And I was expecting a second child,' she found herself saying.

Dashwood sat up at this, and began asking her for more details. Ellie realised he had only known about Anna. After all, why would Louis have told him what he had found out about her?

As she unfolded her tale to Dashwood he increasingly fell silent and she again became absorbed in her memories and the feelings they evoked. In spite of her distrust of the man, she had an overwhelming sensation of release as she reviewed her life during the early years of the war. She described the break-up of her marriage and her flight to Kufstein, where she had finally received her certificate of divorce.

At this point she found it hard to speak, remembering the

awful loneliness that she had felt at that point in her life. She
had been rejected by her family, forced to sign away her right
to be a mother to her children, alone in a country where her
neighbours saw her as an enemy alien.

But Dashwood again urged her on and she managed to
recover enough to continue. She told him that her neighbours
in Kufstein had been relentlessly hostile to her as a woman
who was both divorced and English, so that she had fled over
the border to Rosenheim in the hope of better treatment. She
described the man at the Arbeitsamt there, who had a quota to
fill for Luftwaffe telephonist trainees, how he had ignored her
protestations that she was English-born and put her name
down anyway.

When she got to her time in Munich learning how to use
the telephone switchboards, she found that Dashwood questioned her very closely, asking her exactly what the training had
involved, about the phone numbers she had been told to
memorise, but which she had now forgotten. But as he did this
he maintained an impassive front so that it did not occur to her
that this might be a damning part of her story. She described
the letter which Grabner had sent, warning her commanding
officer that she was British and not to be trusted, her subsequent dismissal, her journey to Graz, and then her work stack-
ing chains in the factory there.

At this point she began sobbing violently. She remembered
the nights she had spent sleeping on the factory floor, the
starving faces of the Russian and Polish peasants who had
worked there, her terror that some implacable, unknowable
authority might one day force her to share the fate of the prisoners who had worked in the loading bays. But she could not
describe any of these things because she couldn't get the words
out.

Dashwood seemed to be used to people breaking down. He
got up, brought her a glass of water, said he'd go out and come
back in a minute or two. Her longing for sympathy led her to

see this as a sign of his concern for her.

When he came back the interrogation continued. She told him everything that had happened since she managed to get out of the factory and return to Vienna, the better times when she worked in the language school, the bombing that ended all of that, her relationship with Carl Mayer and her detention by the Russians. But she did not tell him about being raped. She could not, would not bring herself to expose that to him.

He was interested again when she told him a letter had arrived for her in the weeks before the Russians came, summoning her to the Gestapo building to explain her absences from the work she had been assigned to in the Siemens factory out in Floridsdorf.

'Did you go there?' he asked.

'No,' said Ellie, 'I was frightened when I got the letter. So many people went to that building and never came out again. Some of them were people I knew.' She thought of the death notice she had seen on the wall of her building in Biberstrasse, reporting the execution of Laura Gadoll, the intense young woman who had attended some of the English classes.

Then she remembered what Poldi had told her when they were standing at Morzinplatz.

'A friend of mine found out how they used to kill people there. The Gestapo had a guillotine to chop their heads off.'

Dashwood took this in without comment. She looked up at his face and it was a blank.

'So no, I didn't go there Peter. Or should I call you Lieutenant Dashwood?'

Ellie was recovering from her tears and starting to feel angry with this man, who seemed to know so little, yet presumed so much.

'I wasn't going to risk it. They never followed it up anyway. Everything was falling apart by then. They must have realised it was hopeless trying to get us all to go to work.'

He waved her through the time she had spent in

Klagenfurt, saying he knew all about that. Then he asked her what she would do if she got back to England; how would she support herself?

It was at that point that she told him she was engaged to be married to Clifford Tarraway, who would be returning to England next week. She hoped to join him there. And she surprised herself by saying suddenly, with a rush of feeling that nearly choked her, that they would be taking Anna with them.

She looked up and realised that he was temporarily speechless at her news. A red flush slowly spread across his face. He told her that the interview was now over.

She left the office a little after eleven. Somehow she made her way back to her place in Jergitschstrasse, collapsed on the bed and slept for the rest of the day.

Interrogation report (extract)

> Throughout the interrogation, subject has stressed that during the war she was continually reminded by the people she came into contact with, that she was an English woman, and as such got little or no co-operation from the authorities.
>
> It is interesting, however, that at no time was she questioned by the German authorities about her activities or sympathies, and that she was never interned.
>
> Her claim that her mother-in-law's Nazi sympathies led to the break-up of her marriage and separation from her children might be investigated further by contacting her ex-husband, who she claims did not take the same view of the political situation as his mother.
>
> If allowed to return to the UK subject emphasised her wish that her daughter Anna should be allowed to accompany her. She was

unable to locate her eldest daughter
earlier this year when she visited Zell am
See, but she believes she is still residing
there.

Throughout the interrogation subject
emphasised her struggle during the war to
make a living, partly owing to her British
sentiments which she claims she never tried
to hide. She is a woman full of ambitions
and schemes, perhaps ruthless in the way
they are realised. It is her intention, if
her return to the UK is sanctioned, to
marry Clifford Edgar Tarraway, Little
Bealings, Ipswich, Suffolk. He was a
British soldier working as Chief Clerk in
Civil Affairs prior to his recent
demobilisation. Through him she will be
able to support herself and her daughter.

Conclusion and recommendations

1. It is NOT considered that the Subject's
answers under interrogation were
satisfactory.
2. This woman as a British-born subject
seems to have been under no sort of police
supervision and to have been allowed
complete freedom of movement throughout the
war. She is unable to give any satisfactory
reasons for her visit to Metz in March
1942, to Kufstein at the end of the summer
1942, to Graz in April 1943. On the
evidence of the interrogation this
Organisation can NOT agree that she
received no assistance from the German
authorities since she seemed to have
enjoyed almost complete freedom of movement
and employment.
3. We should be interested to know also
more about her work with the Luftwaffe,
whose complete confidence she seems to have
enjoyed.

4. A police check on her addresses in
Vienna will see if her story about her time
there can be corroborated
5. We are also interested in acquiring more
information on the Subject's connections
and in particular Josef Marcher. It is
thought that it may be possible for to
contact this man and some of her
connections through CIC at Zell am See.
6. When the checks described in paras 4 and
5 above have been completed a re-
interrogation of the Subject is rec-
ommended.

Lieut PD Dashwood, OC, 428 FSS,
Intelligence Corps.

Police report

SUBJECT: <u>BAUER, Eloise</u>
FROM: <u>291 FSS VIENNA</u>
To: <u>OC FSS KLAGENFURT</u>
<u>RESULTS OF ENQUIRIES.</u>

There is no Gaukt trace of the subject, but
a police check produced the following
results: –
    Bauer, Eloise, nee Picot, born on 22 Jan
15 in Jersey Channel Islands, divorced.
    The subject had a very bad character in
her former place of residence Vienna III.
Rechtbahngasse18/9 and according to
neighbours who knew her at the time, lived
a most loose existence. Soldiers were
common visitors at her flat, and made a
habit of wandering in and out frequently.
    Almost the same report originated from
the address Vienna 5. Schönbrunnerstrasse
14. The Hausbesorger* admitted that she had
heard from the subject herself that the
poor Russians must be pitied, being so far

from their families and wives, the subject
was apparently a mistress to a considerable
number of Russians as well.

At the other addresses given, it was
established that the subject had lived only
a short time at each, and thus nothing much
could be said about her.

At Vienna III, Rennweg 45, the subject
worked at a Language School for adults and
children, from the end of 1943 until the
autumn of 1944, then she went to work at
Siemens-Halske until the entry of the
Russians. The firm's records show that
about three weeks before the end of the war
she was summoned to the Gestapo offices to
explain her continued absence from the
factory, but it appears she never answered
the summons.

Politically, there is no record of the
subject, and similarly in the records of
the Staatzpolizei, a negative result was
obtained.

Conclusions.

It is evident that the subject lives, and
has lived, a very immoral life, and has
left a bad reputation behind her everywhere
she has lived. Politically, she appears to
be uncompromised.

*caretaker

Colonel Baxter to Vienna HQ

To: HQ ACA (BE) Vienna
Date: 16 November 1946
Subject: Frau BAUER, Eloise

No. S/5834135 SQMS TARRAWAY C.E.O., who was
Chief Clerk of this Unit, has reported that
it is his intention to bring the above-
mentioned to Britain in order that he may

marry her. Frau BAUER has, I understand,
applied for her repatriation to Britain in
order that she may regain her former
British nationality.
In order to give TARRAWAY the correct
picture I would be most grateful if you
could inform me of the present position
regarding Frau BAUER's application.
Colonel R.N. Baxter
Chief Civil Affairs Officer,
H.Q. Civil Affairs (BE) Land Kärnten.

Louis Nicholson to Home Office

30th May 1947. To the Under Secretary of
State, Home Office

Sir,
I have pleasure in giving you the following
information re Mrs. E. Bauer.
In November 1945 I met Mrs E. Bauer in
Vienna in my capacity as liaison officer
for Field Security Services in Carinthia
and Vienna, Allied Commission for Austria
(British Elements). I was satisfied that
she was of British birth and had married
and divorced an Austrian National. She was
in some distress at the time, and I
arranged for her employment in the Labour
Section of Military Government in Kärnten.
I subsequently worked for some months in
the same headquarters and can testify from
personal knowledge that she was of very
good character and very efficient in her
work. As far as I know, she's still working
in the headquarters, and I can only presume
that she continues to give satisfactory
service.
I am, Sir, your obedient servant, Louis
Nicholson,
Member of the Stock Exchange, London.

Home Office, London (handwritten note; Miss L. Saunders)

This is a 2/51 case where applicant is living in Austria the country of her nationality. Aged 32 years, she was born in Jersey (C.I.) and became Austrian by marriage in 1935. In 1938 the family went to Austria and in 1941 the couple separated, the marriage being dissolved in 1942. The husband served with the Luftwaffe and applicant made her own way. Since Nov. 1945 she has been working for the British Mil. Govt. and is reported as having applied for repatriation and as wishing to marry a British subject.

The interrogation report from Klagenfurt Field Security Service (F.S.S.) is not very satisfactory and presents the subject as an impulsive and irresponsible person. The Vienna F.S.S. report gives us little further information, but enhances the unfavourable aspects of the case. This woman is of bad character and requires her British nationality for convenience sake. I submit that we refuse to grant a renaturalisation certificate.

In spite of this woman's immoral character there would not appear to be sufficient objection to her to justify the refusal of visa facilities for her journey to the UK. It is a matter for the Passport Control Office however.

I think that we had better refuse this application until Mrs Bauer is in this country; she has children in Austria and may decide to stay there.
L. Saunders 22.7.47

Nr.4, Jergitsch Strasse
Klagenfurt
Land Karnten, Austria
26.9.47

To:- The Home Secretary,
Home Office, London.
From:- BAUER Eloise, nee Picot.
Subj:- Repatriation

In the month of July 1946 I applied to the
authorities in Vienna for repatriation. I
submitted the necessary forms and have been
thoroughly screened by the local branch of
the Field Security Service, and also
interviewed at various times by the British
Consul in Vienna, before whom I declared
and signed application forms for the
British citizenship which I lost though my
marriage to an Austrian in the year 1935.

I was informed by Mr L Nicholson that he
had completed and signed the questionnaire
concerning my person and has also vouched
for me. I therefore presume that my case is
known to your office.

As more than one year has passed since I
applied and I have not yet received
information as to whether my application
has been considered, either to my advantage
or otherwise, I feel that perhaps the case
is being held up pending further
information and I am prepared to give you
any further details which you may deem
necessary.

Some months ago I submitted an address of
accommodation to the F.S.S. and the British
Consul. The address was in Suffolk and was
supplied by Mr C.E. Tarraway to whom I was,
at the time, engaged to be married. Since

approximately three months, however,
relations between myself and that gentleman
have no longer been continued and I should
like to withdraw all information which I
have given concerning my intended marriage
to him.

My reasons for wishing to enter the U.K.
are that I am British born and I wish to
apply for British citizenship, as I have
been divorced from my Austrian husband
since the year 1942. I have no interests in
Austria and no home. Accommodation has been
arranged for me by Mr L. Nicholson and the
address is: Nr. 33, Queensborough Terrace,
Bayswater.

I am fully aware that I am not to be a
liability to the State and I am prepared
and capable of undertaking any suitable
employment offered.

I would very much appreciate either your
views on my case or any other information
it may please you to give me.
Yours truly,
E. Bauer
Copy to: Foreign Office.

Herbert Dunk (Home Office) to Foreign Office

The Under Secretary of State,
  Chancery 8811
Foreign Office
7421/3/Nat. Div.
T.14185/9386/378

3rd November 1947

Sir,
With reference to your communication of the
15th July, enclosing a further
communication No. 107 of the 2nd July,
1947, from the Consular Branch, Political

Division, A.C.A. (B.E.), Vienna, about
Eloise Bauer, who wishes to regain British
nationality, I am directed by Mr Secretary
Ede to say for the information of Mr.
Secretary Bevin, that on the information
now before him he is not prepared to grant
a certificate of naturalisation to Mrs
Bauer.

He would be glad if Mrs Bauer could be so
informed.

A letter on the subject of her
repatriation has been recently received
from Mrs Bauer and it would be appreciated
if the attached copies could be transmitted
to the Passport Control Officer, Vienna,
for his attention and reply thereto.
I am, Sir,
Your obedient servant,
Herbert Dunk

The visa issued by the Vienna Passport Office was securely
packed away in the bag slung over Ellie's shoulder as she stood
in the crowd gathered on the forward deck of the ferry, approaching the English shore. Most of them were soldiers or
civilian administrators working for the occupation forces in
various parts of Europe. A couple of young women who had
had too much to drink were laughing as they sang about blue-
birds over the white cliffs of Dover, arms around each others'
shoulders. A little way apart from the crowd stood a man on
his own in the uniform of an infantry captain, staring out into
the Channel. Tears were running down his face.

She was returning alone. It had taken eighteen months to
process her application for renaturalisation and then for a visa,
in which time Colonel Baxter had written to Clifford Tarraway.
He, on receiving this information about Ellie's moral character,
had broken off the engagement. A part of her was relieved at the
thought that she would not have to share a bed with Clifford, but

it did mean that her plans for Anna had to be changed.

Standing on the deck, she reflected that they had never been very realistic plans anyway. She had no idea how she would have got Anna away from Michael and Marianne. Even if she had managed that, she knew she couldn't have supported herself and a child without Tarraway's help and that would have locked her into her promise to marry him. And she hadn't seen Anna for so long, she wasn't sure how the girl would take to her now. She remembered the vision of Anna as a toddler, her arms curling affectionately around Marianne's neck as she spoke to Michael on the shores of the lake at Zell am See: maybe Michael had been right about Marianne being a better mother for the children.

It was wet and windy out on deck. This didn't seem to bother the other passengers who were focused on the emotions of a return home. But Ellie shivered and turned to go inside, looking up at the weeping man as she passed towards the cabin door.

Indoors, she thought about her own attitude to coming back to England. At some level this move to London was like many of the other moves she had made over the past few years, attempting to find a safe berth in a strange place where she could build up some kind of a life. She had considered going back to Jersey, but she was drawn to London by the prospect of meeting up with Louis again, who had arranged a place for her to stay. She felt she had unfinished business with him, even if he had got back together with his wife. London might be an interesting place to live in too, maybe a bit like Vienna had been: a place where things happen, somewhere with a bit of culture, a city where there were opportunities for someone like her, who knew a bit about the world.

The train from Dover disgorged its passengers at Waterloo. She had never been to London before. She knew she'd have to find her feet in this place, make friends, find work, else she could be sent back to Austria as a foreigner who couldn't support herself in Britain. All around her on the station concourse people bustled around her, directing themselves towards train platforms, tube station or the street. She stood trying to get her bearings, listening to snatches of conversation. Everyone around her was speaking English, which was disorienting. For a moment it felt like a foreign country.

She asked at the tube ticket booth how she should get to the place called Bayswater. Behind her other passengers waited impatiently as the newcomer asked for directions. Ellie sensed their irritation. The ticket man said nothing, just pointed to a tube map on the wall behind her, so she thought she'd better look at it before buying a ticket, even if it meant queuing up again. But the map told her nothing, a confusing tangle of colours and names, so she gave up.

Outside the station she saw the river and decided to go down there to take a look. It was a bit like the Danube in Vienna, bridges in both directions over a wide and powerful waterway. She remembered going to look at the ruined bridges with Poldi after the Russians had driven the Germans out of the city and felt a sudden pang at the memory of her friend.

Then she asked the way to Bayswater from a passer-by who gave her directions and said it wasn't more than a couple of miles. She headed off across Waterloo bridge, through Trafalgar Square, her suitcase feeling heavy, prompting her to stop and look around at the sights. She'd made sure she got hold of a few pounds and English coins before setting out on the long train journey from Klagenfurt, so she was able to buy a bag of hot chestnuts which she ate sitting on the steps of Nelson's column, pigeons strutting at her feet hopeful of crumbs.

She sensed there was life in this city, prospects, potential.

At Queensborough Terrace she surveyed the tall white building before stepping up and ringing on the bell marked Smithson, as she had been told to do by Louis. She was given a key by said Smithson and crossed the linoleum of the hallway to climb the stairs to the third floor. The landings were covered with patches of grey carpet and there was a smell of old cooking that the walls seemed to have absorbed and were now releasing into the damp air.

The room had a single bed with a worn floral cover, brown curtains that had seen better days, a small chest of drawers with discoloured brass handles, an upright chair with a wickerwork seat. Down the hallway was a bathroom. Smithson had told her that the shared kitchen was downstairs, at the back of the house.

She dumped her case on the bed and went over to the window to look out into the street. It wasn't so different from Biberstrasse here. Perhaps city life is the same wherever you go.

There was a cautious knock on the open door and Ellie turned to see a young woman standing in the doorway. She was blonde, with a grey skirt, a cream blouse and a smile on her face. She must have been about the same age as Ellie. Her eyes glittered with a sense of fun as she held out an open tin.

'Hello,' she said. 'My name's Clare. I'm your next door neighbour. I thought you might like one of these.'

Ellie looked in the tin. There were pieces of chocolate cake inside.

'I always think it's nice to give a new arrival something sweet,' said Clare, brightly.

Ellie took one, thanked her, smiled back.

'Have you seen the soldiers riding their horses in Hyde Park?' asked Clare. 'I'm going to learn to ride! Do you fancy having a go? Perhaps you'll find yourself a soldier!'

Ellie grinned back at her new friend's shining, optimistic face. There were indeed opportunities in this town.

EPILOGUE

Many people have asked me what happened to my mother in London and how she ended up in Salisbury with a new family. They also want to know if she ever got back in touch with her daughters. They also want to know whether she was happy in her new life.

She lived at first at Queensborough Terrace, the place Louis had arranged for her. At first she found work, once again in a factory. This time she was painting flowers onto perfume bottles. But she didn't do this for long and her change of fortunes had to do with Ruth Nicholson, Louis' wife, with whom she made friends in spite of everything. Ruth had some relatives who ran an import-export business, dealing mostly in books, in St Martin's Lane. They gave Ellie a job, keeping their records, packaging up parcels for dispatch.

She became a close friend of Clare, her neighbour in Queensborough Terrace. Together they learned to ride horses in Hyde Park. Ellie always used to joke about having learned to ride with soldiers from the Horse Guards. It was a pretty cheerful time in London post war, in spite of the rationing. Peace brought life back to the city and people were determined to enjoy themselves. Ellie and Clare shared in that determination.

She wrote to Anna and to Maria at first, and received some letters back. But then, some time in 1950, this stopped. This was because of her employer in St Martin's Lane, a genial man who had taken a fancy to Ellie. He had offered to visit the family in Austria as he was going there on business. The visit was a disaster as it renewed the Bauer family's fears that there was a plan to kidnap the girls, so they broke off all contact.

Then things got sticky for Ellie in London, for reasons I can only guess at. Perhaps the import-export man got too fresh with her (he was married). There were complications in her relationship with Ruth and Louis Nicholson that I haven't fully understood too, and it could have something to do with that. Or perhaps she just felt like a change: she was an impulsive woman after all and moving to a new place was something she had often done out of a desire to renew herself.

At any rate, she went to live in Salisbury where she got a job as a secretary and type-setter in a printing works. The owner of the works was my father's best friend, who introduced them. Ellie must have told this new man what she felt he needed to know. They married and began a family. I was born in 1955, just before Ellie turned forty.

In Austria, as they grew up, Anna and Maria were intensely curious about their mother. The stories they were told about her by their grandmother, Ilse Bauer, both horrified and fascinated them. In 1962 their father, Michael Bauer, died without telling them where their mother was and their stepmother, Marianne, sold the family home, leaving them penniless. It was Anna who then had the idea of writing a letter to 'Billy Picot, Policeman, Jersey' to enquire about her mother's whereabouts. To her astonishment, she received a response from him. Ellie had turned up in Jersey, he told her, with children in tow, on a visit to the old place. He gave Anna her mother's address in Salisbury.

Anna and Maria discussed what to do next. They had very little money so Maria worked all that summer serving tables in a gasthaus, saving up enough to travel to England where she linked up with her aunt Eva who was living with her husband James in Richmond, where the pair of them ran a small hotel.

Maria travelled to Salisbury with her aunt and met her mother for the first time since she was a baby. She was young enough, and free enough from bitterness against Ellie, to want

Ellie's maternal affection and the two of them somehow formed a warm relationship, so that Maria became a regular visitor to our family when I was a child.

The situation with Anna was more difficult. She visited a couple of times but was a very different character from her sister. Both girls were Catholics, but Anna's religion fed into an unhappiness in her nature, so that she had become a moralist. She decided that she disapproved of Ellie and maintained her distance. I think she was defending some very deep wounds in herself caused by the traumas of her childhood.

I have to say, I recognise something of that feeling in myself, having also experienced Ellie's on-off approach to maternal love. But that's another story...

Ellie returned to Austria in the 1960s, visiting her daughters. In Vienna she looked for Poldi. The Kremenezky family, like a lot of Jews who had been expelled, never came back to Austria and had sold the building, which became a department store. No-one knew anything about a woman who had lived in a basement room. Perhaps Poldi moved back to the country village she had originally come from as a young girl. The bag of coins must have helped.

Carl Mayer became a successful film director after the war and lived a long life, giving interviews from time to time about his activities as a celebrated hero of the resistance. Rudofsky found a place in the post war Viennese art establishment and you can see some of his paintings, hanging next to Böckl's, in the galleries there.

The Pengg-Walenta chain factory in Graz was closed at some point after the war, but the company lives on as Pewag (motto: 'Strong is not enough'), manufacturing chains in nearby Kapfenberg. Siemens, of course, the factory in which Ellie worked in Vienna, remains a household name. At the hydro-electric project in Kaprun there is now a memorial to the unknown number of people who died in the building of the dams, many of them forced labourers and prisoners at the mountain camp where Michael worked, providing them with the food that was insufficient to sustain so many of them.

Then there is the difficult question of how happy Ellie was in her new life. I am afraid people cannot simply shake off their past when they move town and find new relationships, however much they may want to do so.

She had a breakdown after the birth of my youngest sister who for several months was looked after by another woman before being returned to the family. Ellie talked about feeling breathless, asphyxiated, but these complaints were found to have no physical basis. She had a couple of episodes in psychiatric hospitals after she started accusing Richard of trying to strangle her in the night.

At that time, her mind in a state of turmoil, she spoke freely – well, not spoke, she ranted, shouted, accused, screamed, cried out in pain – about her past life and Richard discovered many new things about her. In that respect he was in the same boat as Louis Nicholson, who had run away when he found out her secrets.

My father, though, was much more deeply involved than Louis. He had a busy job, young children and a wife who was in existential torment. Perhaps she was right in one sense, to claim that his presence was stifling. But no doubt he would have countered that he provided her with some stability and containment as the agonies of her past racked through her. And he would have felt that he behaved pretty heroically in holding the family together through this.

In her last years she became addicted to sleeping pills which became a prop to her until her death in 1973, aged 58.

I can't, though, just leave the question of her 'happiness' at that. She was not always in a state of anguish and as Dashwood wrote in his interrogation report, she was a woman full of ambitions and schemes. She had ambitions, for example, to be an artist and she turned a room into a studio and painted in oils and watercolour. She loved music and conveyed that to her children. She read widely – history, biography, novels, poetry. She had educated herself in Vienna and then in London and she had an energetic, warm nature, so that she made friends easily. So her life after Austria was a mixture of things, 'some good, some bad' as she might have said. Asking whether she was happy is understandable enough, but is really too simple a question.

There is one more thing, concerning the mystery of Ellie's father, which was solved just recently.

As you know, the lack of information about her father's identity gave her a great deal of trouble, especially when Ilse – a staunch Catholic – thought she might advance her son's cause by claiming Ellie's father was a Jew. Her brother Billy also felt intensely curious about his father. His mother, with whom he had lived in Birmingham for a while, would never tell him and Grandmère Picot wasn't going to say. But Grandmère had another daughter, called Marguerite. This woman was as virtuous as her sister had been wicked. She was sworn to secrecy about the identity of the father and when Billy visited her shortly before his own death in the 1990s she would not reveal the secret.

She was a very old lady when I went to see her, living in a nursing home in Eastbourne, visited daily by her own daughter who had agreed to me making contact. She had had a stroke, the daughter said, and could not speak, but she thought her mother understood most things.

I approached her bedside apprehensively and introduced myself as the son of Eloise Picot, her sister's child. At this the old lady, her head sunk deep within a pillow, moved one side of her mouth as if to speak, but only a noise came out. Her daughter, from the other side of the bed, moved to wipe some spittle from her chin. I thought it best to get straight to the point.

'I've come to talk with you about who her father was.'

The mouth made another sound and her eyelids closed tight with the effort of trying to speak. Her daughter stroked her forehead.

'I know he was German.'

William Picot, my mother's brother who we called Billy, had a second name: Reiner. I knew that it used to be common for boys who were illegitimate to be given their father's surname as a second name. I could think of no other reason why my uncle had this German name.

The old lady's face did not move at this point, but her eyes seemed to me to acquire a hardened look, conveying a mixture of surprise and resolve.

'I know Uncle Bill came to see you about his father,' I told her. 'But since then we have been able to discover more. We know about the seminary on the hill.'

There was a Catholic seminary in Jersey at the turn of the century. Young men training to be priests came there from all over Europe, although the records suggested that most often they came from Germany.

'We have found his name in their records: Ernst Reiner.' I paused to see her reaction to this news, but she had closed her eyes. 'That was him wasn't it? Ernst Reiner, a Catholic priest. Eloise's father. My grandfather?'

I stared into her face for some kind of response to this news and she opened her eyes. She did not try to speak again, but after a while I saw that there were tears running down the old lady's cheeks.